An unnecessary husband

1st

Published by Favourite Colours, Lillehammer

gavin william wright: editor

a favourite colours book

20   Lillehammer   19

"Civilized life has altogether grown too tame, and, if it is to be stable, it must provide harmless outlets for the impulses which our remote ancestors satisfied in hunting."

– Bertrand Russell

"Fantasy can be damaging. Reality can't hold a candle to it, everyday life doesn't stand a chance"

– Elizabeth Taylor, *Palladian*

Richmond Hill

Onslow Road

Soho

Beak Street

George Street

Ham House

Putney Bridge

Millbank

Victoria Embankment

Richmond Park

Floral Street

Cyberspace

St. Christopher's Place

Union Square

Richmond Hill

Despite the dust and clutter, the mustiness of old paperwork, there was an acrid sterility to the room, the way that hospitals used to smell in the seventies, trapped in their decades-old inertia. It no longer reached me, although my lungs groaned, and my nose twitched at the airborne spores, I had become numb to the dreariness, immune to the atmosphere. Whenever occasional visitors entered, their faces would buckle, confused, feeling transported to childhood, a previous torment, or to some bad place, some sickbed somewhere, and I'd wonder why, mystified, until some brave/hilarious soul asked: "What died in here!"

~

There is a certain type of misjudged confidence that takes over a man with a narrow skill set, a man who knows little about the realities of life beyond the field in which he specialises. I, Christopher Hoyer, confess that I was such a man; I considered myself expert, not just in my field, but regarding life in all its many glorious, wonderful, twisted ways.

'Logistics,' I began to preach – my confidence so uncrushable that I allowed my hips to rotate my chair with a light rhumba. 'Everything in life boils down to logistics. You'll discover that to expedite life's tasks and trials in the most efficient and timely manner, it all boils down to logistics.'

On the other side of the desk, Bilal was unconvinced. He looked at me in such a way as to make me doubt my wisdom. I touched the newly arrived grey at my temples, ceased my happy twisting and reconsidered my comment. No more than a moment was required, I tilted back in my chair, satisfied, assured in my belief that I knew everything about this matter, everything about life; that I was, without doubt, correct.

'That seems a pretty cold and shallow way of looking at life,' he countered. 'You know, just because you're stuck in this dungeon, don't mean that you have to act like a robot.' Immediately he seemed unhappy with his clumsy mixed metaphor, but it conveyed an argument; enough of an argument to cause me to let slip an expression suggesting that it had provoked a thought, even if not quite the one he had intended to provoke.

'Nah, well…you say that,' I hurried, keen to reassert my superior understanding of the matter in hand, 'but does that really apply. Good logistics…the right shape and form, the right manoeuvres, doesn't always equate to a *total* robotic state. Good logistics results in more time beyond the task, more time to *not* be robotic.'

'Yeah, but you said that *everything* is about logistics, so that means that everything you do must also be done by being a slave to logistics, and therefore robotic. For example, do you screw Joodie…logistically?'

I looked up at Bilal, uncomfortable and annoyed at having my logic busted and thrown back at me to prove against my point. And I did not want to think about screwing Joodie – my wife – I had no intention of discussing her with my work colleagues.

'To a degree,' I began – having an answer for everything overwhelmed my desire to maintain a private life. Of course, I remained unconvinced, hoping that I would find an angle by which to justify my claim without making my sex life seem robotic. 'It's all about efficiency...about timing. The application...' Hearing myself, I squirmed – "application" – I could hardly have found a more clinical word. '...application of logistical processes, to ensure that I don't tire or...arrive too early.'

'Sounds like some pretty terrific sex to me,' Bilal butted in, satisfied that he had won this debate...efficiently. 'When I do me wife...'

'Yeah, thanks, no thanks; let me finish – it will be good sex, that's the point. How much bad sex...or no sex...comes down to poor planning and poor procedural...' I squirmed again. '...anyway, as I was saying, how much comes down to...say, having a large meal when your missus is horny – it's never gonna happen...'

'*Never ever gonna happen*,' Bilal sang, badly, not meaning it but unable to stop himself.

'...and even if it does, what chance is there of you lasting the full stretch?'

'I kinda see what you're getting at. And,' he went on, apparently excited by the discovery, 'with the big meal thing, you can add in the danger of letting one crack, or making a little bit of throat sick.'

'Exactly.' I pounced, missing the piss being taken from me, feeling instead that my point was being made. 'Logistics, y'see, isn't just about being robotic; it's about getting as much as possible done with the minimum time and effort expended.'

'So,' Bilal nodded, one of his chins shuddering; happy, it seemed, to have been convinced. 'So, you're saying that logistics is the art...the *science* of being a lazy bastard, yeah?'

I allowed a smile to press just below the surface, smug, satisfied with my logistical evangelism, but I didn't let it show, just rocked the chair seat back and unfolded my Guardian to the sport section.

I tried to read, but something lingered – suddenly I couldn't help but feel that Bilal remained unconverted and, furthermore, that he genuinely thought I was a twat – still liked me but considered me a bit of a twat.

I didn't like this, it bruised my ego, bruised this idea that I clung to that I knew what was what; perhaps I'd looked down a bit on Bilal and didn't give him credit for understanding my life better than I did. This world I inhabited, locked away in this dingy basement, daydreaming, simplifying everything into the simplest, easiest form – perhaps I had given up on life, perhaps my sex life had become a process, going through the motions.

Hiding behind my newspaper, I let my mind brush over the idea that Bilal had sown – the science of being a lazy bastard – this was nothing to be proud of, especially when all the time I was saving, I was wasting – I didn't spend this time with friends, or my wife; I didn't create anything, I didn't offer anything to the world. I was mildly useful but, as a member of society, I was rather unnecessary.

What we had said, what I had put forward – I realised just how boring it made me sound – some grey little man obsessing over schedules and volumes. I am our company's Senior Logistics Manager, I fought for the title three years ago – I mean, that is the reality of my day, I can't escape it – now I am mortified by the idea that people think this about me. And my job title only reinforces it. I wrote the words – Senior Logistics Manager – across the top of my newspaper – it was horrendous, this was what my life had become: a practitioner of practicality. Even worse, the element of seniority established me as an expert in such greyness! No wonder I had recently taken to simply saying that I worked "in logistics", it seemed to get interpreted as having a job in the high-end IT industry, and a trendy IT department employee seemed infinitely cooler than a glorified stock room manager. What a fraud! I'm not even interested, and only basically competent, when it comes to computers. I am one of a select demographic born halfway between the end of the second world war and the millennium, torn with pasts and futures that are part Victorian and part Digital Super Highway – though my daily life is gigabytes and flat screens, my cultural heritage is vinyl records and Meccano.

'Everything we do in life,' I said, not looking up from my paper, imagining the authority and wisdom it would suggest, genius still coursing through my veins, 'everything we do in life is mimicry – from our friends and family, TV…movies…' Now I looked up, Bilal was checking his phone. I coughed. 'Every decision, every mannerism, is stolen from someone, who stole it from someone else…'

'I thought everything in life was about logistics, what's that got to do with logistics?'

'That we are *all* robots! That was your criticism, wasn't it? That by dealing in logistics we become automatons? The point is we're all robots anyway, nothing you or I do is because we create it, it's just a copy of something else, filtered and augmented across generations and personalities.'

'So we *do* add our own creativity to things…'

'No, we simply blend two or more copied traits to make something…not new…just a variant. Do you agree?'

'Ahh, I dunno, I'm too busy thinking about…' and he began to thrust robotically, '…about robots doing your missus.'

I didn't feel that Bilal had been entirely convinced, but that was ok, because I didn't entirely care. No, instead I returned to my newspaper, illuminated in the unhealthy artificial light; a CD clicked around on its spindle, exposed, the thin plastic flap of the cheap player had cracked off; I didn't care about this either – it was Friday, and I was on top of my workload. In fact, I was basking in my efficiency, smugly delighted that I could afford such leisurely moments of downtime.

Mechanically efficient – robotic, if you will – my processes and methods meant that things "got done" –

how could Bilal have not understood this! I had precious little enthusiasm and applied the minimum amount of graft but possessed the key driving force – a desire to have life made as easy as possible. Most days, life washed over me; decisions, when essential, were reached with effort and reluctance, but wherever possible always leading to an outcome geared towards preserving my easy life.

I drifted from the paper; the music – progressive, hypnotic – pulled me from reality, my mind, surprisingly, began to wander towards, of all people, my wife.

I met Joodie on my thirtieth birthday; in the midst of a well-established, drawn-out celibacy (self-imposed, but not the least bit actually desired). As with every other element of my life, I had been procrastinating, shuffling around the necessary activity to meet and secure a partner. At that stage, it had been nearly two years since I had been with anyone, and Joodie presented herself available and interested.

Joodie is five years my junior, the friend of a friend; she was definitely in the "cute" pigeonhole back then, dark hair and overlarge brown eyes, she was not glamourous in any sophisticated way, but she wore pretty things: floral and flattering. She had just finished university and was abundant with optimism and potential and tanned deeply brown after a post-graduation expedition to the southern hemisphere; she was outgoing and filled with open minded exuberance, a desire to explore and to find her path in life. In the spirit of her worldliness, her exposure to men and women beyond the normal narrowness of her student colleagues, Joodie was excited by the idea of an older man – this decently, interestingly handsome man celebrating his thirtieth birthday seemed exactly what she desired. She approached me, the spirit of a boundaryless world still strong in her; all the legwork was on her part and she secured, with little effort, a date with me – I, of course, was only too happy to concede, and she, bypassing the true shallow pools of my character, found herself inextricably locked to a man whose personality glaringly contradicted her own.

Sufficiently intrigued to expend a modicum of effort to please her, I dated her with an unexpected enthusiasm. And when I discovered myself established in her life, like any of my occupation logistical efforts, I approached the new relationship by doing only what I felt to be necessary – I contrived elements of our life together to achieve the most expeditious results with the minimum expenditure of time and effort. It was not difficult, Joodie was enthusiastic enough to take on the bulk of my decision-making obligations, and I was falling in love with her. Instantly, my propensity to contribute and to exert myself rose in proportion to my desire to remain with her. Despite my practicality (I like to think as a result of it), it was good, it was fun. It worked.

Romantically handcuffed, it's true, but we had enough ingredients to stay happy, and so we committed to moving in together. We were happy and after nine months, I proposed and a little over a year later we were married at a civil service at Ham House. I remember it fondly, we sat on the banks of the Thames as the sun set, and decided that we were unmatchably happy, it felt like forever.

As I sat at my desk, newspaper open before me, its content utterly abandoned, I was locked into my thoughts; Joodie had initially been the subject but, oddly, I found myself thinking about another woman. It was actually a woman that I knew well – a friend, Ophelie Wyeth – why was I thinking about her? Ophelie, why her? This was a woman who, like a satellite, had shared the phases and mood swings of our marriage; Joodie's university roommate, her maid of honour – Ah! – she had stood only metres away from me on the great checker-board floor of Ham House – that's what brought her to mind, I could see her among all that Restoration stateliness, dressed (such is any bride's malicious prerogative) in a vile dress the colour of Juniper berries. Ophelie.

It was a peculiar and unexpected sensation; naturally, I had spent many moments in Ophelie's company, days and evenings, the odd weekend away with her and her husband and Joodie, but why suddenly this peculiar daydream? Of all of Joodie's sprawl of friends, as much as I enjoy her company, she was not the friend I would say I am closest too, she was not even the friend that, if pressed, I would celebrate as the best looking of her friends, but I found myself thinking about her – really thinking about her. And, even stranger, I allowed the thoughts to develop – I began to consider certain elements of her appearance, her personality and something...something more arcane about her – a new colour I couldn't quite express in my mind, a detail in my consideration that I had either not noticed or that had not been present before.

Across the desk, several pens scattered as I tossed the newspaper down, realising that I was no longer reading it, needing to involve my hands in the perplexing consideration taking place in my head. I was close to needing a cup of tea, but it hadn't got that far, not just yet. Key in my mind was a new question: I had easily solved the previous puzzle of why I was thinking about Ophelie; furthermore, it was entirely plausible to find her present in my mind – as any one of Joodie's, mine or anybody else's friends might appear – to complement this rationale, however, I added the distinction that she was pleasing to the mind – she was attractive and a sweet woman – I could think of many people less welcome or likely to present themselves in my thoughts. My new question, then, was harder to dismiss and potentially impossible to answer: this wasn't the first time I had thought about her, was it? And, digging deeper, was this the way I had always thought about her? For the previous six, seven years I had known her?

Content that I was not likely to be disturbed by visitors, phone calls or anything else work related, I folded my arms and rocked back into the chair, compiling a list, not specific enough to include dates and places, but a sort of abstract series of recollections of indisputable evidence of my having "romantic" thoughts about Ophelie. Incidents and opportunities flooded in; predominantly isolated moments where I felt free of guilt, others tinged with the possibility of passing sexually motivated associations. It wasn't a surprise, but it was certainly unexpected. 'Oh my God,' I thought, 'this can't be good'.

Immediately it seemed necessary to dismiss the idea: the fear that I might have developed an attraction to my wife's best friend; or was I already there? And why not before: *had* I felt this way before? I started to picture her again, to recall how I saw her, the elements that stood out. It was suddenly undeniable, there was much about her that on any other woman I would surely find attractive or appealing. And yet I was haunted by the conflicting sensation that often I considered her to be the antithesis of the prettiness that was my definitive taste, the prettiness which made Joodie the beauty that she was to me; Ophelie was totally different, stronger, almost more masculine in her features and more athletic and lithe than Joodie.

No. I tried to comfort myself; there was nothing to it, nothing that could justify expending further thought. It was just a moment like any other. I was a man: I was attracted as I was attracted, there was no control over that emotion. Yes, she had certain attributes and it was not unnatural for me to be aware of these, to appraise them, maybe even to highlight and to find favour in them, but...

I was tired, now I needed a cup of tea – there was nothing more to it. Joodie was the one, she always had been, I had thought of no other since I first saw her.

'Busy?' The deep sarcastic voice of Bilal broke into the dark reflection I had melted into. As thoughts naturally do, what had commenced in a very living and real debate in my head, a simple mulling over, had drifted into daydream. I was a powerful daydreamer, and with the swirling organs and rubbery guitar lines, the soft psychedelic effect of the music playing in the background, along with the aridity of the old heating system, I had spiralled into thoughts of a more fanciful direction. If, before, I had had only a hazy awareness of inappropriate past thoughts of Ophelie, now I was rapidly augmenting them with a very specific contemporary example: a composite form of her – scattered shades of erotic imagery, cast back recollections of my experiences of her body, her face when it had pleased me, when she met her potential and shone, beautiful.

Looking up, the face of my colleague standing in the doorway, propped against the wall, I was mortified, as though the incorrectness of my distraction, the subject matter at least, rather than the practice, was transmitted into the room; that Bilal judged me.

'Man, you've been like that for ages; what the hell were you thinking about?'

'I was just, er…music, just into the music; this track, wow – pretty intense.'

'I wish I had time to just sit and listen to music all day. You got nothing else to do?'

I dragged myself upright, searching for a façade of respectability to cover the internal lasciviousness; conscientiously, I brushed the front panels of my shirt and cocked my tie. A blush burned on my cheeks, I prayed it went unnoticed by Bilal. Quite remarkably, I even felt slightly irresponsible from a work point of view, a washy sensation that I was expected to set some kind of good example.

'So, that was all, eh? Just into the music?' We both turned and listened to the current passage of almost inaccessibly peculiar music.

'Well, you know, the music and...other stuff.'

'Ah, you were imagining me doin' your missus – man, I'm sorry, I shouldn't've put the idea into your head; I'm a bad man, a bad fat man.' And he giggled a chubby giggle, whilst I cringed at the idea, oddly more concerned by the gargantuan sprawl of Bilal's body, naked, than the thought of volunteering my wife into such a liaison.

'If I was thinking about that spectacle...'

'Spectacular,' Bilal interjected, his appraisal met with a disturbed glare.

'...then you can expect me to have been a shade of green, if not actually vomiting, right here.'

'So cruel, you know you love a bit of fat Paki love...'

I backed away from the sobriquet, conditioned to finding it distasteful and keen to change the subject anyway. I *almost* wanted to discuss my confusion regarding Ophelie's changed presence in my thoughts, but Bilal wasn't the best person to seek advice from, not because he was likely to turn it all into a piss-take, but because he might actually offer some truth in the matter that, one way or another, I was keen to avoid. Should I be persuaded there was an actual significance, I would expect to then feel deeply uncomfortable and that, of course, was to be avoided at all costs; yet, equally, obtusely, should I be convinced that there was nothing in it...the thought of such a discovery was fearsome to me. There was a part of me, I realised, that wanted to feel this way; that wanted to feel this attraction. So I left it, kept it bundled up for the time being and, like a killjoy child, acknowledged that I should be doing something and proceeded to hide behind my logistics.

Richmond Hill is inimitable as a location; there is no street comparable in the world. The properties that stretch predominantly along its eastern pavement vary in dimension, as of course they vary in their ages, spanning centuries and spanning scales from humble and delicate to sprawling and domineering. The roads that lead off, small lanes and busier streets carry names arcane with antiquity, quaint peculiarities of an esoteric past: The Vineyard, Ellerker Gardens, Nightingale Lane, Friars Stile Road — what fanciful tales, now forgotten, prompted such dedications! It is hard to really encapsulate the uniqueness of Richmond Hill because there is no natural comparison (though William Byrd may have disagreed) — the thin causeway climbing that clings to the fading face of steep topography, magisterially looking down over green land and the curving breach of the Thames as it cuts and fades southwards to Kingston.

From high in the stern-faced properties, along the ridge where the land runs away into the Thames Valley plain, it is almost weirdly similar to the sensation gazing out from Hampshire House on Central Park South — the bird's eye view of lush greenery, trees bunched and clumped. And, whilst the horizon isn't the chalky sprawling expanse of Harlem, it shares the unfathomable serenity and joy of acres and acres of unspoilt flora. From Richmond Hill, archetypal English countryside fills the panorama and, to the possible envy of New Yorkers, the irrepressible Thames curls lazily between intermittent tracts of fine properties cutting through the trees and meadows out towards Kempton Park and Hampton Court. Just to sit on the terrace as Turner and the Prince Regent once did, absorbing the ultimate natural boundary of the great metropolitan capital, buildings seemingly handpicked from Grosvenor Square and Mayfair, looming behind; or to wander from the spectacle, down little alleyways and lanes amongst the relics of older forms of Richmond, little cottages and lawned mansions, the legacy of Georgian and Victorian lust for aspects and status. It is also unashamedly affluent, but then it is also so utterly unreproducible.

Amongst this exclusivity and separatism, away from the celebrated views and the divine property, the streets are lined with semi-detached townhouses, five stories of the inevitable pale-yellow brick, mildly decorative bands of sugary plaster at windows; gabled and bayed, and now split, often clumsily and inconsiderately, into apartments. Not without their charm, of course, the prices still obscene per square foot, the luxury addresses still exclusive, the height and scale of the rooms still enviable, but the narrow streets and excess of parked cars, the nasty eighties dormer extensions, mean accessibility for a less moneyed class, well-off renters or the spoilt children of rich families. In one such street, Onslow Road, such a house exists;

its window frames, the original wooden sashes, freshly painted a glossy black. Yellow and pink flowers in the summer scattered upon plump bushes in the mossy, concreted front yard, a tropical plant out of place in an ugly pot at the top of the nine steps to the suspended entrance. From the exposed side wall, beyond the small entrance hall window, a brick annex protrudes oddly from the raised ground floor, acting as an open but sheltered porch to the door of the basement flat...

Bilal isn't as lucky as us – me and the wife – he doesn't live on the hill, around it or even in Richmond, he lives in the quiet suburbanity of Surbiton, so it was no particular effort for him to drive his Ford up the incline; the mansions, apartments, the luxury homes unseen and uninteresting. Solidly brought up in the contemporary working class – his father worked for the Underground, an insignificant supervisory role, his wife working for the Nationwide – he can't relate to affluence; their finances are safe enough and their breeding has resulted in just the one pretty, infant girl. He can't relate to any concept of excess, it doesn't register to him how a family, let alone a couple or a bachelor, could require so much space or pay so much money to be close to a view, without even possessing it.

Bilal groaned at the decrepit locals creepily completing their short strolls, struggling from their rooms-without-a-view; trudging onwards to the long gravel terrace at the lip of the hill, just to sit and gaze back into time. Back to a place where they respected and were respected; looking out over the low land, remembering when manners cost nothing and yet people were prepared to pay.

He revved the car's engine, forced into an uncomfortable lower gear as one such old couple crossed the road. I sat in the passenger seat anticipating my imminent escape and dive into The Buck's Head, my local pub. The old folks staggering by made me smile, cheered by the sense of optimism that flooded in seeing the doddery pair entwined in history and content familiarity. It created a curious sensation of possibility – that marriage could work; but quickly a coolness washed my thoughts as the realization of the difference between these two geriatrics and myself and Joodie caught up with me. As they might remember their lost, dead world in the green scenery down the hillside, I understood that me and seemingly everyone else was no longer capable of comprehending devotion, we could not be trusted with marriage; everyone was too impatient and lazy.

Seemingly oblivious to the traffic, their slowness was more of deliberation and detachment than infirmity. The man was upright and groomed divinely, she had a slight curvature exploiting and diminishing her no doubt elegant posture – it could have merely been a stoop rather than osteoporosis, a tendency adopted to compensate for the length of her body. They strolled indifferently across the road, crossing at a point convenient to them rather than dictated by the marked crossing further up the hill. It seemed as though they did so unaware of the traffic building up on the incline, until the man, his left arm escorting his wife, raised his free hand, the loose beige sleeve of his Burberry overcoat dragging back up his shoulder; he opened his palm, crooked fingers splayed long, rheumatically unable to wave fully, he gestured an appreciation for the inconvenient pause and continued forward into the path of the downhill traffic. Bilal revved the engine again, no longer with impatient aggression, but to hurriedly set the vehicle back on course, the small distance to make up before he would drop me at the pub.

In front of the building I looked both ways, not about to cross the road, but loitering in the middle of the pavement. It had occurred to me, waving away the back of the Ford and the back of Bilal's head, that perhaps there was an alternative to my customary weekend pint. My observations up and down the road covered two options: option one – stirred by the hanging memory of the finely maintained old couple – was downhill, to visit the terrace and the view, (even though I lived just a few streets back, it was not a place I went; instead, rushing home from the pub for the re-run of a sitcom churned out on a daily basis, a loop of American theatrics that I could consume ad-infinitum, cyclically, season after repeated season), or, option two, uphill, towards the tall gates of Richmond Park – again, another place criminally ignored – I had grown up with the idea that a park was a deep green flat field, marked out for sports, crisscrossed with regulated concrete paths, a fenced off playground, maybe a tennis court – Richmond Park might have been a sprawling Kenyan reserve for all I had previously cared. That expansive undisturbed rough countryside: it would be like going back to the middle ages; save it, I had argued, for the horse riders and bird watchers. If I wanted grass, I could sit on the Green or in the backyard of a pub; after all I rarely set foot in my own garden, let alone that great deer-stalked wilderness.

Today, as my head took in the up and down, something did press at me: a nag, an inclination to go into the park. Even stronger was the lure to go downhill to the terrace and the older folk. Unfortunately, stronger still, I followed the unbreakable call of The Buck's Head, entering, forgetting all about the other alternatives, welcoming the low dark interior of the ancient hostelry and the sour smelling carpet and alcohol.

Of all the charming anachronistic pubs in and around Richmond Hill, I had my reasons for choosing The Buck's Head as my "local", Friday evenings, a kick-start to the inefficient inadequacy of my weekend, slowly mulling over the weak froth of the regional real ale. Chief among these reasons was convenience, second was its aspect, although the seating in my preferred spot, by the window, was low and the view somewhat obscured by the trees. What I had missed, avoiding repose on the terrace, I tried to compensate for, through and over glass.

The large old window, its faint curvature and the small wooden squared frames, from the outside especially, had something of the look of the rear end of a galleon; it felt oddly nautical. Landlocked and almost airborne, yet the suggestion of the historic caused me to cast myself, now and again, as an ancient mariner.

Sitting there, the fractured autumnal gloom and the inadequate lighting made me lose my grip on the "now", I fancied myself as some wandering Georgian journeyman...no, a curate returning from London to some Wiltshire parish; regardless, such daydreaming left me absent, broken from the subterranea of my work place and the effort of staying married.

I took up my current biography of choice (right now it was the over-indulgent, syphilitic tragedy of William Makepeace Thackeray) avoiding any eye contact with the miserable barman and his moronic wife and her tedious over-exaggerations. Mercifully, with a grudging obligation, they only interrupted me on the misfortune of me stumbling into eye contact with either of them – many times I had been forced to dash my eyes back down to my book, hoping that they had missed it, feeling how I used to feel at high school, caught dreamily gazing at some unattainable prettiness with a Princess Diana haircut. So, I took up my book and loosened myself with beer, the cosy anachronism of low ceilings and hand-formed woodworking, drifting away into the past.

What did it offer, these onward journeys to imaginary lives, formed of literary figures and long-suffering artist's wives, but always so different to Joodie, always full of lightness? I'd create with noticeable antithesis as far from my world as I could conceive and be happy until the last drop and the returning drone of large executive motors on the road outside, luckier men returning to grand lives and happier worlds.

It seemed odd as I sat there, appraising myself – the

notion of unfollowed paths; my habitual predictability spun my thoughts inward and, self-conscious, I wondered why I had always been so sentimental. Wasn't sentimentality reserved for the geriatric pedestrians we had revved across the road? Why did my thoughts have to turn backwards to find reassurance and calm?

The window had triggered it – for once it was not the Captain's cabin that transported me away, it was the pure and practical form of the frame, the humble technology that had contrived to bend the panels into this bow; just then, all the flatness of modernity seemed wearying and disappointing. I am prone to allowing my thoughts to criss-cross and with a sip of beer, my book softly ignored over the edge of the table, I began thinking about the old couple crossing Richmond Hill. It was indulgent, but I let the sweetish melancholy grow, disenchantment tinged with the warmth of their affection and the heavy joy and sink of the alcohol.

Entrenched in these occupations, my mind twisted further and discovered a new, involuntarily sought path; the poetry of my mind transported me back to my desk and the still gloom of my office and the exchange I had had with Bilal. Nowadays, there were phases of lust for Joodie; that was all, and that was all it was: lust – such shallow desire, no more emotional or meaningful than the pull to the pub each Friday; no romance, no real affection, just a drab physical placation. I wallowed in a dreamy appraisal of her body, the coolness of her curves, her slim waist and sharp breasts and laughed gently as I conceded the validity of Bilal's implausibly sincere wish to enjoy what I had and perhaps took for granted; my own desire was not so fully directed; at least, not so playfully, happily interested.

Meandering through my frigid indifference, slightly aroused sensually, the path of my thoughts now shifted laterally; still primed by the earlier conversation and my increasingly romantic, or rather, lustful, state of mind, without prompt or control I found my focus had shifted back to Ophelie Wyeth. Again, it confused me why her presence should be so tightly pursuing me. I had let my mind fill with nudity and sexuality, thinking about Joodie, suddenly there was Ophelie – only, and rather oddly, she was neither nude nor with any apparent sexual association – but before me, as a daydream. My mind swelled with the pompousness of the biography I had been reading, the accompanying monologue in my head was of floating femininity, I was audience to an apparition of sudden intrigue.

Beyond anything, however, snapping out of this fantasy, guilt crushed down on me.

I tried to rationalise it: why it was that, whilst infidelity has traditionally been so commonplace, there now seemed to be something grimly incestuous regarding the possession of deeper feelings for the friends of one's wife or girlfriend. Obviously, all kinds of infidelity are considered wrong these days, but this practice of applying grades, levels of misdemeanour, how is this rational? Time and accessibility to one another is the most natural catalyst for attraction, so it stands to reason that relationships commonly blossom between unattached friends and co-workers. Pure physical attraction or "love at first sight" can exist, obviously – in a moment, in a glance – but among those acquainted, a deeper soulful connection must be the more natural outcome? So, to fall for one's friend is not so strange, nor for a relationship to develop – trust pre-established, the intimacy forged on platonic foundations. To fall, then, for a friend that coincidentally happens to be the friend of one's wife or partner, well, can it be prevented any more than falling for a friend when one is unattached? It happens, it is not so surprising when it does, and yet there is such foulness to the deed – yes, it is unfaithful and unfaithful is bad, but somehow it is worse because the person is known! Conventional logic suggests that if one is involved then falling for *anyone*, friend or stranger, is completely unacceptable, but so is parking illegally or taking a stapler home from the office (and almost as common). Trivialities perhaps, but wrong, done and tolerated; without implying justification for infidelity, one must accept that such adultery happens, as it always has and always will – but if it is unfaithfulness with an acquaintance...

I was not being unfaithful. I quickly repeated this to myself, trying to establish that as my state of mind, instead of the guilt, but still I suffered as though I were. Burdened with a comparative guilt, I had not and was not considering leaving Joodie. Ophelie was married, anyway, and there was no moment I could recollect where any suggestive chemistry was present between us – but if ever anything happened, I knew it would be far worse than if I left Joodie for a woman unknown. I mean, I thought about such women all the time – at work, on TV, on the tube – all the time, without guilt; I think about them sexually and not a flicker of disloyalty – thoughts are safely platonic, right? And yet I thought of Ophelie with nothing more than an unplaced curiosity and discovered myself to be appalled.

Onslow Road

Across the hard, stone kitchen floor, milky yellow October sunshine lay between the legs of chairs and the tumble and crash of fur and faces, the playful fight of our cats. The bundle froze in the middle of some intertwined gymnastic game, three heads turned up to my towering figure strolling among the faint shadows. I reached over the worktops, the glistening black and gold and grey granite that Joodie had insisted upon (and it did look lovely, I had conceded this, although I came short of sharing her excitement at discovering that the colour palette of the expensive stone matched the tabby colouring of Shidney, the youngest pet.) As I reached, the sag of my shirt gathered a watery thin coffee spillage that I didn't notice; I tugged down a window-blind, clipping and castrating a chrysanthemum, I took it and tossed it to the thrilled feline sprawl on the floor.

It was one of those brilliantly cold mornings, winter was still distant enough that frost was not formed; the garden, seasonally abandoned – items left randomly on the last warm day, always in mind that another would follow, but the sun shone lower now, and these cloudless days were illuminated only with a frigid sun. There was no frost, but the dew sat on the lawn and sparkled like chrome and the coffee darkness between my hands was warmer than ever as I considered the golds and bronzes, the entire metallic tonal spectrum of autumn.

'You really have to put all that stuff away, the stuff in the garden; it'll go rusty.' Joodie was a local girl, mildly middle-class, but of the normal working part of it; she was born and raised in Sheen, suburb to the suburb, thick still with her family and the school friends that hadn't moved either into the county or into the city, finding the parochiality of Richmond too quaint or too faded depending which way they ran. Joodie remained. She had studied at Kingston, staying with her mother and father, and since then she had worked in television and media, stuff I knew nothing about, famous clients, offices in Soho; everyone involved, as far as I could tell, was either precocious or pretentious or both – a new moneyed class of tasteless brats, forging their ugly dumbed-down cultural stamp on the capital and, thus, the nation.

Joodie's clique are not really my kind of people. I'm not the least bit creative, I don't have a relationship with whatever social media is; but I am conversational, I can talk to almost anybody, so I can interact with her workmates; occasionally I hit veins of compatibility and, more often than not, I'm content, in my practical way. It's this thing with logistics, efficiency, again – finding ways to make my life as easy as possible, so I find paths to navigate those evenings in uncomfortable bars in the West End. My own circle of friends is small, I was brought up around London but never anywhere specific for more than a few years, my decisive teenage years were spent in Hammersmith where it seemed like everyone just sat around smoking weed and listening to NWA, while I was listening to Genesis and Caravan. A few friends lingered, others faded, like so much male companionship, with the break of university; or a shift to new groups through work, until only a couple of people I could call friends remained, and I only saw them once, twice a year, at best, even though they were just a few miles away. As such, Joodie orchestrated any entertaining we did at home; a combination of those friends from her work and her past that she felt, more or less, "got on with me". It became an established core of people; we entertained more than our parents had ever done but with an amateurism that at times made us, well, me at least, feel like we were only playing at being grown-ups...

'Eh, what was that?' She had crushed my autumnal reverie; I hadn't even noticed her come into the room, and yet she was sitting there at the breakfast bar, split between her magazine and her coffee.

'All that mess in the garden,' she repeated, heading to the coffee percolator to refill her cup. 'It has to be put away before it rusts, it'll ruin out there all winter.'

'All winter?' Her careless exaggeration annoyed me. I repeated...I *whined* the phrase back at her so that she could experience the melodrama for herself. 'It's not going to stay out there all winter; I was just looking at it...' (This was a lie) 'I'm thinking about doing it later...'

'Well, you'll have to do it this morning, it looks awful and Phee and Craig are coming for lunch.'

'What?'

She looked up from her magazine, her coffee cup suspended above it; the snap in my tone seemed to have bothered her.

'Why didn't I know about this?'

I did know, at least now she said it I suddenly remembered her telling me, and I let it annoy me, that and the fact that it was assumed that it was down to me to clear the garden, and that I would have to do it in a hurry. And also, disturbingly, I discovered that it annoyed me to hear Ophelie's name mentioned – her name or its juxtaposition with her husband's?

I blushed, this was getting silly now – I hadn't thought about her all of Friday evening, Joodie had opened some wine and we had watched sitcoms until bed; but just her name, just that one little mention and I was mentally twitching and uncomfortable. Turning away to hide my reddened cheeks, facing the kitchen window, deep at the foot of the tall house, I began to warm inside, how beautiful the sunlight, golden against the back wall, and Ophelie – how intriguing, now, the prospect of seeing her. I really wanted to see her, never before had I actually *wanted* to see her; and she was coming, soon she'd actually be here and I could dismiss these ridiculous thoughts.

'I suppose I'd best get started on it, then.' My grumble was part a return to chagrin, part a necessary disguise of this sudden anticipation.

'You needn't do it straight away.' It was a needless and infuriating contribution, offered without looking up this time, the coffee mug still swinging on her hooked hand. Even if I'd answered straight away, she wasn't listening for a response, her arty magazine seemed more interesting than anything I had to say. The tone of my voice, I hoped, would show her I was pissed off, and she expected only excuses or procrastination anyway. Beyond antagonising me with her contrariness, she had no wish to get involved in a debate regarding a task from which she had already excused herself.

'I don't see why it comes down to me to do it anyway?' I controlled my tone and shifted from whiny child to disgruntled co-worker, ultimately unable to drop the whole nonsense. Joodie looked up briefly, wordless, her expression answering for her; she noticed her coffee, took a sip and set it down on a place mat. 'It doesn't,' she advised, contradicting the obvious inference of her look, 'it just would be nice if you could do it.'

This is what I hated; why did she have to sound so bloody reasonable and calm when she was being so manipulative and divisive?

'I guess it's the only way it'll ever get done.' I contributed my own snide remark to the exchange; it was all I had left.

I took a final swig of my coffee and looked out of the window again; there wasn't actually that much that needed doing. Without further comment – it occurred to me that we hadn't even said good morning – I trundled down the corridor to the bedroom to change. It was not like this every day, but the touch-paper was short; mercifully, it was not so often that our moods were naked flames and thus peace was maintained. And yet, should that incandescence occur, ignition was inevitable.

As I had done with my job title, so had I also done, five years ago, for the flat: argued for its cosiness, the idea of me and Joodie tucked away from the world in the snug warm basement – it was beautifully fitted out, a decent height, consuming the entire foot print of the house. At the time I had an office on the third floor of a 1980s midrise in Croydon, admittedly, it was dismal, but it was full of daylight and a vista that, without being interesting, was not to be sniffed at; so, the period appeal of the flat in Onslow Road, the low dark rooms seemed to be the perfect balance to my airborne blandness. Eventually, Joodie was swayed by the reality that this was as good as we would get on Onslow, or any other road, so close to the Hill, the park, the town and her family. Typically, only a short time after we bought it, my company relocated to the current vault I occupy; an almost troglodytical existence, shifting from one dingy hole to another, became my life. I was actually glad, then, to be in the garden, scooping up the various summer goods and forlorn tools from the grass and the path. I even considered, standing frozen, looking like a mental case in the middle of the garden, whether I had the patience and energy to mow the grass, the alternative of going back inside was hardly glowing, so I scheduled the task – once started, it wasn't so difficult to find motivation. My thoughts, as usual, kept me company, thinking again about Richmond Park, that maybe I would try to take a walk there later – but damn it, Ophelie and Craig were due for lunch – apparently. There would be no escape.

The annoyance of losing my Saturday to a visit from a couple I liked but that had never really stimulated me continued to pursue me. There was a chasm of difference between me and them, not insurmountable, but the conversation always floundered, the scope for interest too soon exhausted. But my mind was not finished, its conniving continued until I found myself focused purely on Ophelie. I did like her; I couldn't deny it – she was incredibly sweet and thoughtful. Perhaps it was actually the similarities in our pace of life that raised the barriers between us, maybe we were more similar than I thought. Unsure, I tried harder to think about her accurately – the last twenty-four hours I had concerned myself with her physicality, her slim curvaceousness and grace, but I couldn't really see her, couldn't really press her face up to the light to see what was there, if there was in fact any appeal. It was too difficult; I could only remember the cruel frozen captures of the randomness of candid photographs, the gallery of images seen briefly over Joodie's shoulder, that she shared with the world, that she felt represented her satisfaction with her looks or, braver, those images that revealed how she wished people to consider her and her life. But, as I said, I am not a great believer or consumer of digital socialising and it had been a while since I had seen these pictures, I had no registered social media account, I was reliant purely on memory – I hadn't even looked at any of the billions of photos Joodie had taken of our life, most of which were, like so much of my life, entombed in some little black plastic box next to her laptop, effectively irretrievable. There was very little to go on, other than what my fussy mind had preserved.; relying on this source, I managed to establish that I was content to think about Ophelie, regardless of whether it was accurate or not, to think about her in a way I could neither explain nor voluntarily abandon – she calmed me from my own drudgery and self-absorption and thrilled me slightly with the freshness of new attraction.

'Done.' It seemed important to make a point of my effort. Joodie still sat at the high island in the centre of the kitchen, her laptop opened, a barrier between her preoccupation and my interruption.

'Well done. I mean…thanks.' She balked at her initial sarcasm, I doubt that it was because she felt wrong for it, or even because I had done something that was potentially a joint task, something that she might have got roped into – no, it seemed simply to be because, right now, she had no wish to antagonise me. And not for my benefit, it was utterly selfishly motivated; obviously she was involved with the study of some website, to do with some project she was no doubt wrapped up in.

'You're welcome.' I had no such problem with my own lazy irony, everything was annoying me, and her latest reaction seemed to be a push too far. 'You know that was both our stuff out...'

'Yes, dear, and I *do* appreciate it...really. You know I'm busy with this, I can't just leave my work at, er, work, you know, not like you. Besides, I need to finish what I'm working on before...' and she looked at her watch, 'Damn, before Phee and Craig.'

'Perhaps you should have factored this in when you invited them over.' I was back on to my annoyance at them coming over Saturday lunchtime – honestly, I was up to my chin in her crap. 'I can't see why you've asked them over for lunch...on a Saturday. Don't these sort of things usually happen at a restaurant or café? Surely, if we had to meet them at lunchtime, a café by the river or lunch on the Green would have been more suitable, at least then I would have felt as though the day had purpose.'

'Oh, Chris, must we? I am *so* busy with this...'

'You not on the internet?'

'Um, yes, of course I'm on the internet, but it's work.'

'Right. It just seems a bit of a strange thing to have organised...for a Saturday.'

'What difference does the day make? Look...ah,' she stretched upright from her slouch, conceding the necessity to break from her work and attend to what she was clearly considering to be her problematic spouse. 'Look, I'm super-busy and I need to do this this morning, I wouldn't have had the time to traipse down to town, in all the shoppers, fart about looking for somewhere to eat, it would have ended up taking forever; it's just much easier having them over. Besides, when was the last time we had anyone round?'

'Do you have time, then, to prepare the food?'

Suddenly her dominance was withdrawn, and a child presented; I could see where it was going and let her get as far as, 'I was hoping...' I spun on the spot and gripped the edge of the worktop, it was silly and melodramatic, but... It wasn't an argument, I wasn't even especially angry, but it was so typical of her – I didn't even mind doing it, but hadn't I just spent the last hour in the garden picking junk out of the cold, wet grass? There was no chance of mowing now.

'I wish you'd told me.' I turned back to her, and, oddly, I had to smile; she was beautiful sitting there, peering with her big dark eyes over the top of her laptop – half hiding, half flirting. Suddenly I wanted to sleep with her – now, of all the times! I fumed inside at my misfortune. For a moment I even considered it possible that nowadays I was only attracted to her when I was mad at her – it wasn't so, but it did seem just lately to be the case that we only felt horny at times when sex was completely impossible.

'Is there any coffee?' I distracted myself, returning to the domestic. 'I mean, when *were* you going to ask?'

A sorry looking inch of coffee was all I could pour from the glass bowl, missing the dregs, which I cast carelessly into the sink. I switched off the plate and sipped unimpressed at the bitter stewed drink.

'I've bought all the stuff,' Joodie announced, pleased to have remembered this fact, offering it by way of a consolation, her part of a compromise – immediately, it was now a joint effort and there was no longer a reason to feel guilty. 'You know you *are* a host too.'

I didn't feel very hospitable and grumbled inarticulately. Sensing this to be an agreement and the end of the matter, Joodie slumped her shoulders back down to the screen, her face lit amber from the page colour, back to work.

Early afternoon sunlight shone low into the back yard, the south-western aspect of the rear of the property allowed light to gradually fill the kitchen as the earth tipped over, over and over until it would leave the shy autumn sun, raising the western hemisphere, sending up the houses on Montague Road, sending up the horizon, twilight and then darkness. There was no direct sunlight in the sheltered alleyway along the side of the house, yet it felt like an abundance of light compared to the dim gloom inside when I opened the door, and in this light I saw the happy, fine faces of Ophelie and Craig, faces with that warm message, "look, it's us!"; broad smiles, as much pleasure being seen, as seeing. I took in Ophelie's features – for the first time, it seemed – appraising her on a level more than mere acquaintanceship. It was odd, the way she smiled didn't flatter her at all, it was cumbersome and ill-fitting, although still very natural and reassuring. She was immeasurably different from Joodie and her huge dark eyes and pixie nose and mouth; Ophelie, with her French ancestry was altogether more Gallic, but not in a sleek, dark Mireille Mathieu way, not even with the light breezy looks of Bardot, but more the masculine strength of a Capucine, strong jawed and full lipped, a proud shapely nose and pale oval eyes (yes, I actually surprised myself, my untapped knowledge of dead or dying French women, too many late nights watching old movies, anything to escape modernity). Yet her broad over-smile broke the geometry of her features and, by no means ugly, she became ordinary again – from French starlet glamour to awkwardly attributed girl next door, in the flash of a smile. As I watched her through to the living room, she offered her gummy gesture of pleasure, apparently oblivious as to how it distorted her looks. I swooned a little, she was here and happy to see me, and something, something beyond her features, just her bearing, her presence, suddenly, and for the first time, had an impact on me that at once excited and terrified me – everything in the last twenty-four hours instantly became terrifyingly real.

With my contribution to the preparation of the lunch done and dismissed as such, Joodie was only too happy to step in and act as waitress and hostess; I wasn't even concerned that she would get credit for my work, I just wanted to sit down in the living room and relax. Ophelie was nattering confidentially with Joodie in the kitchen, I just didn't care, they might be annihilating me with slander, it didn't bother me, I'd had enough today, now I was through with my obligations. Furthermore, I discovered that I was pleased to have company; Craig and Ophelie were a sweet couple, of all of Joodie's friends, maybe they were the most pleasant, at least they were the least hung up and self-absorbed.

Craig (or Cregg as he pronounced it in his mid-Atlantic drawl) was a sports journalist; a scratch golfer without the nerves to have gone pro, he had drifted into writing about his sport and, blessed, now spent his time covering the US pro tour for some internet sports service, or something like that, I'd never bothered to set it to memory. He sat on the couch and, decently remembering that I knew nothing and cared even less for golf, started a rather awkwardly male conversation about music. Unfortunately, Craig knew almost nothing about the kind of music I listened to but trusted that he was smart enough to have an opinion on stuff he had only a passing familiarity with. From somewhere he pulled out the name of a Danish band that I was not familiar with but, a lucky shot from Craig, it was a band I had heard of and had been intrigued by.

'Definitely, you really should check them out; you'd probably really like them.' Of course, Craig was obliged to make such a prediction – he had no idea how I would feel about them, but it was the only way to reliably sustain the conversation, a collapse in dialogue now and we would be at the mercy of either or both of the women returning to break us from that awful catastrophe of male social interaction, the inability to use a subject more than once without a different direction being taken first, like a penalty in football that has to touch an opposing player before the missed shot can be salvaged.

'Yeah, they sound like the sort of band I'd probably enjoy, a bit more expansive than your average combo these days. But I haven't bought a CD in months, they sound a bit obscure for HMV, I'd probably have to go into London.'

'You do have the internet, though?'

'We have it, but it's on that bloody Mac thing, I'm not so good with them, I'm barely on speaking terms with my PC at work, and anyway it's not hooked up to the stereo.'

'No, but I meant that you could buy it online, there's plenty of places...'

I was mortified, how pathetic of me for not thinking of this, it must have made me seem dumb and out of touch, but worse – I knew this from my job; what was the point of being Senior Logistics Manager if you couldn't even think to buy a CD online.

'Of course,' I mumbled, ashamed. 'I'm just a bit lazy, I suppose.'

My negativity broke the conversation, fortunately it wasn't noticed, Joodie came in loudly with a tray of drinks, laughing and talking over her shoulder to Ophelie, with her own tray of food.

'I was just telling Ophelie about Cameron, at work...' She had already told me about bloody Cameron, at work, now she had told Ophelie and now she was going to tell Craig. 'Basically, Cameron is such a laugh, but the other day he came to work and he was in such a bitch of a mood....'

I had no choice, I just shut my mind down; I began to watch Ophelie as she waltzed with the tray through the obstacles placed around the living room. She moved effortlessly, her centre of gravity was perfectly balanced for stability and graceful movement; tall, and high hipped. She wore plain fitted jeans and a thick knit sweater, a kerchief tied playfully asymmetric around her collar, her hair was loose and long, pinned casually back over her ears and her face seemed totally unmade up.

'...And I said to him: "Look, Cameron, that's between you and your wife, don't do your laundry in the workplace..."'

The phrasal malapropism cut through my wool-gathering, like nails down a blackboard. Why was she even telling everybody this, nobody cared about Cameron's failed marriage, it was just depressing; I could see Craig nodding and smiling fakely – years of interviewing tedious golfers, I suspected, masterful show of interest, though no doubt hopelessly bored.

Ophelie sat forward, leaning to look at the food spread on the coffee table, looking at it with wide eyes, looking at it as if she hadn't just carried it through from the kitchen. Her body seemed ready to break into a fit of shaking; her knees, together, rocked side to side and her hands, clasped in her lap, rocked with them, whilst her shoulders shifted with a corresponding inverse movement. There was something immature in her ingenuous excitement, even if she was just being polite, it was with an unpolluted freshness, a pleasure to act out. The broad embarrassed smile of her entrance had gone, replaced by the consumption of her lower lip by her upper lip, causing a slight delicate point to form. Seeing this, I shifted forward to the front of my armchair and watched her as she scanned the tray of snacks like a cat approaching its bowl. They were divine, her lips – how had I never noticed this before, how had I never felt how special her mouth was? Of course, I was familiar with the feature, years of watching her speak, watching the activity of expression, how she allowed (as she now did) her lips to hang apart very slightly, anticipating something remarkable – it was all incredibly familiar to me, and yet suddenly it was new and dizzying and totally absorbing; she was remarkably attractive to me right now.

I wanted to kiss her.

Like a child with a comfort blanket, I needed to feel something against my lips. Beauty was before me, but until I felt it against my own all-sensitive lips it would not be real, it would be nothing more than a picture or a scene from a movie.

Ophelie's joy at the spread of food reached its climax and, her fingers pinching like the descending head of a crane, she dipped down to the platter and picked out a single tiny piece of bread and popped it onto her plate with almost fussy delicacy. A few small samples of the rest of the buffet followed and she balanced the plate on her lap, looking around waiting for everyone else to gather their portions.

Consumption of the food caused Joodie's story to unexpectedly climax or rather it reached its painful end, a climax would suggest an element of drama, at the very least a shift in direction or tone; she had introduced an additional character, but this woman was even less familiar to her audience than the protagonist was. So, as her final words were generously shared there was a sensation of breaths held, not from suspense, merely the uncertainty of whether the loop was to begin again.

Sensing a gap in her insinuated soliloquy, preventing her return to the suspense of Cameron's misbehaviour, I pounced into the vacant hush with a spontaneous question. All the time that she had been finishing her workplace tale, I had been snacking violently, getting the most out of the spread, not purely through hunger but for the unacknowledged effort I had put into preparing it. Throughout this gorging I had continued appraising Ophelie and Craig – less about their physical appearance (though more than once I found that my gaze dwelt upon Ophelie; her bored face seemed to sink, the bright life that made her, now seemed withdrawn, replaced with an indifference, stained just slightly with a sourness) – but specifically I considered them as a couple. They were a little odd; I searched to find the dominant partner – it seemed only natural – yet with these two it seemed that while individually they both had strength, together they seemed to cancel each other out until a washed-out blandness of attitude consumed them. Rather than bringing out one another's personality, they seemed to repress each other's character. Maybe it was their dissimilarity – though there was common ground in abundance, there was something more essential that was of an opposing polarity – it was almost as though they repressed their own light to avoid casting shadows on one another.

I didn't dislike Craig. Craig was an ok guy: kind and generous; clearly, he was good for Ophelie – yet I noticed within myself a growing discomfort, a dislike of the man's company. Perhaps – I had pursued the thought as Joodie blathered on about "sweet Cameron" and his "fatalistic sense of romance" – perhaps there was an element of jealousy.

By anyone's standards, Craig had a dream job, swanning around the luxury resorts of America, the finest hospitality, business class travel, the society of the rich and famous – it wasn't even comparable to the monotony of my own work and the views were, of course, much better. More than this, though, I felt bad for Ophelie – it was one thing for me to envy Craig, but it must be even harder for Ophelie to accept; as far as I knew, she seldom attended any of his events. Perhaps she might have been more annoyed by his absences had she not been so busily employed, but, still, it was apparent that Craig did not encourage her involvement in his work – she had said so herself, I impressively recalled, a sighing complaining tone in her voice, confessing that it was a bit of a closed shop – she was left out of this exotic part of his life. Furthermore, apparently burnt out with the business class hospitality and sports star schmoozing, when Craig returned home, he had been telling me, he returned subdued and desirous of simple domesticity, to crash in front of pay per view sports, to cook a little and to take his car out into Surrey or even down to the south coast, across the Downs. All the travelling, he argued, the anonymous hotel rooms and catered lunches, all of this sucked away his personality and apparently only a drive in the country could bring it back and she, Ophelie, was welcome to join him, if she wanted. And, happy just to have him beside her, I guessed, she would do it, getting a movie and his body on hers in reply. It must have been sufficient or acceptable for Ophelie, glad just to be a couple again.

'Your job, Craig?' Sitting forward to eat, I aimed directly at Craig, physically aimed, like a catapult, potential and dangerous; an approach direct and slightly impudent, there was something of the job interviewer about me, the dimness of the room provided an added hostility; none of any of this however was present in my tone, which I kept jocular and matey. 'When is Ophelie going to get to take advantage of it?'

Naturally, Craig had ready a library worth of circumstances and hindrances to counter such an idea; I didn't doubt this, I wasn't consciously trying to upset or annoy Craig, consciously I wasn't specifically trying to do anything. It just came out – the barrier between my conscious and unconscious thought was wafer thin, it was not even a barrier right now, more a sieve – that is, certain thoughts that worked their way through my processing mind were unconscious only by virtue of my failure to accept responsibility for them – not through stubbornness but by disbelief that that they could possibly have been of my own creation. It had all built up in me: my wife disgorging words, Ophelie confusing me and Craig sort of annoying me – the specific motivation for pursuing this trite and socially unfair line of questioning was, amazingly, a notion that I was acting as a protector and defender of Ophelie. Not that she wished for or appreciated it; she, as much as anybody was embarrassed by my unexpected curiosity – they had all heard the reasons before, all of which were defendable and reasonable and so perfectly considered that they were as watertight as if designed to protect Craig from an infidelity.

Craig, beginning this well-rehearsed charade, practiced but still a shade discomposed at having to perform the farcical routine, drew back his shoulders and breathed deeply; his attempt to subdue the physical side of the bullshit had the counter effect of making him look strained and uncomfortable.

'Well, there you go.' He finally began and, it turned out, ended; an ambiguous riddle of a response immediately throwing me off the scent, not quite what had been expected, no lame formulaic cop-out, just a meaningless fragment.

'Really? I do? No, I'm not sure what you're saying.' I attempted to match Craig's indirectness, leaning further forward and, in a show of calm, contrary disinterest, forking a half tomato from the salad.

'It's a job, Chris; you can see *that*, can't you?' He had slipped a little, the sarcasm a crack in the composure that helped seal the lie, the whole acting out of this laughable dance. Whatever the excuse Craig chose to employ, everybody in the room knew that Craig had no particular desire to have his wife in tow – not that he needed her absent, he would survive if she was his constant travelling companion, he would simply miss having the leave to flirt and ogle, he would miss also the liberty to drink freely, to play his little hand-held video game thingy, he would miss the freeness of the quasi-single life. It was understandable, fair enough; it was tolerated. In her own way, Ophelie received much the same benefits, only without the sunshine and the catering, she had her friends and her work, her family and the countryside – she was happy enough. All that remained was to sustain the façade, to ensure that everybody continued to believe the lie that "nothing could be done".

I, however, was ruining it – my hopeless, implausible pursuit, my forcing the game to be played out was putting pressure on Craig, and Craig, not helping, was for some reason avoiding the tried and tested pat responses and the usual sad regret at leaving her behind.

He chuckled, trying to disguise the sarcasm as silliness. 'It's just a job – she has better things to do than traipse around golf courses; it's really not *that* glamorous...' He petered out, realising he had got this slightly wrong, even the weak dismissiveness at the end could not prevent the ill-chosen words before – it should have commenced with the disclaimer flagging how much he wished that she could be with him, and then something about the "strict rules and regulations of his employers and the circuit" – no, this was wrong, it was flawed. I was, in fact, about ready to abandon my ill-judged heroics; the lack of appreciation on Ophelie's face disconcerted me; I sensed her displeasure at the whole dreadful scene. I was ready to quit whilst he was ahead, but suddenly this was something new, this aperture in their tedious harmony deserved to be tested. I leant in, having sat back in preparation for my sad withdrawal, and looked towards Ophelie as I spoke to Craig. She was a picture of bewilderment and disbelief.

'*Every* time? Are you telling me that just a few times a year, Ophelie wouldn't be interested in being whisked away? You're at the golf, sure, but I have a feeling that Austin and, er, Miami and...and...I don't know, LA? – these places all have pretty decent malls and restaurants...and beaches.'

I switched observation between the two of them, hungry for both their responses. Ophelie had turned her own attention sternly towards her husband – the game was a shambles – clearly she was now interested in witnessing his unprotected feelings on the subject of her tagging along. In reality, as far as I had previously understood, she usually got at least one trip a year out of his job, another reason she had initially found my inquisitiveness tiresome, she had even travelled to Dubai the year before last; but this was not about free vacations, this was about his charmed status as a free-wandering man, about the reserve of his life away from her; even more, it was about who he considered her to be these days. What might he say in response to this challenge, where and how did he actually see her?

Craig looked blankly but expectantly back at me, a twist of the neck towards but not wholly round to Ophelie, enough to see her intentness in his periphery; almost, he appeared to be waiting for someone else to answer, like a scolded cat, unsure, wanting to hide but trapped, confused at the nature of his crime. Humanity returned, and he parted his lips to speak, Ophelie shifted her crossed legs, tugging down the edge of her long sweater that folded around her hips like a shift dress.

It felt like a no way out situation, one of those awful traps where every answer is wrong and most will make things worse. Craig's lips were frozen, desperate. He filled his cheeks with air, before exhaling hopelessly into an absent trumpet, clapped his fingers together and...

'This is *exactly* the same situation as Cameron...' Joodie declared, excited by the coincidence.

Tension relieved was greater than frustration caused and Joodie didn't entirely re-tell the story, she hit a tangent that mercifully hit another tangent putting any reference to Craig and Ophelie out of mind. Nonetheless, it was another work-based intrigue that she ended up with; some banal soap opera, cast with unknowns, the characters all seeming alike and virtually impossible to relate to; so difficult, in fact, that attempting to sympathise was so tiresome and unlikely to be successful or beneficial, it was pointless even bothering to try. Still, it gave the three of us an opportunity to snack and take stock of what had happened – though unresolved, there was sufficient revolution to meditate upon.

When my eyes were set upon Joodie, my line of sight allowed only a blurred image of Ophelie; as it was, even if I had sat a foot in front of her I would have discovered no more from her blank expression, nothing more than the determined wistfulness that I could see anyway. Before today, before this sudden increased awareness, I had never considered her to be a deep thinker – quiet at times, absolutely, but philosophical, burdened with perplexities? – no, that did not seem to fit. Looking at her, guessing the likely subject of her thoughts (it was apparent, unquestionably, that she was not following the new revelations regarding Cameron, his wife and now their holiday plans). I felt guilty – the cruelty of my previous opinions, the conclusion that her quietness was attributable to a dumbness – that peaceful stasis that effects the easily mentally satisfied. Horrible; but that had been my classification of the woman; granted I had never really thought about her so deeply, and now I tried to disown the thoughts; had I really been so arrogant to have rated her so poorly? After all, I knew that she was more and better educated than myself.

In a digression of self-consciousness, I phased out of Ophelie consideration, thinking again of the old couple yesterday – how odd I had found their height. It occurred to me that I definitely was prone to a weak kind of prejudice – not commonplace prejudice, but more a prejudice of detail, a subconscious attribution of personality and characteristics – I looked, trying to clarify or dismiss my self-accusatory discovery, back towards Craig, who was happily removing with his teeth the cap of a shelled hard-boiled egg.

Rather by process of elimination, I concluded that Ophelie was probably reflecting on her husband's behaviour – their relationship in general, maybe – regardless of the indefinable specifics. It was a satisfactory conclusion; the nature of her thoughts was a sadness or bitterness rather than anger or disappointment. And it was exactly at this point, something about the way she pushed forward her throat, the rise of her chin, the hard, smooth glowing lines, the need in her eyes, cool and feline, and that incredible suspended anticipation in the parted lips – it was at this exact moment in time that I discovered that Ophelie was unquestionably beautiful.

Simultaneously, the discovery was unsurprising to the point of being expected, while, paradoxically, improbable and unbelievable. She should not be beautiful, I argued with my train of thought: 'there is nothing there that I would normally associate with a beautiful woman – where are the big dark eyes and the petite upturned nose?' They were right before me, as I switched, unable to resist fully focusing, between Joodie and Ophelie, I saw them distinctly in my adorably pretty wife. In Ophelie, I saw only a combination of features that I had never considered to be attractive – and yet there she was: sad and divine. It was just the way she held herself, so classy – her body, obscured by autumnal clothes, hadn't influenced the discovery; in fact, like her eyes, the colour of the ocean in pastels, the self-hugging introversion of her body should have put me off – but nothing, it seemed, was capable of doing that – she was absolute; excellent and drawing me in. And I was – I had to snap myself out of it – transfixed. I watched her with the same degree of fixity with which she currently watched Joodie; only, compared to Ophelie, my distraction was a sappy, doting animalism, like a dog towards an opening tin of food, not panting, but dreamy and flattering.

Nobody noticed. Ophelie in her own world, Joodie in her own cinema of narrative terminal velocity and

Craig, as if unfed for a week, was single-handedly removing lunch from the plates spread across the coffee table.

'And that's it, really; so, I suppose not *that* similar to Craig…'

Craig disconnected himself from eating, hearing his name and expecting to be obliged to respond or listen, to contribute in some way. Joodie's story, lost to the world, but no doubt scheduled for a repeat at some stage, disappeared into the grey stillness of the room; she offered to make more tea without appearing to have any intention of making any. As she looked around at the blank faces, everyone seemed to follow suit. I turned my own gaze to Ophelie, just as she turned hers to me; she smiled at me, not the broad unflattering gum heavy grin that she arrived with, she had completely softened, her lips took on a floral looseness that took my breath away – she *was* beautiful. It was happening all the time now.

Joodie's story had come full circle, she looked terrified, the unacceptable possibility that she had ended up reminding us of the caustic atmosphere she had been hoping to eliminate. Her solution to this potential *faux pas* was to continue as she had been: 'We had this awful client at work yesterday – so rude, you wouldn't believe…' Ophelie, feeling that she was the "you" being addressed, returned her focus to her friend and with a look both sympathetic and encouraging she drew a deeper explanation from Joodie of the foul visitor.

Women, I thought, turning obligingly to feign

interest in the story, could do it; they could absorb meaningless chat and small talk as effortlessly as they could dish it out. Craig had mastered a "lite" version from his media experience and also, I spitefully concluded, thanks to his easily satisfied attention level. Effectively, I condemned Craig to the same standard of shallowness that I had previously attributed to Ophelie – a limited need for intellectual stimulation. To an extent, unlike my newly adopted understanding of Ophelie, the evidence did lean towards such an assessment, Craig actually seemed to have a one-tracked flow of thought – his golf – and rarely raised himself to contributions when the conversation touched on anything more highbrow, or even medium-brow – he was, in fact, a normal sort of bloke: he liked what he liked and was comfortable with his indifference to anything that fell even a hair's breadth beyond this. If I could have been remotely honest with myself, we actually weren't that dissimilar.

I began to fidget, my eyes chased around the room for distraction and I was desperate for the lunch to end, throwing all of my hope onto Joodie remembering her alleged commitments to her work. It was beyond my control – maybe our guests would pull away, but Craig seemed happy enough, he had started work on the chocolatey sugar section – damn, how did he stay in such good shape – and Ophelie was almost certainly counting on getting some better conversation out of Joodie before she left. Catastrophically, it dawned on me that for this to take place, me and Craig would need to sustain a conversation long enough for real women's talk to commence.

I plunged lamely in, accepting the role I'd have to play to progress the lunch towards its dénouement. And it had to terminate – not only was I bored and uncomfortable but Ophelie was... What was she? I had no idea, but I was not at all happy with it – this couldn't happen, I had to stop it from growing further.

'So, when are you back in the US?'

Still discontented from my previous assault and his subsequent lucky escape, it was only natural that Craig might read maliciousness into my ingenuous question. Suspicion rose easily and plainly into his eyes and his expression; not entirely incompetent, I picked up on it and eased the question in with a modification in thrust. 'America's a place I've always wanted to go...' It worked; I suppose I had diminished myself, admitted my failure – not having been to an easily accessible and affordable destination was a point in Craig's favour.

'America's great; it's so different to how you expect it to be – believe me,' he added as an aside, nodding towards his wife, just in case she was discreetly following their conversation. 'I'd actually *love* to take her...'

'Oh,' I jumped in nervously, concerned that the conversation might die. 'I never meant...'

'No, no, it's cool, no worries.' Craig clearly had no wish to start anything here, and rushed forward, keen to get back on to his reinforcing justifications. 'More often I think it's the people, not so much the place – you know, not just about the beach *et cetera*, everyone tends to forget about the people, real Americans. It's always about skyscrapers and the Grand Canyon...and

Hollywood, but it's the people that make it – and I mean *real* Americans, not TV Americans. It's no wonder Brits think of them as loud and obnoxious, they...Americans...seem to have a suicidal desire to present themselves that way – I don't watch those Oprahy shows, but that whole "whoop, whoop, whoop" thing – it's crap, at least in my experience. Sure, they let their hair down – party hard...' It was an unconvincing attempt at the expression, but his general affection was sincere and, leaning into the conversation, I was genuinely delighted at him breaking free in speech, saving myself any effort. Craig continued with a genuine passion and respect for his adopted nationals: 'But in normal life, man, they are so much more civilised and traditional than us Brits. I guess you learn to appreciate things that aren't taken for granted. I mean, we've almost swapped roles with them, they've held onto their heritage, scarcity of it, whilst we've turned our backs on ours – its tedium and stuffiness – and, ironically, accepted their trashiness, the bizarre world some of them have created to sell to the world...'

I sat back, hardly listening; Ophelie and Joodie were already locked into inaudible chatter. The day was settled now, routine would get me through this, take her away; I could move on, dismiss my emotions and return to the everyday.

Even after Ophelie and Craig were finally gone, they remained. I had been confident that having seen her, Ophelie would cease to interest me, yet she hung there, like a new star in the pitch dark of my mind, Craig a mere orbiting rock. She burnt and illuminated my afternoon thoughts: she was the flame in the crackle of the LP playing its concert in my living room. I settled into the yawn of the sofa and relived the moments passed when she had been just a few feet away. Perched on the edge of the couch, I had studied her; the range of her expressions dominated my thoughts – not grand reflections upon her hair, tied back casually, or her body that had remained obscured, buried under the bulky woollen sweater – such things were not on the agenda of my thoughts – only that face, strange and beautiful, the animation and sensuality of her lips; the mystery of her eyes, alight one moment and as still and pale as glacial pools the next, trapped in some unknowable contemplation, thoughts that I could never share. Cruel, I wanted to know them, to feel and understand, I wanted to be part of the process of her, but her's was a world I could only guess at.

Soho

'Tonight. Opening. Soho.'

Despite the staccato punctuation, the first words of the telephone conversation were delivered without enthusiasm, almost a begrudged ultimatum. To the uninitiated, the words could also have had questionable meaning – I even wondered momentarily what response would have been offered had Joodie taken the call. The invitation (for that is what the triplet actually was) did not surprise me, it was the way that Burchmann always talked: succinct and efficient – from a Senior Logistics Manager's point of view, I couldn't help but admire and respect the compact way of doing business that he possessed.

'Really? I'm not sure. It's a bit late notice.' I dribbled meekly into the mouthpiece.

'Absolutely.' The reply was awash with surprise; the notion that any objection could be raised appalled Burchmann. 'It's going to be a good one. It's at BulletPoint so there's bound to be masses of wine and...even better...'

'What?'

'*Even* better, it's Frew Grensen's first view...'

'So? I've never even heard of him.'

'*HER!* Very much *her*.'

'Equally, I've never heard of her; is she that special?'
I knew, merely having answered the phone, that I was
committed to going, but if I was then at least I would
make Burchmann fight for it.

'Frew Grensen? Haven't you, she's huge...'

'But is it worth travelling all the way into...'

'Artistically, no; you'd hate her...'

'Well, that's that then.'

'No, dear boy, no it is not – what's the rarest
commodity of modern female painters?'

'She's hot?'

'Who's hot?' Joodie asked from nowhere. I freaked;
the scare of the unexpected voice hitting first, then the
realisation of the situation driving the panic home. I
kept my back to her and my mind, wonderfully, sourced
an answer; I diluted my tone further, already subdued
from the thought of my newly scheduled expedition,
saving me, allowing for the fabrication, 'Bilal's
daughter, she still has that fever.'

'Oh.' Joodie was instantly disinterested.

A trip from Richmond to the West End often escalates from
the original intention of "just popping into town", escalates into
something more classifiable as an excursion. Beyond the
mundaneness of the walk to the station and the dilemma of which
tube or train to take, where to change (regardless of the declared
duration, this always turns out to be the wrong decision – the
one with the kaput carriage or the defective signal) – the journey
itself, though no great distance, is somehow epic. Even a
fortuitous piece of timing to meet and take the "express" only

Soho

delivers the traveller to the southerly terminus, Waterloo, then it begins again — the onward journey. If it is short enough a distance to one's final destination, it is almost impossible to ignore the lure of the walk, to absorb the ceaselessly inspiring Thames and the over-scaled glory of the Embankment architecture: it is London, after all and for all its faults, its inconvenient Britishness, it is still breath-taking; a rival to all. But the walk, ambling and awestruck, slows, and the journey time extends; so, it is not always possible to indulge, time is passing by, appointments, meetings are ticking ever closer. So then, what? — the bus, the tube — either way, a change is usually required at some point — the bus might lead to a walk, or the tube or to a second bus; the tube alone can become a labyrinthine subterranean trek through ceramic wormholes, Edwardian pipes and clattering spiral steps. And even then, such short distances, such excellent regularity, normally, so good that a three-minute wait announced in digitized yellow dots causes frowns and sighs and rolled eyes. And time slips by, unexpectedly lost and rushing away with the hammering clang and rattle and roar of the underground trains. Finally, arrival, and the town is great, the journey forgotten after the obligatory retelling to all who will listen. The hours tick and the reverse begins; only now the choices are limited. And all the time gauging the alcohol consumed — a growing obstacle to good decisions; the threat of violence, the threat of sleep; the timing of the last toilet visit and the hope to hang on as the night bus crawls a tour around the whole of suburbia, before a last stagger back up the Hill.

It is perhaps extreme to classify the thoughts of a man regarding an everyday excursion to be love/hate, but I was in that state – astrologically speaking, I was doomed. I was born under a Libran sun and a Gemini moon – scales and twins, hardly possible to be a more contradictory, ambivalent personality type, neither of which offered me the balance suggested, merely hopeless indecision and rambling procrastination; every decision seemed to be equal. At the same time, I am also burdened with extremes, the scales of personality rocking dangerously, the axis fit to topple. So, in the case of trekking into Soho the extremes were, on the one hand, a sense of holiday, of freedom and liberation, schoolboy excitement at seeing the beautiful bigness of the capital, the ancient ghosts of Aldwych and Strand; at the other end it was an unforgiving torture that was capable of completely putting me off the idea altogether. The result of this was twofold, it would take something either very special or something of necessity to force me to subject myself to the hassle of getting out of Surrey; and, should I establish sufficient reason to succumb, I would subsequently insist on absolutely making the most of the effort, to squeeze every possible opportunity for experience and joy out of the project. Naturally, once I have made the initial effort of committing to the journey, completed the preparations and headed out the house, invariably, I will enjoy the most part of the trip, never quite admitting that my fears and reservations have been overblown and unfounded.

Smiling, I hung up the phone, thinking now about the thrill of urban travel, the sights and smells of public transport, passing through the metropolitan sprawl, the queer backstreets of Soho, hissing conversation, grinding packed bars: "crouched in their swivelling caves of steel, turning to scent the appetizing enemy squadrons in the distance" – it had been a while and, suddenly, I was ready for it.

Ophelie and Craig had left at about two; the call came at ten to three. Burchmann was one of my few remaining friends from high school, in fact we hadn't even attended the same school, we were part of a group that came together, underage drinkers in Shepherd's Bush and Holland Park.

Moving with ease into my logistics mind-set, I began thinking of timetables and footspeed, compensating for potential amateurism on the railways and awe and introspection on the walk across Hungerford Bridge, up Charing Cross Road. It seemed good. Checking my likely start time, I glowed at the realisation that, all things going well with the train, I would actually have time to veer North West, cut through Leicester Square and have time to get some food at Chinatsu's.

The plan was set, perfected by this allowance for my meal, even allowing for the likely wait to be seated, I knew that I had a decent cushion due to Burchmann's usual appalling tardiness – I could drop into some pub, somewhere like the Crown and Two Chinamen, and meet Burchmann there. Yes, it was perfect – this was the only way to do anything, to factor in every possible chance to sustain my level of comfort and to minimalize the influence of other people's stupidity.

*

Sure enough, my heart sparked as the train cut deeper into London, the buildings changing and revealing unknown fairy-tale pasts, the humour and misery that lay buried within; the treachery, debauchery and domesticity of the now long dead. I was, whether it be biography, a stately home or an old magazine, forever bewildered by the past and, moving through Clapham and Vauxhall, I saw the spectres of history and became queasy at the thought of everything that society had lost – all the dead businesses that owners had suffered or even died for, the unmarked buildings that once held all life, all society: the lost pubs and inns, cinemas and brothels; all the customs and culture, words and clothes, food and traditions – all no more. Such a waste, I thought and felt an urge to get involved in the preservation of something, some moribund tradition, a little fragment of British life to encapsulate, to reintroduce to modern Britons. Who would be interested, though, hardly anyone cares anymore – they just want cheap rubbish, global brands and no challenge. Screw them all.

The train curved into Waterloo, and I felt a little more at ease – the most inconsistent element had been survived, now it was largely under my own control. The route was perfectly well known to me, there was no chance of getting lost, the distractions on the way too familiar to cause overindulgent loitering and the odds of being stopped by an acquaintance were negligible to the point where I omitted them from my calculations.

Squeezed onto a table, my back up against the back

of another diner, I smiled at the oversized portion of steaming Japanese cuisine like it was an old friend; the smell was familiar, the meal the same each time: comfort food in more ways than simply filling the belly. It was nice to have this consistency, the removal of the fuss of finding a restaurant that would satisfy, or paying for a poor quality dish. I had a brief mental list compiled covering most of the food groups and national dishes, the list contained examples not of the spectacular, but the reliable, the consistent. This was not to say that they were safe or boring, I just fell back to my belief in efficiency and practicability – that a certain restaurant ticking all the boxes was a matter of satisfaction.

Chinatsu's was a funny place, it reminded me of many things and many moments, though nothing specific or significant enough to cause sentimentality to spoil my meal. Such a peculiar little restaurant – given its location it might have been more focussed on presentation, competing as it was with a hundred other Asian places and equidistant between Leicester Square and Piccadilly Circus, yet still implausibly un-touristic – it remained humble and unaffected and low budget, cramped and hurried. Definitely, the place had the feel of a works canteen, really rather in the tradition of the greasy spoon. And the ever-changing staff of pretty Oriental girls-next-door were consistently charming and impossibly, uncomplainingly busy, all of which was a refreshing antidote to the predictability of my choices, to have a new cast of faces hurry me to my table and rush my barely finished plate away.

Hot and good; I forgot the ten-minute wait in the

street and up the steps to be seated, my mind drifted as the food filled me and the icy Japanese beer tingled and shivered. Work thoughts were long forgotten, domestic issues rose. I pushed aside a nagging complaint that had followed with me on the train: Joodie and her work tales – did she not appreciate how little they meant to me? I was capable of interest only the first telling; it was that insistence to complete, then update and then, as if unsatisfied that it had been heard, the verbal redraft and resubmission. Maybe she was simply hoping for more of a response from me, but what else could I say? Apparently, it was her ideal job, yet she complained with a wearying regularity – seriously, what could I say? I didn't and still don't understand the social mechanics of the industry she works in, the only lunch conferences I have are at the vending machine and involve nothing more taxing than agreeing to the scores of football matches or which movies had now received a DVD release. When Joodie finished some vitriol about deadlines or agents or rushes, there was nothing much more to add than: "that sucks" or, even more uselessly, the hopeless lie: "yeah, I totally understand". And this problem had occupied my mind as I rode up into town, constantly reviewing the problem in a two-way monologue, arguing in my head the cause and response of the whole disagreeable situation. It had stressed me in place of the stress of the journey, but now, eating the splendid juicy meat and pillowy rice, I had had enough, instructing myself to forget about her and her problematic career. Forgetting Cameron and the others, licking some mayonnaise from the stubble that grew a little thicker through careless shaving at the corner of my mouth, my mind returned to dinner and, once again, I began to picture and muse upon Ophelie.

Saturday evening, Shaftesbury Avenue. The pedestrian traffic, more chaotic than the vehicular, caused me to step into the road now and again, trying to maintain a decent pace. Gathered dawdlers spread across the pavement caused a rolling of my eyes, a grumble – not through grumpiness, so much, but just the idea of my preciseness being cut into; the free flow of my life, its careful orchestration, potentially corrupted – but this evening I was unaware of the flying detours I took into the gutter, oblivious to the passing taxis as they veered to compensate for my side steps, themselves grumbling at the inconvenience and the effort at the few degrees of twisting applied to the wheel necessary to complete the manoeuvre. Such was my distraction; such was the pull of my daydream companion.

As I walked, my pace hungered additionally by the thought of a second beer, a draft beer, my mind was confused, pleasantly, by the continuation of these reflections on Ophelie – there was no doubt that I now saw her in an entirely different light: she had made an impression that, while unexpected and inexplicable, was wonderfully satisfying. Beyond what was occurring in my mind, my body was reacting too – it was silly, but I felt younger, lighter – all the ridiculous clichés I would have scoffed at, had I not been the subject of them. I moved among the pedestrians like I was on skates, passing and swerving. Childish, I was a racing car, the way I used to picture myself on long walks home from school, catching and passing, overtaking anyone I could see in front of me – it was something I had used to speed up my walk, to distract me from the time-sucking consciousness of the endless unchanging houses; this evening I just wanted to be a racing car again. Furthermore, with the domestic obligations of Joodie and home washed away, the tight grip of tension – unnoticed but hard in my abdomen – had softened and released – I felt upright, I walked proud and with the bounce and gait of a sportsman. No, it was not love; it was merely the first breath of understanding.

Chauvinism is a fair accusation when Burchmann is the recipient; not with aggression, not maliciously, but as a result of his innate incapacity to think of women other than as remarkable objects, as trinkets – beauty and femininity. He loves the idea of women, loves them so much that he is almost completely incapable of treating them as humans, and such is the extent of his delight in female beauty, that he is seldom satisfied – there is always someone new to fall in love with. Unsurprisingly, Burchmann has spent an awful amount of time single and has enjoyed less regular sex than his drilling libido demands.

We are about the same age, Burchmann a few months younger than me, and we're not entirely dissimilar in appearance, although he is a fraction taller than me, neither of us is short. Stylistically, though, we are very different: when I go out, I dress decently, well-conceived and well-executed – a combination of new retro pieces and original vintage touches, slightly scholarly, quaint but genuinely modern, saved, I guess by combining articles and choosing the right palette to suit me and, apparently, stay on trend – such are Joodie's reassurances; I fear the "modernness" and "trend" stuff is more a coincidence, because it never used to be – it was always just old-fashioned. All this is light years away from Burchmann, the only element connecting us being the inclusion of vintage garments, for me this might be a Fair Isle style sweater or a pair of tailored worsted slacks, for Burchmann, a floral shirt in boutique colours or a pair of Cuban heels. Tonight he was dressed, by his standards relatively subdued: a beat up pair of long, plum coloured Oxfords, a tight pair of lightly pinstriped pants – part of a suit, historically and slightly gone in the seat, the fabric loose around Burchmann's slim backside – a soft shirt that looked as though it had been constructed from the baize of a snooker table, over this he wore a jacket, the cut of a slim fitting single breasted suit but made of a flimsy leather the colour of his shoes, a shade or two darker. His near black hair, slicked back damply, completed the look.

The pub that we had settled on was too decorative to be anything less than authentic, modern recreations never have the attention to detail, the flamboyant over the top flourishes; perhaps a too small budget, perhaps talent, perhaps simply the modern revulsion to fussiness and ornateness. The place had a history for us, the focus of many adventures and dreary alcoholic afternoons. There was no doubt in my mind that Burchmann was effectively resident there; that escapades, no doubt more hectic, dangerous and probably, from time to time, illegal, took place from this very starting point with other supporting casts. Burchmann was at ease, he knew people that passed by us and the bar staff treated him with a queer blend of admiration, contempt and pity.

He was perched on a bar stool, looking as though he was genuinely trying to appear like a movie still – he was, in fact, suspended in a moment, abandoned, killing time watching the pert barmaid refilling the fridge. At his fingertips, he lightly twisted a tumbler of iced scotch, moving it as though it were the control nob of a microfiche reader; a tall glass of German pilsner accompanied them. Burchmann scratched his neck.

'Burchmann!'

Beautifully and broadly smiling, Burchmann swivelled on his stool at the familiar sound of my voice – it had been a few months, but he had known me for twenty-odd years. Whatever complaints one might have against Burchmann (and most people who knew him had at least a couple), a lack of sincerity was never one of them, he was genuine and brutally honest, and he was unquestionably happy to see me.

'Hoyer!' It was more of a screech than a boom and the use of my surname was inevitable – so used to being addressed in such a way it was almost as though Burchmann had no concept of the idea of people having two or more primary names. I don't know a single other person who refers to themselves by their surname, at least not without the suffix of a "y"; many years ago, I had met Burchmann's mother, even she had used their family name; mind, she had been a little distracted simply by existing, clearly there were genetic mysteries at work.

'Burchmann.' I continued the sharing of family identity, grinning uncomfortably and uncontrollably, returning loosely the embrace that Burchmann threw around me.

'Man, it's been too fuckin' long.'

Between rapid counter sips of his small and large drinks, Burchmann began to fill in the details of what we might expect later. Immediately, it was apparent that he was chiefly interested in the exhibitor, a Californian painter called Frew Grensen, although he focussed less on her work and more on her backside, her "raw creative sexuality" and other embarrassingly explicit adjectives regarding her "talent". For me, I was simply pleased to be going back to BulletPoint, although I tended to be more interested in the building and its quirky Dickensian charm than the works of art displayed on its walls. A pint of golden, East Anglian-brewed Ale was set before me; a glint of affection shone down from my eyes, something between that of a younger to an older brother, or the fascination of supressed sexuality.

Now I was relaxed. I liked being out, I liked the West End – I knew the back streets well. There was an anachronistic quality about the narrow row houses, the occasional grander structure, I liked the narrow twisting lanes, the aura of fiction that transported me again into a world now gone. It was like time travel – if one opened one's imagination and filtered away the cycle couriers and the loud teenagers on mobile phones, it was entirely possible to be elsewhere or, instead, it was possible to not be "now".

'One more?' It was more a fatherly direction than a question. Mindful of my capacity and what was still to come, I looked into the thinning foam across the top of my drink, a shade over three fingers, but it was decent beer and, caught up in the atmosphere and intoxicated by the golden light in the mirrors and my drink, the excited buzz of plum middle class female voices, I nodded my assent.

'How's the wife, then?' Burchmann challenged.

'The wife?' I groaned, mysterious, sounding like I'd forgotten I had one. 'Hmmm, good question.'

'I take it there's not a good answer.'

My voice had a drawling uncertainty as I tried to explain: 'Generally, everything is much as it should be: all right...'

'All right? Huh, I really envy you married types, with your *all rights* and your *just fines* – what a blissful state of agony.'

'Historically, I would have leapt, not *leapt*, you know, but, anyway, I'd have had to defend us "married types" against such a negative summary of us; your typical over-generalised negativity...'

'But...?' Burchmann filled the pause as I took the newly arrived "one more" and lovingly sipped it.

'Cheers, Burchmann.'

'Hoyer.'

'But...'

'Yes, "but" – do I sense trouble in paradise?'

'No, not trouble, not quite; not yet; not paradise either – but, yeah, definitely not hitting the spot matrimonially.'

'You bored?'

'Of course, I'm bored, I've been married for...Christ, how long *have* I been married for?'

'Fucked if I know, Hoyer; fucked if I know,' he managed to disguise ignorance with the wistfulness of regret.

I smiled as Burchmann began to grin at the realisation of how much he had lost it.

'You bloody should know – you were there!'

'Apparently. *When* was it?'

I ignored his sarcasm, drank some more. 'The boredom isn't the problem; I get enough out of the relationship and we still have a nice time together...'

'*Nice.* That's another of those words – there's no passion in words like that.'

'And that's the problem: there is no passion. But the worst thing is not that the passion has died – again, I can deal with that: who wants a life of passion – we're men, we can't cope with emotional intensity for long spells...'

'I can manage about an afternoon.'

'Well, you're hopeless anyway – I'm talking about normal people, in normal relationships.'

'Cheers.'

'You're welcome. What I was saying...yes...I'm not

bothered that the passion isn't what it was – not extinguished, but maybe it could be more...'

'And the sex?' Burchmann didn't allow his point to sneak through, the bar girl looked round, intrigued by the question, Burchmann caught the movement, caught her eye and winked: she blushed, he swelled.

'All right, I guess – not enough by either of our standards; not absent though.'

'*Not enough*; *all right* – man, how can you live in this swamp of mediocrity – if it's even that...'

'It probably isn't. But that's not even the worst thing...'

'No?'

'No; the worst thing is that she's really started to annoy me.'

'Do you annoy her?'

It hadn't even occurred to me to think about that side of the equation, I had been so absorbed in my own frustrations and so distant from hers, that I had never investigated the possibility that it had been the same for her.

'Probably. You know me, Burchmann...'

'You are an incredibly annoying man,' he chirped playfully.

'Yeah, not sure about the need for "incredibly", mate, but I concede, happily, the rest.'

'So how is she pissing you off,' Burchmann retreated; he knew me well enough not to push too far and refocused the bad guy role onto Joodie.

'Little things, I guess – bigger things...she's so self-absorbed, mainly. Sometimes I might as well not be there. Like today, we had some friends over – which, by the way, she hadn't even told me about! – and then she's got me doing the fucking garden and preparing lunch.'

Burchmann giggled. 'Doesn't sound like she's *completely* forgotten your existence.'

'Yeah, well, I know it doesn't seem much, but then…and see, it's not even just about me, all the time they were there she kept going on about some dude from her work that *none* of us knew.'

Burchmann was getting bored, I could tell, probably imagining me and Joodie boring each other to death. 'Look, man,' he interjected, believing that he could resolve my marital disharmony and get our conversation back on a different track with just a few words. 'Life's hard enough without trying to change the behaviour of a woman; fuck it, they're all a bunch of stubborn…you-know-whats…' He controlled his tone, the bar girl passing close by, suspiciously looking, frowning at what appeared to be the gist of the conversation. 'They're stubborn, they look out for themselves and we're not here to…' he mimicked intercourse with a combination of prodding and looped fingers. 'So, you have *your* life, she hers; have you never talked to her about…about…whatever the hell it is that *you* do…'

'Logistics.'

Burchmann pretended to nod off. 'Exactly,' he said, springing awake again. 'Christ, does she get the weekly report on your…logic?'

'You're missing the point slightly – I never really

finished – this thing with the stories, there's other stuff as well...'

'Yeah? Let's save that for later, eh?'

'Er, yeah, sure – anyway, it's not that she tells these stories – I *am* interested, she's my wife, I love her, it's just that she feels the need to tell me the story and, when I've got it, understood it perfectly, she starts over again. I just don't have the patience – you know how I am, I get anxious, I can't redo *anything* – it has to be done – done – bang! – once and finished – I get anxious having to do something twice.'

'So, this is *your* problem, really? It's your incapacity to deal that's getting you annoyed – you're anxious and, admittedly, she contributes to that, she could protect your sensibilities, but why should she? You're both part of the problem, what can you do? Deal with it, or get the fuck out.'

'More and more I want to do the latter – as I said, there's more to it and to make it worse all of a sudden I'm starting to think *a lot* about this other...'

'Drink up, Hoyer – we need to move – you can finish this on the way.'

Beak Street

The side streets south of Oxford Street, that whole tiny city between Charing Cross Road and Regent Street, are full of high, narrow old buildings, so very English, yet so rarely constructed now – four story corridors with shoulder-wide staircases as steep as if they were the inside of spirals. These spindly ancient structures, even the sturdier art-deco infills, offer glimpses of a different world, they make people like me want to buy a hat. Fictional in their histories, by not being of this time, of the living generations, they become unreal, they became the stories of Woolf and Hitchens or further back to Thackeray and that whole brigade of writers and artists that swarmed through Regency and Victorian London. Round here, I could almost smell the mortality of Cholera and poverty – but these buildings were no longer the basic, unhygienic streets of history and literature, they were art galleries and concept stores, boutiques and sushi restaurants, and the family homes were dissected and reconstructed as adequately sized apartments for media professionals and stockbrokers.

The BulletPoint gallery could have been any such retail outlet. Next to its narrow door, the large window could have contained displays of art materials, high heeled shoes, jazz LPs, imported meats, bondage gear or customers along a narrow shelf eating falafel or raw food or drinking coffee or sake. Instead, the window contained nothing, a few flyers scattered along the low ledge, nothing more, the aperture revealing the art pinned to the walls and a crowd – expensively dressed or slovenly bohemian art lovers, art consumers or simply hangers on, sponging the free booze.

Me and Burchmann were mainly of the final persuasion. Although Burchmann had unsuccessfully plodded through art school, I had never been remotely artistic; still I had a reasonably knowledgeable taste, I had even purchased the odd piece; predominantly, though, we came for the drink and the society, by which it should be taken to mean "the women". Not that it was an exercise in drunken lechery, at least not usually; quite rightly – you simply couldn't get away with it these days. Back in the nineties, neither of us had sufficient shame to hold back and, besides, every exhibition in those days of *Cool Britannia* was utterly riddled with cocaine and other such perky drugs. It wasn't like that now, we drank freely – freely – but within our limits and we never hit on the women, not directly, not me at all; if anything of that nature took place, it took place when the show spilled out into the West End. Such was the joy we got from these events; the art, if we were lucky, was a bonus.

Between the pub and the gallery, Burchmann had thrillingly expanded on what to expect from the artist, Frew Grensen; clearly, he was besotted and had prioritised approaching her. He knew plenty of people in the London art scene, he knew plenty of people in general, but he had not yet managed to share a proper conversation with her, a couple of close shaves – four lines of nonsense in a pub in Shoreditch being the pinnacle of this: she hadn't understood him, checked it off as "English Humour" and with faked laughter walked away to air kiss some grossly flamboyant journalist.

Inside BulletPoint, against the decrepit walls and the locals in a seasonally dark wardrobe, Frew Grensen was unmistakable: tall, and made even more so by an amazing amount of hair, independent waves of dark blonde and grey poured from her scalp, wild and dramatic; it framed her face, rather it was like a stage backdrop to her face, which was squarish and dominated by a beautiful long straight nose; her mouth was unspectacular as a feature but sensational in its perpetual motion – smiling, it seemed, was her religion, laughter her drug. She was not pretty; unquestionably, however, she was beautiful – this was my perception, at least, gauged from the back of the crusty wooden room. She stood out a mile – Burchmann's shuffling gesture to point her out was redundant.

Immediately I was impressed by her, and relieved: so many painters I had met were difficult and insular; those that were not tended to be extreme to the point of mania – that most were, probably, in reality, very ordinary, passed me by; qualities of extremes always stood out to me, the middle ground indistinguishable. Frew Grensen had an air of easy-going lightness; eerily phlegmatic, she showed no signs of anxiety or first night nerves. Perhaps it was the antidote to her work, which was violently ugly, brutalist butchery – not bad, not to my taste; not bad, but stark and almost distressing in its angularity and viciousness. She was not my type, far removed from it – but I liked the paradoxical genuineness of her perfect, orthodontic smile, and I liked the twitch of her nose as her mouth broke out of conversation. Soon enough I noticed the parallel with Ophelie's – different in its shape, but expressively identical: the same warmth, the bated expelled breath, hanging ready to develop into talk or rest. So, I liked Frew.

'Fuckin' amazing, isn't she,' Burchmann boasted. 'The sort of woman who ruins my composure and makes me look like an arse.'

'She is…very special. I like…'

'*Very* special. Brilliant – she's with that old drunken poofter, Ahri.'

'The Mediterranean guy?' I sipped the icy white wine, my eyes widened, instantly detecting quality. We were still close to the drinks table, edging forward; the show was popular, and the rattle of chatter was big in the ancient room, like a concert crowd before a symphony. Between adoring glances, Burchmann was considering his approach and best timing.

'Egyptian.'

'Technically Mediterranean.' My inner pedant couldn't resist it, feeling the first motions of drunkenness, the shift from beer to wine.

'*Technically* an irritating, alcoholic poofter; but I know him, and that lets us in to Frew.'

'Can you say that anymore? Poofter?' I asked with

a wondering sincerity, a middle-aged woman turned a long nose disapprovingly towards me. 'I mean, not just political correctness, but...it's all a bit retro, isn't it?'

'Believe me, Hoyer, when you meet him, you'll know that's *exactly* what to call him; it's not mean; that's what he calls himself. Christ, he looks bladdered already.'

It took longer than we planned to find the right moment to approach, so much so that we picked up our second glasses as we committed to our big push. For a second, Burchmann feared we had blown it, Ahri turning away from Frew as we closed in. Burchmann, a slight panic, called his name, catching his attention, catching also that of Frew Grensen as she too twitched to turn elsewhere.

'Ahh, Burchmann – ravishing, ravishing Burchmann.' Ahri exploded into a welcome – it was part outrageously gay, part bizarrely upper-class and part performance art, and just a little bit Fosbury flop, culminating in kisses, heavy, noisily wet, on Burchmann's cheeks. 'You know, of course, Frew – our star – our...oh, the words, the words, I have not the words to describe this magnificent bitch...'

'How about – Magnificent Bitch,' I chipped in. Ahri looked confused; Frew Grensen laughed, Burchmann oblivious. 'Or is that too much like a racehorse.'

'Speaking of Magnificent Bitches...' Ahri fought through the booze. 'Who is *this* little fox?'

'Hoyer...um, I'm Christopher...'

'Christopher.' He said the word as if he were

performing oral sex on it, again with the rolling shoulders of a high jump approach. 'Remind me to find you next time I pop under the stairs!'

We were stood, the four of us, in an uneven loop, Ahri shifted across to stand close to me, continuing his conversation with intimate closeness to my ear, his hot breath damp and ticklish on my neck; Burchmann stepped into the breach and put out a hand to Frew.

'Yeah, we've met,' he began as if nothing had occurred since Ahri's unnecessary introduction of her. She took his hand, the movement of her brow suggested that the news of their having met before was a surprise to her; yet she let it melt into her natural smiling state, just generally happy.

Burchmann talked, mainly; he was doing ok, she was very approachable and happy to talk, but soon enough, under pressure, his conversation grew routine and had started to drift towards bullshit and name-dropping, the pauses growing in number and duration. Frew, like anyone at the centre of attention, felt no need to progress the conversation, if it were to dry up, she could easily excuse herself and disappear, which she eventually sort of did.

'Christopher,' she said, to my enormous relief, the closeness of Ahri's voice had been comparable to standing in front of a Marshall stack and his line of conversation was little more than thinly veiled pornographic come-ons, unconvincing flattery. 'It's so good that you could come to my show; we haven't met before, have we?' Burchmann was sensitive enough to be slighted by this, but relieved enough to instantly dismiss it. That she seemed to like me could only be beneficial to him.

'No, we haven't, but it's an absolute pleasure.'

'Do you like my work?'

'How could he not?' Ahri slimed. 'Such beautiful work and, Christopher, clearly a man with taste...'

'I think it's really exciting; I've not quite taken it fully in yet, but... yeah,' I chortled fakely for emphasis, 'your paintings are really wild.'

'Thank you *so* much,' she said after a good burst of laughter. 'That's exactly what I hope people will think; most people find it difficult to be so...um, frank, so quickly.'

'I'm sorry...'

'No. No, don't be sorry,' she cut me off. 'It's refreshing. It's easy to tell the difference between genuine enjoyment and platitudinous sycophancy...'

'Urgh, I hate those people,' Ahri spat, proving her point.

'Well, ok, then – but, yeah, wild... in a good way.'

'Thank you,' she said sweetly. 'And thanks for being so honest, so un-English...'

'Yeah, Frew,' Burchmann jutted in, feeling ignored. 'Your paintings are fucking...crazy.'

'Er, thank you.' She wasn't smiling.

Conversation was kick-started by the fruity Egyptian – the solid ground of talking about the star of the show – everyone was happy with this. Ahri's natural inclination seemed to be towards sycophancy and, as though faced with a gourmet meal, he was practically salivating at the joy of listing the many proofs of Frew Grensen's genius. Burchmann was pleased to have the attention shifted away from himself, not quite comprehending his own outburst, and with Frew the returning centre of attention, it meant that he could bask in what was becoming difficult to repudiate – Frew's perfection. Aside and only casually listening, I was content with the sensation of being in this group, within the cosmos of the exhibition; I was, say, Venus to Frew's Sun, and it was a cosy place to orbit. Yet it was not my proximity physically to the scorching star that made my cheeks flush a soft crimson – that was the lingering flattery I had taken from her charming and kindly interested attention, that she had requested my opinion on her work and even then remained friendly – did she (I swooned), did she like me? It was ridiculous to even consider it – she was too tall, for a start, to like me; too talented and important, and too confident. Without any great difficulty, I concluded that she was out of my league and it was nothing more than the quickly disappearing Chardonnay that was doing the thinking for me, and to further support this dismissive reality check, I recollected what Craig had said, earlier that day, regarding how nice and well-mannered Americans are.

I was, however, certain that something was wrong with me – such nonsense about Frew's non-existent attraction towards me! And Ophelie propelled back into my mind – something had happened in the electrics of my brain, the regularity with which she now appeared to me and the gnawing sensation – lust, affection, guilt, shame – that accompanied these thoughts; they were daydreams, really, the way they presented themselves: directionless and unspecific; but she stood clearly as the focus of them – the soft focus, more aptly. I discovered my glass suddenly empty and my heart full – Ophelie's presence and Frew's sweetness were all the companionship I needed.

Frew excused herself, spotting a friend of some celebrity entering the building (they were making a documentary, some TV show, I didn't absorb the details, I wasn't impressed by these kinds of things – it was the sort of bland report Joodie provided on a daily basis). Frew's face lit up an additional degree it seemed impossible to achieve, but she did, and she glided away.

We all watched her, her buttocks significant and round, equine, strong and mobile under the slick fabric. I was impressed; even Ahri, from some curious perspective, anatomical admiration, perhaps, seemed absorbed by the globes that disappeared into the crowd of mere mortals.

'I can see you're impressed.' Boasted Burchmann.

'He should be.' Ahri added, as if to confirm his own weakness. 'I'm a ridiculous old poofter and even I'm thinking utterly filthy thoughts.'

'For once, Burchmann, your hyperbole has not disappointed; even before she turned around I...' I tailed off, there was nothing more to be added; I was overwhelmed – despite the devastating rump, the endless legs below, all I could focus on was Ophelie, still in my living room at home as she stared soft and sad into unknown complexities.

Now was not the time to share this with Burchmann, for many reasons – significantly his own pre-occupation with Frew Grensen, and his incompetence at providing useful romantic guidance. Despite these limitations, he was the only person I knew to whom I could confess such a personal experience: other than Burchmann, who did I actually have? – Bilal? I could not envisage myself discussing this over our morning coffee break. I tried to imagine Burchmann's response, to bypass the process of explaining my situation – it was a futile exercise; the unpredictability of Burchmann's response could range from suggesting divorce, to visiting a prostitute; both would be marvellously and complexly argued, but nothing practical would ever be offered. Still, I wanted to tell him at some point just for the relief of sharing – sharing the stress, sharing the confusion.

'It's not just the physical...stuff...' Burchmann, meanwhile was still in a world of Frew Grensen; he was effectively addressing himself – I had phased into my newly, alcoholically enhanced dream world. The Egyptian, meanwhile, already bored by the lack of Frew and the commencement of this whining, heterosexual romanticism, quickly spotted a young guy, alone and staring seriously at a monochromatic nightmare of ink and oil hung on the wall, tilting his ginger afro in contemplation. Ahri, saved by this vision in copper, rushed over and embraced him like a side-on road traffic accident and with an intimacy and completeness that, conceivably, could have included penetration.

'It's her mind, everything about her in fact.' It was rather tedious and didn't fit Burchmann at all – yes, it was intrinsically Burchmann – infatuated and obsequiously enchanted – but there was such pathos in his deference and demureness, that it was embarrassing in a totally new way; while at the same time I was driving into a frenzy that, to me, was totally ascendant from Burchmann's washed out pining. I focussed again, the whine of Burchmann's devotion breaking the serenity of my own forming attachment; I was unsurprised by Burchmann's tone and, as ever, disappointed by it.

'I don't know how you get by, day to day – thank God, I've never been as lovesick as you seem perpetually to be, Burchmann – I think I'd kill myself. You realise you have absolutely no hope with her; she'll probably end up married to some prick of a Hollywood actor...I get the feeling that she doesn't even like you.'

'You kidding? She's just warming up to me. These artistic women...two things you need to know: one – they are notoriously unapproachable – it enhances their reputation – would you want or even try to fuck Tracey Emin? Exactly. And, two – two is the most important – when they break, they're the filthiest women in the world – absolutely no limits – and imagine *that*, Frew, doing absolutely anything.'

'I wouldn't know where to start.' I laughed to show that I was trying to be funny, rather than the incompetence I actually felt.

'I know *exactly* where I'd start.'

*

I took a moment to look at the paintings – Burchmann was right: the more I looked, the more I hated them – but I liked Frew Grensen, so I was determined to like her art. Look for qualities that were satisfying, that would be a start and from there I could nurture my interest and grow to understand – I was convinced of it – even though, deep down, it would remain repulsive and childish, it always would be. I picked up on a textural quality that appealed, at least it was intriguing – she seemed to have at least made that much effort. Half a dozen of the pictures I scanned and dismissed, it really was rubbish; no, not rubbish, I wouldn't allow that – even being objective, there was so much that was worse than this, really appalling art. Still, I was determined to like it; but because I couldn't get excited about it, I felt there was no way I could enjoy it, therefore it must be that I hated it – there was no room for indifference – indifference wouldn't help me – imagine, later, drinks in a moodily lit bar, the darlings of the art world and she asks me:

- So, you like my paintings? – I
  couldn't help noticing that
  you were studying
  them...closely.
- Yes. I had a good look.
- You, er, you liked what you
  saw?
- Erm, they were all right –
  didn't love 'em, didn't hate
  'em...

It would be awful.

'You're Burchmann's friend, aren't you?' a light hand pressed my shoulder. 'Hi, I'm Sonny.'

I turned around, moving my head instinctively to locate Burchmann, he had wandered off, no doubt in further pursuit of Frew, and I was left to acknowledge the woman who had introduced herself.

She was striking. Though rather short she was immediately the most interesting person in the room. It was almost as though she had just stepped out of a time machine – she wore an immaculate and authentic tailored suit, clinging to her figure, the skirt gripped to her knees; her hair flawlessly sat up on her head and her make-up, photoshoot pristine. Entirely, the ensemble was period, specifically sometime around or just before the Second World War. Her shoes were high, she perched on them with a divine posture, upright, and holding a patent leather clutch against her thighs, remarkably, in gloved hands, arms stiffly straight, stretching her short frame further. Instantly, I wanted to like her, as I had a moment ago with Frew's paintings, only with Sonny I genuinely liked what I saw, the whole vintage thing was stunning. I wanted to be attracted to her, my mind was firing that way today: Ophelie, Frew...but I was not, there was something she held from me, protective.

Certainly, she was not ugly, it wasn't that, though it was hard to gauge effectively as her make-up, though finely laid, was a mask. Perhaps it spoilt what naturally lay beneath, more likely, it enhanced what, like Ophelie, was rather plain underneath. No, it was not an absence of beauty – there was something about her that was never going to intoxicate me as the others had done, (although it had taken years for that to be felt with Ophelie, mere moments with Frew Grensen). She was pretty, her face was smooth and oval, her eyebrows high and curved and constructed, her nose thin and long, lips like Clara Bow and eyes, chestnut eyes that swooned with an unusually oriental curtsey. I was really in the mood to be attracted to her – all this female attention – and the whole package she came in appealed to my archaic sensibilities, but I just wasn't, it just wasn't there.

'Hi, yes. I'm Christopher. We haven't met, have we?'

'No, I didn't even know who you were – he,' she nodded her mountainous red hair to an unseen Burchmann. 'He told me to keep you out of trouble.'

She was softly spoken, with a faint lisping accent that I could only narrow down to "maybe near Lancashire?" Her voice was feminine and without the toughness of her tailoring; it wasn't through shyness either, at least not of the situation, it was almost as though she wanted to remain unnoticed, even though she clearly dressed to stand out. I suspected her way of dressing was purely for her benefit – its impact on the surrounding world was of no real concern to her. I said nothing, she moved to the next picture, expecting me to follow; which I did, magnetically.

'So,' she turned and looked up at me, 'I don't think much of the paintings. You?'

'I'm struggling.' I drew my mouth backwards, embarrassed at my failed mission; smiled at her, happy to hit common ground so quickly.

'I need a cigarette; will you keep me company?'

I agreed, unhesitatingly; happy to stay with her, happy to get outdoors, the wine fizzy in my brain; besides, I had looked at nearly all of the paintings on the ground floor, moving with increasing pace past the now repetitive and bleak images.

We stood in the street with the external party of exiled smokers; so many that it spilled across the fronts of several of the neighbouring properties; even then, Sonny drew me a metre or so off the tail of the group. As she smoked, she was silent.

'You know,' I felt obliged to talk and was happy to do so. 'You're not like anyone I've ever met before.' It was a reference to her way of dressing and behaviour rather than anything more personal; she looked up at me, fearful, suspecting a different implication.

'Oh,' she pleaded, 'please, don't – I'm not...'

'No.' I rapidly jumped back in, detecting her misunderstanding. 'I didn't mean it like *that*...' I hoped to prove with my emphasis, how ridiculous the idea was. 'I'm married.'

'You're not hitting on me? Thank God, I get that – I think guys like the stockings.'

I hadn't noticed them, assuming if I had assumed anything that they were just regular tights, that what they appeared to be as I quickly looked to check.

'I'm sorry. Not that you're not...and yes, men, they

do? – but...'

'I'm gay, Christopher.' She jumped in to prevent any further embarrassed, rom-com jabbering. 'It's fine. I'm the one who should be awkward and sorry – you just seemed to be...'

'I like your hair, this whole forties thing.'

'Thank you.'

Expressively, Sonny smoked her cigarette, smoked it as if she had practiced, or was recreating the style of somebody else, or felt the need to justify my complement. It wouldn't have surprised me – she did it so well – but everything about her was out of a magazine or movie. I thought back to the point I had tried to make the day before with Bilal: it was lifestyle plagiarism – she didn't validate my point, but she was an extreme example of it. Not that she was unique; my opinion was that everything and everybody is a forgery of someone else's idea, Sonny was merely a magnified example. Mind you, she did it immaculately. Maybe, maybe that was the quality in Frew Grensen's paintings that I had been unable to place.

'Where is she?' Sonny asked, her cigarette ground into Beak Street; I was miles away.

'Huh?'

'Your wife? Where is *she* tonight?'

'Oh...at home.'

There was so much disinterest and spleen in my answer that my feelings were visibly pushed to the surface.

'Right, so she's...um, she's either cheating on you, or she hates you or...she's just a very bitter woman that's long overdue fertilization?'

It wasn't as funny as Sonny had hoped, at least it was misplaced enough for me to take it seriously.

'I doubt she's having an affair, though it's not impossible and she doesn't hate me; she's not *that* interested in me, though, and I think the idea of breeding repulses her. None of which has anything to do with her being at home – the reason she's at home is that she thinks she's being a good wife by encouraging me to spend time with my friends. Urgh – it's a bit dumb but, to be honest, I'm actually pleased, for a change…I never used to be…but right now I'm actually pleased to be away from her. It's a shitty thing to say, but I don't have the patience for her these days…God, why am I telling you this?'

'I get the feeling,' she was lighting another cigarette as she spoke, 'that you're dying to tell *some*one about it. Apart from Burchmann, you don't have many mates, do you?'

'Hey, that's a bit cruel,' I protested, though good naturedly. 'I don't even see much of Burchmann these days.'

'Oh, poor likkle Chrissy. Look, I'm bored of this place…' She nodded at the exhibition, 'Send Burchmann a text, let's go to the pub and you can pour your heart out. Burchmann's probably looking for an excuse to get into a pub.'

'You reckon?' I turned as I spoke, and we stepped into the quiet street. 'Free wine and his latest obsession, Frew Grensen? – He'll be there all night.'

'That does make sense – her art is pants, but her

pants are art.'

'God, you sound like Burchmann.' Sonny made herself comfortable, side by side with me along an upholstered bench in a reproduction pub, sharing also a bottle of red wine. 'What's with all you boys and your soppy crushes?'

'No, it's not a crush at all; I don't want to be with her or even sleep with her – I just, and only very recently, just started to think about her...a lot. But not "think about", ha, like you say, like Burchmann thinks about women; this is not about creating great romances out of nothing, this is just simply a case of noticing this woman...'

'Ophelie?'

'Yep, Ophelie...noticing her and finding that...you know when you hear a brilliant song for the first time, and you stick it on repeat? You can listen to it over and over again and she's like that, there's just something about her...an aesthetic, a...I just can't explain, but I just keep thinking about her.'

'But even these songs – and I get what you're saying – even these songs, eventually you get to a point and you no longer have that desire to keep playing it, maybe you stick it on once in a while but it's not...look, don't you think that this might just be a result of your wife not showing any interest in you?'

'Not "no interest"...just...less.'

'Less, none, blah – the quality and quantity is not important, it's the state that matters – she's pissing you off, so you transfer your sexual desire to the nearest convenient fanciable woman. Classic. And a little bit sad, I'm afraid.'

For the first time I didn't like her so much. I looked around the pub, looked at the couples – would people think me and Sonny a couple? It wouldn't be so bad, maybe I *did* just want some attention, to have someone closer than Joodie was.

Sonny poured some more wine and apologised, 'I'm sorry, that was a bit nasty; I didn't mean that *you* are sad, you know, *pathetic sad.*'

'I think you probably did and, you know, it *is*...I am. And believe me, I'm not that thrilled about it and, for the record, it is completely *not* sexual. There is attraction but it's not like an, er, a wet daydream thing, I don't imagine us fucking; in fact, it's not physical at all, I mean physical in as much as contact, it's physical in the same way that lions are impressive when you see them in real life. She's not a lion, but it's not such a bad simile – there's something about her I can't quite fathom, but it is kinda feline, the way she moves, holds herself – it's very elegant.'

'Does she dance? She sounds like she must have had dance training as a kid – my kind of woman.'

'I guess; I've no idea – I actually don't know her *that* well...given all the time I've known her. I've never tried to have that much to do with her friends, Joodie's friends. But, yeah, she has this lightness of control – maybe it's just that, in this way and the way she presents herself is just so opposite to Joodie.'

'The grass isn't always greener...'

'Quite; but sometimes you find flowers.'

'Ahh, that's a pretty thought, Chris – you *are* a bit of a romantic, aren't you.'

'I think I'm too lazy to be romantic – I have the odd romantic thought – I surprise myself…'

'I can imagine.'

'But grand gestures…? Hmm, that's probably why she's bored of me.'

'Well, whatever the reason, this Ophelie thing does not sound good.'

'What can I do? I've no control over it – she's there – I didn't ask for this.'

'But you're en*joy*ing it, you fool – why do you think you keep reminding yourself of her. What it is is that this is about as dangerous as your life gets…am I right?'

I didn't answer, reaching for the interference of my glass. 'I am, aren't I? Oh, Christopher, you need to spend more time with Burchmann, or at least with me; didn't your wife encourage you to spend more time with your own friends? We're friends now, we should hang out, take some risks…'

'I'm not quite sure that's what she had in mind.'

'Christ, what possible threat could I be – I am a lesbian, I think you're safe. How could she be…I think maybe *that* is what her problem is, why you are struggling, if she won't even trust you with a gay woman. My God. It makes perfect sense, she doesn't trust you, so you target the ultimate threat to her and you – her best friend.'

'And the real irony is that she'd probably trust me completely with Ophelie.'

'Ah, but that's fair enough because – let's not forget – you don't want to fuck Ophelie, it's just "aesthetic".'

'I don't want to fuck you, either, what's your point.'

'You did…before you knew I liked women.'

'Did I? I liked your hair and I though your outfit was great, but…'

'Outfit? Charming! It's not a fucking costume.' She pretended to take offence, actually slightly offended. 'This happens to be my typical everyday wear.'

'You wear it for work?'

'I wear it for work,' she confirmed, proudly.

'Cheers,' I raised my glass.

'Cheers to you, baby.'

'Not exactly perfect, no; I wouldn't go so far as that, but…so many ways, she's not like anyone else.'

'So, you'll continue your pursuit, then?'

Me and Sonny had formed a little unit to double team Burchmann; we found his assessment of Frew Grensen comical and simultaneously began to tease and discredit his lavish praise.

'It's not a pursuit, I'm not pursuing her; I see her as a potential partner, I have…I'm really interested in her. I think…woo…I think she might be interested in me.' The idea left him breathless.

'She seemed massively disinterested earlier. What was it you said?…it was truly bloody embarrassing…'

'I've no idea what I said, but no one was em*bar*rassed; you don't know what you're talking about.'

'No, no; it was.' I laughed, rubbing my head, struggling to pull the quote from the depths. 'Ah, what the hell was it, something...oh, Christ, it was... Sonny, oh, he said something...yep, something about, ooh, something about her paintings...argh, man...'

'I wouldn't bother, you'll never remember, 'cause you're mistaken,' Burchmann advised, grumpily.

'Nooo, I'll...yes, exactly, that's it – we were talking about Frew's paintings and I, I'm no expert, so I just clutched at a word...' I nodded at Burchmann, smiling smugly, 'and I said they were "wild", which...well, she understood what I meant. And then, ha, then Burchmann just comes out with,' I adopted Burchmann's fake "cool" drawl, '"Yeah, man, your paintings are fucking crazy".'

Full of wine and spirits, it tickled Sonny; I was pleased getting to the story, warm with the memory of the event and so we both burst into laughter. 'Fuckers', Burchmann growled under his breath.

'Oh my God, I bet Frew loved that; you know that...'

'She wasn't bothered.'

'Much!' I ironically contradicted.

'She wasn't. Don't make such a big deal out of it, Hoyer – you don't remember properly, you're just showing off.'

'But you do know,' Sonny returned to her point. 'You know that her ex-husband is a complete nutbar?'

I recommended my laughter as Burchmann's face sank – clearly it was new news, he had grown pale, sick looking.

'Beautiful, absolutely priceless.' I rubbed it in, tired with laughter.

'Fuckin' hell,' Burchmann finally broke his petrification. 'I didn't even know she'd been married.'

Greyly, the austere stonework of Trafalgar Square mooned down on the departing drunks assembled in the night bus blackhole. Sonny had been sent off in a cab, with promises of hanging out again soon, me and Burchmann walked around looking for my bus back to Surrey.

'I'm glad Sonny kept you busy this evening; I hadn't planned to be ignoring you for so long...you could say I'm a bit hung up on Frew.'

'Understandable – she definitely has something, Frew does and, no worries...about Sonny, you ignoring me and all that – I'm sure we'd've run out of things to say, you and I – I guess we both did better...company-wise. Mind you, I never actually got to speak to her that much...about herself, I mean – you know me.'

'Talk about yourself all night, again, eh?'

'Pretty much the whole time, yeah...'

'When you weren't bitchin' about me, huh?'

'Heh, hard to resist that...so, what does she do – she looks like a stenographer?'

'A what? No, different kind of 'ography, mate; she's a model – not like on a catwalk or shit, you know, kind of classy erotic stuff – nothing mucky – not surprisingly, I think mostly retro stuff...and yes, she does have a website.'

'If I even could find it, I think Joodie would check my search history.'

'Jesus, what's up with that? It's not like cheating on her. Men need to look at other women's bodies; it's good for us, especially if we're ten years into marriage. Surely, it's better to have a shuffle over some professional stranger than to do it in real life...Checking your searches, fuck...don't you know how to delete that shit...seriously, your wife must know more about computers than you do.'

'I think the focus here is not so much about the relative computer literacy of the two of us.'

'No, course not – is she really that distrustful? You'd never cheat on her, you're not the type.'

My inebriation was on the decline, still drunk but my mind was clear enough to develop thought, though my judgement was liable to make any such process pointless. 'Maybe I am? I've never really wanted to.' We reached my stop, Burchmann lit a cigarette. 'Before now.'

'Before now?' Burchmann's face showed confusion, the cigarette in his lips flicked like a VU meter as he spoke, 'Why now? What's happened?'

'Oh, nothing specific,' my answer cut anti-climactically, not completely wiping away Burchmann's interest. 'Just that the last few days I haven't been able to stop thinking about Ophelie, Joodie's best mate.'

'Ooh, no...' Burchmann physically drew back, raising his palms as if my confession had been flowing traffic. 'No, don't go down that avenue.'

'Why? I mean, I've no intention to, but why not?'

'Hoyer, dear boy; *never*, never the best mate – always it's going to end in disaster.'

'But it's just a silly taboo; just cause she's...'

'Forget taboos, I'm not talking about taboos; taboos have never stopped anyone who really wanted to get laid from getting laid – this is about the best friend. Someone she works with, that's fine; old acquaintance from Uni, again, go for it...um, friend of friend, of course, no problem; friend she's sort of mates with but can't quite remember why – yes, yes and always yes...but *best* friend..." He drew in a hissing negative breath. "...and sisters – best friends and sisters – never, never, never – they're like one and the same thing – would you screw her sister, course not – it's the same either way, some crazy psychic ESP shit we're talking about here. Just the fact that you've even been thinking about this broad...all the time? Really? Man...'

'What?'

'*Man...*'

'What?"

'She probably already knows.'

'What! Don't be such a bullshit drama queen, Burchmann.'

He half smiled, realising he had got a return on me for the teasing over Frew Grensen. 'Seriously, women talk; she knows.'

Survival is often the only true focus riding a night bus in London. The N22, unhindered, should consume an intimidating forty-five minutes, the reality is invariably beyond this, yet it remains an unavoidable evil. The route is epic – staccato progress to Knightsbridge and Chelsea, opening up on the long drag to Putney, before plunging into the twisting village lanes of Barnes and Mortlake – granted, at leisure and comfortable, a charming enough route through some of London's finest boroughs, but with a bladder full of booze and no option to stop once under way, the test soon begins. To bail, to cut loose from the bus, means waiting half an hour for the next bus, if it is even on time; and the booze, the hunger and tiredness, still clawing, only to start again, to try to make it the rest of the journey, not to mention the ignominy of urinating on the King's Road. And even for those joyously blessed with sturdy enough bladders, the on-board experience is never pleasant; the opportunity to sit down, a seldom and luxurious occurrence, is not always enough to make the odyssey tolerable. Regardless of the season, the interior is always horrifically hot downstairs and, during the winter, arctic upstairs. And the smells – the booze, the kebab and curry-driven flatulence; the vulgarities and obscenities, the intimidation and occasional violence: it is almost not worth suffering.

London, coming home, has none of the ghosts of the daylight version – no peering down from the raised Victorian railway, over the old high rows of wilting property, the endless changes slumped in brick, the shadows of the past in flickering paint, skeletal marks of disappeared construction high on the sides of vacant lots and backyards, chevrons scarred onto the brickwork where ancient roofs once gripped. All the clues of previous activity and existence that stood out like illustrations in an encyclopaedia are lost in the dark, dimly glowing nighttime, deeper in the shadows, the dark keeps its secrets. Along the bus route, the endless neon, the walls of crumbling late century signage and the sleek new signs, the merciful saviour of improved materials and an optimistic return to the pride of the shopkeeper. Even these cast artificial light, rebounding off the endless parked cars, bar-lines of nauseating golden streetlights creating rhythm and the dumb Morse Code of the traffic lights providing unknown text; the reflected reds and blues, flickering road signs – so much light and colour, against this fearsome shadowy darkness. London is lost, a tunnel of back-lit, spot-lit advertising, information and commerce – it could be any place, or nowhere. Yet there is an excitement about it, the drunk blur and flash and glamour of light, stimulated by the cacophony of pissed voices, boisterous friendships forming and failing as the bus swoops down the broad empty streets. The mist of heavenly cooling air as the doors part and the crush eases a little each time, until, as the lights diminish, the whole experience takes a new direction, the woody dimness south of the river and the ghosts of history returning, the old walls and crooked windows of crusty village relics.

As the mess of urbanity streaked past, the colours fusing into a kind of optical white noise, the mix of alcohol darkly toxic inside me, I followed my thoughts back through the evening and back to Ophelie until my entire mind was a flood of femininity; only Joodie failing to complete the day's hand – Ophelie, Frew and Sonny, and all of them without question totally unavailable to me – unavailable from certain points of view, yet all of them, to varying degrees had made themselves pleasant towards me. Sonny, her sexuality designating her disinterested in me beyond companionability, had been the freest with me; like old friends we had clicked and discovered a harmony in our attitudes. Frew had been sweet; for a time, I confess, foolishly I fancied that she might have been mildly interested in me, but her personality was of such an unburdened sunniness that I soon wrote of *that* little ego trip. I was simply benefiting from her natural vivacity. And Ophelie – true, she had never really opened up to me or addressed me directly with any regularity, but she had dotted the general chat of the afternoon with smiles in my direction, smiles that warmed and attracted me, smiles that employed her eyes as messengers. Naturally, the messages that they sent were foreign to me, I did not understand their language, but their tone was kind and inviting; she seemed to be letting me in and even if she was not clearing the path for sexual contact, she was certainly comforting me, offering a forum for interaction between us. Had she always done this, had I just never noticed, had something new ignited for her, too?

Remembering this sensation, dwelling on the soft appealing language of her eyes, meeting me, I raised my projection of her, held her high and with greater fondness; I had already built her up into something she had never been before, that almost certainly she was not. And never had I really been in the habit of celebration, never had I been fixated with actresses or pop stars, in fact I hadn't even staggered through an extended pursuit of a woman – me and Joodie had come together fairly routinely, there had been no drawn out attractions from afar, no unrequited epic campaigns to win the hearts of the hard to get. Ophelie was now projected in my mind as some fanciful ideal; my mind when I considered her was trackless, yet unflinching in its forward thrust. When I thought of her, the associations drawn were romantic and sentimental, there was an overwhelming sense of aspiration. Predominantly, superficially, it centred on her lips; but also, when I pictured her, there was a satisfaction in beholding her, her entire construction, something unnaturally excellent about her proportions, as though I were looking at A DaVincian study of anatomy; it was femininity, remarkable, sublime femininity. It was not about friendship, it was not about sex (though it was supremely physical), it was admiration and pride. She was established as special; idyllic.

I woke up with a flash, fallen into some near-sleep state as my mind forged ahead, fuelled, poisoned by alcohol and Ophelie. The night was darkest, the houses set back from the road – I must be nearly home. It hadn't been a dream, the image of her still filled my mind and the pit of my stomach still a drum, a cavernous barrel. My whole world seemed full of her – even when I stopped, when I changed the subject of my thoughts, she was there, peeking in – a state of mind, like joy or sadness, as thick as depression, as alive as fear. She was in my head.

*

Exhausted by my thoughts, I quietly let myself in; the dark hall silent, the dregs of booze in my system made a final push, my head thickened, the Ophelie-induced sensation in my guts was replaced by the swooning liquid, excessive inside me. Clothes thrown to the bedroom floor, I slipped into the heaven of the deep bedclothes, the cool, flat paradise of mattress and the angelic cupped hands of my pillow.

'Good God, it's nearly four.'

Even half-asleep, it bit into me; I didn't want to get into anything – my body was spinning like the reels of a fruit machine, I just wanted to coordinate the random tumbling motions and collapse into sleep.

'How are you back so late,' she pursued, no answer to her initial challenge. 'Where have you been?'

'Gallery. Burchmann,' I groaned, hoping that the tone of my voice carried additional code to prevent further interrogation.

'Still, these things don't go on that late.'

'Pub. Bus.'

'My God, you're hammered. I sincerely hope he hasn't had you behaving like an idiot. I'm surprised they let him in. His reputation...'

With a superhuman effort, sobered slightly again by my stasis and her accusatory tone, I rotated onto my other side. Joodie's eyes were open, wide in spite of her proximity to sleep – she was beautiful, I wanted to censure her for her attack on my friend but, lying there, her gaze so deeply into me, I managed only to give her a slight kiss on her naked lips, she pressed lightly back.

'I've been good, Joodie; I'll tell you everything in

the morning. I'm tipsy.'

Hopeful that the affair in my head was just a cerebral fling rather than a deep emotional attachment, I longed to return to work on Monday, to have as much distraction as I could wish for, but the weekend dragged on; Sunday, so often the strangest day of the week, was particularly challenging. I managed to take time to enjoy Joodie's company, we drove to a pub just outside Shepperton for Sunday Lunch; even though Joodie was driving, I had a soft drink instead of my usual pint of bitter, she smiled at my apparent thoughtfulness, which she took to be an act of sober solidarity, the reality was a dull aching hangover. The day had been pleasant enough; as the sun lowered, the large meal and painkillers finally pushed the hangover down to the status of fatigued discomfort. Back home, Joodie was soon back online, I watched an old movie and as my thoughts cleared, a figure emerged within them. I didn't have the energy to deny my interest, to even question her presence, I allowed her to dwell as I dozed off before the end credits.

At work, practical thinking tasks consumed me. I had determined that Ophelie had no place in my thoughts, that I had to take control and get her out of my system – it was just a madness and utterly meaningless. The Monday had been wet all day and on the way home it was easy to think under the hypnotic sway of the wipers; Bilal, driving, mercifully absorbed in local drivetime radio.

I returned to my analytical inclinations, taking as fact that Ophelie had physical characteristics that appealed to me, such interest, I determined, did not absolutely imply that I was attracted to her. The logic was, yes, a bit flimsy – I thought on and argued to myself that it was possible to see beauty in all things – men, animals, flowers, the elderly, the young, even machines; none of which I had any desire to sleep with – there existed beauty without sexual attraction. And, genuinely, I did not picture myself in a physical position with her – it truly was, as I recalled, barely, from my deduction on the night bus, it truly was an admiration of her, of her soft lightness, her poise, her breeziness and her sweet thoughtfulness that had caught me. If I were to imagine her naked, it was not associated with how one might consider an erotic image, rather how one might gaze at the form of Picabia's *Nu devant un paysage* – simple, natural. It was all I had to work with and with this notion on board, I vowed to limit my thoughts of her, to restrict any development or expansion.

George Street

'I feel really stupid.'

It was a small risk to confess this to Bilal, he spoke now and again to Joodie, but only when some work event brought them together, such social events were seldom nowadays. I knew that Bilal was not a gossip and not the sort of person that, even in the unlikely event of having the opportunity, would inadvertently reveal personal stuff; besides, the revelation was nothing more than a moment of titillation, if anything, Bilal seemed to find it all a bit dumb.

We sat on the low wall of the bleak Victorian building, its gothic tower stretching away above our heads, giving a sense of vertigo if we attempted to spot the two creepy narrow windows at the top, or the weird little balcony. Eating sandwiches and sausage rolls we had little to say; small talk was always exhausted by mid-morning coffee. It was grey but mild and I, for much needed clean air, had headed outside to see the sky – it made thinking so much easier when then restrictions of interior were lifted, even staring into the grim paving or the thick toneless cloud. However, it was not more thinking that I needed – I had hardly stopped. The idea of work distracting me had proven massively unsuccessful and work was now the last thing I wanted to do, the distraction of Ophelie in my thoughts prevented any kind of efficiency.

Opening the conversation was not as difficult as I had imagined, taking the decision to do so had been the challenge: whether Bilal was a useful confidant, whether anybody else even needed to know about this. Really, I had wanted to speak to Sonny, we had connected so speedily and easily, but she had not replied to my text message and, disappointed, I didn't pursue it, my confidence blunted, I opted to believe that perhaps she hadn't felt the same friendliness afterwards as I had.

I broached the topic in a fashion that I wasn't comfortable with, that bawdy, misogynistic laddish manner of discussing conquests, both complete and fancied and, for that matter, fanciful. Bilal initially giggled, he didn't really know Ophelie – their only contact had been at a handful of parties over the previous years at Onslow Road – his giggle could have been applied had I said any name.

This reaction was actually what I had hoped for; trying to persuade myself that it was foolish, yet my desire and commitment to the idea of Ophelie had swollen to such proportions that willpower alone was incapable of forcing a retreat. Once started, though, I gushed a confession; all the ideas of justification that had raced through my mind recently came forth in an admission of self-ridiculing preposterousness.

'I do. I genuinely feel really stupid – I just can't help it though; I'm drawn to her for no imaginable reason – no reason common to my normal practical self. At first, I just liked her smile; she has this fabulous mouth, her lips and teeth – all completely devastating – but a face is a face, who ever got so worked up about a face. More and more it was her body, I guess... You know what, it's not even as simple as her having a great, er, rack or killer pins...' I was so involved in this deep breath of liberation that such unnatural terminology slipped into my soliloquy. 'She has...she is just so, well...I guess I want to say, um, balanced?'

'In proportion?' Bilal contributed

'Yes, but something more, more, um, balanced, just her poise...'

'Boyzzz,' Bilal again interrupted, feeling obliged to utter something he considered to be ghetto. I stared at him, bewildered, the blush against his dark cheeks suggested it sounded moronic in his head as well; changing the thrust of the discussion Bilal went on, 'I can't say I remember her that well, she's kinda tall, yeah?'

'Not so much tall, more long, but tall enough that she sort of hangs her head sometimes, maybe that's more personality, I don't know. It's weird she's actually rather normal, she makes no effort to stand out – she's kinda pale and almost always covered up – so you might not've even noticed her.'

'Maybe that's it, I'm sure I'd have noticed a fit chick at one of your parties. Tits?'

It took a moment to register this as a question, I was obliged to considered it, 'I genuinely haven't thought about...'

'Yeah,' Bilal blasted out, incredulous. 'Course you ain't, course you ain't checked out them titties...'

'*Them titties?* Is that really how you speak?'

'Stop avoiding the question, tell me about her boobs.'

'Jesus, um, not small not large.'

Bilal sighed, disappointed, but finding motion again, I continued. 'But firm, I'm sure, very firm under her damn sweaters; strong, like so much about her, feminine and elegant.'

'Gay.'

'How can talking about a woman's breasts be gay?'

'You know what I mean, go on, tell me more...but less...'

'Gay? Right. I don't know what to say, it's weird, she's certainly good looking, but nothing remarkable, in so much that she's just a human being, not a fantasy, not pornographic or cinematic, not airbrushed or digitally manipulated, just a girl stretched and swollen into a woman and yet so different to Joodie.'

'Ahh, and there we have it, the crux of this whole infatuation.'

'Infatuation? Hardly...' I looked away, sheepish; looked like a man revealed.

'Whatever. Clearly that's what it is about her – she's not some hot sexy woman, but she's not your wife – which is probably the sexiest thing imaginable.'

'Yeah, but there are plenty of similarities, they're actually about the same height, more or less.' I realised I had run out of similarities; her image was deeply ingrained now and I stared through the grey day out to her. 'I think the *real* difference...the real attraction is their midpoints...'

'Midpoints?'

I turned towards Bilal, bread limply curling from my hand; suddenly I felt like I had said too much, what had started out as a casual reference to a woman I had been thinking about was now twisting into some bizarre over-thought-out analysis and comparison of my wife and her best friend. And yet it was satisfying to hear all these turbulent observations out loud, to realise how distorted my thought process had become

Regardless, like some great stupid unstoppable thing, I carried on. 'Their midpoints,' still looking towards Bilal, as if that helped to make it feel more like a general discussion on anatomy. 'I guess the point where they bend, torso and legs coming together...'

'Dude, can't you just say their muffs?'

'No,' I replied, far too seriously. 'I don't want to use a sexual reference, this really isn't about sex, it's about aesthetics, appearance, the human form; anyway, their midpoints are not at all the same, for me this is such a key dynamic; it's the axis that separates the two of them.'

It was the detail in Ophelie Wyeth that had been making me feel like a horny schoolboy, that tingled in me under my desk. She wasn't, in her features, as pretty as Joodie; a heavy pre-Raphaelite quality was her face's saving grace, something in her physiognomy that seemed to mirror my own. But I was intoxicated, now. I knew quite clearly that I didn't love her; there was not the tenderness I still adored with Joodie, the perfection of an embrace with her; even to envision lying in Ophelie's arms was a struggle. So, was it just a physical thrusting urge, a queer infatuation?

Bilal looked at me in awe, a packet of crisps ignored in his hand. 'What the fuck is up with you.' He didn't seem to be able to choose between laughter and anger, but the tone of his comment naturally indicated the latter, only blended with confusion and disappointment. 'Seriously, what the hell. Your wife is amazing, so cute...I mean I don't know this other one, but it doesn't sound like she can compete with Joodie – granted, her arse may well be a bit further from the ground, as if that makes any difference – Priya's arse seems to be getting closer to the ground each day. Nah, but seriously, you're pushing forty, married for ages, nice house, steady job; you should be looking at a family not your wife's mate's arse.'

'I've never really thought about her arse actually; hips, yeah, legs, yeah...'

'Whatever. You know, whatever you were just going on about – midpoints – it's just details, Joodie is the bigger picture.'

'Look – all I know, right now, I can't think beyond Ophelie. And I don't know why, it's like a...urgh...it's like I can't control it, like brainwashing. But beyond that, I know – Joodie is the bigger picture, she's my wife; but you have to see also, if she's the bigger picture and I'm not happy with her then the bigger picture is...'

'Fucked up.'

'Well, exactly. Ophelie...Ophelie getting into my system is not helping – I really like her, the whole idea of her, just thinking about what she brings, the clarity that she brings...it makes me feel good, turns me and makes me…'

'Alive?'

'Yeah – for want of a better cliché. I guess it's more that she provokes a response in me that is clean and strong, and Joodie…doesn't.'

Two weeks passed and rather than the feeling fading, I had grown to want Ophelie beyond reason. I had tried Bilal, but it got me nowhere, I needed real advice, someone that understood, not so much me, or what I was going through, but someone who understood women, a woman. Sonny.

Because of her sexual inclination, Sonny was the ideal companion – possessing the conversational superiority of her sex, the charm of femininity and the pleasure of physical desirability – she was nice to look at – but, most importantly, the safety net of her having absolutely no interest in me as a potential partner, yet without the self-esteem crushing reason of not being into me.

I hadn't thought so much about Sonny; my initial thoughts about her had got lost along the way, there was nothing substantial I could remember about her; that she was dressed so particularly was about it.

I was caught off guard, slightly defensive, swinging around, not quite in a martial arts pose, but frowning and ready to be mugged. For a moment my fear seemed equally worrying for her, but quickly, clearly, it became impossible for her to keep a straight face. She laughed.

'Steady there!'

'Sorry,' I gasped, relieved, embarrassed – she was dressed so much more casually than in Soho, 'Didn't recognised you without your...'

I was never going to end *that* sentence; she bailed me out, 'Yeah, yeah, "outfit" – let's not go down that path again.'

Inside the Old Ship, it was good to be drinking with her again, she brought out a lightness in me that I hadn't even noticed that I'd lost. We chatted a little bit, it didn't seem right to hit her straight away with Ophelie, it needed at least a half empty glass to broach the subject.

'So, I'm guessing it's Ophelie...Ophelie, right?'

'Right.'

'That you've dragged me out to this distant borough for. Admittedly, it is very lovely.'

'I am afraid so.' I was matter of fact, business-like, I didn't want to sound apologetic – I already felt lame enough.

'Yeah, so I'm pretty much thinking about her constantly, now.'

'What, constantly – every day, or constantly – without pause.'

'Oh God, not without pause, and not absolutely every day. Well, in fact, sometimes every day.'

'Oh.'

'And sometimes without pause.'

'Oh. Shit. Really?'

'It's difficult to explain, it's all about phases. Sometimes I'll just have her in my mind without a break, for days on end but...but then I'll forget about her for days at a time.'

'Right, well, that's pretty normal, I suppose.'

'You think?'

'Well, not *normal* normal, but normal for someone that's developing a lame, slightly creepy obsession.'

'Terrific'

'Or Terrifying. When it starts,' she sipped and looked towards the windows briefly, 'is there anything that triggers it, anything you do that starts you off; look at her picture, see a post from her on...oh, no, you don't do social media, do you.'

'Nope. No, nothing specific. I don't even have any pictures of her. Although, bloody typical, and perhaps this could be a catalyst to the propulsion of my interest in her, she does seem to be at our place more often. Last thing I need, right?'

'It almost certainly can't be helpful...'

'And I do tend to sort of wallow in it. Craig, her husband, is back in the USA and Ophelie, bored, fills her time gossiping with Joodie, you know, over a Pinot Noir. But, and this *is* good, it has the advantage, at least, of sparing me the monotony and complaint of Joodie's conversations.'

'A small mercy, indeed. Bigger picture, Christopher.'

'Well, it's relevant, surely – half of the problem is my issues with Joodie.'

'Fair enough. So, you just sit there and watch them...her?'

'Thanks, you're making me sound like...'

'*I'm* making you?'

'Touché. Not quite as bad as it seems but, yeah, there are elements of me sitting there...looking. But I'm trying to understand why, why I'm thinking about her so much. And it's actually the strangest thing, I can sit there and feel like I'm absorbing her – absorbing her femininity, absorbing her presence...and yet she is not especially feminine, not like you...'

'Aww, you love me.'

'I wouldn't put it past me right now, but no, sorry.'

'No great loss, I'm sure.'

'But, anyway, I feel like I'm taking these qualities from her, but...even though, sometimes, her company can be a dead blindness...that she doesn't even offer me these treasures. I mean, she doesn't ever say much, just sits there, kinda blank, listening to Joodie blathering on. I can look at her, the same woman who drives my musing mind wild, look at her and nothing stirs: her aura is mute, her chemicals inert, her manner and personality aseptic. Other times it takes nothing more than the narrow parting of her lips, in profile, the hanging parted teeth and I am a complete madman again, mentally punching out my frustrations.'

'Wow, you really do overthink, don't you?'

'Do I?'

'Yup.'

'Oh, 'cause I've got a lot more than this...' The flood gates had been opened, it was blesséd just to say all these things, had I really thought all this, or was it just spontaneous thoughts on subjects that had been rolling and thrashing, undefined, through my head all this time?

I couldn't stop: 'Curiously, at times it's Joodie that starts these phases, like I think about the superficial flaws of her personality – normally I've just accepted them, they're so familiar now, but recently I've stopped and said...not literally, I'm not talking to myself...'

'Not yet.'

'Well, I sort of do have conversations...in my head...but anyway, back to the point, recently these things...about Joodie...are just so laborious, and that makes me *ache* for Ophelie – just because she is different. I have to admit it, you and Bilal were spot on with that...element; but it is far from always the case. With Ophelie, sure she has her own set of faults and flaws, but much less known, fresher, if you will...'

'I suspect I *must*...'

'...and her contradictions, the little antitheses between her and Joodie, it makes me forget the problems of my wife. Ophelie is an escape route, only the door is locked.'

'Oh, Christopher...where to start. I don't think there's anything wrong, at least not with having a crush on her. What is *wrong* is trying to turn it into something...you sound like a schoolboy.'

'I feel a bit like one, like I felt years ago, virgin and bewildered.'

'So, you've got to learn to give it a rest. I mean nothing's ever going to happen, and by that logic you have to see that nothing *is* happening. It's not real.'

'I know but those days when all I can think about is Ophelie, seeing her, seeing her sitting there or walking around my flat, seeing the uninhibited way that she laughs, quiet, but still hearty; she moves like mist; and, when she is still...it's like she is suspended. Her face is like part of my own consciousness. Can't you see, this is beyond my control, I know it's juvenile, overly romantic but...fuck...I'm just stuck.'

Sonny took me in her arms, she could see I was breaking down, I think she'd underestimated what was going on, even I had! – it wasn't the trivial silliness she had thought it was, she could see I was messed up.

In her arms I felt wonderful and safe, I realised that I didn't have this kind of protection, protection from myself and the world, not even Joodie did this for me. I just abandoned myself to her, allowed her to gently cuddle me, not quite sobbing, but shaken, emotional.

Calmer, she released me, smiled and asked if I was ok.

'And what is the most destroying of all this?' I still couldn't stop, but I was steady now, controlled, back to my practical self. 'More than the crushing lust, more than the cruel regularity and cosy proximity of Ophelie – what crushes me, whenever I see her, is that I *do* know, I do recognise this, that it is never to be – I will never have anything more of her than I have at those moments. I will never caress her, never behold her nudity, never possess her affection, never share in her spirit. And, you know, when I first understood this, it was as final as knowing that I would never bring back the dead, the lost and missed. I accept it, dismally, but I *have* accepted it, and I accept the futility of my enthrallment, because I can't stop it. It is absolute; on an everyday and commonplace level, I know that I will never enter her, as my body forcibly demands my will to desire. I know that I'm not brave enough to risk anything. Besides, Ophelie would never buckle from her domesticity or loyalty to Craig; it is impossible to conceive of Ophelie having any passion for infidelity, and probably not even any passion for me.'

'Passion. Wow, well, you're certainly not short of that.'

I chortled, unimpressed. 'No, but I am certain that there is something she feels for me: like a dull respect, a wan affection, a soft daydream at the very least, but never a passion.'

'Maybe. Maybe she feels something, but, like you said, would she ever act on it?'

'No. I don't reckon she would.'

'Why shouldn't she? I'm not into guys, as you know, but I work with a lot of guys, models, cool guys, hipsters...so I know what's what, and you're a handsome guy, Christopher. That you're married to Joodie, she's good looking, right?'

'Absolutely.'

'Successful, popular?'

'Very much so.'

'Well doesn't that suggest that you must have some decent pulling power.'

'Exactly, and me and Craig do have a certain similarity in our looks, so it's not impossible to believe that she feels some pull towards me.'

'Exactly.'

'Exactly. So, how does that make this any easier, how does it make me stop – knowing that if things were different, we couldn't...'

'Because things aren't different, you moron...urgh, I'm sorry, you're really frustrating, you know that?'

'Christ, welcome to my world. Overthinkers Anonymous. But you see my problem, you see why I can't break this. This is my logic; this is what I am fighting against, part of the trap I am in. Even to the point of such arrogance that I believe that, surely, the same conundrums must press on Ophelie's conscience, that she is sitting there obsessed with me and killing herself knowing that she can't do a thing about it.'

'Do you really think that? I mean, there doesn't seem to be much basis for it.'

'No, there truly is something; something more concrete in the way that she looks at me – this soft kind of intensity...'

'Is everything about her soft? Have you noticed how much you use that adjective?'

'It's all part of the dream, I guess; so much of this is my projection of what she is...I don't know, maybe even what I want her to be...it's...'

'Anyway, you were saying...your argument for her...'

'Sure, yeah, she looks at me in this way...'

'Soft.'

'Ha ha. Yeah, soft, but it's quite definite, there's a strangeness to it too, as if it's being driven by puzzlement – she seems to look deep into me as if asking something, as if on a second plane superseding mere eye-contact. It is full and lingering, and it seems to intensify, midway through a bottle of wine, as if freed from her monstrous repressed coolness.'

'Oh, come on, Chris, that's too much; she's probably just a bit drunk, maybe she's just trying to focus on you. Is that all you've got – some soft, puzzled, drunken stare – hardly grounds for breaking up two marriages...'

'That's it, you're right, that is it – that's as much as we have; the strength of our connection is this unspoken unknowable knowledge of one another – not even the cliché that we are both thinking the same thing (it isn't impossible, but I don't have the faith to believe it), merely that we share a common intrigue.'

'I'm not sure if you even have that.'

I wasn't listening now; wallowing in my gloom, stuck in my own head and feeling sorry for myself, I couldn't even hear her. 'We have nothing else.'

Speaking with Sonny did not miraculously solve anything, but it followed that something of the intensity of my feeling was worn away. Times passed when my indifference was remarkable, when Ophelie's face had no appeal, less than zero – I would actually be put off. Ophelie, during these periods, projected stiffness, a sort of compression – her appeal, her softness was lost, strained out of its cushiony delicacy into an exhausting shape, a grimace almost, hard work to absorb compared to the effortlessness of the very same features that normally enchanted me.

And then there was an odd similarity I had started to subtly feel: a familiarity beyond the years I had shared her company. A knowingness closer to the feeling of looking at a cousin or an aunt, the traces of genetic parity, manifestations of antecedents, surpassing simplicity – eye colour, ear lobes – a deeper link, a mannerism, a posture, the inset of the side of her nose, the incline of the wings of her lips. Inbuilt and disturbing, it both drew me in, narcissistic, and repelled me, my self-confidence was tumbling with the doubt over my own value as a husband, which brought with it a dissatisfaction with my own looks. Some days I understood my handsomeness, remembering what Sonny had said, other days, lower days, days when Ophelie's smile slipped from perfection into objection – then I too felt ugly; I saw the fine characteristics as rough flaws and, knowing myself to be imperfect, I transferred the gloom and disenchantment onto Ophelie.

So, I could not look at her, thinking only of how I had too purely lusted after her, guiltily repressing the memory, repulsed by the thought of my desired infidelity, questioning how I could ever have been so attached. Magic or mayhem, by the hand of some other power I had torn my focus from Joodie; and whatever it was that drew me in to Ophelie, was not within my command – Ophelie was an enigma and I was a pilot, a navigator lost and enchanted by some arcane witchcraft, a majestic lust that crashed like oceans against lands, a tumble of white water over rocks, fast moving rivers; volcanic. I wanted her beyond understanding, or she was nothing – hard and ugly. And released from the spell, bewildered by her ordinariness, I fell, thankful, into a stillness; only the low subsonic groan of guilt and shame kept me from petrification.

Even if I had possessed the scale of vision to project myself mentally into Ophelie's bed, between her thighs, heavy on her ribcage, if I had possessed the bravado or idiocy to threaten the placid lives of so many, to risk all on the chance that she would take me and that it would be good – I knew, or rather I felt it and feeling it so completely it became a knowledge, I knew that I could not proceed. Within me, blinded by the lust that rumbled like an allergy through my body, that pricked and drained me underneath, deep within there was a kernel, a knot so tight and bound that held me somewhere, that reigned in all my thoughts and my charades; almost ceaselessly it dragged me down and back. It was a weird condition, seemingly rooted in the physical but affecting only the emotional – I felt it as if a dull pain, a cramp and a fever aching through to my limbs, enslaving my spine, and yet it twisted my thoughts, it restrained me and shaped me.

Somewhere, deep within, I could not escape a sensation of adolescence – that painful dysfunctional era of nervousness, shyness, paranoia and inadequacy – a time of sexual nascence, alone and individual, without outlet or resource, only fleeting seldom softnesses of stimulation – late night movies, glamorously monochrome, or mainstream titillation in print and the limited brilliance of a faceless blind imagination; the non-consummation of pointless crushes, nights of ineffective praying, days of sulking for attention. This pit of passed existence was the knuckle upon which my adult psyche rolled, my maturity corrupted by this lingering essence of youth that rose from the belly through thought and feeling and left me a boy in a man's body.   No longer the symptoms of shyness holding me back, a greater pressure, a thick sensation that I wasn't ready, that life was not yet available to me; surrounded now by younger men, I felt the youngest and, thinking of Ophelie, I felt unavailable to her: incapable.

Ham House

We motored up Richmond Hill; slouched in the passenger seat I stared up at milky clouds, bubbling against cerulean softness; the divide sharp and stark. In spite of the fineness of the day and my joy at recalling the colour I needed to classify it, to reaffirm some kind of reality, the car contained no conversation, no happy dialogue as the week drew to an end. My preoccupation had regressed again, the indifference was harder to muster, and once again Ophelie was my constant companion, like a perched bird on my shoulder or some illustrative conscience whispering in my ear. It felt unwholesome and controlling.

With no outlet for this desire, the arcane connection I had created with Ophelie tore at me. However, rather than inspiring frenzy, which it was capable and prone to do, I was as if in the eye of a hurricane, everything had become still in my mind. I had not seen her for some time, her visits to Onslow Road had ceased with the return of Craig earlier that week and, as with any burning, with diminishing fuel the flame only fluttered lightly – my thoughts remained dominated, only the mental images were fading, more reliant upon imagination and recall than an imprinted impression.

The soft purr of the car as it pulled up Richmond Hill sent thin vibrations, perfectly resonant with the thoughts that echoed in this eerie stillness, my own thoughts became this soft sinusoidal drone, easy and steady, the murmur of an engine; my mind rang out – Ophelie – the automotive ramble of this vision of her. Everything was in my head: I had no sense of location; my motoring companion, my day, my past, my connection to everything – all was lost, just this blissful hum and the hanging face, the slim perfect movement of Ophelie.

Instantly it burst, she was gone. As clear as she had been there, now she was removed. The car lurched heavily and now stood still; like confetti falling to the ground, the world around me rematerialized – Richmond Hill – I focused on my surroundings and slowly, emerging from behind the cars in front of them, the old couple shufflingly appeared. For a moment I watched them, considering whether their pace was a necessity of their aged bodies or whether they simply chose to dawdle, as though they didn't care for the urgency and unreasonable hurry of the motorists. Everything about the old pair was calm; it seemed not through indifference or senility, but simply the consequence of knowledge – the experience of understanding that there is no benefit to haste, that worry and anxiety are admissions of ineffective living; energy burnt needlessly in anticipation of the potential. They saw no need to pay in advance for that which is never guaranteed to occur.

With the car stationary in the impatient traffic, it

drew no shocked attention from Bilal when I popped my seat belt free and, opening the door, announced that I would get out at that point.

'You not going for you usual, then?'

I bent back down into the opened door, looked ahead and into the trees through the car window. 'Maybe, but as we've stopped...' I had no intention of going to the pub, and no reason to hide it, but something embarrassed me about my intentions, that I was doing something different and unpredictable and that it was so personal. 'Have a nice weekend, say "hi" to Priya.' I swung the door closed and skipped in front of the car, motorists behind tooted disapproval, the traffic liberated and moving forward again. Bilal ignored the flatulent prompts, raised a parting palm to me and revved away pursuing the tail of the commuters.

Under the wobble of a black iron railing, the terrace, the long sandy lip sitting below the pavement, gave on such clear days an uninterrupted view over the treetops out into an almost silent countrified suburbia; spoilt only by the traffic behind, thinning now as the rush home completed its daily shift. I stepped forward, the surface crunching, golden beneath my feet; the breeze came softly up the slope, catching and brushing through the trees, scattering the dark dappled shadows of leaves, calming and flickering to rest. Instantly the cars became forgotten; I ambled along the edge, the deep slope away to my right, yet my focus was not the ancient villages, clustered trees and lawn-like pastures, instead I scanned the uneven row of mismatched benches, serially occupied by elderly people, nursing mothers, bored students smoking over laptops perched on raised crossed legs; a pair of dogs circled under and around one bench leg, intrigued and flirtatious. I was looking for the old couple, wondering if maybe they hadn't stopped but headed instead down the steeply inclined path through the meadow running away to Petersham Lane and the curve of the Thames.

At a scruffy gap in the otherwise neatly kept hedge, I checked down the slope, two youngish looking men in suits headed downwards, whilst a very heavy woman laboriously, probably quite dangerously, struggled up the final twenty metres. The old couple could not have passed this way; their pace would have rendered them still easily visible. Just ahead of me, on the opposite side, I noticed a break in the fence and a set of steps cut into the pavement, I glanced from here back down the road and discovered the slow progress of the tall pensioners.

They edged closer; so as not to feel idiotic, standing waiting, I continued a little way along the terrace. At one point the area curved a semi-circle into the hillside, a heavy tree centred in it, I stood here and looked down to the river and the islands, my breathing grew deeper, expansive and luxurious. I forgot about the couple, forgot about Joodie and my unhappy home, even Ophelie did not trouble me. As I might have experienced in the window of the Buck's Head, I was transported in time, taken to some fantasy history, utterly unspoilt. I passed back decades, somewhere Regency, imagining the tenants of Ham House as they might have been when it was young and when the sprawl of Twickenham suburbia, of Kingston and Teddington, were mere villages; I imagined the meadows and woodland not spoilt by 4x4s and beer cans, but occupied by the deer that have now been limited to reservations – Richmond and Bushy Park. The mellow breeze pushed up the hillside, pushing kindly behind the final few steps of the obese woman. I turned to the reality of early Friday evening, scanning the banks of benches and spotting the elderly twosome.

With the majority of benches on this stretch of the terrace occupied, it wasn't unnatural to sit in the space next to the gentleman of the couple. My urge – everything just lately was urges, I had no solid direction or ambition, the only fuel currently driving me forward was compulsion, insignificant in the scheme of life but coming so regularly that it provided a clanking momentum carrying me – right now, the urge that possessed me was one of wishing to speak with the pensioners. To clear a path, a kind of invitation for them to feel unintimidated, I asked if they would mind me joining them – of course, they replied with a pair of matching smiles, a warmth felt at the rare semblance of politeness from a member of a younger generation, perhaps – kind smiles of acquiescence and a jumble of hurried words.

Reward was almost instant; the woman leant forward as I sat down, across the still broad chest of her husband, a small rose struggling upon it, she looked at me. 'It's fine today, isn't it, for just sitting and looking out into the world.'

'Yes.' I needed more and after a useless pause, 'Yes;

I can't believe I live a few streets away from here and I don't think I've actually just sat down here and looked at it.'

The man nodded and managed an "oh", his wife also nodded and confirmed her original observation. 'A fine day and a fine view.'

It killed the conversation, the couple returned to absorption and I remained uncertain how to proceed – I wanted to know about them but could not fashion a question that didn't sound nosey, even invasive.

'You only just moved here, I suppose?' His voice, the old man's, was dry, hissing on certain tones, his rounded elocution was refined, upper middle class, slightly magical, almost childlike.

'Sadly, no. I've been here over five years.' There was an urge to call him 'Sir' – it made my thoughts drift to Craig, what he had been saying about America, the retention of tradition over there, how they had retained so much that England had lost – to me, calling this stranger "Sir" would be patronising: how ridiculous it was – why should being respectful and polite be construed as offensive. Only in my own mind did it seem that way, conditioned by modernity – surely, the fellow would be flattered; if anything, it would have surely been the norm in his youth and adolescence, even throughout his working life. But I held back, treating him instead as I would treat Bilal or any of the other guys from work.

'And this is your first visit?' The wife took up the astonishment; her naturally sweet voice, still crisp and sure, rose with a melodic cadence that surpassed even her husband's, whose face still glowed with bemusement, as though my actions had registered but did not compute.

'I'm afraid so; I get dropped off further up...'

'Buck's Head, eh? Good jar of ale they used to do there – not my scene anymore though...'

As he tailed off, he visibly drifted into a dream of some time ago, much as the Buck's Head inspired me to do, only these were real histories that he visited.

'We never go as far as that; this is our spot.' She nodded generally at the area where they sat. 'Usually not so far, back a bit, where you can see Ham House better.'

'Oh,' I leapt in, suddenly at ease, the conversation established. 'I got married there.'

'Really? Oh, how charming. Lovely. I had no idea they did that.'

'Yes, Acantha, yes: they do them anywhere these days.'

'Well, really – I suppose they do – yes, I've seen pictures in the paper of Warren House...'

'Your great niece, um, yes, she got married there.'

'She did. We didn't go though, did we, Paul? Oh, but Ham House – that must have been wonderful.'

'I guess,' I conceded. 'I'm pretty inadequate at things like this,' shifting back to the original, more preferable direction of the conversation, 'you know, sitting and staring; I need to be doing something – you know, busy hands.' And I did a little Jolson wave.

'Sitting and staring,' Acantha smiled, charmed at the thought, comfortable with her own passive acceptance. 'That is what keeps us alive. That's what I think sometimes – we have the radio for conversation, when ours wears thin – and it does – but the radio is much the same as sitting staring.'

'The difference being,' Paul slipped out of his own private gaze, 'that when one stares at the view, one must provide the dialogue oneself...'

'And I suppose,' his wife turned the ball back, 'listening to the radio (our flat really isn't so very much to look at) one must provide something visual.'

'Which is easy enough if it's a play.'

'Quite,' Acantha agreed.

'Quite,' I, remotely controlled, added my own assent.

'It's barely enough,' Paul pursued. 'After a life largely spent overseas, this life becomes humdrum, especially after twenty something years of retirement. 'I'd've kept going if they'd've let me.'

'I can imagine. So, overseas – seems like everyone's getting their chance at that these days – were you military?'

'Briefly – I served, as we all did, caught the end of the war and lingered a bit, but they moved me into Government – cushy number, and it made my father happy.'

I fought to stay with the conversation: the dusty antiquity of this old man's father was a morsel of excellent time travel – the idea of someone living in, surely, the end of the nineteenth century was a considerable fascination. I forced the image to the back of my mind for digestion later this evening, a morsel for my mind to chew on during one of Joodie's over-telling of some adventure in media.

'Your father was never happy,' Acantha protested and Paul, with a sideways nod of his ancient crinkled skull, gave an agreeing "aye", that contained almost a century of weary contemplation and he wandered, mentally, off to some distant location in another distant memory.

Ten or fifteen minutes passed, dragging rather pedestrian; unlike the couple, I was not dressed for sitting on a bench on an exposed strip of autumnal hillside. Besides, I was beginning to feel uncomfortable, my intrusion into their habitual peace and introspection; it was not that I suspected my presence bothered them, but I did feel that I had stayed long enough. My departure, quickly enough decided upon, was textbook: a stretch of the shoulders, arms pressed out forward, a glance at my wristwatch, a small sigh and my palms, declaratory, patted down onto my thighs.

'Ah, it's been lovely to talk to you both – time for me to go, though.'

'Swift one at the Buck's Head?' Paul speculated, amiably. Acantha smiled at the notion of my having enjoyed their company and her own enjoyment at having someone different to share and to stimulate their own ideas.

'No,' I stretched the vowel, reassuring the unlikeliness of such a visit occurring. 'No, actually,' I acted surprised at the thought, unconvinced that I really meant it, 'this has given me the urge to work in the garden – it's a bit neglected…'

'Just like these views?' Acantha suggested the parallel, knowing that I sensed it, my eyes returning as I had spoken to the vista before them.

'Very much so.' I turned back to them, standing now; raised a hand. 'Well, see you here again someday, perhaps.'

'Ah, we're always here if it's dry,' Paul declared, solemnly.

'Ok, well, bye.'

'Good day.'

'Goodbye.'

I walked away, up the small uneven steps and deliberately back down the hill, away from the pub; neither of them noticed, they had returned to the view, Acantha's head tipped onto her husband's shoulder.

'Hi hon.'

Joodie seemed to be in a good mood. It upset me.

Wandering home among the fine old buildings, thoughts of dead people and non-existent historical situations raced; it was the furthest I had been from thinking about Ophelie all day. How easily and sweetly I had been distracted by Acantha and Paul, led comfortably into a normal conversational world, it had set me up nicely for my nostalgic walk home, thoroughly appreciating the beautiful random architecture of the crowded villas and apartments. Just two words from the mouth of my wife and, not love for her, but the infiltrating adoration of Ophelie returned to me with the punch of an ocean; I was floored, devastated – I wanted to turn away, to close the door and head away into the ivy lanes.

'I've just made tea. Want a cup?' Her voice was sweet and kind and called out to me with honest affection. It went unheard, the tones did not translate in my mind, only her presence; so her kind gesture became a pressure, a nag. I didn't respond, took my shoes off and walked into the kitchen.

'Been to the pub? You won't want a tea, then?'

'Um, no, I'll have a cup, nice and strong, please. No, I didn't fancy it...'

'No?'

'No. I went and sat on the bench.'

'*The* bench?'

'Yes,' I allowed my patience to stretch, as my body tensed. 'One of the benches on the terrace? On the hill?'

'Oh, I didn't know you liked it there. Not your scene, I wouldn't have thought. No beer, no windows to keep the world out.'

'What? I don't know what that's supposed to mean.'

'Nothing. Wow. Here's your tea, take it easy, darling. It's the weekend. Ooh, guess what...' She perked up at the thought and the chance to change the subject. I winced, sensing an oncoming drama from her work. 'Phee and Craig...'

'Don't call him "Cregg", his name's Craig, he's from Ealing.'

Joodie looked at me, as if at an extra-terrestrial, she took a deep breath, ready to challenge my attitude;

thinking better of it, however, she hadn't the patience, she went on, happier to share her news about Ophelie and Craig. 'They invited us round for dinner tomorrow.'

'Oh?' My monosyllabic question was pregnant with curiosity. Immediately, the idea of getting to see Ophelie invigorated my soul, a voluptuous swell of emotion – her bright cool eyes, the potentiality of her lips, I wanted to hold her, wanted to kiss her. It was all so purely physical, now; I knew I would share her space, beside her, communicating again with her.

'Don't say you're not coming!' Joodie guessed completely wrong.

'No, no.' I quickly clarified my position, childlike, my voice pitched up. 'No, that'll be nice, we haven't seen them for a while. I didn't know Craig was back.'

Watching a movie, alone, some trashy eighties teen comedy, it was easy for me to delve into the froth of my state of mind, happy to let Joodie vanish into the depths of the internet – separate rooms for our separating lives. My fancy was awash with Ophelie, I knew that I adored her; she was so much more interesting to me than Joodie. More and more Ophelie's presence had been the grind of my daily thoughts, like dreaming of next summer's vacation, she sat there; not even a mechanical figure – limbs and breasts – but a concept; her name rolling around my head like a mantra. Now it was every day and commonplace, like flatulence after pizza and beer. Walking to the coffee machine, up the cold, echoey stairwell; during meetings – flipchart ignored –

softly she was there and softly she teased me with her inaccessibility and the stupid inevitability of never being with me. And now I was going to see her. Dinner, tomorrow; it wasn't so very much in itself, but it would mean everything that my harangued brain could not currently supply – the living movement of Ophelie; monumental things like the penetration of her blue green eyes, the curve of her thigh extending from the taught tidiness of her buttock.

The movie was sucked into the oblivion of the dim forgotten living room, my thoughts traced a memory of Ophelie's dangling fingers, fine and thin, an elegance about them that was absent from Joodie's – perfectly good in their way, slim and compact, strong when they gripped me – I loved Joodie's hands, but I saw in Ophelie's something new. Something new.

I lay there, trying to understand my own lust so specifically directed, how had it grown from a flicker of attraction into this heavy desire? Why? And why now? Maybe it *was* just the need for something new, maybe it was just boredom. And not necessarily boredom with Joodie – this insanity in my head hardly seemed to be about her anyway, she was not part of this fixation – no, it was purely about me, totally selfish, egotistical and self-perpetuated – maybe I was just bored of being me, of what I'd become; superfluous. Thoughts of Ophelie, thoughts hurried and busy in my head, increasing and strengthening, they were not just tumbling from nowhere, they were not accidental or unexpected, I triggered them, brought them forth by my own wish to have her with me. Youth returning – to be again the sweaty teenager: sleepless nights and tortuous days, painfully studying the pretty girl in the form room, forever there, forever unavailable.

But even this new regularity of meditation was false – these were not devotional thoughts, idylls of love or even charm; I was not intoxicated by her beauty, I had not fallen for her as I had fallen for Joodie – the attraction was without romance. Visualising her, hers was not the majestic face that dreams are formed of; I knew and accepted that she was not like the models in magazines – flawless and unimaginably lovely – so, when I failed, lost, thinking about her, her name roaming and slipping around my head, on my lips, I admitted that it was nonsense. I thought I was falling in love, but I knew that I did not love her. Base, then, that was all – an obsession, like art, her movement and her shape, the idea of her, the idea of something glamorous. Of course, the illicitness of her – something so wrong about this attraction – guilt and pain – the need for me to suffer guilt, to wrong and to be a bad person, deep inside and unrealised, and to cause pain; the thrill of discovery and the thrill of the secret – psychological and physical – to suffer, to inflict and to lust.

Where then was the emotion? Was the affection between Joodie and myself so strong and constant that I didn't need it or anything similar in this fantasy relationship with Ophelie. Non-existent, though; the whole thing was a figment of my hormonal, cock-driven imagination and in the unreal there is no place for emotion – it was cold and cinematic. Of course I could not feel; I could never even begin to love her, not until I might lie there with her in my arms, her eyes grasping for me, searching and seeing and needing me; the full realisation of those maybe-glances that had escaped from her over dinner tables, over the misty tops of wine glasses. I hung to these memories, the fluttering looks that she allowed me, tenuous hints that I was right: that she desired me; that she would desire me, how key was that? Reality and reciprocation – the components absent, the force of emotion – to hold her and to be held; to consummate and compliment, to complete – to be without these, was to be without emotion and without emotion was nothing.

It was like climbing ropes in gym as a kid – nothing changed form, but the sensation was surprising, dizzying; it felt like it had to be clutched and squeezed, squeezed hard, the life numbed out of it, but my hands were busy with cutlery so all I could do was cross my legs and press. It was embarrassing – could they tell? I felt like I was flushing; maybe even, it seemed my eyes were rolling in, like some comic hit-in-the-nuts sketch.

The plate of food had to take me away – if I looked up from it, Ophelie would be there and, the conversation at an impasse, she could easily take my attention and draw me into dialogue. I had become obsessed with the way that she talked, the way she pressed her tongue to the back of her teeth – cruel; was she doing it on purpose? Of course, she was not: 'so how come', I asked myself, 'how come I'm noticing it now?' I *had* noticed it before, it was just that previously it hadn't been sexy, it was an odd glitch, a fault, a cause of discomfort, slurring her speech and making it heavy, woolly. She had got it from her French mother, genetics or affected or the consequence of being drilled in French at a pre-school age, and I loved it: it was my new favourite thing about her. Last week it had been her fingers, seemingly independent from her as a human being, their movement had the elegance of limbs, tiny dancers, fluid. The last time I had seen her – a coffee morning at Onslow Road – she had been maternally tousling the feathery hair of the sleeping infant son of another of our friends, obliviously lifting the fine strands and letting them cascade back through her long digits; and now it was this quirk of dialect. While she spoke my eyes were focussed on her mouth, its beauty unmissable – I had read somewhere that looking at a woman's mouth while she was speaking made you seem more attractive, it was worth a try – I found myself tingling just by her spoken word. And sometimes, the word delivered, she would leave her tongue there, pressed forward, her teeth parted revealing the curving pad, her eyes wide and smiling above, excitedly awaiting a response, sometimes I would reply and make her laugh and her whole mouth opened to a full silent laugh.

Beyond the torture of my unproductive and mercifully inert arousal, the discomfort of Ophelie opposite me was psychological; furthermore, the disturbingly banal small talk of Joodie was currently emphasising the gulf between my needs and the grind of reality. It wasn't that she was uninteresting, her stories were just rather parochial, and diminished in impact without intimate familiarity with any of the protagonists, and no one at the table possessed this. And her method of retelling was cumbersome and, at least for me, had the potential to make the listener feel impatient and uncomfortable. Sometimes, compounding the disorientation, she would contrive to fashion a punchline, mid-paragraph, which delighted her and bemused everyone else; it was her nature to consider that everyone felt and did as she did. Craig was lucky, possessing this handy way of stretching his thick lips and releasing a plummy guffaw that he could realise quickly, sensing the requirement, that sudden breaking of Joodie's laugh – it served him well and annoyed me, me with my fake laughter, which was exactly that; and, besides, I was tired of indulging her pointless inside humour.

Angry with Joodie, the guarded Ophelie, stately and subtle, seemed all the more cruelly absolute. The prohibition of contact with Ophelie multiplied the faults of Joodie – small quirks and imperfections of her personality that jarred with me and, under pressure of my frustration, the sense of my own inadequacy, were blown up into unabideable antagonisms, huge chasms of annoyance. I wanted to walk away, my mind fried by the grossness of being trapped with one and segregated from the other.

Neither of them were right for me – would any woman be? I imagined the type of woman that could achieve such a level of demands and squirmed as she grew to a dimension far beyond my reach, a scale of idealness so far out of my league; and, again, I shrivelled into my adolescence. Even if such a woman existed, I would never move in a world she inhabited. So I was stuck here, trapped at the dinner table with a woman I could touch but could no longer reach and a woman who brushed so close that I could actually smell the scent, hot on her collar bones, knowing that I would never get closer than that.

I became drunk and impeded as such, but I had been drunk in her company before and not felt the way that I currently did. I was losing focus, the thrill of this otherness was overpowering; the idea of her long body against me was no longer an abstract, the shift from an obsession with an idea to a distinct belief, meant that now I could picture myself beside her, the cool malleability of her stretching thighs like a warm breath gliding over my own, the hard swell of her abdomen curving in to meet my own, the sink of her waist under my palm, breaking with a crease in the paleness of her flesh, a dark prohibited line finally real under the inspection of my fingertip – all of this I could now feel as a potential reality. For the first time, my mind took the adventure of this living experience, together and touching and yet still without believing that I could ever do it; still the barriers in my mind, my protracted youth, blind duty, sensitivity to order and my loose comprehension of karma.

Although not quite an enlightenment, I was seeing things in a changed way. Entirely new and enormous, this feeling sent my pulse racing and I set down my fork. Looking up, hoping that she was looking at me, to see her eyes warmly caring and with a stillness upon me, empathetic. It would be awful if she was so, but a desire to feel that she was connected to me or at least that she knew what I was feeling, gripped me. They were not. She cut her beef, studying it as she did so, her head tilted down towards it, her hair falling forward revealing an ear. I was knocked out – thank God she wasn't looking at me – an ear, an ear! How absurd my thoughts were, ridiculous – no, she was not a prize-winning beauty, no, she was not on the cover of a magazine, yet an ear peeking out blew me away. My heart thudded, compensating; my stomach was a pit, nerve endings scintillating almost stood me on end – an ear! – It drove me to a madness, I wanted to punch myself, rip mine and her clothes off – I wanted her. I wanted to be stood there, naked, pressed against her, clasped; her cool skin healing and my salvation. Quickly I excused myself and hurried from the room making no real distraction to the form of the meal: Ophelie chewed, Joodie talked, Craig smiled – a ripple in a lake. I moved from them – a whirlpool, a waterfall, a tsunami.

Ophelie would never have me, I accepted this as she and Craig stood to say goodbye, as the well-tempered clavier played oddly, interrogatively, in the background. In spite of the looks she had bestowed upon me throughout the night – the depth and curiosity I felt to be exclusively for me – the embrace she allowed me as we said goodbye was loose and without heart. Here was her chance to show if a sympathetic emotion also touched her – but she declined the invitation, letting it pass with the weak hug reserved for lapsed acquaintances, my thick coat between our bodies denied me the compressed hardness of her breasts, their longed for pressure against my own pounding chest.

It was natural but unconvincing that my immediate reaction was the result of her own fierce caution. And her caution was immense, on a scale to compete with my own. She was by her very essence a reserved woman – flashes of vivacity juxtaposed, producing a grand desirability. She was tender and mellow and serious: the warm lisped fuzziness of her voice, her soft femininity presenting a semblance of playfulness, childlike almost, that slipped out unexpectedly and breathtakingly. It was all revealed in the embrace: Ophelie placed her forearms up the length of my spine, those unforgettable long fingers creeping unseen and featherweight against my shoulder blades; I mirrored the hold, awkward and afraid, the dumb schoolboy in me breaking at the crisis, and we came together at our collar bones, my face sinking into her hair, placing my farewell kiss somewhere within it, somehow incapable of making contact with her skin, the powdery cloud of her cheek, so close to her mouth it would have been exquisite, the finest separation between reality and fantasy, the inconceivable manifestation of hopeless dreaming into splendid actualization. I kissed her hair and she made a sound near my ear – it was as close as we could get; shoulders flat to one another, the sexual realm of her breasts withheld and miles away; arms loosened and then withdrawn.

*

Saturated with exposure to her, the whole night face to face had been dumb hypnotism, staring mutely at her at every opportunity – grateful for her desire to talk this evening, allowing me to sit transfixed, watching the pretty mechanics of her speaking mouth, drifting up to the cool stillness of her eyes, queerly shallow, dramatic in their metallic calm; drifting down to the frill of her blouse, disappointingly protecting the form of her bosom today, a faint treasure of a curve escaping the ruffles on the lower outside arc. I had taken my fill of her, of her living actuality, as if it were her death that was imminent rather than simply my departure home. I had drunk her vision dry, every detail of light in her hair, every dipped eyelash; I had sucked her dry, her flimsy beauty, suspended on a fine thread between plainness and perfection and now I was full.

Back home, in the dead moments as the night failed, a night cap by candlelight, I suddenly felt hit by the unknown alcoholic volume of the evening, the tipsy heaviness crept up and, without the hum of the music, without society, the evening was over. I reeled and wilted among the consumed images of Ophelie that clashed harshly with the peculiarly out of place chatter of Joodie, gushing about how delightful the evening had been, swooning at its excellence; at the success of the mundane. I was unable to adjust to the dinner party terminating, my whisky brutal, I declared a desire to sleep.

'What's wrong? Can't you stay? It's so nice, just us sitting here.'

It *was* nice; it was nice that she was aware of me but, with my attention distracted, provoking negativity again towards her, my calculation resulted in the reality that she was happy because *she* was happy, not because *we* were happy. I stood up and extinguished the candles with soft kisses of breath; kisses spilt wastefully – the intended lips streets away. I created the darkness rudely, not thinking, leaving Joodie on the couch with her drink in her hand. She stood up, close to me, looking deeply into me, searching, confused. Blissful with her own state of mind and the wine, she tucked her hands between my arms and my waist, squeezing herself into me, my chest a pillow to her dreamy thoughts; the top of her head smelt oily beneath my chin. She simpered romantically, drunkenly reclaiming her love for me. The room was dark around us; I looked up from the star of her scalp to the dim blinds, backlit by streetlight. Carefully I offered my arms around her, devoid of commitment and she tugged me closer, snuggling sounds and slight rubbing of her cheek, cat-like on the fuzzy cotton of my shirt. I could hardly even feel her.

'You didn't enjoy it – tonight – did you? You seemed edgy, distracted.'

'Maybe. Distracted, yeah, I guess I am – I'm not quite at the races at the moment. Not sure why, but I'm a bit out of sorts. I did have a nice night, though.'

'Don't you like them?' Joodie slipped past the plea for attention that I had vaguely tossed, I rolled my eyes, disbelief that her only concern was how I felt about her friends.

'Of course; Craig does my head in a bit, Ophelie's sweet, you know I get on with her as much as any of your friends...'

'I don't know why you find it so difficult to relate to them...my friends, I mean...generally.'

'Oh, I don't want to get into this, it's too late, I'm tipsy – look, it's just that it's a different world, I don't think I dislike any of them, I just don't have much in common with any of them – even Ophelie...'

'You and Ophelie have...' Joodie stalled, unable to bring to mind the connection she believed existed.

'Anyway,' I saved her the effort – I'd spent weeks searching for something to tie me and Ophelie together, however tenuous, and came up with nothing. 'It's not about whether I like your friends or not...tonight, I had a nice evening, I chatted to both of them...'

'When you could be bothered.'

'It's not about being bothered,' I defended, my voice toughening, my arms separating, Joodie withdrew unconsciously sensing the shift. 'Jesus, what kind of thing is that to say – I actually had a great night, I chatted a fair bit, I enjoyed the meal, enjoyed being out with you; like I said I'm just not on top form just lately.'

'Yeah, well I know all about that – don't think that it's fun for me when you're moping around the place.'

'I don't mope; you're never here anyway. Maybe, if you thought less about your work, and more about your commitments to your family...'

'Family, so that's what this is about – you want to start the whole baby thing again; Darling,' she pleaded, bored rather than considerate, 'I've told...'

'It's got nothing to do with babies; Christ, I wouldn't bring a baby into this...'

'This? What the hell do you mean by that.'

'This. This fucking routine, the fact that you don't care about me or our lives...you're so damned wrapped up in your own world...'

'*I* am!' She was staggered by this suggestion, the antithesis to her reality.

'So selfish.'

'Me? How the hell am I selfish.'

'Well, self-absorbed, then. Everything revolves around you and what you want, or feel, or what your friends think of our life – and I'm a distant consideration – at best; at the end of the line.'

'Oh, that's just bullshit.'

'I'm going bed. This is what I mean, you live in your own world; you're incapable of seeing things from my point of view.'

'Well, maybe if we ever invited your friends for dinner or...anything. Maybe if you actually had any friends...and not bloody Burchmann.'

'Huh? What's wrong with him?'

'What kind of person doesn't use their first name.'

'Fuck. What kind of person calls themselves fucking "Cregg"?'

Joodie parped a little giggle, she couldn't help it and its effect was instant and complete – I saw the funny side and the ridiculousness of the fight.

'Don't give me a hard time, Joo; just understand that it's really difficult for me right now...I'm doing my best; can you accept that? I had a nice night tonight, and I *do* like Ophelie – of all your friends, I really think she's my favourite. Ok?'

'Ok.' She re-established her embrace, holding on to me, a necessary thing, whilst my arms re-circled her, a deep satisfaction in knowing that I had just confessed my feelings without saying anything, this underhand declaration of the sensation that ruptured through me. I squeezed her, re-pressing in my mind the incomplete, unsatisfactory hug, parting from Ophelie.

Such small reward the earlier farewell embrace from Ophelie had been, yet it lingered and whorled among my humoristic agents and thundered in the sexual as I undressed. Lying in bed she was still with me in the failed closeness of our brief attachment. My hand, carelessly, reached for my privates and I began to manipulate the over-responsive tip, the cell that had consumed me throughout the evening with its nagging presence, hot under the dinner table, false alarm, alert and active, yet slumberous. With greater subtlety I massaged, a completeness calming, familiar and fresh, long awaited and, in its raw exposed availability, the flesh broadened and firmed under my secretive fingertips, the silent bedroom confessing the flex of my wrist, expanded movement uncontrollable as the pleasure both tumbled and ascended. Joodie's breath came with a hum through her nose, not quite the deep inaccessible sleep she would eventually succumb to, on the cusp, seemingly gone, she stirred, groaned, I suspended, my pulse still rumbling under my frozen fingers; she groaned again, shifted and lightly began to snore, a queer giggle escaping – even in her sleep, out of time punchlines tickled her, unexpected. I began again, but the focus was lost, the intimate ghostly world I had built to house myself and Ophelie in, the revealed sleekness under her clothes against my real nudity, it was there before me, in my imagination, but only superficially against the dark skin of the night; the trance was broken, I was alive again and reality was my master. Beneath my fingers, the rubbed sensation was intense and sharp, unpleasant, I had lost her and let go. Joodie, beside me, contorted her body with the movements of her own subconscious, contorted and curled up; the base of her spine, a huge curve, pushed hard and heavy into my hip.

Putney Bridge

Dream littered and hungover, my sleep had been erratic; the nagging, daybreak reality of the household pets cut through the deep treasures of the final and finest moments. Two of the three cats waltzed recklessly around my legs as, heavy-footed, I crossed the cold, kitchen floor, blindly and fortuitously managing not to kick them. It was too early; furious at the ingenuous felines for stealing away the delicious erotica of my dream, replacing it with cold tense aching reality.

The simplest of dreams and thus utter perfection: I had been sitting or, rather, surrounding Ophelie; she was stretched prone on a copper and orange sunset, her legs stretched long like a silhouetted desert skyline, rising in smooth waves of nature, rising to the neat swell of her buttocks, the leopard skin of her bikini briefs puffed loosely over her cheeks and the fine, downy *piste*, two remarkable hypothetical dimples shining either side of her spine, sloping into the small of her back, twisting and becoming her ribcage. And, such is the perfection of dreams, I had absolute vision; like the camera suspended on wires over televised sports fields, I manoeuvred, drifting like the stealthy cats tickling between my legs as I stood dishing out the meaty lumps of fish – I hovered and swooned around the imagined rounds of her backsides; unknown domain, I had accepted the dreamed interpretation of how they might conceivably be shaped, they seemed right, seemed to meld with the denim reality that was my known experience. The dream, a pleasant surprise, was all legs and buttocks and, heavenly, untouchable, she remained. But how sweet this last phase of sleep, how cruel to be woken.

I returned to bed; Joodie's corpse-like, somnolent body sprawled towards me. Dehydrated, tired from the incompleteness of my interrupted sleep, the room was too light through the curtains to feel sleep returning; my body, knowing that it was existing in morning time rather than night time, stubbornly refusing to close down, to give in and fade out, unresponsive to the need to complete the night's sleep. My mind was full of the dream as I drifted close to sleep, failing, waking and drifting again in a cruel cycle of drowsy awakedness.

The following days were a fever. Unable to focus, irrational and physically crumbling, I needed to break the cycle. Constantly I fought with my thoughts, attempting to diminish or dampen the overwhelming female presence. It seemed so gross and childish to be so lovesick, but there was no escape route – I was incapable of changing the thoughts that dominated my mind – desire and salvation – this double-team controlled me – to satisfy the first I would achieve the second. Yet it remained inexplicable – even now I could not fully grasp the source of her desirability. Periods washed over me where certain things seemed understood; some grinding, physical lust; the niceness of her limbs and body, somewhere unseen and denied; the elegance of her movement – but so possessed a million other women.

Sonny called me, out of the blue – she was in Putney, she'd been working there, on a shoot, and figured, by London scales, she was "in the neighbourhood". We'd just finished dinner, Joodie was straight on to her laptop, so I mumbled that I was meeting Sonny – without curiosity – it was the first time I'd mentioned her – Joodie mumbled in return her understanding of this fact and I dashed out before she had time to become curious.

We sat in the Star & Garter, looking out at the river; I thought to ask about her "shoot" – it hadn't been great, she confessed and, seemingly unenthusiastic to talk any more on the subject, she hit me straight back for an update on my "Ophelie-thing".

'My Ophelie thing? Well, it's not a "thing" anymore, it's a frightening fucking monster.'

'Oh, tits. I was hoping it had passed – go on then, what's the situation now? Still entirely in your head.'

'Obviously. Although, despite it being so much confused thought, I still haven't got to a place where the *desire* is head-based…'

'It's *all* in your head, what are you talking about?'

'I mean that my desire isn't cerebral – I don't have any particular interest in her… in her thoughts, what she likes or thinks. This element is completely absent. Needless to say, though, I am hopelessly locked into her.'

'So, is it just this image you're into, this idea, like

this photographer today – he just kept trying to get the same shot, he had this idea of what he wanted and we wasted so much time getting to it, and then wasted the rest of the time just shooting the same thing.'

'Kinda...in so much that we're both locked into this idea, and that the idea becomes so dominant that we can no longer understand the reasons why it is this particular image we like – so we just stick with it, hoping that one day it'll come back to us...maybe? I mean, she's above average, but her looks are difficult; she's intelligent, but not exceptional; she is often quiet, and serious; and if she is poetic or creative, she keeps it concealed or subdued entirely; even as a romantic, there's no signs that she does it well – I've never seen any public affection between her and her husband; I don't think I've ever seen them kiss or embrace. She's not exactly dream-woman material, but then...'

'No. Oddly enough, I don't see how you've got into this state.' she seemed to be at a loss, understandably, I'd wasted hours...days mulling it over, even from her external perspective there seemed no explanation for what I was doing. 'Well, do you think they're happy, her and "Cregg"? I mean, if they are, then perhaps she's not even close to being the woman you're obsessed with...'

I started to interrupt, to challenge this accusation. 'Oh, Christopher, you *are* obsessed.'

'Yeah,' I sulked, 'but you don't have to say it.'

'Oh, boo hoo. So, is she? Are they?'

'I'm unconvinced. Based on what I've seen and, by way of Joodie's loose lips, what I've heard, they're not exactly blissful – but who is?'

'I don't get it then. Her deficiencies are noted – nothing about her is obviously remarkable or capable of making men swoon, so all you really have is this general aura, a certain sweetness, a softness, grace and calm.'

'All true. There's not much, but it really hits you...one...me...'

'Ok, but also there is the fact that she is so different to Joodie...and the mere attraction of her presence and her unavailability. That's it? So why,' I grimaced as she drew this mortifying conclusion, my hands through my hair, 'why are you so destroyed, so lovesick and so embarrassing?'

'I don't know! I want it to stop, the futility and inappropriateness...I know, it's glaringly apparent...but nothing is giving, no reduction, no denial; I hate it, it is starting to ruin me and yet, urgh, there's a part of it that I love.'

'Are you in love with her?'

'I don't think so. I don't think I'm capable of that. If it's love, then I love her as I might love a vapour. How can you love something that doesn't exist?'

Cruel or blesséd, this rare moment of honesty was followed by a period where Ophelie was once again absent from my world. Craig was working from home and whatever constituted a love nest in the Wyeth household was established and remained, apparently, uncrackable. Terminated were the coffee mornings, wine and movies in the evenings and any hope for another dinner party was given up to time unimaginable in the future. Even studying, tracing and retaining all that I could recall of her from that last meal at their place, Ophelie was in danger of fading into an inaccurate blur in my mind.

Yet I had one treasure, something new and radical by my standards, one piece of evidence that she was what I believed her to be. Despite, my failure to embrace modernity, I was in the possession of a mediocre mobile phone; the device was barely acknowledged, let alone utilized; yet over the years I had clung on to it, as technology swept by, leaving the device to fall horribly into antiquity; as such, I was too inhibited to hold the cracked and crusty contraption in the faces of my friends, so the vast majority of images it held were of interesting buildings, pictures of the cats and a couple of Joodie. However, incredibly, I now had a picture of Ophelie. There it was, one low resolution image had found its home in the little yellow digital folder and, sitting in the enclosure of my office, I flicked through the gallery of images searching for the one I had braved to take at the Wyeth's dinner party – a nice picture of the hosts and Joodie; Ophelie was smiling, not too prettily, but she held my gaze, held it and it soothed me; in the grey loneliness of my office, she was with me.

The isolation of my workplace could be dangerous, not just for the ennui that festered in solitude but also for the time and freedom allowed for introspection, and always, now, my thoughts turned to Ophelie. Nights often full of dreams had imprinted her among my basic functioning thoughts: the drive to work, the tasks pointlessly passing before me were all littered with images of her face, her body, clothed or unclothed, the details of her movement – all the turbulent visions and scenarios that had been playing out in my daydreams were now running constantly, everything, one after the other. At times it was a thin, intense heaven – the comfort of her warm features gently gazing out of the fantasy, kindly knowing, knowing me, understanding my desires, easing my frustration; or the tingle of desire, fireworks in my stomach at the passing thoughts of obscure parts of her body recalled. Predominantly, though, it was a hell; the nightmare of having her constantly beside me – all that I wanted right now was to have her as my own, but she wasn't there, she was, as I had admitted to Sonny, nothing more than a mirage. The whole idea of her and me lying together – kissing, rubbing close, feline – was just a madness, a crazy unrealizable fantasy, schoolboy daydreaming that had somehow mutated into, and again Sonny was spot on, an obsession. I hated it; I just wanted to be happy with Joodie.

Perhaps with bad humour, perhaps kind empathy, the clouds gathered throughout the morning, swelling plump with their dismal waiting load, and broke, mid-afternoon. Discovering the grimness of this early evening, I was cheered – if misery loved company, then the weather was my new best friend. For the first time that day I smiled – it had been a gruesome day, impossible to focus on my work, decisions hard to come by, the hours had dragged by with glacial weariness, plastic flow, the eternities of the minute hand; I had sat and suffered. Ophelie lingered cruelly now; any confusion or doubt that I had initially supported had now wilted, no questions remained – this woman meant something to me, I wanted only her in my world. Thoughts rang without romance, a returning cycle of thoughts, schizophrenic, demanding my attention – it was beyond my control. Colleagues coming and going were met with a cold indifference, almost from oblivion came the grunted laconic commitments, responses to questions barely heard. My outward appearance was a pure dead calm, yet underneath obsession bubbled and twitched, crossed with anger, dejection, fury and hate – a mess of emotion, wild and demanding.

Out to the suburbs, there was no conversation in the car; Bilal was fully focussed on the conditions: water blowing and thrown up from the tarmac, whilst I was calmed by the rain, that sound, always enveloping. Every visual perspective was distorted by the film of moisture, constantly shifting, kaleidoscopic over the glass – it was not perspective that eased me – I wasn't exactly eased – it was as if I had nothing inside me, only vapours of awareness of Ophelie and her presence in my life. Bilal swore at the traffic, he swore at the car and the weather – as if in the North Atlantic, fighting through the silver sheets, through the saturated hurry of pedestrians in the High Street; the river was lost in a grey haze and the climb up Richmond Hill could have been a climb anywhere.

'I can drop you off at your house, if you want; you don't want to be walking home in this, do you?'

Blinking free from the moribund reverie, I "hmm'd".

'Do you want me to go straight to yours? Quick, 'cause I have to turn off...'

'No; actually, you can drop me off at the Buck's Head...'

'Dude, it's not the weekend, yet.'

'I understand that...I fancy a beer, and I don't want to be at home right away.'

'Joodie'll kill you...'

'I doubt that.' I missed the hyperbole, or felt that it was too close to being accurate. 'Besides, why do you think I don't want to be at home.'

'Urgh, like that is it? That explains why you've been so boring all day.'

Wanting to know, worried that people might think I'd lost it, I braved an explanation. He spared me any sarcasm, visibly concerned about me and I didn't even tell him the half of it.

No one, apparently, had guessed, but over-desk conversation was of "Christopher's mood", speculations from death to divorce to destitution were offered as justification for what had clearly been picked up on, my distraction and moodiness.

'And no one spoke of passion, no one spoke of adoration?' I clutched for.

'Mate, no one has ever used those words in a sentence about you or any other Senior Logistics Manager'

Like the sky above the buildings, I sat still and darkening, whilst the pressure within built and the downpour pressed to fall.

'Really? I thought I...maybe...?' We paused at the kerb.

'No, not even close.'

I climbed out into the noise and volume of rain, instantly soaked. 'I'll see you tomorrow.'

After so much intensity, I dropped fully into a lull. It had been a while since Ophelie had sat across from me for those indulgent hours, and as I stared into the unsatisfactory foam skinning the top of my drink I blandly tried to imagine her sitting on her couch, the meal finished, adequate alcohol in the four of us and a game, a word game being played; I had lost, it was guys against girls and I was uncomfortable having to partner Craig, feeling for perhaps the first time in my life since I married Joodie the cringing bite of jealousy; furthermore, how could I even concentrate, when all I could conceive was Ophelie, sitting with her legs tucked up, her feet curled cosily, like shrimp, as she drank her wine, stretching her fine torso to place her glass on the side table, comfortable in her home, her own world surrounding her.

All the reality that had so luxuriously been placed before me, in spite of the useless image on the little screen of my mobile phone, had receded, melted back down to imagination again – the knowledge of her sadly interrogative look, the light movement of her limbs when she had danced in her socks, strong slender arches gliding over the parquet, and she was a good dancer, odd and languid but her rhythm was spot on and her coordination allowed breathless movements of her arms, shoulders, her head – now it was all gone; a new distant memory, small moments hopefully retained, my own private chest of thoughts and recollections of her. There was nothing new – time had passed during which I hadn't seen her, no new details had been made available to that dark repository, and no new adventures for sexual accompaniment. I longed for a new vision: a new dress, blouse, skirt, some gesture or comment – God, maybe even a sign, a slight flirtation on her part, some new reciprocation – but there had been nothing and all that I had was faded and dull, a dreary annex to my marriage – was that it then, was it simply the newness that I craved, after all? With only the worn-out images of her to feed from, I found the passion subduing, like a habit overcome, like a change of diet, with less to consume the hunger faded and the norm adjusted. It was a relief to be in a trough after such a peak, only now I was bored, now there was no passion in me at all.

From the window of the Buck's Head, today there were no voyages into imagined history; with such indifference washing through me, it was without romance that my mind functioned; picturesque outings into contrived fantasia were absent, shrill rain dominated and wearied. I looked over to the terrace, expecting it to be empty and, indeed, no one sat there, but under an umbrella a couple walked, her arm tugging his tightly towards her – it made no impression on me, such sweet companionship that normally would have warmed me, propelled me into the imagining of some tryst or liaison, now it was just a shivering couple, increasingly soaked. My trousers were damp against my thighs, I wanted to go home and change and curl up with a mug of tea, but the very idea of being in that dreary buried place sent the cold sticky patches of my legs aching and dull.

It was Acantha and Paul that I was most inclined to be with; there was a reassurance about them, an understanding. I had lost my own collection of grandparents in childhood, my parents had emigrated; no conduit to the bygone existed for me now, save my biographies and histories, but only through the empirical experiences of generations preceding can real knowledge be gained.

Yet, this lull, while it lasted – by the evening I might again be intoxicated by the strange beautiful curiosity of Ophelie – it was a blessing to me. Rather, right now, to feel nothing, to be free of her pervasive clutch, than to struggle for clarity and rationality; beyond which the guilt had worn me raw. I could no longer think or act with any definition or direction, even a demanding desire simply to walk out into the rain, to find solace in the pure nature of the heaving storm was discredited and refused, the idea of the effort of discomfort seemed too much of an effort, too onerous.

By the time my beer was drained the rain had settled into a drizzle. Damp already, I didn't take a second thought about stepping into it. It was sublime; the cold dots invigorated my scalp; a light breeze created a soft colourful noise in my ears. Strangely, I noticed how, compared to the moribundity of my soul, how alive the streets were, how full of fragrance and sound. Part of me awoke from apathy and I thought of the surprise expressed by Acantha and Paul when I had confessed my neglect of my surroundings – it was ungrateful to live in such a beautiful corner of England and not to have even attempted to appreciate what was around me, and the trees in abundance rattled wetly to emphasize their considerable presence.

Caught up in this comprehension of the local environment, my focus turned to the park – Richmond Park – the great reserve upon the crest of the hill, the wild space that, to me, was a place for families to visit, tourists, birdwatchers – certainly not for me. It wasn't that I didn't like nature, but that I could only deal with it for a short time before my attention demanded occupation and the park was so vast that to wander into it, alone and unladen, I would be trapped in isolation, a frantic hurry to be out and home and busy, if not in body then at least some distraction from the thoughts that, unchallenged, roamed my head like the herding cervidae.

Maybe, I pondered, maybe I'll try it this weekend, take a portable CD player, headphones, listen to *Nine Feet Underground* – that would be enough to get me in the grounds, see what it was all about, satisfy my neglect of my surroundings and still have me out, without stress, a half hour later.

As I made the final turn into Onslow Road, with satisfaction I recollected that Ophelie was something of an advocate of walks in the park – madness, I had always considered – so, then, if nothing else, the next time I met her, we might at least have one more piece of common ground. I smiled, a rare smile, at my own pun.

Dimly lit, the flat confused me into feeling welcome. It was home but I had feared returning to it as one fears visiting a headmaster, knowing that there was nothing wrong but equally the feeling that being there was far from right. Yet, warm against the cold and damp of outdoors and my now awfully clinging clothes, the low lit hallway, the smell of onions, frying, this against my passivity and dead emotions, the slight shove of the brief euphoria, now waned, of the wet leaves and the delighting suburbs – somehow it eased me, but it was unpleasant in its undesirability – ennui had served me well, saved me from the churn of obsession and disenchantment – but here, home, I felt a lunging desperation forming, a desire to be with Joodie.

Dragging the wet clothes from my limbs and taking a precautionary peek through the crack of the door (naked and spontaneous I may have been, but a cautiousness in me remained, paranoid that my absurd and risky gesture could be exploded by lurching in and discovering the mother-in-law, for example, sipping rooibos at the kitchen table); it appeared safe to proceed. The initial intention of making a dramatic prancing entrance had been rapidly scaled down to a more romantic, more erotic stroll. As I reached the centre of the room, I called out Joodie's name, low and husky, aroused by my own nakedness and the potential. Joodie was at the counter, facing the back window, dark and reflecting her downturned eyes.

'You're a bit late,' she grumbled, unmoving from some chopped mushrooms. 'I couldn't wait, so I've started dinner – you're lucky, I might have done it an hour ago.'

I rolled my eyes, her prosaic complaint almost destroyed the mood entirely, but I was there now, cold from my still damp skin where the rain had seeped through.

'Yeah,' I continued in my imagined sexy tones. 'I had to *pick* something up...*for you.*'

'Oh,' she suddenly brightened, looked up to the glass and, not sure what she saw, spun around, the knife comically erect in her hand. 'Oh wow – I haven't seen one of *those* for a while.'

How she always managed to do it; I fought not to frown and cringe – why did she have to draw attention to the negative? Here I was, stark naked in the kitchen, offering unexpected sexuality and her reply managed to turn, unconsciously, critical. I had to move on, she was beautiful, her face bare from the normal excess of paint and plaster, her trousers, fine, showing her slim legs, flattering her form, elongating her frame, a simple pastel sweater, short to the waist stretching her frame further, and her smile, there it was, I had missed it, finally breaking, sweet as ever and for me. I stepped forward and embraced her, the knife, with a clang, tumbled onto the floor.

Millbank

After extreme vividness of desire, followed by extreme tepidness of indifference, I found myself in a dark, foul restlessness. A manic shift from trembling infatuation, nerves a constant pulse of excitability, fast-breaking thoughts, ideas, plans, whole futures, Ophelie, Ophelie – until now, down to this, the penetrating guilt of despicably lusting after my wife's best friend – so great a risk for a non-existent reward. My mind no longer raced hot and sexual, drooling on the female aesthetic, but remained a pounding fullness that distracted me and laboured, my whole life seemingly filled with Ophelie – myself and her – non-existent yet ubiquitous. Now the thoughts that came to me came to punish. My thoughts were no longer just imagination, they were an infidelity; cheating with my devotion to desiring Ophelie, with my leering fascination and desultory masturbation, my sexual side-tracking when I actually made love to Joodie; the punishment, like the obsession, was self-inflicted: no one judged me, no one even knew, not the real depth of the obsession. Joodie, always so self-absorbed, lost in the sound of her own voice, despite her distrustful nature, was likely to be too preoccupied with her own world to notice – even if an affair had become reality. And still I hoped that Ophelie knew – not of my obsession, but I prayed that maybe she had an understanding of my feelings, feelings that I dressed up as a kind of romantic and heroic dedication, an interest flattering and dignified – I flattered myself, I know, it was just a sham to try to protect myself from the sad reality. I hoped that she knew, maybe then she would respond – it was back to high school again, praying that the object of my affection would initiate, too scared to push my own cause.

November began, a Saturday afternoon, the sun a distant memory behind clouds that would never clear. I lay twisted and bent over cushions heaped into the corner of the sofa, propped loosely on one hand, supported by the corner of some soft furnishing. I had decided to begin Ackroyd's book about the River Thames; it was a diversion from the historic lives that normally occupied me, but seemed to fit in ideally with the new interest I was taking in the place I lived. It had been recommended to me as the current reading matter of Acantha; earlier that week I had contrived to join them on the bench, a cool but dry day, I was better dressed for a stay – eventually it would be me who was abandoned, the chill in Paul's bones, unsettling him, his mood turning and Acantha devotedly keen to keep him at ease.

'It doesn't seem as relevant as the Hill or the Park, but it's the river that really makes Richmond...'

'It's Richmond upon Thames, Acantha – how can that not be as relevant?'

'Richmond *Hill*, Richmond *Park* – that they say what they are in the name makes no difference, that doesn't separate them, what I mean is that the park is such a specific landmark and the hill so much more human, with all these grand buildings, it's easier to consider them the reason why Richmond is how it is – so perhaps they are more relevant – regardless, it's the river...without the river we wouldn't even be sitting here today – so, learning about the river is a good place to start.'

Paul dismissed this with a middle-class grunt, shaking his head. 'If you want to know something about Richmond, then study its people: Turner, for example, and, of course, Russell, that's where you should start – you don't need to know about some damned river, that'll teach you nothing – read Bertrand Russell, read about him, and you'll learn something of life too.'

'I always thought he was Welsh, for some reason,' Acantha dreamily considered, then giggling playfully at her own silliness. 'I had no idea he was a local. You could always turn to Dickens, he often referred to this area.'

'I don't really read novels,' I had sheepishly replied, the confusion evident on the old couple's faces reaffirmed my own sense of inadequacy on this point.

So, for the second time I walked away from The Terrace having been made to feel incomplete, lacking in accomplishments essential to the person I had so far believed myself to be.

In my local bookshop (I tended to buy second-hand, as much for the fragrance as for the value or scarcity) I had looked at Russell, but was immediately terrified; indeed, feeling briefly powerless, as Russell's "slow, sure doom", made me fall, pitiless and dark into some chasm of mortality entirely inappropriate for a Tuesday lunchtime. So, I had gone with the Ackroyd book and suddenly felt the calming breath of the English riverside transporting me out of the present and out of the gloomy November.

Washed away in the heavy progression of the Thames, sleep began its overpowering flood of my mind; soon I slept, the book, heavy and ill-supported fell onto the laminate floor with a crack, then a rustle as the pages crushed into line.

I didn't dream to recollection and, waking a half hour or so later, I groaned miserably, wishing that my vacation from reality had been extended. It felt later – the same song seemed to be playing in the kitchen, the same beat and nothing to distinguish it coming through. Days had passed since Joodie and me had made love in the kitchen, my hands gripping her buttocks, pressed flat against the stinging cold glass door of the oven – it had been fine, she had felt good and I had been in love with her – today, there was nothing but resentment. Her presence in the house sternly controlled the atmosphere – she was in decent spirits, as ever swamped in work, yet she seemed perpetually engaged in other matters; I was no longer able to comprehend the true activities of her work, everything seemed to be a long session of coffees and her laptop. And I moped in the bay of the living room window, watching grey figures pass under the lamps in our windblown street.

*

I was starting to like text messages, thinking of them as telegrams for the 21st Century. Today, I was just pleased to have some contact with the world beyond Onslow Road – my phone screen flashed, I figured it might be Burchmann – another Gallery, another gig: something alcoholic and socially interactive – but Burchmann usually called…it was Sonny.

The message used less than half of the available characters, so that, even by text message standards, it was brief – simply: Tate Brit, Tomorrow?

I considered a reply, commenced and then deleted it – not that the reply would be any different later, but some mechanical trip in my head warned me to delay, not to reply so hurriedly. Silly, like a teenager and his crush – but this was Sonny, I liked her, we'd met a few times now, were we not buddies? – apart from the fact that she wasn't interested in men. Why then? What part of me was without control – it wasn't my own natural response; I knew it was preposterous and I knew that my crush (as stupid as that was) lay elsewhere. Why? What function of my brain released such an odd and improbable thought which I, a rational adult human, had then expedited? This was new, I trembled, the thought of what this Ophelie madness was doing to me.

I was bored and isolated; after that period of disinterest, Ophelie had seemed to drift away from me; her clutch, in the brownness of my mood, had relaxed, let slip; a heavy rope slapping with a thump into dark cold waters. But now I was adrift and rudderless. At the same time that the peace was liberating, it was also devastating – with nothing to stumble through, the journey had become turgid.

Getting out of the house was exactly what I needed; to spend time with serious pursuits, blended with laughter, the sardonic humour that Sonny and me shared. The prospect of imminent escape still wasn't enough to take the gloom away from the Sunday morning; Joodie was quiet, lost in her own mechanics of thought, her world whirling as a separate galactic experience. I could not understand her, could not connect; I could see her consumed, and there was no way in, nothing revealed; as it was, then, I left her to it, sipped my coffee watching the day develop outside.

The clouds condensed into a lighter greyness as the day rolled on and my focus, thankfully, shifted to preparation. As with my previous trips into the centre of London, the journey was a factor there to be dealt with – it was never likely to put me off going, there was nothing that I would rather be doing. Such was my way that I sat with my timetables and established a departure time that would give me a fifteen-minute cushion; content with this plan, my time margins and directions, I set off suddenly chirpy and excited five minutes ahead of the allotted time.

So very rarely did it happen that it was almost as frustrating as being late – perhaps the train had hurried, skipped out of the empty local stations with the minimum of pause, perhaps there had been fewer people blocking my route from platform to pavement – it seemed unlikely and certainly I could establish no explanation for the fifteen minutes I had managed to cut from the journey. The idea of standing in the foyer was limited in its appeal, even though we had arranged through a flurry of mid-morning messages exchanged to meet in the great chamber of a staircase, the modern side entrance, I knew that a half hour wait here would be unbearable. It was an ok day outside, even though the sun was dismally absent; the Thames, gunmetal in the meek light, I opted to pass the time in the quiet back streets of Millbank, thickly residential, dotted with Victorian legacied pubs and sterilized modern equivalents, endless delis and food vendors of interminable description. Below leafless trees, the periodic bite of the wind, northerly, cutting down roads and across junctions, animating dogwood bushes, a shock of red and green Ilex grew and wandered across the forecourt of a mansion block, a dozen floors of smooth rolling modernism, boasting its superiority as it approached its centenary, still majestic, still as sleek and cool as the great glass boxes, the cladded dynamic infills aging in infancy. Everything around me was grey and red, the sky and the pavements above and below, the endless brickwork, valley walls either side. It was nice to walk here, aware that no one in the world knew where I was at that moment, no one might guess; then the sadness associated with such realization – no one knew, to infer then that no one cared. I reached the great chess board mansions on Page Street, as I headed towards the river, checked my watch and turned back to the Tate, suddenly late.

She was standing alone, dead centre in the stairwell, like a photograph; the broad flat stairs rising to her right. She wore an A-line coat, buttoned up tight around her small curved silhouette; her hair, blonder now than I remembered. I wasn't in love with her; I knew that straight away. That this was even a conscious thought suggested to me that I always tended to believe that I was in love, emotion built up and an inclination towards the romantic. Sometimes I had thought about Sonny, imagining her to be the *kind of woman who'd make a very sweet wife*, she was attractive, she dressed how I liked to see a woman dress, even Ophelie was not as I would have her in this respect – and so much of my fantasy would see her presented in the way that satisfied my tastes, rather than the casual, non-descript clothes she usually wore. But, no, I looked down at Sonny, she was good-looking but not what I was after, my mind so full of Ophelie, it was that model of woman, that classification of facial, physical type that I demanded: Sonny did not fit it, neither I knew right then, did Joodie.

'I can see why you like this entrance, though it's a bit modern for you, isn't it?'

'You'd think. I guess it's not just about things being old that I like, it's more that they have an effect on me, they transport me to some other place – see, I like the width of the stairs, the height and the light, it makes me feel like I'm someplace else.'

'That's nice.' Sonny wasn't really interested, I could tell, she was gazing around. 'I usually come in the front I guess…' I giggled, smuttily, fortunately she didn't notice; she turned to me. 'Shall we go? I want to show you my favourite.'

We began upstairs and wound our way through the mess of chambers, the static art around us, eye-catchingly bad and subtly brilliant; sculptures, installations, oils – all these treasures, so much inspiration. I looked down at Sonny through the temporary silence, the nervous muteness of a church interior, I looked down at the fluffy mess of her loosely pinned hair, glad to have a friend.

'I've been meaning to ask,' I had been meaning to ask. 'How are you called Sonny, is it short for something?'

'No,' she said without looking up, as we reached a closed door; she swung it open for me, meeting my eyes as if to suggest that was the only answer I was likely to get.

'Do you not like to talk about it?'

'It's my name – I *like* my name, it's just a bit of a cliché to focus on something so obviously inappropriate, like asking me about having sex with women.'

'I've never asked that; it's not my business. I have no relation to that…'

'But you too sleep with women, don't you? So you do have some relation to it?'

'Different. I don't approach it with the same goals or requirements as you.'

'True. Fair enough. My parents were rather hippyish, they loved Sonny and Cher, but they didn't like Cher's name, they thought that "Cher" was too similar to "share" – they felt that was *too* hippy."

'It's a bit male, do you think it...'

'No, I don't. Don't be stupid.'

'It's *really* nice round here,' I digressed, well aware of the fact, yet I shared it with what seemed, oddly, to be surprise; almost, there was a hint of aggression; but it was neither, it was a curious embarrassment that tinted my opinion. 'I wouldn't mind taking an apartment round here...The cricket field – have you seen that? Incredible.'

'Can't say I have. Anyway, you live in bloody Richmond, it's not exactly a slum...not like us poor buggers in Mile End.'

'Mile End's all right...isn't it? I guess it's a bit Whitechapely. Last time I was there, near there, was when Burchmann was crashing at that place, you ever go there, the Swedish guy, a painter, I think...I don't remember, but – no, I mean I'd like to live here after.'

'After what?'

'After...er, nothing...in reality; but, you know, if I left Joodie.'

'Are you going to? Do you plan to?'

'I've no idea, and I don't exactly do planning when it comes down to life decisions – trains and buses, yes – can you believe I was fifteen minutes early?'

'You have mentioned it.'

The painting that she wanted to share with me was Meredith Frampton's portrait of Clive Cooper, an ordinary sort of man, with a juvenile looking collection of bones. I hadn't seen it before, but instantly I was charmed by it. Sonny embarked on the retelling of a great list of the details within the painting that she loved, everything from the way the book rested open, to the queer plan on the wall; there was little left, superficially for me to comment on, I muttered, ineloquently, an opinion on the texture of the palaeontologist's suit. We stood and admired the plastic perfection of the painting for a minute or two, piping from time to time an occurred thought, a sensation derived from the talent displayed before us. At a point we became exhausted and overwhelmed by it and falling, it seemed, from a weak trance, with in-taken breath we turned and attempted to consume the rest of the room.

Futile, though, we soon discovered it to be – so taken by Frampton's art, it was hard to enthuse about anything afterwards; we had already passed through the pre-Raphaelite room, the unreal presence of their prize Waterhouse, nothing else now could inspire us.

'We could try the Turner exhibit?' Sonny idly suggested, as if it were a chore, at best as if it might present a surprise or two.

'Turner?' I enthused out of nowhere.

'Yeah,' she replied, wondering. 'They have, like, a whole wing of his stuff.'

'Really? Oh, then we have to go see that.'

'Jeez, you're a real fan, then.'

'Me? No, he did some blurry seascapes, right? No, not someone that I've paid that much attention to, but apparently he lived in Richmond, or maybe just painted there.'

'Oh, a neighbour, gotcha.'

Increasingly fatigued by the strolling, it didn't take long before the repetitiousness of Turner's masterpieces became unbearable.

'He *really* did paint a lot of blurry seascapes. Fuck, Christopher, you do know your art.'

We sat in a pub, a dingy little hole in a back street, the alcohol sweet after the exertions of observing frame after frame of inert history. 'So,' Sonny, challenged, 'you're leaving your wife?'

'Am I? No, probably not, I don't exactly have the balls for that sort of recklessness.'

'The same kind of recklessness as telling Ophelie, telling her how you feel about her.'

'And how do I feel about her, I'm not even sure anymore.'

'Last time, you were besotted.'

'Besotted, heh, you use some real proper words don't you. Yeah, I guess I was "besotted", huh? No, Sonny, I just don't know any more, she bothers my thoughts. I'm still thinking about her...all the time; it shifts, which is why I'm pretty sure I've not fallen in love with her. Sometimes I don't know what I was thinking...when this started...well, I wasn't, of course...and we've nothing in common.'

'You know, it is possible to be interested in someone just physically – it's just as legitimate an attraction as liking someone's personality. Granted, physical desire is probably not worth fucking up your marriage for.'

'What's to fuck up? She's not that interested in us anymore, she's always been...well, let's just say she's become increasingly self-absorbed.'

'Sex?'

'Pretty mediocre, I'm not bothered if I don't get any and she's never really put much effort into it – it's weird, but she's always been too easy to please, and now she'd rather I satisfy myself because she's always uncomfortable, there's always something; it's hard to touch her body without her flinching.'

'Good God, it wasn't that bad before, was it?'

'Possibly, it's not really the focus of my attention anymore. Maybe it is worse now, now that I've stopped caring, it's allowed her to feel at ease with her own...'

'Frigidity?'

'Not entirely; it's not that we're barren sexually – the last time,' I remembered the kitchen, 'the last time it was fun. It's just that...it's more about indifference. I guess it's the idea of having to sleep with someone that you're just not inspired by sexually. She wears too much make-up.'

'You can never wear too much make-up,' Sonny, with relief, brought lightness back to the depths of our conversation. I laughed, brief and sad.

'Well, if it's done well, sure, but...'

'Kinda ugly, sure. Have you ever thought of talking to her about it?'

'Are you kidding? I know you haven't known me long, but...'

'Oh, I know you well enough for that to seem unlikely; I guess it was more a prompt than a question.'

'No, no, I don't think I could.'

'Because then you'd both realize you were a complete mess and have to split up?'

'Whadda you know! You *can* read me like a book.'

'A comic book,' she teased, and I played along, gasping fake shock.

'So, my marriage is a joke; I'm besotted with a woman I'll never have; what else have you got?'

'It's your round.'

Sitting either side of a pair of half emptied beer glasses, the familiar breath of an old pub, there was something deeply comforting about sharing a table with Sonny. We were laughing, easily finding humour – for me the release was tremendous, the sensation peculiar; my body hadn't at first known how to respond and as Sonny cracked me up about something, an update on Burchmann's calamitous and now abandoned pursuit of Frew Grensen, I had ended up gripping my stomach with a stitch and briefly trapped a nerve in my neck – which resulted in Sonny bursting into uncontrolled laughter of her own.

Talk turned, inevitably, back to my problem with Ophelie and Joodie. My complaints were drawn out and predictably tedious, going over old ground, I concluded with an admission of my disinterest in women in general.

'Maybe it's time for you to be gay,' she joked, half-heartedly, dead pan and with rolling eyes.

'I think it's more relationships in general, rather than gender...though I think I've sufficiently overindulged thinking about Ophelie's body parts that even the vaguest hint of female anatomy is difficult to palette – like too much ice cream...'

'Too much? Too much *ice* cream – how does *that* work?' she feigned shock to lighten the tone.

'You know what I mean, I'm kinda sick of the thought of femininity.'

'So, you're gonna start hanging out with the guys, doing guy stuff, finding your masculine groove?'

'No. Actually, I thought I'd spend more time with my wife.'

'Try to make it work?'

'Not really trying. She seems happy enough, so...I guess I just have to learn to accept the situation and...if not, call it quits.'

'Such a shame.'

'Is it though? Really?'

'Of course. All that time you've been together and built...' She faded, unsure of her line of argument

'Exactly. What have we really built in that time? Sure, most of it *was* good, now it's not. I know I should be more grateful – not everybody gets so many years of what I had. What I *had* – that's the thing – it's not there anymore.'

'I think that's apparent. So, maybe, this Ophelie thing, maybe it's just a way of expressing the larger problem – that you're no longer in love with Joodie? I wouldn't say it's very unusual – I mean how many relationships are screwed when the guy...'

'Or gal.'

'Or gal...cheats, leaves their partner for the new guy-stroke-gal and, what? – within months, no time at all, they've left the new person as well.'

'Quite often, I suspect. But I couldn't be

unfaithful; it's just not in my nature – Christ, even lusting after Ophelie has left me crippled with guilt...'

'Crippled?'

'Ok, well...but I *do* feel bad, I feel unfaithful just thinking about her.'

'But that's so weird – guys spend half their lives lusting after women who aren't their partner.'

'I know; I don't get it – the only thing is, is that...their relationship...like doing your wife's sister, almost.'

'I can't see why it should make the blindest bit of difference – there's no scale – who says?'

'Society?'

'Oh, fuck society – you don't even know the first thing about social displeasure.'

'True. You lot have been...urgh, let's not go down that line – it's just sex – it really shouldn't be that important, but our society has turned sex into the ultimate fascination. But, yeah, I've always thought homosexuals tend to make it worse for themselves by creating this whole "scene"...'

'Scene?'

'You know, this community – just 'cause you have a specific sexual taste, why the necessity of having groups and parades and magazines; why can't you just sit at home and be gay, like I sit at home and be straight?'

'It's called being proud.'

'Fair enough; but it's common-place now, you're not outcasts anymore – people love a gay.'

Sonny laughed. 'I understand what you're saying;

it's just about personality – the reason that I'm not a flamboyant fag is probably completely alien to someone like...Ahri...'

'Who? Oh, the fat Egyptian from the opening...'

'Now fat people – they deserve everything they get!'

Sunday had been a new sensation: safer and with dangerous hints of tranquillity. Obstinately, I still longed for the insane experience of the peak of my desire, the frantic thoughts and the sublime pureness of passion; I missed it but at least today was a better feeling than the oblivion of the indifference, the listlessness that had retarded my life.

A week later, an oddly warm day, I sat in the garden, tucked inside a thick sweater, a baseball cap insulating me against the unfelt chill that crept up on tricky days like these and screening my eyes from the low sun. I sat on the summer furniture, dusty from the inclemency of a long, disappointing summer; leaves, striking and bold, fallen from the trees, occupied the empty seats – there was a peace surrounding, a litter of neighbourhood children played politely behind the Victorian garden wall, two of the cats played in the golden autumnal blanket just behind my bench, the play and rush of the leaves like water sounds, tranquil and hypnotic, and the oldest cat sprawled lazily, heavy, delighted by the unexpected day of sunbathing. I sipped at a cappuccino, cooling as the breeze drummed at the surface tension; I found myself with time and peace enough to pick up my book, back to a biography, Turner; I had bought it last week at the Tate, in spite of the antipathy I felt towards the work – there was beauty in the art, I knew that; the life on the pages passed into me at the pace of the life actually lived, a slow but enjoyable read.

Ophelie was still with me, of course. I imagined her, her face bare – she could easily survive without makeup – her cheeks, flush from the weather, and the warmth of her cautious smile were the only illuminations her face required. I sat her, notionally, beside myself on the leaf strewn furniture; what controlled my vision was indeterminable; she sat there and I felt at ease, as if all were complete, as if Joodie and Craig had never existed; I sat there, known and treasured by a woman to whom I felt absolutely connected: marriageable and splendid. Was this a new understanding, this peaceful, respectful, more tender imagining of her, or was it simply a new manifestation of my obsession? There was a sweetness and a gentle satisfaction that I had not experienced, my heart did not race, my soul was not heavy – it was natural and easy and without pressure. The pressure had been the force that had turned a casual interest into a foreboding chase; without the pressure, I did not feel the same need to possess her, to know her unclothed beauty, there was no feeling of incompleteness, as though without her I was not human, not alive. Today there was a freedom from the pressure, just a vision; a woman seated in the light. For the first time in a long time I remembered the friend – I had known her for years, known her personality, danced with her, laughed with her, got drunk with her – I realised that I liked her. Suddenly it was no longer a competition; the sensation of pursuit was washed away.

Easy and blissful, sun-kissed face; I gazed at her straw-coloured skin, the light freckles unobscured on her clean skin. It was only a daydream, but I had known her like this; many times we had sat within our group of friends – around a country pub picnic table, in the park after an impromptu kick-about, her cheeks red from the effort, her less-than-girly but still slightly random pursuit of the football, and in my current daydream I was able to bring forward this version of her. She sat there in simple clothes, her figure, unimportant, obscured; her face untouched by powder or paint, her hair loose over her shoulders, ears sneaking through strands pinkly, small and sharp. It was a surprise to envision her like this, so free from the clichéd sexual allusions of the last weeks. For all of my desire to see her nude, to caress and hold her (and it had initially been only that visual element, to see her undressed; her coy body despite its length and inevitable sweetness, she would not, I assumed, posture or flaunt; almost, she would be embarrassed by her nudity), but for all of this I was happiest right now thinking of her, quiet and pale and thoughtful in the dappled sunlight beneath the young sycamore tree, a child of nature. She was, anyway, an outdoor spirit, it was one of the things that convinced me, now and again, when I allowed it, that we would make a hopeless couple; but for now, I was happy to marry myself to this autumnal beauty, that was enough – a foot-of-the-mountain daydream. Yet I had damaged it, my musing on her external lifestyle and its conflict with my preference for the internal, just a doubt, a doubt about the validity of something that had always been impossible, that it might prevent an event destined never to happen. It upset me to think of such potential incompatibility and the image of her faded as she bored me. I snapped alive to find the big old cat asleep on my lap.

Suddenly I was just a guy at work again, the normal problems and challenges that defined me returned to prominence; from time to time a thought of Ophelie would pass through my consciousness, usually it was easy and sweet – I could rationalise her: she was just a friend, a pretty girl that I happened to know. Other times, it was at work that this apparent tranquillity of conscience and consciousness was hardest to sustain. Solitary in my underground annex and with insufficient occupation or distraction, with no lingering boss to control me, or subordinates to manage, I was left to my own company and so, in the windowless chamber, my mind would, if left unchecked, run and run – a sexual steeplechase, an ideological pursuit – each thought shifting my unstable psychic apparatus first one way and then, sharply, the other.

In general, the calm dominated, but each day was littered with random attacks of insecurity and confusion, my mind vaulting in unsteady rapid shifts of borderless and confusing micro moods, indistinct obsession segueing into a necessary and wilting guilt. The shifts in my moods were no longer over days or weekends as had been the case in the past, they came instantly, during the daylit coffee breaks or enthroned in the lavatory.

One moment I might find sufficient fault with her looks to abandon my interests; the next, I cherished the imperfections, charmed, accepting them as intriguing facets of her attractiveness, a step developed in my interest and connection to her, no longer looking for a route out, but overlooking; smoothing and overlooking.

The degree of the fluctuations caused me consternation; during these brief confusing explosions of thought I feared an approach to loving her, and my heart skipped as I pursued an angle to take the possibility away, focussing for a while on Craig, on her stubborn commitment to him. I had never been a huge fan of the guy, but, generally, with a manly, offhand disinterested lack of interaction, I had always ended up quite liking him; increasingly now, I felt that Craig was an arsehole. And where I had focussed on Ophelie's flaws, that analytical part of my brain now looked for them in this poor dumb innocent fellow – why? I panicked, was this yet another sign of impending love. I tried to control my thoughts, but this will and paranoia were too competitive. And so, at times like this I hurried to the CD player, greyed with dust, sitting on the filing cabinets, and put on a calming ballad: *cures for measles and cures for colds and cures*, I appreciated, *for my soul.*

Deep, subterranean at work, I was thinking about Richmond Park. My experimental tours had proven a rather unexpected success – I was actually enjoying the walks, the liberty of space, the discipline of the increasingly poor weather – true, I was not so involved that I would risk rainstorm and gale, but there was something undeniably healthy and cathartic about a brisk breeze. With the cold in my bones under bleak grey clouds, naturally, I shamelessly cast myself into some noble and heroic portrait – an Earl or a Squire – periodically wishing for, even considering the purchase of a dog.

All of this exploration, such an unpredicted shift in my lifestyle, had returned to me for the first time in months a sense of myself as an individual. For too long I had not been able to see past the idea of myself as part of something – myself and Joodie, myself and Ophelie – finally, I was able to consider myself just as I was – Christopher Hoyer – a man: that was what I was, just a man.

And, deep in the confines of my office, surrounded by files and files of problems, situations that I had investigated and resolved, this was my world. I didn't love it, didn't reasonably care for it, but it satisfied me – it was my role in life, one that I had accepted; one that, in spite of my indifference to the reality of actually doing it, I found satisfying to complete, to see results.

Pages of documents blanketed my desk, a crude system of order; the ignored monitor flicked onto the system default screen saver and I teased an obscure patch of stubble at the corner of my mouth, inadvertently missed whilst shaving.

'Coffee,' called out Bilal, entering the room, two mismatched corporate mugs held aloft.

'Excellent.'

I was pleased to accept a break from my work. 'Sit down. I need to stop; I can't get any of this to work out.' I exhaled noisily as Bilal placed the coffee mugs on the desk, on the paperwork, creating as yet unknown beige rings.

'Still brooding over your woman troubles?'

'Christ, you make it sound like I'm having a hysterectomy – no, actually not...for a change.'

'No? So, you've filed for divorce and ran off with your mistress.'

'Careful! That's a dangerous word to use in this place – they have antenna upstairs – not my...you know what, and no, I'm still with Joodie.'

'But you are still thinking about it all, yeah?'

'A bit, but not *brooding*; there's still some issues.'

'But you've quit with the obsession? We can get back, sort of, to normal again?'

'Yeah, schoolboy crushes *seem* to be a thing of the past.'

'Moved on to someone else? Gone gay?'

'What *is* it with everybody thinking I'm suddenly gay – no – no I've not "gone gay".'

'Me thinks you protest too much, mate. So, what detail is screwing with your work, now?'

'None of the above – I still think about her, about Ophelie, not Joodie, all the time. Horrific, I know – but I can't help it...but just not letting it overwhelm me – not even that, actually, I don't need to control it, I sort of just...under*stand* it.'

'You understand it? You must be the only one who

does...'

'The *only* one? The only one out of me and you? Right?'

'Er, yeah...totally what I was getting at. Carry on, anyway – you understand it...'

'What I mean is that I feel the way I feel, and I understand that that is how I feel, and to feel that way is not right or wrong...it just *is*.'

'Is what? – never a day to miss 'cause Saturday is Tiswas day...?'

'Huh?'

'Nothing, I just got carried away – I loved that show.'

'Right.'

'But at least you've made everything much clearer!'

'Good.'

'No, I'm still bullshitting you, I ain't got a clue – something about it not being right or wrong, it's just...?'

'Just is.'

'Justice? It's justice? I don't...'

'No, it *just...is...*'

'Just is what?' Bilal smiled, I growled and Bilal backed down. 'Ok, no more piss-taking. But I still don't get what you understand about this whole mess...'

'Mess?'

'Yes. Mess. Very much mess. So, you fancy her and you're too big a pussy to do anything?'

'I *can't* do anything, that's the point, that's part of the point; besides, I don't think I ever *wanted* to do anything about it.'

'You don't think? I thought it was all settled, understood?'

'I guess. No, I'd love to...you know – she's so sexy – but I'm sure there're a million women *you'd* love to be with but never will – you know, actresses, singers...'

'Porn women – mainly porn women; but ok, yeah I get that.'

'So, you see, I "understand". I can't fight the, ahem, feeling – but at the same time I know it's not going away and can never be satisfied.'

'So, you're stuck with it.'

'Exactly – and the obsession, originally, grew from wanting to *do* something about it and the frustration of failing to do so.'

'You really are a screwed-up man.'

Bilal adjusted his big hips in the barely adequate confines of the office furniture, holding his mug between his fingertips, sacred, as if it were the source of all knowledge. 'So, where does that leave Joodie – now that you've sorted out the Ophelie element, where does that leave you as regards to Joodie?'

'With regards to Joodie?' I confirmed the question, altering the ugly disliked phrase selected by Bilal. 'I really don't know – if I felt that there was something legitimately saveable, things would be a whole lot easier – knowing that she still wanted to be married to me might...'

'But, come on, do you actually know – for a fact, like – that she doesn't want to be......I mean, indifference to you and a mediocre sex life, the fact that she has priorities in her life that are before you – after being married for x-amount of years – it's not exactly grounds for divorce. I'd say, worse case, she doesn't love you anymore – worse case – even then that doesn't mean she doesn't want to be with you. I'm pretty sure most marriages, after a certain time, really are nothing more than very good friendships – sex is a bonus; but a lot of people wouldn't expect it, if they actually even still want it. At best, it's probably just a patch, a bit of a bad patch.'

'Bad patch. I don't want to be in a marriage with bad patches.'

'You want to be in a marriage that doesn't exist then – everyone has bad patches. You telling me that this is the first time either of you have been unhappy?'

'For this long? Yes. There have been times, odd weeks, the collateral from depressing winters...fights, of course – but nothing like this. Anything before was at least a passion-fuelled fall out, a conflict, temper at frustration, whatever, but this is just cold stark indifference, no hate, no guilt, nothing...unless you count irritation as a dynamic, which I don't.'

'But, still, that doesn't mean it's the end of everything – there must still be *some* love – you must feel something.'

'Yeah, but it's very domestic.'

'You mean like a pet?'

'In a way, yes – not in a masterly sense, just in that way of comfort and familiarity – she makes me feel reassured. When we're close it's still very special – I know her, she knows me. God, it's almost the worst thing about it – the bleeding familiarity.'

'Which ties in with what you said about this concept, you know, that Ophelie was a distraction and that she was just a way of showing you you need a change.'

'Exactly; and that's where I get stuck trying to convince myself that I want to continue with Ophelie...Joodie, I mean. I need to know that it is worth it.'

'To stay?'

'To stay or to leave – both of them are stupendously big commitments, right now. I used to think that staying was the easy option, and it is, I suppose – go with what you know – and change is always the biggest upheaval, the biggest chore – yet staying, urgh, I actually can't even bear the thought of it at the moment.'

'No decision it is, then.'

'I just don't know. Ultimately, no decision, by default, means I'm staying with Joodie. And it's not like I'd be leaving her – if I did – for Ophelie, or anyone for that matter.'

'So, go then. You'd probably get someone before long.'

'Would I? That's the other thing – firstly, would I be able to find someone and, even if I did, would they necessarily be any less annoying than Joodie? – well, it's possible.' I defended my cynicism against Bilal's challenging expression. 'I'm talking worst case scenarios here. Anyway... And secondly, the real unknown, what about the things I'll lose – how much of what I take for granted now would I sacrifice if I left her?'

'You'll never know, until you blow…Um, but, yeah, gain or lose, you want to be happy and you're not right now. Chris, this *isn't* about logistics, for once in your life…this is about gambling – whether you are more likely to rediscover something or find something new with Joodie or whether there's a greater chance of trying your luck elsewhere. Maybe you won't find what you're hoping for; to be honest, either way you'll be lucky if you do, but maybe if you take a risk you might find something good, even if it's just something different.'

'Maybe. Maybe I'll just carry on procrastinating and acting like a child until something comes along and forces my decision?'

'Probably.'

'Heh, yeah – but right now things are at least calm…*ish*…for a while – my head is steady enough to spend more time with Joodie – I'm not completely sidetracked with the Ophelie thing, I'll spend some time and effort; then, one way or another, I should understand how that *really* is.'

Victoria Embankment

When Joodie picked me up from work in the car, climbing into her coupé's low bucketed seat, I instinctively did a double take. She wore too much make-up for my taste – with her barcode colouring her skin shone white against the darkness of her hair and to compensate for this she created an artificial doll of herself with a creaking layer of expensive make-up. Today was no different and there had been no specific reason for my attention to be drawn other than my head still being full of Ophelie.

These thoughts that lingered were of the tranquil, garden variety, tinged with a corruption of the sunset dream I had enjoyed. At leisure, with the weekend arrived, I felt sufficiently content to conduct the movements of a fantasy vacation with Ophelie; I had her, inevitably, in a bikini – nothing slutty, her skin tinged with a little burning across the shoulders. Momentarily, I questioned why I had conjured up such a condition, a blemish in my faultless created world: a kink in my tastes or a flaw to punish her, perhaps just verisimilitude? There she had sat, tarnished only with ultra-violet, her hair tied messily back from her face, littered with freckles but, crucially, untouched by brush or pen.

Seeing Joodie so waxily presented in the driver's seat, I sank at the heaviness of the way she presented herself. As we drove away, Joodie talking, my eyes set on her as if following the inaccessible turgidity of her gossip, I couldn't keep my eyes off the overkill of crumbling foundation. Hours old, it lay corrupt in the warm cavities of her pores, breaking the loose ground at the wrinkles in the corners of her eyes, almost worn away completely by the constant expansion and contraction of the giving flesh at the points of her mouth. I looked away, ahead, the road in the rain rushing towards me, her voice endless, repetitive like the windscreen wipers; at peace, I allowed myself to drift into bikini oblivion.

Unlike the idyll of the previous weekend, there was no surprising sunshine to illuminate the autumnal pleasantness of our garden – it had soaked through in seconds, the bleak charcoal sky sending down platoons of icy winter shower, a harsh east wind sweeping the infantry of raindrops across the window. And yet it was ideal, it suited my mood perfectly – I was tired, disillusioned: the past weeks of furious internal debate, the variability of my psyche – manic shifts from base to bliss – suddenly it had all gotten too much. Frustrated and angry, understanding that I was never going to get what I wanted, I couldn't care about Ophelie anymore, her limbs bored me, her softness was just more dumb cloud. And Joodie was no more than a living headache, I couldn't even stand to be around her; she was sweet and peaceful, but I could not see this, I couldn't see beyond her presence and, unwanted, it ground down my patience. Women. No, I could live without any of them right now – split between constant imaginings of Ophelie and disinterest in Joodie, sex no longer seemed real to me, just a blurry pornographic daydream. Nothing was real, women were simply shadows that I fought, swirling hopelessly, chasing and chasing as they faded and reappeared elsewhere, my feelings shifting the light as strobes at a disco. My libido was doused and castrated, beauty no longer existed in the combinations of skin and bones, Ophelie was no more beautiful than she was plain, she was neither: less than a statue. No woman seemed to project towards me, movies and magazines, nothing stirred me, just one blank face after another, bodies that would have bewitched me were now no more than formless clay.

Suddenly finding myself temporarily (I assumed) disinterested in women and all things feminine was something of a mixed emotional state. As much as it freed me from the perpetual nag of my crotch, a looseness now experienced across my abdomen, dizziness gone from my heavy swooning skull, at the same time I missed the sexiness of Ophelie. I missed the way that I would get excited thinking about her buttocks and her navel; I missed the schoolboy abstraction, dressing her up, stripping her down, redressing, manipulating her elegance into all manner of delicate enchanting situations. It was a game, or at least it had been and, like a child whose toy has broken, I looked down sadly at the split pieces, the remains of the once unstoppable fun, holding back the tears. I wasn't about to cry, but I missed the feelings and found myself trying to conjure up intoxication, the highlight reel of her best moments, dredging the treasures reserved for solitary intimacy. The reel ran in my mind, a cavalcade of limbs and swishing flesh, of ponytails and eyelashes, flashes of forearm, flexing feet and parting teeth – without response. And so I threw in the reserves of my imagination, fantasy blended with empiric knowledge, scenes and situations new to me, dirtier and more explicit than I had dared or desired to consider before. Still, there it was, my body had blocked such processes, shut down my libido; my need for her sexuality, her sensuality, was purely cerebral and I was left with the mood of the upset child, empty, without occupation, wandering from room to room, the toy abandoned to history, lying discarded. I was bored, and with nothing to stimulate me, no sexual exhaust, I found myself alone and having to deal with my thoughts, I would have to live again: some distraction was needed; I had no option but to be a man, to be Christopher Hoyer again.

Twilight had passed prematurely, submerged under the dirty rain. Onslow Road was a trail of scattered illumination; light from windows breaking into the dark, picking patches across gardens into the trickling tides running downhill. Rain still spattered apathetic, streaking the windows of our flat, the cats idled around the neglected food bowls, expectant of service, moodily balled into lumps stubbornly protesting with stillness, a sleeping presence. The expensive kitchen threw down a clean glow from under its overhanging upper storage and the screen of Joodie's Mac cast its own shadows, weakly and at contradictory angles.

Immediately, entering the room, my teeth set hard and ground down, unconsciously. Was there ever a time when she was not on the computer?

'Working hard?' I grumbled.

Joodie left a group of happy women on her screen, they laughed at nothing; glowing, tanned. She swivelled to me, 'Not right now, just browsing the stores. Probably have to get back to it later though.'

'Do you not want to come to the pub?'

'That ghastly Buck's Head? No thanks.'

'It's all right.'

'Not to me.'

'No, I suppose it's not very Soho.'

'Hardly.'

'No. Anyway, I meant in town, down by the river, or on The Green...if you preferred.'

'It's still raining,' she objected, making an over-conscious effort to stare out the dark window. 'And I'm working. I'll have to pass, babe.'

'You're not working now; c'mon, just an hour or two...'

She looked at her watch, it provided no assistance, she couldn't really argue timing; she looked, frowning, at the hopeless traitorous screen – no help there.

'I'm not really in a pub mood; we could watch a movie?'

'At the pictures?'

'No, Chris – it's *raining*; I *don't* want to go out – that's the point.'

'You never said that, you just said you didn't fancy the pub – you weren't in the mood for the pub.'

'Well, that's obviously what I meant, part of it at least.'

'So not just the rain? But, helpfully, the rain eliminates any other activities away from the house.'

'Helpfully? What's that supposed to mean? No, I'd have liked to have gone out and, yes, the pub doesn't appeal, but equally I don't want to have to sit around soaked through. It's not because I don't want to...'

'But you're hardly keen.'

'No, not on getting drenched and catching cold in a germy old cinema.'

'So, it is because it's raining?'

'Yes,' she confirmed, bewildered and annoyed.

'Which is very convenient,' I countered, sulky.

'It's got nothing to do with it being convenient; it's about...Jesus, what's your problem? I don't want to go out...'

'See, that's what this is all about?'

'*What*?'

'Why don't you want to go out – what's wrong with going out together?'

'I was about to say...for the millionth time...go out in *the rain*; how many times! But, right now? – no I couldn't deal with having to go out with you – you're acting *very* weird and you're being a right old grump.

'Is it any wonder – so much negativity.'

She had half-turned towards her Mac, but my words had caught, she sighed, turning back.

'*I'm* being negative? Are you kidding? Jesus, I'm

doing this, I don't want to catch cold or get soaked, so I simply said I didn't want to go out and you've...you've turned it into some...ugh, I can't even be bothered...I just don't want to go out.'

'With me. Thanks. You specifically said you didn't want to go out with me.'

'*Now!* Yes, 'cause you're being a prick, you're being a complete fucking nightmare.'

The cats, in unison, turned up their confused sleepy little faces – the peak of the exchange reached and the ensuing creepy suspension, like the eye of a hurricane – they sensed the tension and, reluctant to abandon their vigil at the food bowls, decided to take their leave and shuffled off to the living room.

'So, you won't come to the pub?'

'What? No, absolutely not; are you even...'

'Then I'm going...to the fucking Buck's Head!'

But the pub wasn't all that much help, other than that it took me away from the dysfunction of my marriage and the obnoxiousness of Joodie – such was my perception of her behaviour.

What if it was for real, for good; that I hadn't just ducked out, hiding away in the pub, what if I had actually gone, left her, broke from my marriage and, with no return possible, taken a step into the new uncharted world I had feared so much in my thoughts of late? The idea seemed wonderful: the notion that I would never have to go back to those dismal tribulations lifted me, paradisiacal ease, taking leave of all obligation, commitment and challenge – what could possibly be better? Prematurely concluded, it turned out, as my thoughts meandered onwards and dystopia grew around me – silly things, practical matters, logistics: the extra costs, the tiresome dissection of possession and, naturally, the solitude – but wasn't all that just laziness? The overwhelming threat of effort, even the effort of accepting and reacting to change exhausted me; but really, none of these objections were anything worthy of stopping me – I could afford to live independently; although I would regret leaving Richmond Hill. Onslow Road was as much a bitter complaint now, a virus lingering and causing discomfort; and, thinking about it, what possessions we had were almost exclusively split already, the result of our increasingly disparate tastes, anything that remained debatable I could abandon with only the mildest regret – what was the point in moving on and not discarding the baggage so currently resented. As for the solitude, I tried to give myself credit for believing in my social capacities and my eligibility as a newly created thirty-something bachelor – I could tell myself this but, barely below the surface, I was less than convinced.

The dull beer suddenly appealed as the realisation struck me – perhaps Joodie was my reward, the fine gift to compensate for the instability and treachery of my thoughts – perhaps I was lucky, perhaps I should be grateful even to have her.

Such was the cyclical nature of my emotions that before long my disinterest in women had bottomed out.

A general indifference to most things took over; I ghosted through the days, unable to find the right thing to put my heart and soul into. Desperation marked my pursuit for distraction – I did not want to allow space for my feelings towards Ophelie to swell once again, to swell to the obsessive scale I had experienced, knowing that it would consume me. Just thinking about how badly it had possessed me, how it had retarded me, and how irresponsible it had made me, a feeling of discomfort hung around me, so I pursued distraction to occupy my limits of careless thinking.

Meanwhile, at the other end of the scale of undesirable trains of thought was Joodie, who, at times, was becoming even more unlovable. I played her off against Ophelie – even though Ophelie was not currently my paradigm of womanhood, she remained a gauge of what satisfied my taste. Anything that remained of my desire for Ophelie was the pure still pool of autumnal clarity that had intoxicated me – this picture of her free from the need to be made up, simple and light in her movements – contrasting so severely with Joodie – some immovable power, constant and drilling and present. This falsely overdressed, over-lacquered woman; she was like furniture, like some vast couch – despite being an average sized woman, she had a certain mass about her, the steely movements and the inertness of her repose; and if she were a couch in my world, then Ophelie was an angle-poise lamp, hardly there, flexible and illuminating, whilst Joodie cast deep shadows. And me, I was a rug, the rug beneath them both and, like a rug, right now I could only think with a flatness, everything was so very flat. From the centre, at the level of the rug, I could not see the edges, the boundaries, only ceaseless flatness, with a couch towering above and a lamp casting light that shone around me but never touched me, obscured of its pureness by the shadow.

Time had passed, the dinner party, the last time I had enjoyed any prolonged interaction with Ophelie, was forgotten, consigned now to the heap of other occasions where me and Ophelie had shared company; it no longer offered familiarity. On my mobile phone the photo survived, a relic, a museum piece like the phone itself and, whilst it had lost its impact, no longer a treasure, no longer a device for transportation, merely a jumble of pixels two inches high, her face still sat in blurry high contrast, motionless and silent and looking back at me. So long had it been since I had seen the zoetic form of her, that I still wistfully studied the image. It was a periodic indulgence, my thoughts of Ophelie came and went, cruel and tortuous – and when they came, they brought with them a heavy longing to be with her. No longer was my desire sexual, I thought only of her character, as it had been at the beginning – pining for her particular blend of the serious and the playful. Her physical bearing still remained with me, yet no longer the focus upon breasts and limbs, but of her vitality; a blend of memories of standing close to her, just talking, or sat on an adjacent chair to her, perhaps in conversation, maybe just that she was there. Verging on maternal, something about her seemed to surround and comfort me. And I needed soothing, my mood was bleak and heavy, like a man in need of food or water – I needed some affection or intimacy.

Joodie seemed almost hopelessly absent now, impossible to access. Perhaps it was my infatuation that had split us, divided the fragile connections that held us together – the apparent superiority of Ophelie combined with the ever-increasing disenchantment with Joodie. It was difficult, and I found myself always returning to Ophelie to compensate for the void in my marriage. The gloss of my fantasy life with Ophelie was a bare and acidic comfort, compensation for the milky nothingness of reality. And Ophelie, she could provide in my imagination exactly the sensation of emotion that I felt to be necessary. Gloomy and disenchanted and without hope, I had no need for the sexual physical manifestation of Ophelie, nor the intellectual version – I sat alone wistfully staring at the blanked screen of my phone.

'So, updates, updates. Where are we with Ophelie?'

By now, Sonny was intrigued by the saga, I suspect it was a great living soap opera for her, but I was happy to indulge this, sharing gave me some relief; the problems no easier to solve, but easier to understand, spoken out loud. And I liked her, she brought me down to earth, and took me away from the fantasy worlds I lived in.

'She's sort of settled in my mind now,' I began. We walked along the embankment, another visit to the art in Pimlico, another lost afternoon staring at Clive

Forster-Cooper. 'She's settled there, like a...'

'Like a bug?'

'Yes. That's exactly it. Like a harmless bug in my mind. It's like the narcotic has passed through my system – I had the high and the comedown and now the damage, the haunting physical knowledge of the intoxicant lingering.'

'Well, it's not exactly closure, but it seems healthier to be in rehab, than...'

I laughed, 'My God, that's it, I can't believe she can be summed up that way, but it's true. I even, from time to time, suffer flashbacks...of a kind...to the peak of my obsession, days or even just moments when she returns forcefully into my ideas, when the notion of her body...um, that unfathomable desire takes over and again those limbs, those fingers, those lips, revealed and recalled, they spin me around, a trip. And I'm cracked, lost in her, the idea of her.'

'I'm not sure if that's technically a flashback, it sounds like you're indulging yourself again.'

'Well, no, kind of, but...no, I said days but more often it's just short bursts, out of nowhere, before it was...'

'Embarrassing?'

'Looking back, yes. But that's the point, that's the difference. I was out of control back then, and it was my normal state of mind, now it's more flashes of...'

'Insanity? Self-indulgent bullshit? Juvenile wank material?'

'You know me so well! There is all that, yes, but other times I might return to the lows of antipathy, just to think of her at these times fills me with gloom. There's like this state of disenchantment that prevails, I can even despise the thought of her, her image becomes an unscrubbable stain.'

'And right now? Up or down?'

'As I said, it comes in flashes. Right now? I'm much more positive, I think I'm over the worst of it. Chiefly, my life passes with mundanity, with Ophelie completely...*mostly* absent from it.'

'And Joodie?'

'Joodie I avoid wherever possible. That is not getting any better...'

'So maybe, after all, that's all this Ophelie thing was, that the real issue was your crappy marriage.'

'Maybe. I mean, I do find sporadic moments, moments of rekindled affection when I remember that I loved her. And that's good, that's positive; it's really special, I can understand – she is mine and I don't think of Ophelie at all, I don't allow those comparisons.'

'Which she always loses out on, because what we don't have always seems more appealing than what is deadly familiar. Wow, I'm proud of you, Christopher Hoyer. You've made some real progress. One day soon, you'll be able to consider yourself an adult again. Bravo.'

'But I'm still not happy, not like I wish to be, at least not how I imagined it was possible to be. Some part of me accepts this, it's not so bad, and this alternative happiness is only a suggested state, there's no proof – it could just as easily be that my life with Joodie was the pinnacle of my happiness.'

'You mean that what you see as greater happiness in others is unattainable, that each individual has a certain limit of fulfilment...'

'Specific levels of joy...based on who you are...yes.'

'And that maybe you have reached your allotted potential...'

'Sad but true. And maybe then, that the inequalities between people results in their relational disharmony – is that it, could it be?' The thought that I was at my most happy crushed me, I was so terribly unhappy.

'It's strange, the path that this...adventure is taking. Now, there's none of the fire and none of the relentless confusion, the misdirection, that had threatened to swamp me. I don't feel any more that I am obsessed with her, the pace has changed; there's still regularity but the intensity is gone, it's a degree down from obsession.'

'I have to say, I'm a little sceptical. You're here talking about her...'

'You asked. You started me off.'

'This is true. Continue. Sub-obsessive...'

'Ok, so there are flashbacks to the more intense times, but generally I tend to just think of her in this one specific way. I've developed a sort of light calmness which focusses my thoughts so that when she comes to me, I imagine a long future, a marriage – if not on paper, then in some way spiritual or symbolic.'

'Ok. This is new. You're not obsessed with her, but you imagine yourselves married. I can't see how you're going to explain this one...'

'But,' I winked, 'you know I'm going to try. So, these thoughts, they tend to be filled with a sense that we are ideal for each other, despite, of course, the unchangeable fact that we should never be together and that, were we to somehow realise a liaison, it would be truly hopeless.'

'So, you know it's rubbish, but you can't help thinking it?'

'Yes. Rubbish is a tad harsh, but, yeah, it's really difficult to rationalise how easily I understand this – I know our communication is pretty ineffectual as friends...'

'Would it be any better as husband and wife, as a couple, even just as lovers?'

'No. I'm pretty certain it would not be, still I persist with fantasies of this very outcome – and not just fantasies, like lonely late-night imaginings...'

'A crafty hand-shandy whilst she's removing her make up...'

'Um, no, yes, not *that* kind of fantasy, but actual belief that such possibilities exist.'

'It is kinda ridiculous.'

'I know. At a stretch, maybe as lovers – if anything could ever occur between us, it would probably be as lovers.'

'If either of you had the spark or nerve or creativity required to bring such an outcome to fruition.'

'Exactly. With each other we're oddly alien, whatever exists as an attraction is almost entirely unsaid...'

'Or in the case of Ophelie, entirely non-existent.'

'Maybe.'

Sonny laughed.

'You can laugh, but it's not going to explain why I pursue this relationship of wifeliness, this queer matrimonial closeness. My fixation has drifted such a distance – we're talking continental here – that from my initial frantic incapacity to imagine us together, physically, I've now come full circle, to where I find myself in a constant walk up the aisle. I picture us on park benches, casually around the house, a house, neither of our existing homes – all startlingly domestic, almost mundane, but always close. And the irony is bewildering – this simple, near sexless sweetness is merely a more satisfying, if wholly undesired version of what I actually have.'

'Maybe it's got nothing to do with wanting to be married to Ophelie, maybe it's simply the outcome of a metaphoric mind game – just a train of thought to press Joodie from your mind – to be rid of Joodie, her inadequacy as a partner?'

I had heard this before. The idea had been pushed so strongly at me earlier in our talks, as the reality of my situation that, stubbornly, I had forced it away, dismissed it as interference. But it did make sense, could I have saved all this stress if I'd just accepted this from the start.

'Probably. Maybe you've been right with this idea all along.' Sonny smiled as I admitted this. 'I am unhappy with aspects of her character, as much as I had loved her and loved so much about her; as a wife she is deficient. In so many areas she fails to satisfy; and her attention towards me is arbitrary, at best. Equally, it fits at the other end – Ophelie only pleases me with her beauty intermittently and her personality doesn't seem to fit so well as even Joodie's did...does. Perhaps it is just a representation of something longed for? Ophelie representing not my dream woman but merely acting as an indicator that an alternative is required to fulfil my need for happiness.'

'There you go, so maybe you haven't quite reached your peak happiness.'

'God, I really hope I haven't.'

'I'm sure I'm right. I mean, think about it: Ophelie is a convenient symbol for what you need to make you happy – certain qualities she possesses that are wholly absent in Joodie. Like Craig...'

'Craig? That guy doesn't make me happy...'

'Christopher! Don't be an idiot. Listen to me, it'll do you good. Although she is not especially attentive towards you, she has demonstrated a fierce loyalty to the seemingly unworthy Craig – her qualities as a wife, viewed from the outside, easily surpass those of Joodie. As an example of matrimonial desirability, she ranks high on your scale. In the blindness of your infatuation – infatuation simplifies everything, reduces it to the things you *want* to comprehend – you've become unaware of the potential difference between the ideal and the reality. Perhaps Ophelie might live up to your prejudice, but not knowing any better you wallowed in your speculation. Add to this...this connubial utopia, the superior physical attributes that she possesses, conveniently forgetting those she is deficient in, it is irresistible not to raise her on a pedestal as an ideal, as a longed-for alternative.'

'Wow, where did that come from?'

'I'm a smart fucking woman, Christopher – if you'd ever give me the chance to show it.'

'But why her,' I pursued, happy to shift the subject back to myself, hoping also for more of these insights. 'Why not any one of the beautiful women in the marketing department?'

'Why are marketing departments always full of hotties? It's uncanny – the position seems almost magnetic…'

'Ok, focus…Why must it be my wife's closest friend?'

'Well that's obvious, in a kind of…um…oh, a kind of *amicable transference*….'

'Seriously?'

'Oh, I'm serious. What I just said…blah blah transference…you've attached yourself to the most known, most trusted associate available to you; it was simply the most convenient solution. If you'd met me first, it would have most likely been me that you attached to. It explains why, at no stage, have you ever felt in love with her.'

Richmond Park

Clarity had not exactly been my best friend. Throughout this phase of my life I had tried to keep some degree of perspective but always the emotional extremes and plateaux made it near impossible to remain rational. If I were at a peak, libido dominated and, as a man, any kind of considered functioning was out of the question, only chemical reactions and electrical pulse: I had made decisions based on the needs of my body and my needs were dictated by the thunderous angst in my crotch. Conversely, when I was at a low, the negative aspect destroyed my perspective – the vast distances perceived between what I had, where I was at and where I wanted to be. The turmoil of this disenchantment was multiplied by the sense either that I didn't know what I wanted, or needed, or that I wanted and needed nothing. Even in that strange twilight of indifference, sometimes that was the most painful and the most difficult place to find perspective, simply because, in that place, I had no interest in obtaining clarity – I had no interest in the human world, human interactions: essentially I became a shell, a fragmented extant object that neither loved nor hated nor cared; misanthropic but without the detestation – I was without feeling for people. So I played music, read lightly – a glimmer of a connection with mankind; I would plod through a history or a biography – formless, bodyless lives described and logged: mechanical, practical, clerical. And I would tease the pets and walk through Richmond Park in the open air.

Drilled by a fluctuating desire to attach to Ophelie by developing another shared interest, I found that, taken alone, the outdoors were not so bad – at least for now. Yet I found no real clarity there, no solution to my problem, as if a key to liberation from Ophelie would just appear in my life. Still, I found a degree of peace, free from Joodie, distracted from thoughts of reality by the fresh winds, the swooning trees, green, black and brown, inhuman.

Bewitched and heated, Ophelie remained deeply significant within my conscious routine. Bewitched – it seemed the right word to describe the emotional, now rather affectionate fix she maintained upon me, the undercurrent of sexual attraction accounting for the pulse of temperature that, from time to time, drove me insane, wild with unsatisfied demand. Her spell, then, was twofold: the charm and wonder of her limbs, form, the manner of her construction, combined with some near enigmatic ideal, a concept of male/female interaction that seemed to satisfy my ideals of completion and efficiency, a logistical solution for a domestic problem. So there she remained.

I turned the situation over in my mind much the same as I would a problem at work – but it was a false deliberation. I might imagine a situation that pleased me and an outcome where me and Ophelie would be together, overcoming the conflicts of character, the passivity and milkiness of our friendship – or a solution in which I would sleep with her, satisfy the visual presence of her, her potential nudity. That experience alone would relieve an ocean of frustration and intrigue. Neither outcome had any chance and so remained pointless and defunct. Stubbornly, or incapable of desisting, I continued to while away the turgid hours at my desk proposing increasingly romantic, daring, more ludicrous paths whereby every paradox and perplexity regarding Ophelie would be solved. I contrived a whole catalogue of manageable programs to ease my troubles and satisfy my desires. And at night I might lie awake sore and swollen, disregarded by my deep sleeping wife, longing to possess Ophelie, longing to know if we would be happy and each morning I would set out my newspaper, sip my greying coffee and begin again – indexing and refining models and solutions for happiness.

Now I had this escape route, to appraise things coldly, as though they were no more than a logistical conundrum, then, surely, as I had boasted to Sonny, the worst of my fixation was done? But I knew that was not the case – it was no more than under control. Her presence was a vibration through my life, sinusoidal, rising and falling, it was pure energy and energy indestructible. So I lived with the presence when she rose in my conscience, made the best of it – whether it was the tranquil pastoral matrimony or the sensual visual mobility of her form; even if it was the more turbulent frustration of desire, never so intense now but still persuasive and nagging, I dealt with it and whilst I did so I grew ever more disenchanted with Joodie.

Walks in Richmond Park had grown regular, now; as much as anything else I desired to escape. At the height of the crushing obsession, the roll of the land, the call of the serene blowing of the air through the trees, the perfect lolling white noise of the shivering leaves, all of this soothed and liberated me. My mind settled on normal issues – work, music, food, nature – and I began to imagine living away from Joodie, without Ophelie, just to return to being a man again. I imagined taking a place of my own and living, not a bachelor life, but the life of a divorcee; it was a clear series of thoughts, greater clarity than I had employed on any matter in recent weeks and it was an idea that grew. In the same way that imagining a life with Ophelie had helped me to understand my feelings towards her and towards Joodie, imagining a life without either of them gave me the beginnings of understanding myself. I wanted to go now – life was unbearable knowing that as much as I loved Joodie, I would never be happy; I would always be conceding to a compromise. The only thing that remained was whether to sacrifice the surviving goodness of my marriage to pursue a potential improvement that might never be found.

Wilderness, then – this was what I had inherited. My view back to normality had become obscured to the point where it was difficult even to consider normal to be a reality, that normal even existed. Even in the midst of one of my periods of indifference, she occupied my mind; sitting the way she did on my couch: refined, yet a suggestion of immaturity, with her besocked feet tucked up, her head tipped down in a mixture of shyness and introspection. I could never guess what it might be that occupied her; I found that I adored the fact that she often seemed lost within her thoughts. Joodie was bright and a good thinker but never seemed to lose herself in consideration, instinctively I knew that Ophelie's thoughts were bigger, universal, whereas Joodie's were personal and intimate, self-focused.

I had never been convinced that I was in love with Ophelie, but I knew absolutely that I loved her elemental qualities. I loved the image of her – not as an attraction but as a thing to be admired: sculptural, or like nature: a plant or a stone; or even like a footprint, a curving chord in soft earth – she was aesthetics and form, she was a mathematical formula, balanced and equated; she was a still pond or snowfall. And all of this in her inert state, tranquil on the couch, a captured memory or photograph – when she moved, she was outer space, the stars and planets, she was animal and she was ocean. Was it any wonder that I could not remove her from my cinematic internal vision? And yet she was so oddly plain; I never used to feel this much about her. Her features, I continued to admit, dumbfounded, were independently very ordinary, save perhaps her mouth, but generally, the parts of her face were inconsequential; when they moved together, ordinary elements became theatre, they satisfied my aesthetic paradigm, satisfied it and destroyed it; transfixed and bewildered.

Slight breaks in the pale clouds did little to take the chill off the day; it was almost too cold to walk in Richmond Park; I imagined a day, soon enough, when I would have to abandon this growing enjoyment of navigating my little corner of the park.

If it wasn't yet too cold to pass time walking, then surely it was too late in the year to sit on the exposed terrace. Undaunted, leaving the park, I walked straight past the Buck's Head and down the little steps, hoping to discover Acantha and Paul there; the cold air suggested it unlikely, but I had to pass by, just to check. As pleased as I was surprised, wrapped deep in old, expensive looking overcoats and newer, oddly hi-tech hats, I discovered the old couple.

From a short distance, they saw me, smiling shyly as I moved towards them. They sent obliging smiles back, the unoccupied part of the bench offered in this way to me. Rather geriatrically, I groaned and sighed and made an over-elaborate gesture of taking a seat, unmistakably intending this to represent the weariness and the burden of my life.

'Long day?' Paul obliged.

'Yes. Well, I've actually been in the park, that's why I'm...I've taken quite a liking to it actually.'

'Good man.'

'Thought you might.' Acantha leaned around her husband and twinkled, then she frowned. 'Bit wet though, isn't it?'

'Damp. But not so bad. I'm not quite so advanced that I venture off the path and I only cut through from

Sheen to the top of the hill, there's a couple of nice little woods – obviously, sometimes I go further, you know the gate down at the bottom...?'

'Petersham?'

'Yeah, I guess, I don't know the names; that's Petersham Road...down there?'

'Yes.'

'Well, along there to the entrance at the bottom and then carry on towards Kingston, cut back in halfway and back up to here.' I gestured the gate at the top of the hill. 'It's nice...on the paths, still...' My attempts to swell my pioneering exploits crumbled and I felt, again, rather dismal and sorry for myself.

'What are you reading these days,' Acantha perceptively stepped in.

'Oh, I'm in between books just now – story of my life, just lately...' I wasted no time and, whilst my matrimonial metaphor was subtle, it jarred and stunted the conversation.

'Er, work is it,' Paul tentatively ventured. 'Looking for something new or, damn 'em, they let you go, Christopher?'

I smiled at the old man. As stiff as Paul invariably seemed, he really was a sweet and soft fellow; only culture – my ignorance of it, how little I understood this upper-middle-class world on the hill – culture was to blame: good manners and good diction equated, by default, to stiffness and unfeeling disinterest.

'No, work is fine – not fine, no, but not the problem...I'm, God, I'm thinking of leaving my wife.'

'Oh dear, no.'

'No; never the right thing to do – never.' Paul looked dismayed at the thought, already piqued at the idea of me being made redundant. 'You're a man, aren't you – a man wouldn't walk away; a man would fix it.'

'There's nothing in love that can't be fixed,' his wife qualified. 'Look at us, look how far we've come...'

'Despite everything.'

'Everything.'

'Exactly. Look at us – you don't think we're still here because we never had our calamities? You make a commitment, you see it through.'

'Yeah, I get that – believe me, I really do – and I really want it to work, but it's got to a point...'

'No, it hasn't,' Paul disagreed, defensive. 'Nonsense; I'll wager it's not even close. What? You've had a couple of tiffs; she doesn't look after her looks? Right, something like that?'

'*Some*thing like that.'

'Puh. Nothing at all, Christopher, nothing at all – pull yourself together, man...'

'Seriously, it's more than just arguing – we actually don't argue that much, relatively...'

'Oh,' Acantha interrupted, a past life wearily returning to her. 'We used to have blistering rows...'

'Really? You don't seem...'

'I told you,' Paul cut back in, oblivious to my disbelief. 'You've not reached "that point"; you're not even close...I'm sure of it.'

'It feels like it.'

'This woman,' Paul gestured with his head, stiffly packed down into his collar. 'This woman forgave me an affair.'

'More than one, if we're going to be confessional here,' the "woman" contributed sullenly.

'Yes, yes, yes, as you say – not that that is the point...'

'No, the point is that I forgave him, in a way...how else can one sustain one's marriage?'

I was thinking about Ophelie again, I couldn't even imagine having the guts to cheat on Joodie, but my stomach cramped with desire to do so. 'I have no idea; I'm bewildered, now – I'd never have thought...'

'Yes, well there we have the problem of the youth...'

'I'm nearly forty,' I laughed shortly, incredulous.

'Youth to me, my boy,' he giggled, relieved that my humour had broken the tension. 'The problem with all of you nowadays is you don't think *nearly* enough; you have no obligation or need to think.'

'Believe me, it's overthinking that's got me in this mess.'

'Ah, but that's not thinking – not real thinking...you never read Russell, did you?'

'No, it was a bit much.'

'Bit much thinking, eh? When you sit there and stew over your marriage, you aren't really thinking – let's clarify this, you're not opening your mind, grasping the problems and working for solutions – you don't *think*, you dwell; you line up your problems like trophies and you indulge them, stare at them, fallacies all, and admit defeat. If you thought, you would understand – clearly you do not. Have you ever for a minute sat down and tried to work out, logically, what the problem is?'

'Ah, now logistics is my thing – yes, of course, I've *thought* about the logistics of staying...or going.'

'No, no, no – not log*is*tics, she's not a piece of bloody luggage – I mean have you looked, without emotion or self-indulgence, at the logic behind the struggles in your marriage?'

'I don't know,' I sang, dolefully. 'I can't even think...'

'Ah, there you go – it hurts, does it not, hurts because you seldom do it,' Paul laughed, I sulked. Acantha, listening, but leaving her husband to it, stared out at the greying clouds and the dark lick of river.

'So, what is it then?'

'Eh?'

'What is the reason? What do you mean?' I asked, confused.

'The reason? I've no idea – probably you. What do I mean?...What I mean is, that you should stop looking at the symptoms, the...dear God...the logistics of staying married, and concentrate on discovering what it is that's driven you apart – if you believe it's something that she's doing, whether it's snoring or cheating on you or...'

'Or both,' Acantha giggled.

'Hmm, yes – whatever it might be; look deeply at her, think logically, objectively: why is she doing it? – and there you'll find the problem, or something closer to it than you have right now – no doubt you yourself will be at the centre of it, unless she's just become a "bad person". Find that and you can then work on a cure.'

'Wow. That seems so...logical.'

'Life, Christopher, is always much easier than we make it.'

'Because we forget to actually "think".'

'Absolutely right. Now, Acantha, time for...'

'Oh, of course, let's push off.' She stood up and her forgotten height and bearing were revealed again, her movements seemed strangely agile after being so settled into the bench. 'Nice to talk again, Christopher. Please try. You don't have to make do with unhappiness – but if you can't find a way, come and see us – don't forget that.'

'My pleasure. And thank you *so* much.'

I stood up and offered a hand to Paul, rock solid was the grip I received, solid but a tremble shuddered through it and I looked up into the old man's cloudy eyes.

There was that darkness, then, that comes uncannily, arrives too soon; the afternoon was tinged with unreal twilight, the clouds, bulked and gravid, slid from a dismal grey, like a pavement under rainfall, to a grim charcoal. Though I had risen to depart with Paul and Acantha, I turned and returned to the bench, staring at the heavy black limbs of the leaf-burgled trees. I stared down into the plains of this sprawl of Thames Valley; the first streetlights flickered awake, queer pinkish dots, downstairs rooms by shady gardens suddenly exposing their interiors.

Inner thoughts rose like boiling water, at times it seemed like the clarity I had been hunting; other moments it felt like nothing more than the first burdensome steps of a destination-unspecified journey. The notion that a kernel could be found, that a true source of the failing of my marriage existed, an explanation beyond what I had so far perceived – this would be such a revelation! Out of nowhere there was a chance to believe that not all was lost – how much better to save my marriage than to abandon it or to struggle unhappily onwards. As difficult as it was to believe, it was harder still to accept that, should it exist, why had I not already realised it – had I not thought endlessly over the problem? Naturally, the thought followed that maybe I was incapable of recognising it even if it appeared to me. As much as anything else, I was convinced that the problem *was* known – hadn't my obsession with Ophelie made that unquestionably clear – that Joodie was not the right person for me? Well, it was true – even if it was not the essence of the problem, it was at least a good place to work back from. No doubt it was where I should have commenced this exercise in "thinking", however, staring blindly into ever darkening suburbia, I slipped into daydreams of Ophelie.

What pulled me out of it and returned me to the backtracking process, was a sudden urge to drink. The day had reached that low of temperature that made sitting outdoors unbearable, rain gathered ready to fall and I gathered in my introspections.

The beer seemed as close to rainfall as the sky had been and almost as cloudy, yet I sucked it down and genuinely started to think about the problem. Working from the known value of Ophelie and, for a change, not what it was that she offered but why she had changed my mind, I searched for a trigger to this change in feelings.

How right Paul had been – it did hurt. In spite of what I thought of my previous endless cogitation, as Paul had speculated, I had never really thought about my situation, I had only ever stood apart from it and looked gormlessly at it, watched it deteriorate, watched it convulse and contort. Untended, like a difficult shrub, it had become a wild overgrowth, with no apparent means to uproot – the original foot lost below the leaves. I smiled at this unexpected thought, realising that I had only ever tried to prune it; as such it would never go away, only appear neater and more manageable.

Light, evening traffic moved darkly along Richmond Hill, metallic headlit shadow and flare. I gazed unfocused through the old grid of windows, every burden and pointlessness of life seemed to be represented in the wet night-time street. I had made it to a fourth beer; watching the slur of passing vehicles through the sticky downpour, the thickness of the alcohol in my head, I was still waltzing through the turbulence of my marriage – thinking. Trying to, at least, but inevitably guilty of meandering and tripping into vapid lustful liaisons with Ophelie; even Frew Grensen had served to distract me – a slick adventure, ruminations on buttocks – I wondered momentarily what a life with her would be like – no point asking her ex-husband, I joked to myself. The light humour passed and vague circles of fantasy resumed – a chalet style property in Northern California, a soft-furnished living room, as Frew drifted back and forth to the chaos of her studio, the indomitable power of her hips as they ground me into the inexplicably conceived home furnishings.

My mind meshed back into the business of actually thinking – all of this happiness existed exclusively in fantasy, these moronic schoolboy daydreams – if Paul was correct and the root of the problem was myself, then this, this fantasy fulfilment, must be close to the core. Hiding in fantasy, these implausible romantic worlds so dominant that the ordinariness of my reality seemed smeared with a film of subnormal dreariness – perhaps my disenchantment and perceived boredom was merely a symptom of my being so very full of extraordinary, unattainable delight. The concept fit easily with and explained the inconsistency of my fascination with Ophelie – how she could shift from a nice handsome woman to a breath-taking goddess in the blink of an eye, the way that I could be saturated with desire for her, an ache of longing, and yet clearly had no intention of ever breathing a word to her about it. I no more desired a relationship with Ophelie than I did with Joodie; what I wanted and what I got from Ophelie was a vehicle for escape, not real but imagined – a body to contain fantasy worlds of idealistic impossible romances.

Was that it? Was this the essence, the cause of my failing marriage? Should it be so, then logic would dictate that all I need do is suspend these useless adolescent intrigues, a spell in the real world. Could I manage even this, would it make a difference? Or was it still only another step on the path? Were these fantasy worlds simply the symptom of some other factor, deeper, rooted even further below? And so the pursuit reignited – was there something? Of course, there was. What, then, was the trigger for my straying mind, what drove me to live in this non-existence – something led me to crave escapism, to seek solace in these private individual romances. I had no clue; tired and feeling the drink, I walked out into the downpour.

The rain tapped down on my skull like flicked fingernails, sharp, and the wetness spread and grew quickly, soaking me. Everywhere, the streets were full of water and the dark scent of seasonal plants disturbed into life, shaking with raindrops; the night felt clear and uncanny in spite of the mistiness of the light from the streetlamps, blurred with the shifting prisms, falling uncountable. More and more intensely the rain built up, violently crashing onto car roofs and hissing as though falling on hot fat; becks rushed down Onslow Road. I was pathetically wet now, my hair shone, flat and slick down my forehead and over my ears, pouring along my eyebrows, heavy gathered drops slipping and stinging my eyes; icy cold, the rain cut under my soggy collar, droplets tortuously down my spine; my clothes ineffective, colder and wetter than the rain itself. It was glorious: in spite of the hopelessness and discomfort, it was hilarious. I couldn't guess why; at first a smile, a giggle, then laughing as I walked, dangerously close to skipping – I was simply exhausted with the endless thinking. All day, every day (whatever Paul might say), a constant train of interminable analysis – what the hell did it matter why my marriage had failed – it had, it was failing; what could I do? I didn't love Joodie, I didn't want to be with her, I didn't love Ophelie, I didn't really want to be with her – I didn't want any of them and I understood, free from thinking, digging – logic or logistics – suddenly I knew, alone and intoxicated in the pouring rain: I didn't want anyone, I just wanted to be alone.

Ghosts seemed to occupy Richmond Park. Low gossamer nets of mist hung across the folding ground, trees in the middle distance identified only as heavier more solid shades of grey.

It had become formulaic in my life to walk into the park, the weekends needed such escape. Joodie, when not out shopping or having lunch with girlfriends, was poor company, and she had scant interest in mine; often online or among magazine editorials, her phone alive with communication. At these times, I was actually happiest; when she wasn't talking, the still redundant retrospectives of people I didn't know and places I never went to; the disconnection suited me. What made it unbearable was seeing her active relationship with 'living'. It depressed me hugely as I thought of my own life and how inadequate my activities had become.

Since I had spoken with Acantha and Paul, my

subsequent torrential realisation was that I needed to be alone, I had regressed into a state of inertia and introspection. As never before, my mind was filled with the intricacies and practicalities of leaving Joodie – I had no time or focus for books or films or conversation. It was unfair that Joodie should trundle along, seemingly unphased, enjoying her social world whilst I struggled and fought just to keep straight. Walking in the park, even if it didn't free me from the concern, at least it gave me peace of mind to feel that I was (I hoped), in her eyes, just as relaxed and phlegmatic as she was.

Walking through the gates freed up everything, that first lungful of air– it was no cleaner, no cooler than in the lanes that skirted the park, with their overhanging gardens, saturated with oxygen and tranquillity, but inside the park walls, immediately, every breath that I took was liberation; and knowing the separation, the first breath was always the freest. Truthfully, in certain ways it was a perpetuation of the daydreams that ruled my world, false as they were – a temporary occupation of a safe and content place; however, rather than a sanctuary of unattainable sexual adventure, the park at least had a foundation in normality. Instead of the images of fine limbs and melting smiles, walking in the park was a fantasy of time travel and individuality – the fantasy here did not manipulate others, only me.

In the park I could become someone else, I could find comfort not being me, I could find comfort not having to associate the real Christopher Hoyer with another person to solicit happiness. I drifted through

time, taking on identities; windswept dramatic heroic
figures – not like Nelson or Byron or Fitzwilliam Darcy,
but obscured imagined strangers, scraps of
characterization unconsciously rendered from movies
and biographies. Each one charming for their simplicity
or complexity – either way, as long as their individuality
shone. And I knew: the more I indulged, the more
disenchanted I became with the man I had become – an
underachieving, isolated employee, a friendless
nonentity, an unnecessary husband, a ghost.

It sickened me and, sunk to that depth, my natural
balancing mechanism rolled out, the process of denying
my inadequacy began. I searched for positives by
dismissing the negatives, by seeking justification for my
failings; faking perspective by lowering expectations and
parading the even greater inadequacies of anybody I
could – and there were many: no one I knew lived up to
the lives in the books I read, no one deserved a
biography. Again! – this hapless fantasy; why was I
trying to draw parallels between the ordinariness of
ordinary people and the stars and heroes, the handful of
extraordinary, racked up over hundreds of years of
culture and society? I could do this in the park – crash
and fly – I could look at myself, try to understand; in
the park I was an individual.

The ghostly span of mist had drawn me deeper and
longer into the park than I had been before but slowly,
unnoticed, it had thickened and I started to worry; I
wondered if I had walked close enough to Kingston or
Wimbledon to take a bus home.

The cool mist pressed in until the distant tress

were lost and only the plants hard-by were soft black silhouettes; I remained ever cautious, sticking to the formed path and hurrying on a little; chilly and fatigued, the thought of a safe destination added to my tiredness.

Closer than I would have expected, the bobbing forms of two figures appeared ahead of me, moving towards me. I followed the expected routine, as if controlled by some demonic adolescent, imagining Ophelie, elaborate and magical, appearing on a walk of her own; her wind-blown face, rosy and cold and, hopelessly, set to a flash of thought of her nudity and the long grass. I couldn't help it, even when the smudge of their outlines became sufficiently sharp to establish the female shape of the couple to be too tall and too shapely, beyond Ophelie's more athletic slimness, and never had Ophelie had such a voluminous spray of hair exploding witchily from her head.

I sighed, the endless reality of nothing happening and I sulked at my lack of adventure.

'Christopher?'

The zing of her accent snapped my moping stare up from the path; metres away, smiling impossibly, Frew Grensen approached.

'Dear God. Frew. What on Earth are you doing here? I didn't think you were an outdoors type.'

'Nor you. But then we hardly know each other, do we?'

'No, I guess not; but what…this is your neck of the woods?'

'Oh, no,' she turned, suddenly recollecting. 'This

is my husband, Benjamin, he lives in Fulham, but we just fancied it, but...' and she looked up at the mist to complete her point.

'Your husband...Hi.' I reached to shake Benjamin's hand, wordlessly accepted. 'I thought he was...I mean, you guys were...'

'Oh, sure, yeah, we're divorced but I feel like a schoolgirl saying "ex" – how's your divorce going? Took the plunge yet?'

'Me? I'm not, well, I'm...did I say something?'

Frew laughed and reminded me of a conversation, irretrievably lost.

'I must have been more drunk than I thought.'

She laughed again, reduced in magnitude but ever sincere. 'Speaking of which – I don't think we're going to get any further than this today – let's go to the pub.'

'Oh, I'm not...' I began, never likely to finish.

'Come on, Christopher – Benjamin can't drink anymore; we can send him home – and you can keep me company.'

I found myself agreeing without resistance, she clutched my arm and laughed. 'Let's see what we can get you to forget this time!'

Floral Street

London clambered for a closer look.

I felt as though I had been easily led, and that I was blushing – the treat of being with this attention grabbing, spectacle of a woman – and I was guilty on both counts; with a separate strand of guilt from the thought that I was doing something that I should not be doing. These were mere details; the overwhelming sensation was pride and a queer virgin glamour – for these reasons it felt as though every face was turned upon us. And for the first time for as long as I could remember, I didn't feel like I was part of a couple, yet I felt that I was with Frew; that we were together.

That she was a little taller than me didn't prevent her from putting her arm around my waist as we crossed Waterloo Bridge, taking my elbow as we ascended on the Middlesex bank of the Thames; it didn't even have the effect that I had expected, of feeling some unwanted creepy maternal feeling, it just felt good, natural and with no pressure. No pressure at least to perform, to satisfy or be something – pressure however I did feel, because I wanted to sleep with her. I wanted her and had no idea how to go about it – Frew was no simple wispy English office girl, I would be...I *was* punching well above my weight. It did seem, though, that she was flirting, offering herself rather openly to me – but I'd fluffed these signals before, time and time again. With everything from cultural differences to the insane delusion brought on by the cracking shell of my marriage, I could no longer trust myself to make healthy decisions regarding women – and yet I knew that if the opportunity arose, I didn't care, I would take it – there was nothing left to risk.

It began to rain, we dashed to buy an umbrella; instantly I felt safe, as if entering a world I knew better. It was my safety net, of course, surrounded by the antique dwellings and chambers along the Strand, monuments of past lives. I pitched myself and Frew into some other existence, favouring this time a pre-war adventure; I was Meredith Frampton, soon to paint Frew, as Marguerite Kelsey. We strolled past phantom stores, the retail experience of that dead world; I phased out the gaudy Gore-Tex and ripped denim, the diesel grime of panting buses and Transit vans. Under our umbrella we walked undisturbed, close now, she clutched at my arm and I felt an unexpected scintillation – so quickly had it all changed from the deathly isolation of Richmond Park to this freezing urban intimacy.

Frew turned towards me as we waited to cross to Covent Garden, 'This is so cosy; I'm glad I bumped into you – you're a stronger man than you think, Christopher.'

'Am I?'

'Well, *that's* not very attractive, but…'

'Sorry, I'm just…'

'And that even less so.' She laughed lightly to take away the pressure she sensed she had created. 'Well, I like you – I'll tell you that, if it helps; I do, I think you have something you're hiding, something in you, some great...'

We continued, not hearing the traffic pause, moving with the clustered pedestrians beside us. I wanted her to continue, fearing that she'd lose her train of thought, needing the reinforcement.

'I think within you there's a huge creative force.'

'Really?' Surprise that she might think such a thing, disappointment that she hadn't thrust the greatness of "lover" upon me. 'I'm not sure about that, I can't paint at all, or music, I haven't a clue.'

'No, I shouldn't think you have – no, I see you,' she turned as if to demonstrate her visual capacity. '...you have a great vocabulary, expressive...I see you as a writer – maybe not a novelist, you wouldn't have the patience, no – a poet, like Robert Frost or Ezra Pound or, no, like Robinson Jeffers.'

'I don't know them – not their work; I've never heard of Robinson...Jeffers?' I confessed, making a mental note to investigate, to improve my chances.

'Yeah, I can see it, you should move to Big Sur. Have you ever been to Big Sur?' She was rolling now, excited by her own ideas, creating something – my existence her canvas, painting with her imagination. 'It's fantastic – that's what you should do, dump the little woman and go to the Pacific Coast, write all the crap that's filling your head.

'Hey!' she called out, breaking the daydream, 'look

at those awful things.'

She was pointing at one of the dreadful tourist shops that sold knock-off football kits and plastic models of obsolete phone boxes and Routemaster buses. 'God, I normally hate these places, but I have to get one of these for you.'

I looked out from under the time machine, the real world remained, resting beyond the dark of our umbrella, with Frew's enthusiasm, drawing me in, like a bell ringing around my head.

'Oh, God, no – nothing from there for me, thanks.'

'Yes, I have to – they're perfect.'

We edged through the streaming pedestrians and approached the stall, the greedy little man, greasy from the rain, shuffled across as Frew giddily skipped closer.

'Ok,' she said, placing her hands on my shoulders, looking right into me. 'This is a one day only offer, today is a special day for us...today, today only, I'm going to be your girlfriend and you,' she reached and grabbed, looking momentarily away, 'are going to be the proud owner of this...'

She pressed the square of cellophane wrapped fabric into my chest, her eyes wide, smile wider – pleased with herself. I looked down cautiously, a small laugh broke, confused as I read the "My girlfriend went to London..." motif. I wanted to be grateful, I wanted to join in the joke but was blocked, held back by the reality, the confession of the garment; it was a colossal disclaimer and disappointed me by the same magnitude, the idea that such a position only existed for today; it overtook everything else.

'Don't you like it?' she asked, bewildered.

'Yeah; I guess. It's bizarre.' I forced the reply, realising that it was a damn good offer; in fact, it was the best offer I was going to get. 'Yeah, I just can't believe it, that's all – you're nuts!'

'Put it on, put it on,' she yelped, re-establishing joy, quickly paying the vendor. I removed my coat and pulled it over my sweater.

'How cool am I,' I laughed, finally accepting the joke.

'Oh, we *have* to get a picture, Mister,' she called the vendor over, pulling her phone from her pocket. 'Can you get our picture?'

Behind us the rain drizzled, the canopy of the umbrella framing our faces tilted together for the camera.

Being easily led was not a dilemma for me; with Frew Grensen leading, it became something of a guilty pleasure. So, close to Covent Garden, rather than waste money in a dark tourist-laden pub, she encouraged me to return to her apartment – not that it needed sweetening, she added an offer to see some of her work, the temporary studio she had established in her rented loft. In the end, it was less me being led and more me tripping over my own feet, metaphorically, to get in there. Regardless of whether I expected her girlfriend-for-the-day offer to lead to anything more than a self-proclaiming "lousy" t-shirt (I didn't, but I sincerely hoped it would) I was genuinely interested in seeing how she lived and worked and the lure of obtaining access to the inside of an old Covent Garden property was in itself irresistible.

If the evening were to consist of a series of disappointments, then the first phase arrived quickly. The old building, inside, had been scraped clean of all its personality and refurbished with a predictable cool sterility, and cheaply; the minimalist surfaces were not elegant stone or marble, but some bland industrial chemistry. The batons clasping the flooring to the stairs were a ridged steel, screwed down with the most soul-destroying countersunk screws – everything about it was flat and plain, the plastered edges so crisply sharp that they looked machined; even the windows had been replaced with sealed single sheets of thick immaculately flat, actually rather dirty panes of glass.

Round the first turning flight, I felt the electro-mechanics of my mind defaulting to a pre-set, for complaint and dissatisfaction. Looking around, disappointed and angry at what might have been removed, all the ghost of lives lived in the Floral Street structure, their shadows and footsteps removed, painted over, cleansed. It was empty to me. After the next turn of the stairs, I cared less about the building than if it had never existed. Instead, before me, striding upwards, I watched the march and rumble of the Grensen thighs, ascending, pulling here and there the cruel mess of fabric that surrounded – even just a glimpse of these, bare, would have pleased me. As I had longed for the fantastic unreality of Ophelie's limbs, the unknown terrain of her uncovered flesh, now I wanted the expansive, the bewildering posterior twisting before me.

In my heart I accepted the unlikelihood of anything happening between us, and if I was honest I probably wouldn't want to anyway – I didn't feel sexual, there was none of the urge to be invasive or raptured, it was all still so oddly cerebral, at least visual; again, it was all fantasy. Almost as if the only thrill I could command derived from the idea, rather than the reality – some unnamed sexual quirk where the satisfaction is in the anticipation, and the anticipation was for the impossible. It was a play on the idea of wanting what one does not have, the desire exceeding the reward.

By the time we reached the top floor, the gruesomely simple, converted loft, I was as exhausted by the climb as I was with the overdriving imagination that I had carried with me. Frew turned at the doorway as she let herself in, a blush of embarrassment caught her cheek, a crack in the hyper-confidence she had apparently only worn over some deeper unrevealed personality. Childishly, she offered me the secrets of her home – the real skeleton of an individual – all that she loved and that she had complied to accompany and comfort her life; exposed, she offered it open to me, available to be judged.

Some practical or tedious reason no doubt existed for why Frew had taken this apartment, the content in no way reflected the style of the space. It wasn't cluttered, and it certainly wasn't full, but the plain walls, stark floorboards, the general flat emptiness was littered with a seemingly random collection of what, at first, second and potentially final sight, seemed to be junk. The furniture looked uncomfortably corrupt, perhaps once stylish and costly, the couch was missing an arm, a tarnished strip of chrome reached only three fifths of the way around the lip of the coffee table, which was loaded with shabby paperbacks with gaudy, illustrated covers; delicate yet chipped and stained china cups. On the wall opposite the room's (and it was bedroom, kitchen and salon all together) inadequate windows, stood a huge and gruesome bookcase loaded almost entirely with typically oversized art books.

Frew threw on a bolt of overhead lighting, clearly designed to compensate for the gloom and I headed to a window, for the rooftops and other possible hidden architectural relics.

'I'll open some wine,' Frew called, her voice bouncing back from the wall of glossy white cupboard doors. 'I think I have only Chardonnay; I've tons of it, I got a whole case for some dreadful little sketch I did. Some guy liked it, it was me nude, but so abstract you couldn't...I guess he had a good imagination. Turns out he has good taste in wine, 'cause it's actually damn good.'

'There's not much of a view,' I advised her. 'I thought we'd be at the back...must have lost track up those stairs.'

'Everybody seems to,' she said bewildered by the coincidence. 'The backside is much better...'

'It certainly is.'

'Huh?'

'Oh, nothing – where did you say?'

'Through there,' she indicated nowhere in particular. 'In my studio. We'll go in there; the couch works in there and I have music.'

'Cool. Through...? Oh, I see; am I allowed...'

'Ha; sure, go ahead.' She turned, two wine glasses clinked, hanging off her fingers. 'We're ready here.'

Her building was one of the narrow four floor blocks along the tight little path of Floral Street. Upon the protruding out-buildings of the lower floors, appearing from the back wall of her apartment was an almost entirely wood and glass structure, evidentially plagued by decades of leaks streaking along the greyish white woodwork, mildew hugged the edges of the glass panes. I considered it wonderful, so odd and unlikely.

Beneath the creaking greenhouse, surprisingly well-organised, was the working existence of the artist – Aztec forms of stepped canvasses, complete or untouched; buckets, tins, plastic boxes of a lifetime's collection of paints and brushes, tools and edges. Metal shelves were stacked and wilting under the weight of papers and more books, packets of clay, sealed unknown boxes, even a half-shelf of ancient silty jars. Her music (CDs and a crummy little stereo) filled other shelves, alongside more boxes, overflowing with genuine trash, bits of plastic and cables, grotesque broken toys and obscure shaped metal, fragments and forms, paper cones and rusty coils, hunks of Plexiglas with sharp broken frames. I assumed these were props, three dimensional elements to be absorbed into her paintings; I recalled the fascinating textures of her work, the one factor I had managed to appreciate and, looking around, I was reminded of how brutal and hideous her work was.

Above the glass, the London sky had darkened;

thick sinister clouds and weird high-contrast light. The studio was twilit and everything creepy and gothic; the bars of the overhead structure were like the bars of some diabolical menagerie.

When it suddenly flashed stripped light, the outside, the view over the cluttered shambles of roof tops vanished with an accompanying clinking of glasses.

'This is the place,' Frew suggested as I swung around, 'take a seat.'

I searched the room, I hadn't noticed a couch anywhere in the long narrow space and even when it revealed itself along the side wall to my left, the furniture in question was barely distinguishable; low and broad and disguised, buried under so many rugs and blankets, vast flat cushions, heavy and sunk into the couch's depths.

'Thanks. This room is amazing.'

For the first time in a long time, I stopped caring, stopped thinking and simply settled into conversation with Frew. The first bottle of the admirable Chardonnay vanished with a helpful promptness, and by the midpoint of the second we were sprawled like cats or lazy children across the flat bed of the couch, laughing and teasing. If there was flirtation on my part, then it was without calculation or cleverness, it was a mere natural expression, a seldom shown attribute of my mind – even the usual social debilitation of attraction did not affect my play. I was deeply aware of what she did to me, but the way she was, her uninhibited ease and careless tactility, helped me feel comfortable and capable, as her embracing amiability drew me in.

I wanted her, craved her; the scale of the woman was phenomenal, she was a wholesome, desperately healthily formed woman, just on a large scale – there was a lot of her and all of it tight, in exactly the right places. It was like looking at the newly built Empire State Building, colossal and wildly over-scaled, but fine and slender and impossible not to stare at. So, of course, I wanted her and yet, unlike the clumsy overwhelmed incapacity I had when my desire for Ophelie submerged me, here I was within the attraction, controlling, steering it. And it was because I knew I could survive without it, I would take it if it came and if it were not to be, no matter. As it was, I was blissfully happy; Frew didn't care enough about me to expect anything from me – in the same way that Sonny allowed me to be myself and an individual, so Frew gave me this opportunity, only with it providing some delicious flirtation, the power of the possible, the power of her expediency.

The strip lighting had been eliminated, replaced by localised table lamps; the veil had ascended and a snow-white moon burnt behind fading fingers of clouds, the ghosts receding; and to the north, phallic, rising into the clear shining night, Centre Point, its matrix of dotted light, majestic and iconic. I stared out, awestruck, trying to fathom the situation I had stumbled into, surrounded in this queer chamber by art and music and a pale magic. I was thinking about ghosts (we had been talking about how Frew was obsessed with how haunted the ancient capital was), I had naturally twisted the supernatural theme to my own psyche, painting a picture of myself haunting Onslow Road, an unreal figment, as I swept through the dark rooms, nothing more than a chill down Joodie's spine. Here, on Floral Street, I was substantial again, a solid form, seen and known. The clearing sky above me was as beautiful as the woman I turned to see, draped over the bohemian mess of a couch.

'Jesus; don't you start with that.'

'What?'

'That thing; I'm sick of the bloody things.'

She had been staring into the shiny rectangular screen of her phenomenal looking mobile phone, filling her palm and, in my eyes, surpassing anything I had ever seen – I wasn't sure if it was even a phone, perhaps some freaky super hi-tech mini-computer.

'Oh, shush.' She slid past my complaint, knowing her advantage to be played. 'Bring me my drink – you'll actually like this.'

'I doubt it,' I defied, drunkenly pouring myself into the crevice of cushions, tight up to her shoulder.

'Look,' she said, taking her glass, 'this is so funny, you'll die…'

'God, if it's some idiot getting run over or a bloody animal farting – I'm not interested.'

'Huh? Oh, lighten up – no, it's not a video, I'm not that bad; 'tis an idiot though…'

The phone was hidden, pressed against the blouse section of her dress – she stared at my close-by eyes, wicked and teasing with a twisting vivacious smile. A child, she was enjoying her game, playing with the grumpy boy, knowing the outcome, yet very much adult, like a striptease pulling only half-way back a flap of clothing, she faked revealing the contents of her phone, each time pressing a little further at my impatience. Judging my limit well, she finally released me and held the screen right up to my face. I stared at it blankly, unimpressed and she, disappointed in not getting the rise, no victory, sulked a little herself.

'Oh, you old grump; don't you think it's cute?'

'There's nothing there.'

She checked my accusation – the screen had timed out, blanked, and she rolled her eyes.

'I take it back,' I enjoyed my tiny sarcasm, 'you know about as much about these things as I do.'

'Yeah, I'm a ditz with technology.'

'I'm pleased to hear it.'

'See!' she exclaimed, playful again, holding it right up in my face. I angled my head back to focus and a wry smile formed, unrestrainable.

'Yeah, that is pretty cute – handsome couple and an awesome t-shirt!'

With the phone held up in front of our faces, the temptation was natural, at least in Frew, to take a picture; her fingers slid into the space between mine with an obscure charge and I relinquished the device, allowing her to reassume control. Her thumb, with a series of dabs and swipes, removed the foolish characters from the screen, replacing it with peeks of the room opposite and a thick peachy blur where her finger crossed the lens.

Already our faces were side by side, yet we moved in, not to make a difference to the framed image, but because it was good; the weight and softness, the vibration of our bodies pressed close; our heads touched with a velvet rustle of hair and we smiled with the happiness of mutual closeness and contact.

She clicked and then flicked the thin slate around; left glowing was a grotesque cheesy close up of our faces.

'Urgh, that's bad – try again.'

'Christopher! – suddenly so vain...'

'Not vain,' I complained, taking her teasing still a little too personally, 'but I don't want you to remember us like that.'

'Oh, say "cheese".'

The process repeated, I was posing, 'You're so fake,' Frew laughed, disappointed at the new attempt, '...again.'

Several further, poor attempts we had not improved on our snapshot, the arm's length was, as always, inadequate and the whole episode of failure was becoming tedious to both of us, as she clicked this time, she turned and set her broad mouth, puckered onto my cheek.

'Oh? Interesting.' Excited, I rose to her flirtation, 'Then here's one back...'

She depressed the soft button, and this time we both turned in and she carried on clicking as we kissed, thickly, involved.

I had passed on from thoughts of the phone, my mind muddled; it was extraordinary to be kissing someone, someone who was not Joodie; it was a wild sensation and for the first time my imagined world had become the real world. Here I was, in this incredible space under the stone-cold moon, nestled among rooftops, kissing this extraordinary woman.

Yet there was queerness; I was confused, the peculiarity of unknown taste and texture, the strange implausibility of it actually happening, the exoticism of the incorrectness, tinges of damnable guilt and, threatening to destroy everything, the undermining horror of discovering how awful a kisser Frew Grensen was.

Despite the breadth and volume of her often joyous lips, she pressed her caresses far too hard, the bones of her jaw, her teeth, felt beneath the skin, clashing with my own face, her nose clumsily striking mine, my own nose pressed against her cheek bones. Her head darted and switched rapidly, passionately and hungry, ruled by an apparent desperation; it was frantic. To ease the attack (I had no immediate wish to stop, in spite of the disillusion and discomfort), I pulled back, Frew compensated, leaning in further and further until, bent to the point of fracture, I slid to my side, Frew collapsed alongside me, her tongue taking on the invasion.

The phone fell from her hand to the floor.

Now that I had committed to this, and with the effort of keeping up with her over-active kissing, I fought to hold my place and tried to make the best of the opportunity. As she pecked incessantly at my face, my ears, my neck, I dropped to three–quarter time, dabbing one kiss, one beat for every three of hers, allowing her to carry on as she was intent to do and for myself to relax into the adventure. I reached my hand around and swept up the full length of her hard, broad thigh, the stiff ridge of her underwear across her backside, leaving my hand, as if magnetic, firm and clasping her buttock.

Without pausing in her staccato blast of hard bony kisses, Frew remained content to let my hand rest, gently kneading the callipygous extreme of her body; but as my hand slipped round, the blade of fingers running through the fabric lined crevice and down, pressing her skirt in between her thighs, she slapped my arm down, sudden and harsh, as her lips hurriedly resumed work and pressing.

'What the hell,' I pulled my head, my body clear, pushing her aside.

'Huh?'

She seemed to be as if just awakened; her eyes bleary, her hair across her temples in tangles.

'Was that necessary?'

'Yes. We're only kissing, aren't we? It's nothing more than that.'

'Well, that's just...' I looked at her, bewildered, as though there was a joke in there somewhere, and then, grumpier, 'What the hell happened to "girlfriend for the day" – we can kiss but I can't touch you?'

'Not like that; I said "girlfriend" – I'm not your wife.'

'Who said anything about being my wife; besides, you know what's wrong there, you don't need to bring her up.'

'Sorry.' She was bashful now, peculiarly unflattering. 'I have my own wife-based issues too, you know; there are more problems in the world than just yours…'

Inert and quiet, conversation was briefly impossible. We looked at each other, different shades of guilt, 'Oh, come on, Christopher – we shouldn't be sulking – we were having fun.'

'Yeah? Well, smacking me kind of killed the mood.'

'Let's have some more wine,' she suggested, as if nothing had happened.

'I think I'm drunk enough.'

'I'll make coffee.' She rose and touched her hair ineffectively. She called as she left the room, 'Are you worried about your wife and…this?'

'Actually not.' I followed her into the kitchen, surprising myself to admit it. 'I don't care anymore – I'm going to leave her.'

'Well, remember: I was only yours for today.'

'Yeah, I get that. But, no, I can't do it anymore – there's nothing there anymore. Naturally, I'd rather she didn't know about this, it's not really the way I would want it to come about.'

'Sure,' she said, looking up from a suspended spoonful of instant coffee. 'It's none of my business, besides, I like you, Christopher – you need to be happy – I wouldn't want to screw that for you.'

Without any reason to stay, it was a straightforward departure – coffee, wine and a trace of her perfume accompanied the soft kiss she left on my cheek. Around the corner from the building, I wiped it, ignorant as to whether she had been wearing lipstick or not, a pang of guilt and paranoia sent my knuckles to my face and any potential confession was erased.

The journey home flew in a whirl of frantic thoughts, peaks and valleys of emotional flittering – the fear of discovery weighed greatest, and even within that the sensation drifted back and forth between terror and ecstasy – trapped as I remained in the limbo between leaving and staying. Even if I were to leave, I did not want it to be through foul means; if anything, it would be preferable if somehow I could get Joodie to make the decision – I knew that that was impossible, in spite of her apparent dissatisfaction, she remained inexplicably content and, it seemed, committed, as if her marriage was a mere tag, something she could wear as an accessory.

But there was no doubt in my mind, as I walked up Onslow Road, that the events of the evening had done nothing to encourage me to separate from Joodie – the taste of another woman's lips, the sensation of a new closeness had been marvellous, but it hadn't changed me, hadn't been the emancipating cleansing I had expected. There was no new sensation, only a better, at least a newer version of the old sensation – if the source of my desire to leave Joodie was to find something better elsewhere, this insight proved depressingly inconclusive. And yet I had had a fantastic time with Frew; one cascade of kisses and no sex was hardly a thorough investigation of life on the other side of the fence – that I had been happy all day, however, hinted that enhanced greenery might be a reality.

The apartment echoed with a queer abandonment, punctuated with a heart-breaking croak of a meow from the despondent ginger cat, sitting primly in the centre of the hallway. I thought to call out, a quick glance at the clock on the far wall halted me and I slid into the bedroom.

Immediately I knew the room was empty, the sensation of absence gripped, the lack of a human scent, the coolness of the dark – more hauntings – I knew that she was not there and, oddly, I didn't care.

Sitting on the edge of the bed, I slipped off my trousers and tugged my shirt and sweater off in one go. Prudently, I had abandoned the foolish t-shirt at Frew's, a faint suspicion of her perfume seemed to remain suspended in the fabric of my own clothes; breathing heavily at it, sadly there was nothing. Concerned, paranoid, I took the precaution of removing my socks, burnt from the walk across the park and the city, and folded my clothes around their musty reek. I was exhausted, I was due to leave for work in a few hours and battled my conscientiousness with a desire to take a day off – either way I would have to wake, even just to call in. I picked up the collapsed heap of my trousers and took from the pocket my phone to set the alarm; I unlocked it, the grey and black illuminated, peculiar and unexpectedly different – a missed call and a message. Further investigation revealed the same thing from both sources: Joodie had gone out, annoyed: why hadn't I called? She was at Ophelie's.

Cyberspace

The alarm did its job and woke me at seven; I called in sick and stayed in bed. It was odd, the reality of last night's events seemed washed from my mind with the re-emergence of Ophelie. I had fallen asleep thinking about her, and my dream had been full of her, and it was wonderful; I knew it was only a dream, but it had made me happy, happier than I could remember being.

So much of this confused me. I thought I had reached a point where she no longer influenced my day, that I could control my thoughts and secure her absence from them. I looked at the picture on my phone again, seeing her made me maudlin, great surges of sadness, a sense of loss, as of death, hollowed me. But it was really nothing more than feeling sorry for myself and the knowledge that however much I wanted to cross the boundaries of Ophelie's nudity, to kiss her hallowed lips, I knew that it was beyond my power to do so.

I knew that my mind had gone, corrupted as it had once before been; I couldn't think of anything else, all I wanted was to hold her and behold her – the entire morning passed with ceaseless erotic daydreams – every thought was Ophelie and with each came the frustration of her impossibility. It was as if no time had passed, I was back at the peak of my obsession; she, in my head, was just so beautiful, every thought compressed and moulded into a decent composite – I adored her.

Indulgently, I slobbed around the house for the rest of the day, as though I were actually ill – the apathy and indifference were real, even if the malaise was purely psychological. I made a pot of tea and a dreary sandwich and watched *Marnie*, wistfully imagining escape. I didn't care if Joodie never came back.

Selfish and self-indulgent, I needed to move, the film failing to interrupt the ceaseless trash of thought. The kitchen seemed a better place to be, the cats, hungry, were pleased to see me and the sun was warming through a tight angle of the windows. At the open fridge, I gazed sightless at its contents, I didn't know what I was looking for, something sweet? I took out a half bottle of wine from the door shelf, the probable remnants of Joodie's disenchantment last night.

From the neck I carelessly drank the slightly sour wine, like I was drinking juice. Joodie's laptop occupied its usual spot on the counter; I no longer cared and went straight to it. At my touch it sprang to life and, within my computing comfort zone, I opened a browser. Not expecting anything, my adrenalin surged, my heart thumped – the thrill of discovering the assumed forbidden – unlike the normal blank search engine that usually greeted me at work, that I therefore expected here, I was face-to-face with a cluttered gathering of lists and thumbnails, the nerve centre of Joodie's preferred social networking site.

I swore out loud, brightening spectacularly; my mind didn't need more than a few seconds to compose a plan. A little bit of hunting around, I arrived at a long list of her friends; there she was, a scroll away, the only 'O' in the list. My heart was crazy now, pumping like a schoolboy discovering his father's stash of Playboys; I clicked on the link to her photos and a neat grid of tiny portraits and group shots filled the screen. Even the disappointment of discovering that the page scrolled only a few photos further was short lived and, delicately, as if it were her intimate body I was touching, I clicked open the first image.

Treasure, it felt like – discovery and awe. Picture after picture rolled at the touch of a button across the screen, the fabricated memories and the inconsistent fantasies seemed as nothing – this was close to her actually being there, better in some ways as I could just stare into the digitally frozen eyes and she, silently and without question looked back at me, and each picture a different outfit, a different day, a new location. Often it was just the two of us, alone at last, but even in the group portraits she stole the frame – I imagined her in the group as the picture was being made, looking back at me, casting myself as the man behind the camera, the click and separation, Ophelie skipping towards me, the day, the night proceeding. Most of the images she had clearly posted as representations of what she was happiest with from her looks, and so the parade of portraits reflected Ophelie in her finest state of exploded beauty, rather than the also familiar plainness. A couple of such stray images coasted past, I didn't mind, though she was not as appealing, just to see her, not to be reliant upon my memory was so great a luxury,

I could feel nothing but joy and disbelief.

What if I had found this collection before, if I had discovered it during the height of my infatuation, what control would I have been able to preserve? My heart, calmed, surged again at the thought. Here, with these pictures, something was satiated. As I had been left feeling by last night's dream, so I felt again – happy.

It was almost breathtaking to share the afternoon with her – those lips, ah! – what would I give to actually possess them?

I made more tea, mumbling and swearing to myself how great the internet was, checking and refreshing the images, desperate not to somehow become locked or signed out of the site. I resumed flicking through the electronic gallery, each image poorly shot – ill-focussed, cropped, limited by the quality of mobile cameras – yet each of them a work of art that thrilled and satisfied me as much as anything at Tate Britain might have done.

As the cycle repeated again and again, the adventure and excitement of the discovery and the newness of the images gradually diminished and I sat on the high stool, sipping my tea and really looking, searching the images for something, finding new things to know, new details. She was beautiful – it was my only possible conclusion.

Without becoming completely weary with the two or three dozen pictures, eventually I had to stop; a queer sense of overdose swept through me – there was nothing, though, of the sensation of having had too much, instead the crushing urge to have more, only to have different.

Against the low back of the stool I pressed and

stretched out my spine, realising that I had been hunched for some time, leaning into the glow of the screen; I stretched back my arms and yawned and almost didn't hear the metallic clunk of the front door being unlocked. My rapid movement to the upright pulled a muscle in the lower part of my back, jerking panicky to the computer and amateurishly and incompetently trying to close the page to remove Ophelie's screen sized face from my company.

Miraculously, as Joodie entered the kitchen, I had somehow scrambled to bring up the front page of the BBC website, reading the blur of headlines with a completely unnatural poise.

'Jesus,' her first word, spiteful, aggressive. 'Have I caught you looking at porn or something?'

I didn't have the composure to brush it off, snapping instead, angrily, 'What? Huh? What?'

'Seriously, it'd probably do you some good. Well, you're bright red and look as guilty as hell.'

'Really? Huh, well it must be the tea,' I submitted, reaching for the stone-cold cup.

'Whatever. I don't care – nothing would surprise me right now, that's all.'

'What d'you mean?'

'Shift,' she said, sliding the laptop towards herself, 'I need to show you something, an email I got this morning.'

'Oh...oh,' I eased a little, assuming the worst to have passed; happy, for once, to endure more of her tedious work news.

Joodie flicked the cursor around the screen expertly,

locating her email; bringing up the two-tone list of popularity. Halfway down she clicked on one of the greyed-out messages; I hadn't enough time to be certain of it, it was too unlikely, impossible even, but I could have sworn that the unmistakable name, Frew Grensen, was in the "sender" field.

Instantly the flush and sweat of guilt returned to my face – if it were so, I speculated – the bitch – had she tracked Joodie down and told her? The mail opened, it was true, her name was right there at the top of the page.

Hey, I read, *I've uploaded some candid stuff that you might want to use for the website – sorry, didn't have time to sort it or edit, bit of a bulk delivery, crap from the last month - hope you don't mind, but I have to catch a flight in a few hours...*

'I didn't know you knew her,' Joodie murmured, oddly calm; she clicked on a link and then on an icon at the bottom of the page.

'Hardly...' I mumbled, pointlessly.

On to the screen, grotesquely, nightmarish, the image of me and Frew under the umbrella, grinning – I was physically petrified, it was hard to breathe – my mind rushed through the hazy alcoholic memory – what else had we photographed? Nothing – I was certain, just a few blurry close-ups, cropped heads and weird angles. The notion, however, that I was leaving Joodie had pathetically vanished and guilt and a sense of disloyalty caused me to feel nausea.

'"*My Girlfriend*"? Don't you think that's kind of inappropriate?'

'Oh, come on, Joo,' I tried to breeze by it, if this

was all that she was worried about. 'Like I said, I hardly even know her, I bumped into her yesterday and we went up town – come on: she's an artist, she's American! She thought it was funny – you know I hate that ghastly stuff.'

'Right,' Joodie continued, icily calm, seemingly placated. 'If that's all it was…right?'

'Course.'

'Ok. You just met up and were having a bit of fun…'

'Wouldn't even go that far; it was all a bit silly for me.'

'Ok. You didn't know she was one of my clients, did you?'

'No, not at all – like I said, I barely know her, she's one of Burchmann's…'

'Burchmann, ha! *Quelle surprise.*'

'Look, is this all you wanted, 'cause I don't need this crap – it's just a silly picture. I *am* allowed friends, aren't I? I may have fun from time to time?'

'Sure,' Joodie said, all the time frighteningly calm. She closed the image and clicked another icon, not from the expected series of bad attempts at taking a picture, but a blurry close up of a mess of hair and torsos twisted at a queer angle, two people embraced. 'And this? What the fuck is this?'

'I've no idea. Nothing to do with me.'

'It was with her images.'

'Is it a person? I don't know, must be something else she took, didn't she say in her mail it was just a load of different stuff?'

'Do you not remember her taking it?'

'Me! It's not bloody me; Jesus, it's so out of focus, it's...it could be anybody.'

'You're still wearing the damn t-shirt!'

'Oh,' I whispered, turning my head to the angle of the picture.

She slammed down the screen and stormed out. I watched her leave and gradually I began to smile.

With nothing to say and no real desire to add anything, I felt, once again, completely surplus to requirements – Jodie had reached, as one might reasonably have expected, an incontrovertible opinion on the whole situation: she had accepted it and responded appropriately; I chose not to pursue her. Even now, such was her way with me, she had left me out. The whole problem, in spite of me being the centrifugal force, had been absorbed into the mechanics of Joodie's world: she had made the discovery, brought it out into the open and taken on the responsibility of action. In the space of five minutes she had swept through, a tornado, ripped our marriage apart and withdrawn, leaving me twiddling my thumbs.

For the briefest moment, diabolic, I considered checking to see if the gallery of Ophelie's images was still accessible; more out of the fear of pushing my luck too far than any dignified sense of respect, I abandoned the idea – besides, the images, under such heavy rotation, were still freshly, hopefully indelibly, imprinted on my mind.

Pointless. My presence in the flat made uncomfortable and restless – not that I had any idea where I could go to reverse the feeling – I wanted to call Frew, clearly she bore some of the responsibility for this calamitous situation – hadn't I warned her that this was not the way I wanted to get out of my marriage? – had she actually thought she was helping? Why the hell hadn't she told me that she knew Joodie – she must have recognised the name?

I grabbed my coat, these questions grinding at me. It was the manner in which things had come to fruition, rather than the situation itself that troubled me – I had been determined (after all, I still loved something of Joodie) to not be a coward, to at least attempt to be dignified and respectful – now it all seemed so juvenile. What could I do? – it had happened now, I hadn't planned it, but I would have to accept it; and Joodie, by walking away, had removed the problem, how could I alter the situation now? I was utterly without use. So I left.

The day was bright, and the clearness left a rather nippy chill, but my coat was heavy, adequate, and without a breeze there was no harshness, only a stiffening, almost a discipline about it. Picking my way aimlessly down the smaller lanes, the beautiful properties seemed to possess a kind of conspiratorial warmth, cruel hints of fine domesticity and happy families, and the isolation grew. The sense of my own unimportance – if I no longer had Joodie to care for and if she were to no longer care for me (clearly, she still did; her anger displayed that explicitly – at least next to my own indifference, it seemed to...), then who did I have? Not Frew, certainly not Frew – "girlfriend for the day", I recalled, cringing at the stupid naivety of the thing – she only cared for herself. But did Joodie really care about anything other than herself, either? – was her anger directed at the assault on our marriage or just her half of it? Nobody cared: not Frew, not Joodie, nobody at work! – even Burchmann, would he care or just laugh it off as a stroke of good fortune? Sonny? She might – but she'd blame me, there was no hope for sympathy there.

I laughed. 'Oh, God,' I began to think, 'how pathetic is that, that I don't care if people care – I'm just looking for someone to feel sorry for me!'

Richmond Hill appeared at my feet, unknowingly I had drifted west and now began to wander back up the hill towards the terrace.

'Cristopher?' The voice interrupted my introspection, I looked out again, seeing the sprawling mansions of Richmond Hill Court – surely, I heaved my chest optimistically, surely interaction would liberate me from the torture of my perceived solitude. The voice, behind me, repeated my name and I turned to follow the sound, a strangely familiar feminine tone.

'Hello, Christopher: I thought it was you.'

'Acantha,' I beamed, gloriously, 'how nice to see you!' And, totally selfish, I meant it.

Seeing her waiting there, a dear sad smile warming the cold day, I accomplished a neat, if slightly awkward shuffle, coming and then going, choosing an adequate response. There was no doubt that Acantha was expecting me to wait and chat a while; equally, I was unsure if that was something I was in the right frame of mind to do – my marriage had, after all just been blown out from under my feet, casting me, I suddenly realised, as an adulterer – I cringed at the horror of such an idea, yet I was guilty as charged. The idea of standing in the cold having an uncomfortable conversation with a pensioner, either side of some out of season rose bushes was just something that I had no wish to enter into, and yet there was something persuasive about the way she stood there, something in her eyes urging me to approach.

'So, how have you been? Where's Paul today?'

'I'm all right, Christopher,' she said, clarifying the situation it seemed for her own benefit, as if she had just discovered this statement to be true. 'It's a beautiful day and I'm busy – what more could one ask for?'

'Absolutely; you off to the bench?'

'No, sorry – I'm on my way back.'

'And Paul, run on ahead?'

'No; no Paul, I'm afraid.'

'Oh. That's unusual; is he under the weather?'

'Under the ground, actually,' she sighed, joking blackly, unexpectedly – so much so that I failed to grasp it.

'Eh? I don't...what d'you say?'

'Nothing, dear – I was just being a bit macabre. Christopher...Paul passed away, last week.'

Every indulgence that had been doughily polluting my mind suddenly choked me. Suddenly I knew I was an imbecilic pig – all the criticism of Joodie's self-absorption suddenly became as nothing with the reality of my own grotesque egocentricity thundering down on me – what hypocrisy! Had I ever thought about anyone other than myself? All through this, every decision, every appraisal had been utterly focussed upon myself. The thought of it was bile in my mouth; I licked my cold stinging lips, biting them inwards, the psychological sourness unbearable.

All of this realisation a flash in time; even so, the seconds passed and Acantha, patient, must have been allowing for the news to sink in.

'Oh, Christopher, I'm sorry, I didn't mean to give you the bad news so abruptly...thoughtless of me, I'm sorry.'

'No, no, no...' I bleated, snapping out of my headspin. 'No, it's me that should be sorry...I mean sorry about...for your loss. Actually, no, I just can't believe it. Such a bright and fit...'

'Sadly not, he's been very sick for a long time.'

'Really?'

'Yes.'

'I'm sorry. Just...he seemed so...such a bright mind, so witty.'

'And you only saw the fading shade of it – when he was a younger man, even in his later years...ah, you can't even begin to imagine.'

And I couldn't, for all my fantasy skills. Paul seemed so much brighter and insightful than I could ever hope to be and yet that brilliance was, I now knew, merely a fading ember of what had been before, and now was gone.

Somehow, I had not noticed before, or I had forgotten, just how tall Acantha was; accounting for a slight stoop and her frame twisted to allow her to stand easier, she was at least as tall as I was. Why, suddenly, could I see everything so clearly; what had this man's death and the exposure of my incompetent adultery done to my mind and vision to allow reality to now pour through?

'I say, Christopher – I'm on my way back to the flat…it's awfully chilly out here, would you like to come back for some tea? You'd love to see all Paul's old stuff. I'm sure.'

'I'm sure I would,' with inappropriate eagerness I agreed. 'I'd be fascinated.'

I explained my new situation as we walked. Despite her grief, Acantha found room for sympathy for me, and some well-meant platitudes. Not unreasonably, I sensed that deep down she was disappointed in me, and considered me to be a fool.

The apartment wasn't huge, but it was beautiful, full of mid-century furniture and older art and porcelain; as ever I was hit in the face by the discovery of my own prejudice, having expected a room full of chintz and dark brown furniture; but it was of the era of their prime, littered though with inherited artefacts and memories of travel abroad.

Sprawled over the coffee table were a number of books and several elaborate astrological maps and charts. I sat and flicked through the stuff while Acantha made some tea.

'Do you follow your stars, Christopher?'

'Me? No, not really, I'm too much of a control freak to believe that my life is pre-destined. I believe that we create our own futures, not that I could look at Orion and know I was going to have a bad day.'

'Well, of course, it's not like that at all – we're all part of nature, can't you believe that nature, the stars and planets, can influence the events in our life?'

'Yeah, for sure; but no more than that, no more than, for example, that a cloudy day makes us less open and receptive than a sunny day does.'

'Ok, but that's a start. You seem open to the idea...'

'Absolutely. To a point. Influence, yes – prediction....'

'Well, what do you know about yourself – astrologically?'

'Well, from what I have gathered, what I've learnt, inadvertently, over the years...astrologically, I always thought my world made sense – I'm Libran, though I don't see it as being about balance, rather about extremes.'

'Possibly,' Acantha, curious, wanted to stop me and correct me. 'There's more to it than just your birth...technically, Sun sign; anyway, go on – I'm interested.'

'Ok, well, first and foremost, as I say, I do not believe in portents or the predictability of life – my world is such a mess, so ridiculous, that no amount of cosmic alignment could have caused it, only myself, me and my feverish loins.' I glanced away to the exquisite furniture, away from Acantha, regretting bringing up my loins. She was looking towards the window, at the sky outside. 'But, ok, I'm open to the possibility that lunar and solar and stellar influences are significant on the...on the human...experience.' And for a moment I recalled the times when, awfully, I had cited menstruation at dinner parties, maybe proving a point but causing mass abandonment of cranberry sauce and other sanguinary food stuffs – but it did make sense in my mind.

'For example, I have a suspicion that the fluctuations in my feelings towards Joodie and Ophelie could have been influenced by cosmic phases; I would even go so far as to believe my very characteristics are, in their essence, determined by the confluence of stars and galaxies. This much I will allow: designation, timing triggers and, to an extent, action, but I would never include decisions and outcomes, these I do believe are the results solely of my own behaviour.'

'Goodness, and you said you were a slave to logistics! Ok, I think you are starting in the right direction, but I suspect there is more to it than you have even considered. The first thing we need to do is to work out your moon sign and ascension.'

I wasn't really in the mood for this, not this seriously, at least, but any distraction seemed welcome. I offered up the personal details she asked for; she rose from her armchair with a swiftness that belied her age and went over to a bureau tucked behind the door. Surprisingly, I suddenly became really excited, I had never had an astrological reading or known more than I had just confessed, but with my world so messed up, direction so needed, I was ready to be guided, and as people hadn't really offered up anything worthy or helpful, why not put it in the hands of the universe. The idea of learning something about myself, too, was an inspiring notion. I turned, looking over the back of the sofa.

'Acantha? Your charts are here, on the table.'

She laughed a smiling little laugh, as she dragged something from the bottom of a stack of papers, 'Oh, that takes too long, I use this now,' she turned around with a rather chunky laptop computer. 'There's a web site you can just type the details in...'

It didn't take long, she flew through the procedure, making my computer skills look laughable, so much more proficient than I was, and quickly she had something.

'You were born under a Libran sun and a Gemini moon, hardly possible to be a more contradictory personality type, but yes – neither of them offer you the balance such signs might suggest, merely hopeless indecision and rambling procrastination.'

'Well, there you go, that's me in a nutshell.'

'Every decision seems to be equal...yes? Is that what's happened, why you couldn't work out what you wanted?'

'Naturally. I always factor in the merits of either side of the equation...'

'And at the same time burdened with extremes, the scales of personality rocking dangerously, the axis fit to topple?'

'It does make a lot of sense. The whole of my life

seems to adhere to this and, startlingly, it underpins every emotion I have suffered these last months: the love and loathing of Joodie, the patterns of joy and despair regarding my feelings for her. And Ophelie, she is either the perfect enigmatic beauty or something forgettable and incorrect, even the juxtaposition of this new...liberty? God, that puts it into perspective, I've only ever thought of it as being isolated, cut off.'

'That's how it works, in your mind – extremes and opposites.'

'Yeah. And like the difference between my now regular traversing of the Park and the dark tomb of my office. There isn't and there never has been any consistency, no middle ground, save the bouts of indifference...'

'But even your indifference is just one side of an emotional imbalance, its polar counter being an almost manic surge into intensity and obsession, yes?'

'Yes. The surging hormonal lusting or the petulant disenchantment and misanthropy.'

'But it isn't all gloom and tragedy, Christopher – you have a very bright, personality, a magnetism...' I contorted my mouth, intrigued, she continued, 'Yes...chatty; you know how to get your opinions across...but still keep people attentive...yes?'

'I suppose, in a way...not sure it's always that way.'

'Well, this isn't a law, it's...an insight.'

'Ok, keep insighting,' I smiled.

'Courteous, intellectual, adaptable...'

'Not so sure about that, I'm pretty stubborn when I get stuck on something.' And I thought of my

"Ophelie thing", mortified.

'Well, not so much that kind of adaptability, more that you have the kind of mind that will dive into all kinds of different things...'

'Hmm, closer. But I wouldn't say that's a key part of my personality...what else have you got.'

'Oh, there's plenty, you're a very complex type. Let's see...' She opened a book and began to skim read, calling out traits that hit me, hit the nail repeatedly on the head. 'Mind tends to overwork...but doesn't believe in hard work...hard to figure out...head in the clouds...glib...? Would you say 'glib'?'

'I'd like to think not, but...'

She hurried on, 'not keen on responsibility...' I laughed, she nodded agreement. 'Not great under pressure...clearly. Restless...nervous...academic...oh, but something of a dilettante?'

It was all too much, I put my face into my hands for a moment, Acantha paused.

'I feel completely exposed; I don't know what to say...'

'It's not, as I say, the law, maybe it's not all appropri...'

'But, dear God,' I threw my head up, 'it is, it is true, it's terrifyingly accurate.'

'But it wasn't that awful, was it.'

'No, no – it's like looking in a mirror, you're never completely happy but the familiarity is reassuring. Honestly...I'm just a bit in awe, that's all, it's been a long day.'

'Well, I hope it's made things clearer for you...for

the future.'

'Crystal.' I smiled and topped up our tea.

As with any moment of clarity, it was soon followed by an anti-climactic awkwardness – nothing more to add, and an urge for me to be elsewhere, to put this newfound understanding into practice, or at least to see how it related to my existence. The small talk that followed became prosaic, even the usually reliable offering of another cup of tea couldn't save us. It did, though, allow me to look at my watch, to discover time had moved swiftly forward, giving me a point to excuse myself. We said goodbye, with a hug and a promise on my part to return.

I sat on a bench midway along the terrace, the flat gravel expanse was deserted now, a few birds pecked satisfactorily at a chunk of hamburger bun, the tissuey wrapper caught on the light breeze that swirled from the balustrade, it tumbled little cartwheels towards the abyss of the hill. The county below was etiolated in the expanding twilight, tiny suns of gold perforated the gloom, windows and streetlights sequentially sparking as the shadows swelled. Knowing, believing what Acantha had told me about myself, I could only look deeper. Immediately, I could see the patterns and shapes that defined me, ruling my choices and functions.

I thought of poor old Paul, I owed it to him – I needed to finally start thinking, to actually use my brain. So, deeper I delved, closer I looked, needing to understand what my response had been, how then had I survived, if I could call it that, at least how had I got to where I was now. For as long as I had been divined to exist, surely, I must have equally devised a system to cope with this inconsistency, the whole imbalance of conflict and reasonableness. My first revelation was that I attempt to blank as many elements of my life as I can, oceans of repression; that I try to limit the number of potential extremes and to furthermore restrict wherever possible these potential dead ends from forming. It was all so apparent now, suddenly I was aware of times when I had deliberately forced out all thoughts of a particular subject to prevent me feeling anything, even to talk myself out of particular thoughts. But wasn't this normal? If one is dissatisfied with one's opinion or train of thought, is it not natural to pull up the carriages and chase away the thought? I knew that I did this, I felt that it wasn't so unusual, but equally, looking deeply into the clouds slowly blending the view into nothingness, my head no longer among them, I had to admit that I did it far too often. Surely it is better to live a life where thoughts, opinions, feelings are free to forge their own path?

A jet climbed up from Heathrow and made the turn steeply away from this sedate county and, as it did so, the tiny mechanisms of my mind, like a slot machine, whirred and clanked and aligned and I realised that I was doing it again, arguing with myself, incapable of distinguishing a solution to my quandary, the rights and wrongs held in equal regard. Another failure, another unsolvable indecision.

As the intensity of the revelation and my tiring thoughts shifted back to a more tranquil state, I quickly began to feel the cold. Abandoning the bench, I made the slow stroll home, flickers of questions remaining in my brain. The little side streets, the old village lanes of centuries past that broke up the swooping climbs of the last century, closed around me and the peace and warmth of other people's kitchens and salons took over in my mind. Like a mantra taking over, I had the sudden realisation that the reason why I felt these extremes, and the way I had dealt with their presence over the years was through the process of, I smiled at the pomposity of the only title I could attribute to the situation, a sort of natural selection. That is to say, I figured as best I could that I simply focus the extremes in my life and try to hold onto those streams of compulsion that are likely to be, at best, the most favourable and abideable. And at the other end, indulgently, a retention of those extremes that were the most satisfying – I shivered at the thought, realising that this included all of those phases of sumptuous melancholy; the wallowing in self-pity and, worse, the immature and regretful fixations on women and other toxins.

With these thoughts predominating, I needed help. Acantha had been sweet, but there was nothing more I could discover from her – her insight into my personality had triggered this new contemplation, my brain no longer swam with thighs and lips; there was, for the first time, something real to occupy my mind.

I called Sonny, she refused my invite to come to

Richmond – I shared the news about Joodie, and she was on the next tube down.

'I have a feeling...I hope, anyway, sincerely hope that you might agree with me on this, but I think it's probably best that this has happened.'

These were Sonny's first words after I had explained everything. She had sat patiently through my adventures in Covent Garden and with occasional grimaces, shakes of the head, and a few smothered laughs, she had followed the catastrophe in my kitchen.

'I mean,' she continued, 'it wasn't the best way to have gone about it...'

'It's not as if I planned it...'

'No, but still...It's not going to make for an easy break up, this way...if you'd sat down and...'

'We haven't broken up.' I wasn't sure why I'd said it. My mind had been chasing so many different ideas, I wasn't sure if I'd assumed this or not.

'Haven't you?' It was rhetorical, but I couldn't differentiate such subtleties.

'I actually don't know. Not officially. She just walked out.'

'You've broken up.' Sonny seemed convinced of this; she added, perhaps just to soften the blow, 'Well, if you haven't, you will.'

It didn't make me feel any better.

'Nothing's impossible.' I wasn't convincing, not my tone, nor my body language.

'Chris, she's not going to let this slide, is she? It's bad enough that you cheated on her, but with Frew Grensen...I mean, come on, the woman is out of this world...'

'Out of my league.'

'Absolutely – how do you think that makes Joodie feel?'

'True.'

'And also, she knows her. Ok, they're not exactly friends, but it's got to be worse than if it were some anonymous bint.'

'At least it wasn't her *best* friend.' It was nice to smile, to start to see the funny side, Sonny laughed and, awfully, suggested that "that's the spirit".

Well, it helped, but Sonny went back on with the reality of the situation, 'By all accounts, neither of you were happy, neither of you seemed particularly enthusiastic about your marriage before this – why would she, or you, suddenly want to fight to save it? You were one incident away from leaving her – this *is* that one incident. If she does decide to forgive you – which I'm sure she won't; I wouldn't, given everything – what motivation would you possibly have for staying? None.'

'I love her...don't I?'

'Do you? Really? I don't see it...Look, I've not known you that long, but in that time you've been ter*rif*ically honest with me, and because of that I feel confident in advising you that whatever you feel for Joodie, it is not love. Maybe you used to, and some echo of those old feelings remains. A pulse here and there where...kinda like a love *deja vu* – certain situations occur or a look or...some song, a film...it could be anything, but it is so similar to a state or situation that you experienced together, when you were actually in love, that your brain mistakes this new moment for the old one. You've spent the last month obsessing over Ophelie, drooling over Frew, curious about me and my lingerie...'

'What! No...'

'Don't deny it, you know you have.'

'Damn it...Go on.'

'...you've spent all this time wondering about new situations, with new women, and all the time whining about how,' she put on the voice, whiney, mocking me, *'Joodie doesn't satisfy me – Joodie doesn't care about me – Joodie's not interested in me – Joodie bores me.* Frankly, you're a spoilt little whiney bitch, Christopher, and if I wasn't such a nosey old bitch myself, if I weren't so curious to see how all this ends, I'd have sacked you off weeks ago. You don't love her; you don't want to be with her. This is good. It's what you needed, and quick and painless, too. It is meant to be.'

I sat dumb; a kid censured by the mysterious wisdom of an adult. And, of course, she was right – about everything.

'I guess,' I finally managed, 'you could say it was in the stars.'

'You could. If you were Russell bloody Grant. But you're not, you're just an unhappy guy who did something stupid, who might have just made the best mistake of his life.'

St. Christopher's Place

There we sat, paralysed under plastic lighting, sitting in the squared-off circle, tables manipulated from conference to committee. Someone was talking, a thin drone of managerial opinion, a woman that I didn't know. Her appearance distracted me from the page I was filling with doodles; she was a welcome break from the suited males that had preceded her. She wasn't especially attractive; it wasn't that that made me look, just that she was feminine. It made me feel happy.

I sat there, not listening to her voice, but looking at her, her wavy, light brown hair and the well done, but over-done make-up that made her look like one of the girls at John Lewis. I had no doubt that she was confident about her appearance, that she considered herself good looking – she had that completeness to her that unconfident women always lack – either over or under-compensating – many people probably agreed with her, but I didn't get it, she didn't do anything for me. But I liked that she was feminine. I missed femininity. As I followed the curving tops of her bra, I wondered if she knew that the tight black fabric of her top was slightly see-through.

I hadn't the faintest idea what she was talking about. I knew I wouldn't be called upon, challenged to give my opinion – any impact on my working life would be dropped on me, with little notice, through the cold silent medium of email. Right then, I knew – I knew I wouldn't be around to receive it.

I couldn't do it anymore. This job. It was nothing to me now. I had to leave.

Joodie and I had separated. It happened. The divorce was plodding away, and I had ceased to care; the fear of change, of isolation, no longer worried me. I wasn't upset, such things existed, I now understood, to raise the ordinary, safe periods of life into life worth living. Trying not to focus on the worst-case scenario of finding the same thing somewhere else, I believed that I was still young enough to secure something new, something that meant something to me. I had planned a trip, and now I knew it was the time to take it.

The trip, or at least the idea of it, was the motor that was keeping me moving. It was what Frew had said to me – I couldn't remember her exact words, but something about being a poet, in Big Sur. I considered it something I had to do, not because I agreed with her – I was no poet, I didn't see the man she saw in me – but because I needed a place, an idea – something to lead me. So, California beckoned. I flicked through Robinson Jeffers as I had flicked through biographies; I was never going to write poetry, but the freedom, the space and the peace of nature in Jeffers' words took me to the past, to this place I knew nothing of – but away, away from the now, and my job and my loveless life.

There we sat, and onwards her voice droned. Her femininity was no longer interesting to me – now I was focussed on the plan. My eyes fixed on the bleak white surface of my table; the sour energy of the irrelevant people around me enervated me – even my doodles seemed uninspiring. Deeper I sank into my own thoughts, a ramble of disconnected themes – the past, the future, places I had been, music known, family, friends, and out of nowhere, Ophelie.

So, you return! It had been a long time since I had wasted thoughts on her, after so much had been wasted before. Why now? Was there something about this woman in my meeting? Not really, maybe a little. It didn't matter – she was back with me and instantly I felt different; I could feel that pull in my stomach, locked in the beam the idea of her shot out.

Since Joodie had left, my inclinations towards Ophelie had briefly accelerated; a replacement for the lost nearness of marriage. The discovered social media library of images had, to the surprise of the few people I connected with, caused me to create an account of my own. To my own surprise, Ophelie had consented to connection, which, even more strangely, lead to Joodie herself reaching out a connection to me – I accepted, and rapidly regretted it, overwhelmed by pictures, posted, of all the many things she was already doing – without me. I couldn't help keeping her as a connection, sentimental perhaps, but it was good to see her face from time to time.

Besides, I had Ophelie. It wasn't the relationship I had dreamed of, yet somehow it seemed ideal – the reality of my obsession always being chiefly visual.

Inevitably, this kind of relationship had a rapid

half-life; the pictures of her soon became familiar – at first, I had returned daily, hoping for a new addition, but she was not prolific. Joodie, however, was as she had been as a conversationalist, endless very samey pictures of seemingly random people and places. After a period of enthusiasm, optimism, Ophelie also seemed to represent herself online in a similar fashion to real life – as much as she could thrill, often she was bland and inert. And, static in personality and in pictures, Online Ophelie lacked the qualities that had drawn me in – the poetry of her motion in real life, the warmth of her smile – all was absent. As my obsession had fallen away in the past, phases of disinterest and indifference, so too did this new phase – she ceased to interest me. And, again, female company in general became irrelevant to me – after so long desiring what I could not have – specifically – I began to reject what I could not have – universally.

Bilal had given me an old laptop, I didn't love it, but I became quickly quite fond of it. It brought to me new and interesting pictures of femininity – a new face every day, a new dream, infinite escapism, and soon I was having my cake and thoroughly enjoying eating it – safe from the inconvenience and effort of having to deal with the real thing.

This had become my mentality – the flash of brassiere through the opaque fabric of my colleague's dress became a mildly erotic photoshoot, the kind of gentle, old-fashioned erotica that, I had now discovered, no great surprise, satisfied me. This woman – I could imagine the subsequent images, her disrobing, the unfailing pleasure of striptease.

It wasn't really enough, but before I had access to these everyday women, often my inclination, the archetypal girls-next-door – before my computer, I had no outlet. Instead, I made the mistake of my dangerous fantasies of Ophelie or my devastating indiscretion with Frew. This new release, until I could triumph with...what? – a soul mate – for now this was my world, and it worked. I was ok; I had neither indifference nor obsession, just a satisfied schoolboy naughtiness.

With my sexual world thus placated, my domestic and vocational worlds rose to dominate my capacity for stress and concern. Never had I been so frustrated, so disenchanted; I no longer cared about logistics – logistics became the most tiresome and needless practice on earth. I realised I would have to leave my job and, today, sitting here, I knew when it would happen.

The faces around the table, garish under the strip lighting, all emitted the same understanding – an overwhelming disinterest – no one here cared, and nobody mattered to me.

Shuffling my papers together, a needless show of professionalism, I pushed back my chair and rose from my corner of the arranged tables.

Maybe one or more faces looked up, surprised by the unexpected movement; maybe no one noticed; I neither knew nor cared, I made no explanation, asked not for leave to be excused – just walked from the room, dropped my papers in a bin in the corridor and left the building.

Outside, inevitably, the impact of the gesture faded

with horrifying rapidity, the awkward moment of reality overwhelming emotion. Hopeless, I stood there, no idea what to do next – all rather ridiculous. Naturally enough, the first impact of rationalisation was to go back in – it wasn't too late, slope back in, retrieval of the abandoned paperwork and return to the meeting – *just been to the loo* – if anybody asked. But there was to be no return; it hadn't been a whim, this was something built up for months, probably even longer, years perhaps – no, the more I satisfied myself that this was done, and without regret, the more the normal functioning, logistical qualities of my brain regained their dominance, their control.

In the street, nothing leapt out at me as an obvious indicator of direction – no passing taxi, no public house – I looked around for inspiration, but remained in the dreary built-up greyness of deep West London.

Without a car, and in a tubeless pocket, my only method of escape from this increasingly ridiculous immobility was to jump on a bus. As an idea, it wasn't a bad one – drifting through unknown streets, a fine perspective above the haircuts and hats; regardless of where it went, it would be good. It was to travel that my heart pulled, this was a reasonable way to start.

Not caring where my final destination might be, I took sufficient care to assure that I was at the right stop for buses into town. I climbed aboard, bought a ticket, went upstairs, and took a seat on the driver's side, two-thirds of the way back.

It reminded me straight away of the time I had travelled to Soho, to the Frew Grensen exhibition –

Frew: wow, what a woman. Of course, she had been the trigger for the death of my marriage – I was, in more or less equal parts, both glad and annoyed by this – honestly, I knew it was the best thing that could have happened, but on the other hand I had come out looking like a shit; but then again, I had done a pretty shitty thing. Yes, Frew was the trigger, but the gun, I loaded myself – the weeks of lusting over Ophelie; I had felt guilty almost perpetually, and rightly so; although the way I had behaved was not something I recognised as the "the sort of thing I'd normally do" – but, it was something I had done! – it was not pleasant to recognise, but it was all my own work.

Gliding past the upper stories, those familiar relics of Victorian London – all those lives – it made the scale of my own living universe seem grossly insignificant, pathetically small. Pathetic that it meant so much to me, the time and energy spent analysing all these thoughts and emotions – nobody cared; I was just one more figure, in one more net-curtained existence, living and dying in one of thousands of places.

Gloomy, but contradictorily, it lifted me, lifted the burden of self-awareness. I didn't matter, nobody cared – I had been a shit, done a shitty thing and now...nobody cared. Suddenly, the worry of people thinking: Christopher Hoyer – what a twat! – suddenly this was no more. No one was wasting any time bothering about my mistakes and misdemeanours – no one but me.

Again, I drifted back to that night in Soho – Frew had liked me from the start; this cheered me – and Ahri, and Sonny, too – perhaps that was the world I should be moving in? That said, Burchmann, he was always popular in this set, and he is a complete arse – he's had more infidelities and shameful liaisons than anyone else I know – and he has a busy life, popular and social – perhaps I misunderstand the world, perhaps being an unfaithful shit is normal? Maybe women *do* like a bastard? Well, obviously not including Joodie.

I looked up from my introspection as we passed the Wellington Arch, the shaft of the Hilton, massive and modern, gliding upwards – my mind was a part of the wider universe again, bodies and cars all around, the noise of conversations on the seats behind me. I stopped the bus at Marble Arch and sent a text message, a request for Burchmann's company, the inevitable acceptance bounced back in a flash.

I stood in the little pedestrianised precinct, my namesake, St. Christopher's place – it always made me feel comfortable being here; it felt like an extension of me, a tendril holding me to the city.

Being "in between jobs", (I had learnt not to ask about his occupations) Burchmann arrived swiftly. It was good to see him; I needed a drink and I needed Burchmann. Yet, his first words, were not the reassuring words I had optimistically hoped for; at best they passed as a mildly backhanded compliment. I thanked him, with all due sarcasm, Burchmann smiled and, not going as far as withdrawing the comment, he actually paraphrased it, and delivered it again.

'But it's true – it was a dull job that made you not only sound dull but act dull.'

'Seriously?'

'Deadly serious. The moment you started there…I felt I lost you.'

'Rubbish. I hardly saw you before that, no more than I do now, at least.'

'It's not about frequency, it's about quality – the you that I met after you started there was a shadow.'

'Really?' My gloom was complete. I could trust, to a degree, Burchmann's opinion – on matters like this, he was fair and adroit.

'Yeah. That job, and Joodie…you lost your soul, brother.'

'When have I ever called you my "soul brother"?'

'No, man. *Your* soul…brother…bro…dude…'

'Oh right…God, my brain's a mess.'

My focus was a little off; the bitterness I was currently dealing with perked me a little, enough to force a snarl as I returned the additional suggestion that Joodie had contributed to my…what? – my soul destruction? I could accept that the job had sucked a bit of life out of me, it had, that's why I was here and not still stuck in that interminable meeting – but Joodie, she had lit up my life, surely she had only brought improvement to my soul?

Such anger that I mustered over these accusations, quickly faded and, apathetic, I could only add, 'Yeah, and now I have neither of them.'

'Thank fuck for that – I can see the blood returning already.'

I hadn't seen Burchmann since the incident, quite a while – it was January now – so I hadn't told him about Frew, it wasn't something I was going to tell him by text or phone, and I was generally reluctant to relive the experience that broke up my marriage, and his own wished for connection with Frew made it feel even more insensitive. Being accused of becoming dull made any such considerations immaterial, I had to show I had some sense of the wild in me.

He took it well, his interest in her had clearly faded – some other flame of womanhood had no doubt since scorched him. Was he impressed, well, yes, he was, and he began trying to motivate me with this – to him it was an achievement – he used the word "scalp", less, I think in the sense of Native Americans, more in the sense of an FA Cup giant killing.

'Such a result,' he suggested. 'Boast-worthy. To have got-off with such a woman – a celebrity...'

'She's hardly that.'

'No, it's close enough...A celebrity, no less. I'm proud of you, Hoyer. I mean it's a shame you didn't dip her, but...'

'Thanks,' I cut in quickly, not wanting to go down that route. 'I'm not exactly proud of myself.'

'Should be. Why not? She's...oh yes, she's...'

'It's kind of doubled edged, for me. As a man, my masculinity is somewhat buoyed by the experience...I mean, when I see her on TV or in a magazine, there's a little flash of...'

'Achievement?'

'Hmmm, yeah, I suppose. I was thinking more...an

accomplishment. Anyway, at the same time, it was the cause of my marriage failing.'

'I think it was already failing.'

'Ok. But it could have been saved. Frew was the nail in the coffin.'

'No. Not so. Hooking up with Frew wasn't an issue. Taking photos of yourself and letting your missus see them was the nail in the coffin.'

'I didn't bloody plan it, mate.'

'No, but you'll be more careful next time.'

'Next time, I...No. There won't be a next. The whole Frew thing – and let's face it, it wasn't quite the monumental affair it could have been – well, that wasn't me, that was her. I was the seduced, not the seducer – she just happened to take a liking to me and made a move.'

'And you moved back. You are capable of infidelity, Hoyer.'

'Yes, but the point is I wouldn't have done anything if she hadn't initiated it. That's not me, I don't...I couldn't initiate something like that. That's why it won't...I can't see it ever happening.'

'But it could,' Burchmann persisted, I began to feel he was just winding me up.

'I doubt it. It was Frew that made that happen, not me.'

'Lesser men would not have survived her,' Burchmann drifted from the debate, a weary look in his eyes as he imagined Frew; I hoped not with me. 'She's a lioness.'

I left him to indulge his daydream into the past of

his own obsessions, while I pondered just how big a part I played in my downfall.

'And...and this is important,' Burchmann snapped back to life, startling me. 'She wanted you – not every man, sadly, is interesting enough and attractive enough to trigger a woman like that.'

'I think she just liked my honesty,' I guessed, meekly.

'Yeah, I suppose that's what fucked up my chances...'

'Honesty has not been your friend over the years, man – not a tool you have quite mastered.'

A tepid melancholy sank over us, a chance to catch up on our drinks, to gaze around the pub, the other afternoon drinkers.

Burchmann re-emerged before me, an idea tickled him and he pursued it, keen to get the conversation running again.

'That other one, what happened to her, do you see her?'

'Which other one? What are we talking about?'

'The other woman – the name's gone – something foreign – Joodie's mate.'

'Ophelie.' I answered with neither hesitation nor enthusiasm.

'I feel you too, man...'

'No, Oh-phee-lee-ah, that was...'

'Yeah, I know – I was just being a dick. But her, Ophelie – you ever bump into her – I assume she took Joodie's side.'

'Surprisingly enough, I see almost nothing of

Joodie's friends – not unless it's accidental, around town or whatever. No. No, I haven't seen her since.'

'And you've stopped moping over her?'

'Well, yeah, pretty much – not moping, anyway. There's still a desire there – she was...is...pretty special. But nothing...*nothing* was ever going to happen with her.'

'So, all signs suggest you need to move forward. I think you'll be fine – just get yourself a less dreary job.'

It had been mid-afternoon when we started drinking, now the place was filling up with workers finished for the day. Now we were drinking with a little more seriousness and chatting with much less; the urgency of my gloom had diminished simply by sharing – within a few drinks it was gone. The conversation grew nostalgic, healthy nostalgia.

Around us the change in the atmosphere of the place went unnoticed, until that point where our voices became raised, and suddenly the heat and the fragrances were almost tangible, clearly the working day was done – I felt a little additional relief that I was no longer, technically, absent from work. I looked around, a crowd filled the bar area, tables were taken; the clink of glasses filled the room with the finest percussion.

A new excitement gripped me – the drink, the noise, the presence of, ah! – femininity, again – even Burchmann's broad smile as he struggled to accurately re-tell a well told anecdote, all of it made me buzz – it was new, or rather it was a long time since it had been present: a sense of possibility. Burchmann carried on as

I casually absorbed the faces and figures around me; inevitably, I risked spoiling it with my tiresome obsession with relationships – big or small, blonde or brunette, realistic or ridiculous – as always, that urge to possess. Why could it never be enough for me to simply admire, even to taste – always that belief that happiness came only through possession. And it wasn't "possession" in the sense of controlling – that genuinely wasn't my way, but to possess in the sense of "to be with", to establish connection, permanent exclusive connection. Each of these women around me, oblivious, perfectly lovely in their own individual way, each of them might be someone – why could I not be with her, or her, or her? It was a need, and the need overwhelmed any idea of want – and limited purely to desire, I rendered them all absolutely unavailable.

I had drifted out of range of Burchmann's conversation, so it was no great loss to either of us that it was terminated by a sudden interruption. Burchmann's face lit up and he began gesturing, directing movement, apparently between the door and our table; moments later we were joined by a guy and a woman. Fortunately, the pub was not so full that the extra chairs at our table had been claimed, and so a foursome was made.

Clearly the guy was known to Burchmann, much more so than the woman; immediately, they were locked down in deep conversation, leaving me and her to negotiate a brief silence, a clumsy introduction and the start of some acceptable small talk.

To sustain our newly formed social connection, I

played the shall-we-go-and-get-some-drinks card. It worked well, the change of pace, the movement, the activity returned us, brimming with familiarity and a tray of drinks sufficient to get us through the next social stage of "like old friends".

She was pretty enough, a little thin, long brown hair, nice features, nicely dressed, a nice smile when she tried it, and interesting without seeming to be specially knowledgeable, at least not on any of the subjects we brought up.

Gradually the conversation drifted back to a four-way exchange. The fact that she, Sasha, and he, Jeff, were cousins came to the surface. So far I had not been drawn into consideration of her as another potential "be with", marking her off as already taken; now the cogs and keys ticked and clicked, and out of nothing she was the subject of frustration – the inevitable question: why can't she be mine – how ideal she is – she could be mine.

I shook my head and consciously slowed down my rate of drinking.

'Fucking hell, Hoyer.'

'What?'

'Sasha was flirting with you...I mean *really* flirting. You're pretty bloody hopeless. Didn't you notice, or don't you care?'

I was not quite slurring or spinning, but I was far enough gone for such an observation to seem like a joke – I rewarded it with a laugh.

'Fuck off, Burchmann. Don't pull my leg.'

'You could have pulled *her*!'

'I don't "pull" women, Burchmann – I'm not a nern…nearn…ne-dethal.   And by the way…bullshit! She wasn't interested in me.'

'Course she was.   And all that fiddling with her phone…when they were getting ready to go…'

'Yeah?'

'Have you no clue?   Man!   Seriously?   That was the definitive ask-me-for-my-number move.   Textbook.'

'Oh.'

'Oh, indeed.   How the hell did you ever get Joodie and Frew into bed…'

'I didn't,' I dropped my voice to a still slightly too loud whisper.   'Joodie picked me up, and I didn't fuck Frew.'

'No?   Well, good.'

'Yeah.   You knew that.'

'Did I?'

'Yes, I told you that less than 6 hours ago.'

'Oh.'

'Oh, indeed,' I proudly, tipsily threw his own sarcasm back at him.

'Even so, do you not have a clue about these kinds of things?'

'I do not.   No, sir, I do not have the textbook.'

'Because I fucking love you, I will get her number for you and I will explain to her that you aren't an actual arse.   Beyond that…you're on your own.'

The idea of pursuing Sasha sat uncomfortably in my mind.   Burchmann had had a call from a group of friends, a crowd I didn't know, he made me an offer, his reluctance barely concealed, for me to tag along. As it was, I had no intention of going, I was borderline hammered, if I didn't get home now... So I walked away into the cold London night.

As I walked out of St. Christopher Place, I got a sense that maybe he was protecting me on my journey – as catastrophic as it seemed, I had to admit that I was better for it, that I felt like my life had turned. And it was to travel that I yearned, not to get straight back into a relationship, as much as I felt I needed to have someone.

I came out of Gee's Court, on to Oxford Street and hurried straight across and into Duke Street, suddenly surrounded by all that fabulous red brick; calming, looking up into the past, the architecture and real lives above the shop fronts. I walked loosely, free; the drink, lessening now, outdoors and active, and the night and the escape from my job all lifting me. I came out at Grosvenor Square and just froze. I had a sensation similar to when I walked through the gates of Richmond Park – space, it was as simple as that, but I loved it, and the same as those days when I looked out from Richmond Hill at the enormity of the Surrey landscape. The square was not, of course, on this scale, but coming from the inside of a pub, the high brick channel of Duke Street, suddenly there was space, the bare plane trees, their branches sprawling, open-armed, it was pure liberation. I slipped into the memorial gardens, an empty bench under the pergola and, such was my thing, I began to think of Sasha.

I remained uncomfortable with the notion of calling her, should Burchmann's promise lead me to her number. She was attractive, yes; interesting, yes; ideal – that remained to be discovered; yet, even after one meeting, she seemed, compared to Joodie or Ophelie or Frew to be an improvement in one specific way – as a balance to my own imperfections.

A new thought bit me. Rationalising this balance, the compatibility she offered, something nibbled and caught – was balance actually the function that was going to save me? Joodie had seemed that way, and it had ended up a disaster and, according to Burchmann, she had washed me out and destroyed me. Frew was the polar opposite, and that had been a joy. Ophelie? I couldn't even equate her, she was as if unreal, as though we'd never even existed.

It shocked me. I had, for so long, sustained this understanding that I was searching for someone to complete my half, a soul mate, as they say, and Sasha seemed to be such a person, we were very different but, I thought of Acantha and the astrology, Sasha was the balance I had always felt I lacked. But would she just be another Joodie, in a few years' time – was balance the solution, or did I need, as with everything else, an extreme. Like Frew. Had I learnt nothing from all those silly romantic comedies – always the jarring of personality, and the conflict, before the understanding and the conquering of incompatibilities.

No, I would not meet her – it was not a future I could be sure that I yearned for. It was the right decision.

With this decision made, I became restless and decided to walk on – aimless as far as the route was concerned but knowing my destination to be The Thames. I wound my way through St. James', breathless at the architecture and history, buoyed by feeling as though I had made a useful life decision. Northumberland Avenue delivered me at the Embankment and the river spread wonderfully beyond it.

From Richmond Hill it always felt like I could see the whole of Surrey, from Waterloo Bridge the same could be said of London – or at least it felt like the whole city was within reaching distance. I stared west and then east, looking at the city, alive, illuminated; thousands of windows awake and providing the starlight absent from the orange sky. Such an aspect! - It stirred life in me, softened the rigor mortis of my unloved soul. Adventure, it was so simple, everything that my life lacked, the reason that I had become such a dull unnecessary husband – a dearth of adventure. The affair with Frew – such a little thing in reality, yet in the scale of my life, monumental – so daring, so unexpected; I was even comfortable enough to admit that it was pathetic that this was my standard of recklessness – making out on a couch – it was the stuff of teenagers, but I felt like a playboy. Such was the comedy of my world. Even the obsession with Ophelie – yes, it had all been in my head – but how invigorating, how exciting it had been. Unacceptable, incorrect, taboo – such thrills.

I swallowed hard – this discovery that the greatest

thrill of the last year had been an unfulfilled schoolboy crush. Really? – this was the peak of my excitement? – a fantasy, a daydream. And a snog that didn't even get me to Frew's underwear. Surely, I was capable of more than this? Well, I had walked out of my job – again: risk, excitement – it had been wonderful; it was what I had needed to do.

I ticked my thoughts away and headed east, breathing in the night, the city; enthralled by the great curve of river, the fantastic structures alongside it, the groan and fizz of traffic, the chatter of young people – more alive than myself, still open to the thrill of untested life. It was wonderful – I wanted a part of it, so glad to be out. I felt the deep twist of alcohol, still there, pushing and pulling my emotions, but my mood was set, I was happy. I knew exactly where I had to go.

Union Square

Never in my life could I have ever laid claim to being creative. Frew had teased me with the idea of being a poet, and I admit that I fell in love with the idea of losing myself gazing into Pacific sunsets at Big Sur – this is the thing, to a mind devoid of creative sparks, it is easy to see everything as wondrous, even when, to many people, such things are considered clichéd and predictable.

On Burchmann's coffee table – I was crashed at his place, Onslow Road was someone else's reality now – I laid out my airline ticket – LHW-SFO – to me it was incredible, a complete thrill, to Burchmann and Sonny, who had the creative perspective I lacked, it was deeply ordinary. All night, the best response I got was, with groans, 'Well, you do look like you need a holiday.'

I didn't see it as a holiday, this was to be my Grand Tour, my voyage of discovery – Monterey, Carmel, Pebble Beach – there was magic and mystery, it was an escape route – away from London, from Richmond, from obsession and wishful thinking.

In the lobby at San Francisco airport, their dismissive words were long forgotten, all that had happened felt distant – it was a first breath of freedom, only sterilized and chilled. As obvious as it may have seemed to Burchmann and Sonny, as I stood there, surrounded by the thousands of other, possibly likeminded individuals, just another pale tourist here to see the sights, it seemed to me an inspirational decision, momentous. I breathed in the conditioned air, allowed the reality of where I was to phase through me; almost congratulatory I felt cool, smart for having taken myself away.

In keeping with this adventure, extending the cliché in the minds of Burchmann and Sonny, I had made no specific plans, my itinerary did not stretch beyond the next two evenings; in fact, so hung up had I become on spontaneity that I hadn't even done much research. And, I suppose, fate, too played a part in my decision making – I hadn't changed my belief on astrology and its capacity to predict the future, but I had spoken to Acantha, needing reassurance that this was the right destination, the best approach. All that she could read or understand of my situation suggested to her that it was. She didn't actually say it, but the implication, clichéd, I know, was that this idea of mine was, indeed, written in the stars.

So, I had no plan and knew little of the area I was heading for, hoping to have my breath taken; just the words of Frew ringing in my mind, and an old paperback edition of Robinson Jeffers. Burchmann and Sonny, had found this all very comedic, laughed at my expense, and it hurt – to me this was the epitome of romanticism, of poetic drama – admittedly, not areas I could claim to have the slightest expertise in – but to me it was my fantasy world made real.

The inspiration of Big Sur and the Pacific was close now, the memory of the claustrophobic dungeon of my old workplace seemed ever more distant. But dreams never seem more extreme than when reality hits home. The cab pulled away from the airport and the suburbs; the cold, bleak industry of the Bay Area were my travelling companions. This was no liberation – nothing but beige and grey, phases of greenness as the country returned, phases of blue as the bay appeared through the passenger seat window – exciting because it was new, and different; oppressive because it was just more reality, more endless life, the mundanity of work and life and just moving on. Right now, it was just London but without detail, without history.

The freeway curved, as it had routinely and tiresomely done since we picked it up; it curved again, the off-ramp to Vermont Street and, framed under an ugly footbridge, the city finally revealed itself – it was what I needed, what I wanted to see, and it hit me – this was what I had to see, the ocean and the cliffs were fine for poets, but these great skyscrapers, this mass of energy, this was what fired me. Yes, it had happened before that I could be unexpectedly turned on to wild nature – Richmond Park had absolutely won me over, the sprawl of Surrey countryside from Richmond Hill – no doubt the Pacific coast would similarly inspire something in me, something unimaginably great – but I knew from that second, in the same way I would come to life setting foot in the heart of London, I knew my heart was really an urban heart.

It was a city of spectacular lines and depth, the

unmistakable America of skyscrapers formed as a cluster downtown. As I went deeper, I felt the place deeper – the Bay Bridge, curling off into the distance to Oakland, the hills hiding unknown districts, the queer sci-fi spikes of Sutro Tower. The possibilities were endless, the scale of history, even in such a young town, were monstrous.

My plan, as vague as it was, was that this would be a stopover, my heart set on Frew's imagined poetical road trip south, and, as such, I had only booked for two nights, yet pushed the boat out and arranged to stay at the Marquis – it was sort of an expensive joke on my part – this great big eighties monolith – but it felt special in a way I had never treated myself to before.

Utterly without glamour, the taxi dropped me outside on 4th Street, an overcast day – I could easily have been in London, but the voices, something in the air was present, different to what I knew, what I had grown up with; it was enough to make me feel out of control, as though my next move would be something unique to my life – something untried and exciting. How on earth had I ended up here, in this spot, in this city that had never meant anything to me before today, other than as a movie set – unreal. What strange device had manipulated my life so that I was stood in front of this tower, the buzz of an unknown, increasingly mysterious culture, all around me? Accents flashed past, accents so familiar from television, but coming from actual human beings, real people, working, shopping – the tone familiar, now seemed crazy, impossible, totally different – everyone catching me out, expecting the voices to be predictably English.

If I had learnt anything from the failure of my marriage, the events that built up to it, Ophelie, that entire mess – it was that my life had been sheltered, that I was endlessly introspective, and that such behaviour had been utterly unproductive, standing in this big noisy city, everything unfamiliar, suddenly I had no conscience of my living self, suddenly the world dominated. Overwhelmed, I functioned slowly, the bustle of humanity raced and shoved past me. I had imagined, hoped that the isolation of nature might free me – but already I was liberated, set aside from the traumatic thoughts that had driven me here, nagging, pursuing.

Eventually I got it together enough to move from the flow of human traffic, through the glass doors into the queer cream stillness of the hotel lobby; the only sound a hum of small conversations, spare footsteps. The cool cling of the air-conditioning, even without it being hot outside, sterilised; it felt as though I were in a laboratory, yet at the same time – the stillness, the murmur – also as if I were in a library.

The hotel, my self-satirical plan, was not old; the entire city was a modern city by the standards I normally associated – the house on Onslow Road was older than most of this city – there was no historical daydream to hide in. Yes, I had taken a room at the Marquis as a joke, but now I realised that by doing so I was forcing myself to feel modern, forcing myself to live in the now. It was all oddly spiritual; perhaps I should have been staying on the Haight.

Behind the reception a man fussed with some unseen task, his attention occupied, but a sixth sense active, looking up, smiling the moment I approached. I was welcomed. As an Englishman, immediately I was uncomfortable – it seemed forced, over the top, ingratiating; but it was the warmest of welcomes. My mind hurried to rationalise it, and I thought of what Craig had said about "normal" Americans – away from Hollywood – I went back over my own experiences, so far: the courteousness and correctness of the immigration staff, the deferential manner of the cab driver – it was real, it was sincere, it was natural in a way that made most English seem uncouth and ignorant. I smiled, prepared to be "Sir-ed" and "nice-dayed" into submission.

Recalling Craig's words rekindled events on Onslow Road; 'Bloody, Craig,' I mumbled to myself in the lift, knowing that a train of thought, unwanted, had been released, my mind was now set and dominated by Ophelie.

It was exactly what I had hoped to avoid, and I had done so well up to now – the grand scheme behind this entire trip was to remove all the insecurities and hang-ups of recent times, to remove all focus and direction; to dismiss, once and for all time, the plague of women on my thoughts – Joodie and, of course, Ophelie.

And I had been doing well – they rarely occupied even the remotest spot in my mind, and when they did, it was brief and undemanding. It was only by random prompting that I returned to that online catalogue of her existence, her social media – an indulgence, a pleasant novelty that never budded into anything significant.

The fear, now, was the possibility that, despite the distance, physically and socially, between us, that thoughts returning could contain the poison of those old obsessions. Yes, we were so far removed, now; so free from the temptation to consider impossible eventualities between the two of us – but, suddenly, it felt as it had felt right back at the height of my obsession, some chemical charge, that I wanted her beyond anything else.

High up, standing in my hotel room, luggage unpacked, still in my jacket and trainers, I looked out, inert, into the city below. It spread before me, there for me to lose myself in, and I could not even move, the fear that it would never go away, I could only admit to myself how lovely Ophelie really was, how wonderful it would be if we were together. I imagined turning from the picture window and the city, turning to see her – on the bed with – it seemed so natural, yet so ordinary – with a magazine. Such a sweet, satisfying thought. I shifted it, uncontrollably, now she walked from the bathroom, wrapped in a towel, clean, still glistening, her hair turbaned under machine-white cotton; and I imagined making love to her on the ocean-sized bed, her long, stockinged legs constricting me.

Finally, released, believing somehow that the fantasy might be real, I turned, the bed was untouched, my suitcase, lonely by the door.

Dear God. I needed her, I cursed my misfortune – the corruption of the universe, the carelessness of the alignments of stars and planets – that it was not her that I was destined to be with. The city was huge, the land unimaginable; I had never felt so isolated.

She was with me as I walked up to the reception-recommended pizza restaurant in North Beach, she joined me as the unmanageably large pizza was suspended before me, and she remained as I walked out into the nighttime and night life, as I peered into windows, looking for a bar to escape to.

It couldn't have been further removed from my local, the Bucks Head, with its nautical fenestration – instead of being some dark wooden ancient tavern, it was a compact place that seemed to be the result of a collision between a butcher's and the set of the *Club Tropicana* video. It seemed an obvious and perfect choice as a "change of scene".

Naturally, I felt ridiculously out of place there, awkward in my collar and sports jacket, relived that I had chosen to wear a pair of Wranglers rather than my usual cords, and my old Adidas tennis shoes rather than my Loakes.

In this spirit of doing things differently, I opted to sit at the bar, rather than at a table; it felt natural – drinking alone – to sit at the bar. If I had learnt anything from American movies, anyone with troubles and no friends makes the bar stool their resting place. Where everybody knows your name? Not at all, but, with a beer and bourbon chaser (I couldn't help it), the unknown mysteries of a ball game playing out silently on a boxy old TV, male and female chatter behind me –

I certainly felt at ease, at home.

I sipped away; mercifully, my mind began to drift to Big Sur and what my plans might be.

But it couldn't last, this tranquillity. I began to feel the weariness of the day's travelling; the addition of the chaser catching me, vulnerable to the strong alcohol, and tiny waves of conscious sleep brought little dreamlike hallucinations to my thoughts. Frew Grensen. I imagined myself, an old Mustang, driving out to the coast. It was time to head back.

Alone in the city, alone in my thoughts, not just the returned neediness, periodic as it was, but the apparent futility of all things in my life – when a strange bar feels like home – it was annihilating. Sad cars, solitary passengers were the most regular signs of life passing by, it was hard not to feel sorry for myself – at least these motorists had a destination: journeying alone, but heading somewhere, and even if that was no more than a room, alone, still they were fixed – their homes and vehicles – they had something. I knew I was to return to London at some stage, but nothing awaited me – I had nowhere to live, no job, no wife – my friends, at best inconsistent and sketchy. Even if the stars had aligned and Ophelie was free and, I hardly ever considered the relevance of this, if she was actually attracted to me – would she really take on such a lost cause: a homeless, jobless loner.

But this place, I was in fucking San Francisco! I had to snap out of it, not allow the comfortable misery and self-pity to warm and enclose me – how could I not be inspired by this place, how could I not drive forward surrounded by this great city? – so big, so bright. I had to realise that I was insignificant, that my life was not the most important thing in the universe – I was not alone. I was no more important than anyone else – I should just move on.

I thought about another beer – no longer to simply drown my sorrows, but to be among people, to watch and listen to the lives of others – not self-absorbed with my own; no more imagined worlds of history, but actual life, to establish some kind of yardstick as to what was happening in reality. I liked the idea, but it seemed a better plan for another time, I was nothing if not honest with myself, and I knew that I was dead tired – the day had been long and more than anything in the world, that oceanic bed suddenly seemed like a heaven on Earth.

When I turned the street to see my hotel, its gaudy massiveness, my ironic choice, I couldn't help but smile, couldn't help but think of my grotto of an office back in London, the dark basement on Onslow road, and in no time at all I'd be standing at that window, looking out over... It seemed ridiculous, but it reaffirmed the idea that anything was possible. It was doable, each time I pulled myself back from the shadow, from the obsessions, it became easier.

I wasn't exactly skipping, but I did feel lighter on my feet; buoyed, it seemed, by a willingness to allow optimism – the will, at least, if not the actual belief. Active. All I needed was inspiration, some focus to push forward with my life, but the important thing was that I could be ready for it, that I was in a position to move on.

Once in a day was annoying, twice was not only unexpected but, of course, absolutely horrifying – and after I'd got myself into such a good, clear frame of mind. Craig. That bastard – why was he constantly returning to my thoughts and returning Ophelie back into them. The first time, recollecting what he had said about Americans, couldn't have been avoided – it just popped into my mind; this new visitation was absurd. I walked into the hotel lobby, fatigued, but inspired, I paused in front of a TV showing what was happening in the hotel, in the city, a novelty for hopeless tourists like me – and there he was! I was dead certain – groggy from transatlantic flight, too much pizza and the bourbon, certainly – but I was convinced Craig had just walked across the lobby and into the lifts.

After the first moments of bewilderment passed, I headed up to my room, holding back, avoiding any possibility of meeting this doppelganger, not wanting identification to be confirmed. As the lift climbed, I began playing the event down, dismissing him as no more than a lookey-likey – Craig was, after all, a very ordinary looking bloke – and I only caught this guy's profile, but...ah, it really did look like him.

I stood at the window in my room, looking out at the city lights, but thinking about him, and if it was him...was he here alone – as seemed to be the case – or was he here with her, with Ophelie? It seemed so unlikely, the two factors it depended on being so unlikely – for him to be here, it could happen, it would be an odd coincidence, but Ophelie? – Craig never took her on his trips, I knew that as well as anybody...

I went to bed, worn out from travel and thinking, dreaming of that woman.

San Francisco was here for me – I was unsure of venturing away. The plan had always been to live out some bizarre Robinson Jeffers return to nature in the wilds of Big Sur, but I was a city person, I knew it just looking out of my window, late the next morning. The ocean was only a cab ride away – or a cable car! Yes, my mind ticked as I dried myself, refreshed and ready to move forward, dismissing the nonsense of Craig; the warm feeling of Ophelie, with me, somehow, but not possessing, not dominating my thoughts but simply recollecting her goodness – without fantasy; thinking only about actual things we had done together, time spent in each other's company, real time. And I was thinking about cable cars.

It had been a while since my daydreams had not involved women, now, wonderfully, once again I wallowed in an imagined history, I thought of the cable cars, chugging mechanics, wood and metal, the hills and the past. I imagined myself as Leyland Stanford or Mark Hopkins, dominant in this fledgling metropolis, building a mansion the size of a city block, patronizing the good and great of California; driving to business as the cars rattled past, the cable car man doffing his cap to me. I wanted to go out and discover – I accepted that, regardless of whether I was in the city or the wilderness, I was here to find new inspiration. So I headed out, bought a muni pass and began a day saturated with culture. My mind flashed back to Tate Britain and I was soon filling my day with all the art that I could find. I smiled at people, talked to strangers, I even tried to overcome the awkwardness of calling people 'Sir' and 'Madam'.

The day was drawing to a close, I had spent most of the early evening around the corner from my hotel at the Museum of Modern Art, my brain trying to contend with the whims of the contemporary art world, one of the staff there suggested I also visit one of the smaller galleries nearby on Howard Street, that there was some really good local artist exhibiting there. Had it been further away, I doubt I would have bothered, but they were right there. Typically, the small amount of precious energy I used to walk across to it was wasted – it was closed. It was however open again from this weekend; the artist was Frew Grensen.

I walked back to the hotel, my mind thrilling. Right now, a familiar face, that wasn't bloody Craig, was exactly what I needed. Saturday could not come quickly enough.

'Fuck me!'

These were my first words, as the door of the hotel lift slid open. Ophelie said even less.

I had wanted a familiar face, I hadn't expected this

one – even if last night I had hoped for it, seeing her now, I was paralysed.

'Christopher? Oh, wow – what…?'

At least she recognised me; almost laughing, she was clearly finding my presence to be inexplicable.

I made way for her to step out of the lift but made no attempt to enter it; the doors closed, ignored.

Still we stood there, speechless; our facial expressions in the same realm of disbelief but wildly different the impact on each of us, me: wide-eyed, grinning, foolish, exhilarated; her: confused, now, awkward, embarrassed, yet intrigued.

'Christopher. Wow. It *is* you. What are you…what on *earth* are you doing here?'

'I'm a guest. I have a room here.'

'No, I mean what are you doing in America, in…'

'I'm on holiday. My life has been a little stressful just lately.'

She turned away; the reality of what had happened between Joodie and me coming back to her. She turned away and her jawline was magnificent, her long neck, stretching twisted, was fabulous. I couldn't cope. I waited for her to speak again.

'Sure,' she said, her eyes struggling to make contact – I couldn't work out her feelings, but it was clear that she no longer wanted to be with me at that moment. 'Well, how long are you here? We, Craig and I, are…'

'I don't know.' I answered quickly, saving her the awkwardness of committing her presence, unsure whether she wanted it to coincide with mine. 'I haven't decided where I'll go next…or when. But at least 'til

Saturday, I just booked extra days, there's a…there's a play I want to see.'

'Oh, exciting. We're here for the golf…' She seemed underwhelmed with this reality, and genuinely excited by mine. 'I think I have you to thank for that.'

It was hard to tell if I was being thanked or blamed, her voice was always rather flat, not dull, but calm and expressionless; I felt guilty, it hadn't been any of my business, I hadn't been able to shut up.

'Me? I…?'

'Don't you remember? You bashed poor old Craig about not taking me on any of his trips…here I am! Yay!'

Again, I was unsure if she was being sarcastic, it certainly seemed that way, but why should she be – wasn't this a great place to visit? As such, not wanting to be dragged into any of her issues with Craig – I had, at least, learned that much – I erred on the side of ambiguity and ignored the tone of her voice.

'Well, hey, San Francisco, what a place, you couldn't have ended up anywhere better.'

'Yes, it's nice.'

Nice? What was wrong with her; was there something she wasn't telling me, something amiss between her and Craig? It couldn't possibly be this city. Nice?

No other word in the English language can slam a conversation to a halt as efficiently as "nice". We stood for a moment; she no longer seemed to be in a hurry to leave, despite this perfect window to do so. I stood there, as calm as I could manage, a new train of thought that maybe her relationship was faltering surged through my mind.

Something had to give, I noticed she was dressed incredibly, 'You look amazing,' I braved, the bliss of finally being able to complement her, not afraid of the flirtatiousness always present under the surface of such admissions. 'You must be on your way out somewhere; I should let you go.'

'Oh,' she recalled, looking down at herself, surprised to find it to be true. 'Yes. Supper with some...I've really no idea,' she laughed lightly. 'Golf...businessy people; they're off to Pebble Beach tomorrow.'

She sounded sad, I didn't want to gamble on her ambiguity again – sad they were going, sad she was being left here, sad to be alone? – I could have offered her my company, but everything was such a blur – I still couldn't even be certain she liked me as a friend after what I'd done to Joodie.

'Oh, well, have a nice evening then, good night.'

'Good night. Christopher, listen,' I was turned, the lift already opening, 'I'm stuck here on my own from tomorrow, would you like to hang out tomorrow evening? You don't have plans, do you?'

'No, I don't,' I sadly agreed, but brightened immediately, her invitation finally sinking in. I pressed back the insistent lift doors.

'Ok, meet me down here...sixish?'

'Great.'

'Great.'

Again, I could not sleep.

*

So, this was it. This was what our life together would be like. All those fantastical imagined days and nights, and this was the reality.

We sat across from each other, a little bistro, candlelight, local wine – it could easily have been romantic, but it felt as though we were just two work colleagues, having a business dinner.

Inevitably, the entire day leading up to this point had been an uncontrollable, juvenile, wet dream of a day; I slept, eventually, late, had breakfast out of the hotel – avoiding at all costs any chance meeting with either Ophelie or Craig. I went to the shops, but bought nothing; I went to the cinema, an animated fantasy – I left early, unbearably uncomfortable being a lone man in a U-presentation. I went back to the hotel and took a bath. Throughout, I thought only of Ophelie – how she had looked last night, fantastic, dressed to impress Craig's colleagues; I thought of nothing but her and the opportunity, finally, to be alone with her, intimate, in a nice restaurant, a little wine to loosen our tongues and what might possibly happen...

It wasn't that we were not interesting people, it was simply that we never really found the courage to talk about anything more personal than her job, Craig's job, my role in pressing Craig to let her join him more often – 'I really do appreciate it, honestly, but it always feels more like an obligation on his part'. And I could tell her nothing – that I had quit my job, was deadly single and had a week at Burchmann's before I was out on the street.

Small talk. Not unexpected but so crushingly disappointing. What I considered the right direction of our conversation should be, honestly, was a mystery even to myself – that she might tell me how glad she was that I was no longer with Joodie?

So we sat and ate, and the wine, eventually, did its trick, and yet the conversation, more relaxed, never got any more personal, falling back, instead on going over old days together, even a little about her and Joodie, when they had been young – not a joy for me, I went to the toilet to be able to start a new conversation on my return.

It was not bad, but equally it was, of course, miles from that green grass I had dreamt about. It was nice.

Walking out into the mild evening, I considered what I had just experienced: that it had been such an anti-climax, that it wasn't really that different to what I had had with Joodie. Joodie had made me laugh; there had not been much to laugh about over the dinner table with Ophelie. Joodie, at least in the past, had always made me laugh – but that was it, all the stuff that had been great about Joodie and me was the stuff that had gone before. By the end, not even by the end, quite some time before the end...well, the difference here was that I was out, enjoying an evening out with Ophelie, that never happened, that was a pleasure I had lost with Joodie.

Comfortable with the wine warm inside of us, we walked across the city, back to the hotel; I was no longer expecting any magic, I just walked, happily beside her, silent and thoughtful. Ophelie, suddenly proving all that I had hoped for about her, proving that there was so much going on under her rippleless exterior – suddenly came alive, inspired – a romantic creative soul. She talked of the buildings and the streets, of history and the past; she talked of the world and the stars and the universe and destiny. And as she talked her face opened: eyes wider, those lips, those teeth that had so moved me, now were hung with wildly romantic ideas. She had never been more beautiful.

After the meal I had been convinced that every wonderful quality I had attributed to her was rubbish and miles from reality, but now, hearing her talk this way, it was apparent that we were, after all, so alike. For the first time – all other occasions a deceit – for the first time I was in love with her.

'It's amazing, isn't it?' We had crossed to the centre island of Union Square and she just stood there, in awe of the construction surrounding her; me – I was in awe of her. 'I mean, we do have stuff like this in London, but this is so different, so...'

'American?'

'Actually, yes – there's a difference. Ah, it makes me giddy looking up, this building is wonderful...what is it?'

I followed her line of sight upwards, and then down, to the awnings, 'The Saint Francis. We should have stayed there.' My mind rushed to the suite we would have, overlooking the square – me and Ophelie.

'It's good to be out.' She turned back to the square,

either not impressed or not interested by my suggestion. 'To be away,' she continued, 'somewhere new, somewhere special.'

Her words resonated with me, and I couldn't help but include myself in the wonder she was feeling – not that I believed she considered me in any way special, but that, by being there, I contributed to her good feeling. Naturally, such was my mind and my heart, watching her, those beautiful lips poured apart, the line of those teeth, the way she turned so lightly on the spot, her neck and jaw stretched, like a figure on a music box – being there, being beside her, it was as though every longing, every lustful wish I had asked of the universe, everything I had felt, hit me and I began to confess.

'Ophelie?'

'Yes,' she said, her slow pirouette not pausing, her eyes still brightly consuming her surroundings – the wine and the evening inspiring us both so wonderfully, so differently.

'I have to tell you something.' She didn't acknowledge me, I paused, nothing, I continued, 'When Joodie and I broke up...'

'She left you.' It was harsh, true, but harsh, judgemental – at least, though, she was listening.

'Yes, that's true. Well, the reason for that was Frew.'

'Well...not just her, you as well.' She turned to face me now, something twitched in her lips – a smile? – she was teasing me, it seemed, pushing me a little. But I had started now, the hard part done, I was going to tell her.

'Ok, what happened between Frew and me...not much happened between Frew and me. I mean, not much, but it was enough, but the thing is, what *you* need to know...' any trace of that unexpected teasing smile had gone, wiped out by the focus falling in her direction. 'The thing is, all the time, even before I met Frew, I wanted me and Joodie to break up, deep down...maybe not even that deep, by that point, I knew it had to end...you saw us, you knew her, we weren't a good match...and, besides...I was in love with someone else...'

Ophelie nodded gently, swung her shoulders, awkward, looking for, but finding nothing to look at to avoid looking at me. She was blank, her face in that stasis where little of it appealed – but, Ophelie, now, it was more than just about her looks – I wanted this woman more than any other woman on earth.

'You were in *love* with Frew? You wanted to ruin your marriage for her? I think that she was, despite your little affair, out of your league.'

Harsh again. True again. But... 'No, it wasn't an affair, it was just a kiss. And, no, I wasn't in love with Frew and...and our marriage was a dud; anyway, none of what I'm talking about, or Frew, *ruined* my marriage, it was already gone. Besides...no, the person I was in love with...*am* in love with...is you.'

It hardly seemed real, saying these words to her; it seemed like the most terrifying confession that a man could make: "it is you that I love". And then there was that moment, that frozen space and time, with no response, nothing, just an expressionless face staring back.

How I had got to this point still seemed unfathomable, but my heart, my emotions had been through so much, my world had changed beyond recognition; it was as though I had passed through a chrysalis state and emerged into a new world as a different person. And now I was just standing still, my hand played, the universe humming, waiting, my heart breaking. Nothing could be done now, whatever we had been before, we were now to be something utterly changed.

She just stood there, a blank look on her lovely blank face. My heart raced, waiting for the response, waiting for the smile to break – hoping for the smile to break! - the understanding, the loveliness returned and the reply, positive, wanted, needed.

'Seriously?'

It could not have hurt any more. It wasn't sarcastic, just bewildered, as if the idea was beyond belief, or at least beyond expectation.

'What!' I exploded, not angry but passionate, insulted. 'Of course I'm serious, how could I not be? I've dreamt for months of a moment like this, the two of us, alone, me saying those words; it's all I've wanted. And, no, I don't expect you to leave...um...leave Craig, no, but you should, he's a tool – but I don't expect it, I just needed...this is something that has been building up in me for...argh, so long – I had to tell you. And tonight, God, look at you...amazing. Tonight, I finally did it. It's why I could no longer be with Joodie, for God's sake – how could I possibly go on seeing you all the time, wanting you...'

Finally, her blankness cracked, she had just stood there letting me rant, giving nothing away, now she released – a slight grimace; disgust.

I was burnt out, I knew I'd just be repeating myself if I carried on, and that look told me all I needed, I knew it was a waste of time...even just explaining.

'For months? Really? That's a bit...'

'Yes. Since October.' I was like a schoolboy in front of a teacher – done wrong and made to feel pathetic about it.

'Oh. Oh, Chris. This is all just too weird. I mean...that you think about me...like that. It's all a bit off. Don't you understand that?'

'It's not something I chose to happen.'

'No, but you let it happen. Think about how that makes me feel...'

'That's all I ever do...think about you, about what you might be thinking, feeling. Not every minute...I mean, I'm not insane, not so much now, anyway. Christ, I didn't see it coming, and I *did* do everything I could to stop it...it is so hard to know that nothing would have happened, that it wouldn't ever have worked out, but...you are *so* beautiful, and...'

'Thank you,' she blushed, maybe, but didn't seem to know what else to say, the shock, the discomfort still overwhelming.

'I *never* wanted it to get so bad...and now it really isn't. In fact, if I hadn't seen you here...'

'How bad was it?' She said it as though I were her physician and the results were in; turning her head, only bearing to peep from the corners of her eyes.

'A bit obsessed, really.'

'Oh.'

She turned and began walking towards Market Street, back to the hotel. I walked almost alongside her. After a minute I apologised again, pathetic, a little boy, 'Sorry.'

'It's not fair,' she said; we were walking slowly, her eyes locked ahead. 'You can't think of your friends like that...it's kinda disgusting.'

'Do you think I don't feel ashamed? We're not talking about something I *decided* – just like that – to feel. Attraction is not something people have control over, it's just there one day. This is just how things happened to me, one day I looked at you and you were the most beautiful thing I'd ever seen. Not just good looking, but everything about you: your character, your smile, the way you sat, the way you talked, it was all...' Words failed me.

'It's very flattering, all of those things, don't get me wrong, I appreciate it – it's not every day I feel so complemented...it's just...that you've been thinking these things – for so long; that you imagine me, us...it's not the best thing to discover.'

'Fair enough, I get that, I really do. Perhaps, I shouldn't have said anything...though it wouldn't have changed the facts – I'd still have...'

'I get it. Don't need to finish that thought.'

'Look, I'm sorry, I didn't have to share this with you...I did actually...have to share it...but for me, for my sake, to end it all. I won't have to second guess your feelings anymore; I can move on…that was all I needed. And you'll probably never see me again, so you won't have to worry about it much longer, you'll soon forget it…'

'Less than you think – I've always liked you, Christopher, just not…'

'I know. Let's change the subject.'

We turned into 4th Street, the hotel illuminated and calling us to safety, just a few more feet away. We said nothing more until she left the lift with a thin embarrassed, 'Good night.'

Confusion and inconsistent thoughts had ruled my life since my discovery of an attraction, an unexpected attraction; now I was released – no longer would I play a game with my heart, no longer the fantastic unattainable pursuit of an idea. And yet, in place of those furious emotional shifts from obsession to apathy, I was still left with a sensation that was both high and low. Mellowness ruled. I woke up the next morning, opened my curtains to a new world, a world free of questioning, of "what ifs" – the idea of anything happening between me and Ophelie had died, and with it went any remaining romantic ideas – take away that open-ended potential and there was nothing left, as though the bulk of my attraction had simply been the mystery of what *might* have happened. Knowing for certain that there was nothing, suddenly Ophelie was once again just another woman.

Over the next days, the other side rose up, shy and demanding – a gloom, feeling sorry for myself. For all my faults, I was not so much a kid with a broken toy, or whose ball had rolled down into a sewer, not that kind of self-pity, it was sentimentality, melancholy reflection on no longer having that passion. Good or bad as it might have been, or seemed at the time to have been – how much of this, so much, I now knew was unreal, make believe – but, no matter how I had felt, I had truly felt something intense, unforgettable...and now I had nothing.

I couldn't even feel anger, there was no one to blame for what had happened or how things had turned out, not even myself – as self-inflicted as my angst and moods had been, the motivation, the cause, had been involuntary – as I had argued to Ophelie: this attraction was thrust upon me, I didn't choose to fall for her, it just happened.

San Francisco was now a brilliant distraction. I went to the Pacific, to the parks, to the cable car museum, I breathed in the city, the life; I let my imagination run wild – not for Ophelie, but for me, for the history I love to create. I ate well, I even shopped – all of this while making every effort not to run into her.

And she didn't come to mind at all, at least only as I reflected on the events of that evening in Union Square. To be honest, the whole evening was fantastic – thinking back – just to have that one "date" with her – girlfriend for the day? – to walk those streets, to see her brighter than I had ever known her to be was fully satisfying. Inside, only one thing lacked, one detail missing that still maddened me – I still had not discovered, and knew that I never would discover, how her lips felt.

To be able to move on, though, was the best I could possibly have hoped for from the situation – to be able to do so brought about an ease that I had not felt in months. That was a reward I had hardly deserved, but at least now I could try to right the wrongs I had done, to refocus my life and find direction.

Frew Grensen. I walked along the Embarcadero thinking about meeting her again this weekend, thinking about the brief liaison between us, thinking of how she had generally been interested in me. It had been a rush, that night – I pictured the studio, the roof tops of Covent Garden, her tall wonderful body, her incredible charisma – I was dying to meet her, imagining how surprised and pleased she would be to see me – and now I was single, now I could allow her flirtation, I could be tactile and drink wine and the glamour of the evening, the City – it would be wonderful. I couldn't wait.

It wasn't long now, I filled every moment imagining our reacquaintance – the look on her face as I stood before her, how charmed she would be, introducing me to her Californian friends, inviting me to the after party – my thoughts ran riot.

I lay in the bath, lathered with dirty thoughts, reliving the kiss we shared – only now, now I could move forward, now I could undress her without guilt, her full grand body, that tumble of wild hair. It was all fantasy, but for the first time in months my body accepted my erotic thoughts; it was bliss, I was as wild as a teenage boy with a copy of *Escort*.

From outside the gallery, looking in from a distance, I knew immediately that this experience would be far removed from the exhibition in London – gone was the reassuring warmth of old wood and low ceilings, gone was the impetuous blundering of Burchmann, leading the way – I was alone. The interior was like some kind of science fiction autopsy room: the walls, brilliantly white, the lighting strong enough to flood right across the street, to where I stood uncertainly waiting. And it was packed; the noise, like the light, flooded the street, the ricochet of laughter and wine glasses. Typically, I immediately felt horribly, awkwardly British; juvenile insecurities and a crippling inferiority complex rose up and the likely option, now, was to go back to the hotel, to think better of it – a nightmare avoided. But I needed to be strong, and I had to see Frew, had to see that woman – as much to impress her with my presence, as to marvel at her. I couldn't walk away, I couldn't accept that future – I forced up memories of the night on the Strand when she became my "girlfriend" – she digged me, she always had; something about me had appealed to her from the very first moment. I stood at the window, terrified, exhilarated, and I saw her, saw that massive plume of hair. I went in.

'Well, oh my – if it isn't my most favourite, majestic, little bitch!'

I was hardly five metres from the door when I was accosted by Ahri, just as large, just as sweaty and just as flamboyant as I recalled.

'It is you, isn't it? All the way from...Lonnnndon! Of course it is...Christopher!...I'd never forget my own little Isherwood.'

I had no idea what he was talking about and, given the five minutes or so that we had spent in each other's company, I struggled to understand how he felt so possessively towards me, 'Hi, hmm...yeah, it's me. You're the guy from when Frew was in Soho. Who'd have thought it?'

'Well, sure it's me – Ahri! Saaaay, I know what *I'm* doing here, what, for goodness sake, the hell are you doing here?'

'I'm on vacation. Just a coince...'

'Vacation! Ah what I'd give for a week in the sun and my peach mojito...Oh my God! There he *is*!' And he just went, rushing back to the entrance, throwing himself at a bewildered, beautiful young Cuban guy.

It threw me and eased me, seeing Ahri. Safety in the knowledge that this wasn't really any different to meeting Frew at BulletPoint. I focussed on the art – it was all still a bit rubbish, but there remained something honest about it; something wild. I stared at one piece until the glare from the white walls made it difficult to focus; I needed a drink, I needed to find Frew.

Such is the magic of the Universe that I found her at the bar, immediately recognisable from the back, the hair and – there it was again – that phenomenal backside; it was all I could do to keep my shit together

– nervous, excited, horny. I prayed that I would get to her before I bottled it, before someone joined her or she left.

I was right on her shoulder when she turned around, her drink landing plumb in the centre of my chest – I reassured myself that this was the reason why it took her so long to recognise me; my relief complete when, having realised who I was, she gathered me up like a soft toy and crushed me to her breast.

'One moment.' She released me and turned back to the drinks table, 'You'll have something too, right?' She called over her shoulder, practical and domestic, no trace of amazement remained. It had been great, the hug, but it seemed like it should have meant more, that she should have been bewildered and impressed by my appearance there. I tried to shift my thoughts: to appreciate what I had, rather then what I thought was important and necessary. She passed me a glass of wine and smiled questioningly.

'So, you're a little out of your comfort zone, are you following me?'

I held my response, knowing that I was offended. That stalking her was the kind of thing I actually might do, didn't occur to me, but that she should think it, suggest it...I was hurt.

'No,' I said, trying to sound as though the idea of such a thing was absurd and confusing. I felt, though, that my tone was more likely to come across defensive; a small contraction of her smile suggested this was the case. I forged on, 'Actually, I had no idea you were exhibiting, but, I suppose, I am following you...in a sense, that is...following your advice.'

'And what was that?'

Any hope I had that my presence would be sensational had now vanished, we could just as easily have been in Covent Garden as California. I let go of that wish, my preoccupation of the last few days, as if it had never occurred; instead I looked at her, trying to relive kissing her, trying to believe that such a thing could have happened – as Ophelie had said, Frew was out of my league. And I was about to ask her to come to Big Sur with me, to guide me through my transformation, that she had inspired, into some kind of modern-day Robinson Jeffers. What a dick.

With zero conviction, I explained: 'You told me I should go to Big Sur...and write poetry like...'

'Robinson Jeffers! Right, yes, I did! And here you are, bravo!'

Oh God, it was so patronizing, and to think I had envisioned a new and wonderful sexual encounter with this woman, imagined her and me, naked in some cool San Francisco loft apartment – morning coffee, Chet Baker, her curves, her hair – such ludicrous fantasy – I had no hope. Even our fling – nothing – it was nothing and probably meant nothing to her.

I really wanted to leave, but I knew that I had to hang around for a bit, I couldn't just wander off, putting thoughts into her head – that she would think me weird: so far from home and disappearing after ten minutes, as though I had just popped in to let her know, and then dashing off to start my road trip to the coast – I was lost for words and hoped she'd take it as an excuse to move on.

'So, I'm dying to know...' Was she? I was confused, did she really enjoy my company after all, see me as a peer, equal, with interesting news for her consumption? 'Whatever happened with you and...'

'Joodie? Ophelie?'

'Um, Ophelie first – did you ever tell her?'

'Last night actually.'

'What? Last night? Here? She's here in San Francisco?'

'Yeah. And...*quelle surprise*, she ain't interested in me.'

Frew looked absolutely unsurprised by this revelation. 'Ah, shit...too bad. And Joodie?'

Was that it? I was dying to talk to someone about it and...whoosh, on to the next thing; clearly, she was more concerned about me and Joodie, I suppose because of her role in everything.

'Joodie?'

'Right, Joodie. You know,' she softened, leaning into me, I couldn't say if it was seductive or maternal, 'I am mortified about what happened...still. You have no idea, I felt awful when I found out, awful. But you know that, you *do* know that? It was just one of...'

'Big coincidence. Right. Anyway, don't worry yourself about it – actually, you did me a favour, I was desperate to break up with her, I just never had the balls to do it. I'd still be with her, and unhappy, if you hadn't...'

'Intervened. Oh, good, that's such a relief. So, you left her, good for you.' It felt less patronizing, maybe it was just her tone, her manner, I'd never noticed it before, but she did seem to talk down to me, a pet, a project, a child.

'Actually,' I should have lied, let her think that this was what had happened, but I was corrupted by her tone, I felt like the naïve chap she cast me as; maybe I was enjoying the sympathy, 'Actually, she left me.'

'Really? For that one little kiss. Oh come *on*. That's absurd. People do worse that that all the time – *she* did worse than…'

Frew caught herself, the look on her face implying, "Oops, I've done it again".

'*She* did? What do you know…?'

'Oh, Chris; only rumours. Forget it, she's in the past.'

'No. No way. Fuck that, if I'm going to be the villain for…' I softened my voice again, 'for "one little kiss". And she's been…I have to know.'

'It's only what I heard. I really don't know her, we never actually met, but…'

'But?'

'Oh, Chris…I'm just a nosey old gossip; I asked about her…*apparently* she had a thing with some guy…'

'Some guy who?'

'Oh Chris,' she looked around, her guests remained indifferent, chatting, drowning us out, looking at the paintings. 'I don't…'

'Try! This is crucial for me.' Though I had no idea why it should be – putting myself through this seemed a bizarre way to get revenge, or satisfaction, or closure. 'Who?'

She looked at me a little dubious, looked to the ceiling for the lost name.

'Maybe…Callum?'

'Don't know any Callum's'

'I think it was a C?'

'Please tell me it was Craig!' My mouth watered at the possibility.

'No, definitely not, it was more unusual. Er…Sebastian?'

'That's not even remotely similar! How do you get from Callum to Sebastian?'

'I don't remember! C, c, c, c…It was just some guy's name: Caspian, Kane…'

'Cameron!?'

'Yes. Spot on: Cameron.'

'That guy? You're fucking kidding me. The guy with the crap relationship?'

'Hardly sounds like he's happily married, Chris.'

'Christ. That's the biggest kick in the nuts yet.'

'It's just gossip, Chris. Don't take it to heart, it's probably not even true, just some office party canoodle.'

'Canoodle! Seriously, I don't need to be thinking of canoodling, right now.'

'Oh, stop being a baby. You did your own…canoodling, anyway.'

'Yeah,' I sulked. 'But still…I was *going* to try to keep things civil – you know, mutual friends and all that…'

'Like Ophelie?'

'Ha ha. You know what I mean. What a cow, what a deceitful, hypocritical cow.'

'Let it go, Christopher.'

'It's just...so...'

'Let. It. Go. She's just not worth it, honey.'

Now her tone was delicious, I drank it in. She must have sensed it, she pulled me into a hug and I just sank in, lost against her fabulous bust.

I didn't stay too long after that. Frew finally had to excuse herself; she could hardly have stood there all night, at her own exhibition, petting a grown man. Anyway, it was suddenly awkward between us – her guilt, my mood. She promised to catch up with me in England, when she was back and quoted some Jeffers that was hopelessly wasted on me and wished me good luck on my adventure. I sank two more glasses and went to find a bar.

Transatlantic from California to London is actually far too much time to spend alone, thinking, with a head full of bullshit. Ideas pushed and pulled; ideas back and forth – I had taken this trip to discover a new perspective and to clear the scum from the waters of my mind, and ended up discovering nothing other than, as I had always suspected, that all this time had been an utter waste. I'd learnt, basically, that I was a dick. I had burnt so much energy on an imagined love affair with a beautiful woman, who might as well have been a photo in a celebrity magazine; and in doing so I had foolishly destroyed a marriage to a beautiful, funny, intelligent woman. So much energy – the burn of obsession, of fantasy and lust, and here I was alone, gazing into the twilight and the dawn as the plane carried me back...to nothing.

Discovering the reality that Ophelie had zero interest in me should have helped, should have cleared up everything – and in a sense...well, it took away certain problems, it took away the hope, but it didn't leave me free. Months ago, out of nowhere I discovered that I was unapologetically attracted to her; knowing that she did not reciprocate this was not going to instantaneously switch things back to how they had been before – attraction can come out of nothing and nowhere, but it does not fade so easily. Knowing that I would never be with the focus of my attraction didn't dim that attraction, of course not – and for over half a day, airborne, I was forced into a kind of solitary confinement where the recent memories of Ophelie filled my mind's eye – worse perhaps now than ever. So close had we stood, so isolated, and so alive on the streets of San Francisco, she had spoken to me and her perfect mouth was right there, active, alive, calling to me, singing to me, so kissable, so... And this was how my thoughts rolled, over the eastern seaboard, over Greenland, over and over.

And to compound matters, interspersed with the heartbreak and finality of rejection, and the explosion of desire, my thoughts were polluted with anger, hatred of Joodie – what Frew had told me; that all along she had not even been faithful to me. Yes, two wrongs etc...but...if anything, the root of my anger was that I had never got the chance to be as mad with her as she had been with me. It is childish, yes, but at times like this any victory, however small, however hollow, is a fine thing – I wanted my chance to fume, to accuse, to walk out, to ask her to go.

For so long, what I had done had plagued me with guilt, guilt on top of the guilt I felt for my lascivious thoughts about Ophelie – just a whole lot of guilt, and all that time she had got away with it. I failed to imagine her sitting there, worrying about what she had done, contemplating confession, throwing herself at me for forgiveness – let alone that she'd feel bad for her hypocrisy – and yet she had no problem destroying me.

And then it hit me – had she been just the same as me – desperate to get away from "us", looking for a chance to break up? Had I inadvertently made her escape possible, even allowing her to leave in a superior position, free to wallow in the sympathy of her friends? I was absolutely certain of it.

Too much time to be trapped in these thoughts – they were bad thoughts, they did me no favours, did not help me in any way – really, I just wanted to get home; I wanted to get a new job, to be busy. My head cleared on the ground, surrounded by the familiarity of the Piccadilly Line, English faces. Watching real life, I knew that I needed to put my mind to better use – my last job had destroyed me, years of sitting around, overthinking, stewing and rotting. What was it I used to say to Bilal, something about logistics – it was probably a load of old bollocks – I thought I knew everything about everything, and in fact I knew nothing about anything! Everything seemed so straightforward back then, living in a bubble – I didn't want to return to that life, but I wanted, I needed to return to a life where my energy, my thoughts, my over-thinking could be put to some good use, to sort out other people's mess – creating order from practical chaos.

Burchmann, mercifully was out when I got back to his flat. As grateful as I was to be put up by him, his flat was awful. He had nothing, nothing nice anyway, a few tatty old CDs and a few even tattier books, with tea mug stains on absolutely every one of them. And it smelt a bit funny, unclean, it wasn't that he was a scum bag – the bathroom was dirty but, inexplicably, he spent hours in there, taking long baths and fixing his hair, refining his look – countless times I had said to him, when you bring women back here, none of them are ever going to want to come back again, women don't like men who are filthy – his reply was always the same, that his plan was to make them want to look after him. It was a terrible plan; so far, he had had no takers. I didn't want to end up like this, unable to break free from bachelorhood; I wasn't the same as Burchmann but I knew now that, like him, I really didn't understand women, I didn't know how to treat them, or even how to think about them.

I stood in the mess and thought about Paul, about how much he respected Acantha, and how much she respected him – were we, my generation, and the generations following mine, were we now incapable of having those sorts of relationships? Paul had been more of a man than anyone I knew – none of us were cut the way he was; but then how few women nowadays were like Acantha, none of the ones I knew at least – I was so lost in the past and in fantasy, I no longer knew what the modern world was, neither did Burchmann. Did any of us know now how to treat women, what women needed, what they expected? I am not a misogynist, but still I had only thought about Ophelie as a partner, not objectifying, but somehow nullifying her individuality – I could only think about her, and Joodie, too, in terms of my relationship with them, how they affected my life, my world, my behaviour – I knew nothing. I wanted to be with someone, so bad, and not just for me, but to share, to give and be part of something, but I felt I wasn't responsible enough. I felt the need to...not quite punish myself, but to purge certain qualities of my personality, certain ways I had of thinking; I needed to change my attitude. I needed to grow up.

'What? Are you fucking kidding me?

I needed some external perspective – real perspective, not bullshit Californian perspective – I dragged Burchmann and Sonny out to the pub. It was Burchmann's reaction that had turned the angry complaining eyes of the other punters; I'd told him about Joodie, about what Frew had told me, I even included her disclaimer that she considered it just gossip, and I think I would have been inclined to agree with her, had the rumour not concerned that shit...what's his name. Burchmann was even more annoyed than I had been – for all his faults, he was a straight-up guy, mostly fair and mostly honest – and clearly he disapproved of Joodie's deception and hypocrisy.

'I mean, what a fucking nerve. You remember all the shit she gave you?'

'Yes, the memory has lingered.'

'All that shit she gave you over one little kiss...'

'Does everyone,' I sulked, 'does everyone have to keep referring to it like that, like "one little kiss"?'

'Well, it wasn't anything more than that,' Sonny contributed.

'It wasn't *that* little, and there was also some...fondling.'

'Fucking bitch.' Burchmann was determined not to let my complaint interfere with his dissatisfaction. 'You've got to go see her – give her some *shit* over this.'

'The thought has crossed my mind, but I'm inclined to just forget about it, I have to start acting more grown up. And besides, I don't need any more stress.'

'Stress? Give *her* some bloody stress. Cannot believe it. No, you've got to go 'round, let her know that this kind of...her kind of bullshit...let her know, man, that it's...just give her some fucking shit.'

'Oh, Burchmann. Chris, don't listen to this idiot, this freak of testosterone – the last thing you want to do is bring this up with her. What can you possibly achieve by doing so – make her feel bad?'

'Make her feel fucking dismal!'

'At worst, if she actually feels anything, you'll just make her feel bad, and you're not that kind of a bloke.'

'Yes, he is.'

'No, he's not, are you?'

'Well...'

'No, Chris, no.'

'I'd like to think I'd get some...closure.'

'Oh, piss off.' Sonny slapped my arm. 'Did your "closure" regarding Ophelie make the blindest bit of difference?'

'Bits.'

'Not much. And besides, if you go 'round there demanding apologies...'

'Explanations, Sonny – I want explanations: why she treated me like...'

'Shit.' Burchmann spat.

'...like shit, when she was no better herself.'

'Oh, come off it – all you'll get, if she even listens to you, is a list of reasons why you sucked, how you no longer meant anything to her...'

'Surplus. To. Requirements.'

'Shit, Burchmann...'

'But he's right – is that what you want? There's no closure better than your ex-wife telling you you were a waste of space.'

'Seriously, guys, my ego is pretty battered right now, can we please put this in more sensitive terms?'

'I thought you wanted to act more grown up?'

'I do, but...'

'Stop being a baby.'

'Yeah and go give her some shit.'

'Don't go, grow up, be a man, don't go.'

I didn't go.

Epilogue

London has never been as busy as it is in its present form. It can hardly capacitate the current movement and volume of traffic, the unconscious flow of dirt and metal, public and private vehicles and cargo; the narrow thoroughfares overflowing as quickly as the wide urban expressways; encouraged by the government and welcomed by industry, condemned by the motorist trapped in the crawling traffic, and censured by the pedestrian sentenced to walk amongst the fumes and the danger. Pedestrians, clinging to the edge of the pavements as wide as the cramped roads spare them. Pedestrians, weaving in and out of oncoming pedestrians as further pedestrians carelessly cross their paths.

The city heaved and sighed and bulged and climbed, borrowing land and accommodation from its suburban neighbours and evicting them further into the countryside, allowing the phrase - remember when this was all fields - to be passed down to generation after generation. It knows that it stinks under its own volume and vastness and its cancerous stretches of waste and abandonment.

Even in the coldest weeks of winter London remains always a degree or two warmer than the rest of the country, like some urban tropic. London weather, unlike its occupants and its habits has, we are led to believe, over the last two hundred years, improved; no more are the days of the Thames freezing over; no more are the days of the London Particulars. We *are* lucky.

The weather is far from special today. From Richmond Park, the slate grey skyline of the distant city is lost, and the brown treetops become grey cloud at an abnormally close horizon. It is common knowledge (is it not?) that England is a true beauty when it is caught in the glare and brilliance of sunlight: we've all seen the photos, but urban England only really comes to life after a fall of rain; it is only when the pavements are wet and shiny, and the houses and plants are wet and shiny that we are truly aware that we exist. London has a special existence after rainfall: travel to Leicester Square on a damp afternoon, watch the lights and the water finally bring that most tedious and ugly square to life; alternatively go there on a hot day and choke and squint and rush for the safety of the cinemas.

London, no longer England, central London not Middlesex-London or Surrey-London, once apart, then absorbed, now suburbanly discarded, but London, up-town London, the city, the West End, no longer England, a faded echo of an English London decades past, a new London, not English, not even British, but a city. A city, a jewellery box of amazing nationalities, faces in a myriad of shades, in chattering languages bouncing through strangely twisted lips, bouncing, tumbling across each other, indistinguishable. The old remnants of what was English — Strand and Aldwych to Cornhill and Ludgate; teacup sentimentality far from the understanding of generations of the youngest English families, understood better by astute and educated Americans, studied and admired by German, French, European minds — to most English it is unknown, it isn't dumb-assed high street, semi-detached, tabloid Britain, London has escaped the dimness of the English, adopted and globalized by visitors, franchised.

I was learning to embrace London again; to rediscover the sense of adventure and bohemia that defined elements of my youth. Burchmann was right, if perhaps wrong in his explanation of the cause, but he was right – since I'd been married I had lost something – I wasn't sure that it was Joodie's fault, more likely it was my job, or simply my mind recalibrating with the passing of time; regardless, I wanted to find life again, I want to win.

Sonny was my saviour, it turned out, way more than Burchmann; with Burchmann, it was always too easy to get sucked into the same traps, his routines, and always it reminded me of the person I was not. Sonny didn't indulge me, nor did she make me feel any more inadequate than was reasonable to feel; Sonny brought out my sense of humour, she took me to places that were old-fashioned, but new – burlesques, and music halls, and markets – painfully trendy young people understanding the past, embracing it, but not being blinded by histories and regret.

With Sonny's guidance and the passing of time, the obsession that had consumed me, corrupted me, destroyed my marriage and, ultimately, released me, was a thing of the past; my obsession now occupied a place in history that, curiously, seemed no more real than the adventures and histories I had often read in biographies.

Almost, it was difficult to actually believe that it had happened – as distant and abstract as those ever-fewer moments of childhood recalled; it existed blurrily along with all these other regretted cloudy mistakes I had made – lingering guilt, the terror of knowing it could not be redone, only relived, regretted. All that passion that had lit up my days and nights was washed away, a pathetic grown-up schoolboy crush; washed away, its only trace a faint sentimentality for something that I never had, an experience of unrequited emotion. Sentimental by nature, it was my inclination to take that history, the echoes of passion and to cherish them as something special, looking back with half-imagined nostalgia.

But I was improving, Sonny saw to that – any trace of wallowing, of retarded 'what if' moments and she slammed the lid down, brought me around to sense and normality. So, Ophelie remained, but distant, isolated, healthily ignored. It was not too difficult, the hardest part was wanting to be good, wanting to avoid the false heaven of relapse and self-indulgence, but I was close enough – generally, I stayed away.

What was not so easy, it surprised me to discover, was letting go thoughts of Joodie. And even Sonny spared me a little here – that it was normal and not self-destructive to reminisce and reflect on my marriage; it had been real and to remember was not unacceptable and not unhealthy; there was not the same appalling self-indulgent grossness, apparently, of pining for an unfulfilled dream.

Oddly, what I attached to was predominantly

physical. The moments of life we had shared, such memories had faded quickly, the process already started during the dreary, last unhappy year together, our personalities too disparate, her habits and lifestyle grown unbearable – no, my mind focused on her physicality, perhaps filling the void left by Ophelie's removal: those daydreams of femininity and softness; only now, those images of Joodie were easier to come by, easier to make real having an empirical knowledge of Joodie undressed. I missed that freedom, that knowledge I had been allowed, that adventure in curves and limbs and skin. Of course, what I really needed was to find someone new.

We weren't consciously looking, but Sonny took me to a place where I might "find someone suitable, someone compatible". It was good to be out; there was no pressure to meet anyone and, in the meantime, I had Sonny's female company; late night recollections of Joodie would have to satisfy everything else.

Talking bullshit, we sat and drank red wine at a high table, in a booth – a retro bar, but not really overly authentic clientele, very much a mix of people: some like Sonny, dolled up to fit, others like me, like they'd just come from work. Talking bullshit – it was our favourite pastime: people watching and personality assassinations – a trail of punters coming and going and, one-by-one, ruthlessly destroyed by our childish and/or bitchy remarks; and not unafraid to point out those women that either I, Sonny or both of us would like to get to know better.

'Oh my God! Honey alert!' Sonny nudged my rib

as I pointlessly checked my phone.

'Eh? Who? What? Where? Who are we looking at?'

'Not one for you, I'm sure – look at that girl, so cool! She's a honey – totally not your type, but I on the other hand...'

It took me a moment to realise who she was talking about, and a moment longer to register the unmistakeable, now very redheaded Joodie, lightly bouncing among a group heading towards the bar.

'God, she's *so* pretty. Look at that hair!'

'Really?' I teased, 'You think she's cute, the redhead? Kind of small, flat-chested. Really?

Sonny turned to me briefly, my face pulling hard to stay straight. 'Really? Yes, really, definitely... Abso*lute*ly. That is my kind of woman. Great legs, *perky* boobs...I knew she wasn't your type.'

'Actually, you're dead wrong...only I preferred her with black hair.'

I left it hanging, Sonny not reacting, hung up on Joodie. I waited, enjoying this unexpected real-life indulgence, this reprise of, well, yes, great legs and perky boobs – and I agreed with Sonny, she was pretty; and even more so as a redhead.

Slowly, something clicked, Sonny picked up on the peculiarity of my comment. 'What? Wait. You know who she is. What! I might have to ask you for an introduction. Is she...? Do you really know her?'

'I should do. She is, after all,' I was really enjoying this – so rare to get one over Sonny, 'my ex-wife.'

'Nooooo. What!' Sonny exploded, only the noise

of the people and the music preventing the whole bar turning around.

'Shh. Don't draw attention to us; the last thing I want is to have to talk to her. In fact, we should probably go.'

'*That's* Joodie!' She completely ignored my request for a hasty retreat, not quite come down from the shock of discovery. 'That's fucking Joodie!'

'Yes. But as I said, let's not let her see us.'

'Christopher: you utter fucking arse. *That's* Joodie, *that's* the woman you lost because of some stupid obsession and the world's crappest one-night-stand? Are you insane? She's adorable!'

'She's a bloody nightmare – I wouldn't wish her on you or anybody.'

'Oh, I wish she was on me!'

'No, you don't. Believe me. Besides, she's better from a distance...' I wasn't exactly convincing and gave up with a final, 'It's very bad light in here.' The truth was, she looked great, the break-up of our marriage had clearly done wonders for her – she looked ten years younger.

'Anyway, I didn't choose to break up with her. If it had been up to me...'

'Bollocks, you couldn't wait to get away from her. You'd had enough months before it finally happened, you fool.'

'Yeah, but I wasn't right in the head back then – I didn't know what I wanted. Anyway, I never denied that she was sexy - she was...to look at, not to be with. And none of that compensates for how hard she was to be with. You wouldn't last a weekend with her...'

'A dirty weekend!'

'I wouldn't count on that.'

We sat and watched her group, our thoughts no doubt wildly different and yet quite possibly with much in common. The group, about a dozen of them, spread out leaving Joodie standing with a man and woman that looked like they were related by blood, but actually only by a romantic partnership.

My thoughts were washing: now sentimental, now lascivious. I was miles away and hardly noticed Sonny sliding off her stool.

'Woah, Sonny, where are you going? Don't...no, please don't.'

'I'm sorry, baby – I have to.'

I dropped my chin onto my arms, folded across the table, hiding, praying that Joodie's eyes wouldn't reach over to me.

The three of them were chatting as Sonny came alongside them, her hand rested on Joodie's shoulder as she interrupted; Joodie turned, smiling instantly. Opportunely, the couple removed themselves, sensing that they were not required, longing only to indulge in each other. Sonny placed herself for conversation, right in front of Joodie; in her ridiculous heels the two women were about the same height. Joodie stood awkwardly, her toes together, her arms crossed, Sonny, as though she were in a fashion editorial. Bizarrely, they stood there, chatting like old school mates, oblivious of my presence across the room; worryingly, they seemed to be growing ever more relaxed, Joodie's arms came down, there was laughter; Joodie, at one point, blushed almost the colour of her hair – I prayed Sonny wasn't flirting, but kind of expected she was.

And then the moment I'd feared. They turned and looked towards me, Joodie squinted, Sonny pouted; I gave up, sat up and made an awkward childish wave, which Joodie returned, a little emotion clear on her face. They turned back to talk, laughed, loudly, half turning back to me – awful. I felt ridiculous. They continued talking until a guy from the main group moved over to them. Sonny shook his hand, spoke again to Joodie, they hugged, kissed on each cheek and then Sonny left them. As she walked back, I continued watching Joodie, half sad, half relieved; she waved once more to me, I raised a palm, cold, and Joodie turned to the bar and her drink.

Sonny sat down, silent, looking pleased with herself, easily winning the battle between us.

'Well?' I finally demanded.

'Lovely bum.' Sonny nodded to the bar and Joodie, with her back to us.

'No! No. Not her bum – what the hell did you say!' I wasn't angry, just impatient, bewildered. Sonny smiled at me and patted my fingers, motherly.

'Oh, Chris, you are priceless. I'm sorry. I'll share.'

'Thank you.'

'Ok, well, I didn't flirt with her...much...and she seems really nice...'

'Yeah, she's great at small talk, she'd bore you after...'

'Oh, give it up, Christopher, I don't care... I'm not

her best mate, we just chatted.'

I thought about the laugh they shared at my expense, I wanted to know, but wanted to seem indifferent, I couldn't just ask...

But I did, I gave in: 'Well, what about? About me?'

'I'm not going to tell you *that*. I mean, naturally, a bit about you.'

'That's all you're going to say?'

'Yep.'

'Really? That's bloody cruel, Sonny.'

'It's for your own good. You've done so well, you're turning into a fine man; one day, maybe, you'll be wise enough to know.'

I was unexpectedly moved. I still felt like a stupid adult child, my heart warmed at the idea that Sonny actually considered that I'd changed, that I wasn't, perhaps the self-absorbed whiny bitch that I'd turned into. I smiled, and thanked her, sincerely.

'I'll tell you one thing, though.'

'Please.'

'You see that guy she's now with?'

'Yeah.'

'Looks like his mum dressed him?'

'Yeah.'

'Looks like he cut his own hair?'

'Yeah.'

'Looks like he needs to spend some time at the gym?'

'And a visit to the dermatologist.'

'Yes, that too. You see him, that wonderful specimen of manhood?'

'Yes! Oh, please tell me that's her new boyfriend!'

'That, my friend, is Cameron.'

I leapt from my seat, threw my arms in the air, fists clenched, threw my head up to the heavens, jumped from our booth, across the room, spun Joodie around and squeezed her, turned, hugged Cameron, and skipped back towards Sonny, leaping and whooping like an American world cup winner. Yes!

Sometimes victories are small, but the first breath is always the freest.

Thanks....

Ingrid Berg. Anthony Durham. Jilly Wright. Sally Renshaw.

And John Updike for the first breath.

By the same author

Novels

Modern Man is Ultra Quick

Hardback: 978-82-690802-0-9
Paperback: 978-15-406226-8-6

Emily Osgarby's Autobiography

Hardback: 978-82-690802-3-0
Paperback: 978-15-407178-3-2

Short Stories

In the shallows & other Norwegian sketches

Hardback: 978-82-690802-1-6
Paperback: 978-15-406390-9-7

The winter the snow was heaviest

Hardback: 978-82-690802-2-3
Paperback: 978-15-406937-5-4

When now and then is all that remains

Hardback: 978-82-690802-4-7
Paperback: 978-19-812437-8-5

Also from Favourite Colours

Anthony R. Durham

These Quiet Years

Hardback: 978-82-691511-0-7

@favourite.colours.books

Lightning Source UK Ltd.
Milton Keynes UK
UKHW012126261119
354299UK00003B/50/P